JUNE FRANCIS

Step by Step

CANELO

First published in the United Kingdom in 2003 by Allison & Busby

This edition published in the United Kingdom in 2022 by

Canelo
Unit 9, 5th Floor
Cargo Works, 1-2 Hatfields
London, SE1 9PG
United Kingdom

A CIP catalogue record for this book is available from the British Library.

Print ISBN 978 1 80032 795 5
Ebook ISBN 978 1 91159 138 2

Look for more great books at www.canelo.co

Printed and bound in Great Britain by Clays Ltd, Elcograf S.p.A.

1

Step by Step

June Francis' sagas include *Step by Step*, *A Dream To Share*, *When Clouds Go Rolling By*, *Tilly's Story* and *Sunshine and Showers*. She had her first novel published at forty and is married with three sons. She lives in Liverpool.

Also by June Francis

Look for the Silver Lining
A Place to Call Home
The Heart Will Lead
Another Man's Child
Someone to Trust
Shadows of the Past
It's Now or Never
Love Letters in the Sand
Many a Tear Has To Fall
Memories Are Made of This
Walking Back to Happiness
Where There's a Will
For Better, For Worse
Friends and Lovers
Flowers on the Mersey
It Had To Be You

The Victoria Crescent Sagas

Step by Step
A Dream to Share
When the Clouds Go Rolling By
Tilly's Story
Sunshine and Showers

'Keep steady my steps according to thy promise.'
Psalm 119.133

Chapter One

1903

Hannah Kirk and Alice Moran lay on the lavatory roof with their hands clapped to their ears, but the screams from the bedroom of the house on the opposite side of the back entry still managed to get through.

'I can't stand it!' cried Alice through gritted teeth, emerald eyes wide and frightened in her blanched face.

'It'll be over soon. It's got to be,' said Hannah with a touch of desperation.

Screams from the Morans' household were nothing new. Last night, Hannah's dah had gone round there and dragged Mal Moran off his missus. Jock Kirk was one of the few men in Newtown, outside Chester's ancient city walls, who had a wife with the courage to send her husband to face the large Scotsman. Florrie Moran's baby shouldn't have come yet and it was possible that mother and baby might not survive. Hannah could not help worrying about what would happen to Alice, and Kenny, Florrie's stepson, if left alone with their pig of a father.

Suddenly, Hannah realised that the screams had stopped. She removed her hands and, at the same time, Alice's body sagged. Had the baby been born at last and was it alive? They both gazed up at the sash window open at the top.

Hannah raised herself carefully, ears straining for a baby's cry, but then came another scream that was so piercing it threatened to tear the sullen clouds apart. It definitely frightened the life out of her, as well as scaring the pigeons on the roof of the Angel Hotel on Brook Street, five minutes walk from Chester's General Station; the July evening was filled with the whirring of their wings.

'What's happening now?' Alice, her slender body in the neatly darned blouse and let-down but still-too-short skirt, shot to her feet, ready for flight. Her eyes filled with tears. 'I've got to go, whatever your mam said about keeping out of the way. I've got to know what's happening!' She scrambled to the edge of the roof and climbed down.

Hannah heard the click of the latch on the back door and then the click of the one across the narrow entry as it opened. She watched as Alice raced up the Morans' yard and the thin cry of a newly born infant came on the air. A smile created tiny dimples at the corners of Hannah's mouth. It seemed that her mother, Susannah, had been mistaken and the baby was alive. Whether it would live long was another thing altogether. Her mother was over there now with Granny Popo; both women were accustomed to helping the poor of the area give birth and lay out their dead.

Hannah knew that, fifteen years old, Alice would be praying the child would survive; so many of Florrie's pregnancies had ended in miscarriage. It was a miracle that Alice had been born safely considering her mother's curvature of the spine. Florrie had married Mal the year before the old queen's Golden Jubilee, and nine months later Alice had arrived. In those days, nobody had suspected Mal would turn into a wife-beater and terrify his two children out of their wits. Hannah had known Mal's son, Kenny's whole body to shake at the sound of his father's voice, mingling with those of the men coming home up Francis Street, from the lead works situated on the bank of the Shropshire Union Canal.

The girl swallowed a lump in her throat just thinking of Kenny's, and Alice's, fear of their father. She stood up, intending to go down and find out for herself if Florrie Moran was OK. A breeze caught hold of a strand of flaxen hair that had come loose from its scarlet ribbon and she tucked it absently behind her right ear.

Suddenly, her heart jerked beneath her breastbone as she caught sight of her mother's face at the Morans' window and quickly she crouched down again, and flattened herself on the roof of the lavatory, knowing she would get the sharp edge of her mother's tongue if she were spotted. After a moment, she raised her head cautiously and saw the curtains were closed but then the Morans' peeling brown painted kitchen door opened and Granny Popo appeared. The old woman was carrying a galvanised bucket and when she tipped it up, the water ran red, gushing down the grid.

The sight caused Hannah's stomach to heave and she felt a bitter taste in her mouth at the thought of what a woman had to go through to give birth. She decided she never wanted to marry and have babies. What she did want to be was a teacher. Her reverie about her future was suddenly shattered by a long drawn out wail that reminded her of tales of banshees. Guessing it could mean only one thing, tears filled her eyes. She waited for Granny to go back inside the house and then picked up the library book she had been reading before Alice had joined her on the roof, and tucked it in the waistband of her green and blue floral skirt with double flounces at the hem. Then she lowered herself over the edge of the lavatory roof, feeling with her boot for the middle wooden strut across the door.

A hand gripped her ankle and she felt a suffocating fear as a voice said, 'I've got you, Hanny. Let yourself down slowly. I'll make sure you don't fall.'

'I'd rather get down myself,' she gasped, her heart pounding as she clung by her fingertips to the top of the door. She felt her elder brother Bert's hand reach beneath her skirts and climb her left leg.

'Don't be silly! We don't want you to fall.' Bert looked up at her as she twisted her head to gaze wildly at him. How she hated his smiling handsome face, with its straight nose, cleft chin and light blue eyes, a genial mask that concealed a side unknown to most.

At eighteen, he was two years older than her and an apprentice engineer following in his father's footsteps in a company that specialised in hydraulic-powered hoists used for coaling steamships.

Like Hannah, he, too, had inherited their father's flaxen hair and he liked to give everyone the impression that they were close. This was so far from the truth that she wanted to scream out to people to stop letting him fool you, but no one would believe Bert could be such a two-faced snide.

Bert was his mother's blue eye! When it came to her firstborn son, Susannah spared no expense. Wearing his cricket whites, which had cost the family money they could ill-afford, Hannah wondered how he'd known where she was? She could only think he had gone straight up to his bedroom on the second floor, after coming in from playing cricket after work, and spotted her through the window.

All this flashed through Hannah's mind as she struggled to free herself from her brother's exploring hand. She wanted to scream but the sound seemed to have got stuck in a throat that felt swollen with outrage and fear. Her arms were aching and she longed to release her hold on the door but he had his other hand pressed against the small of her back, so that she was squashed against the door. She gasped as his fingers tugged at her drawers and this time she let go, knowing she had to do something to stop him going any further.

He dragged her down with his hand inside her drawers and a flounce of her skirt caught on a nail and tore. Her mother would go mad about that! She lashed out at him and found her voice. 'Let go, you filth!' Her fingernails found the back of his hand and raked it. He swore, overbalanced and fell heavily to the ground. Hannah landed on top of him and she struggled desperately to get away.

Somehow she managed to wrench herself free and made for the back gate; lifting the latch, she dragged the door open and fled across to the Morans' yard, which was situated at the junction of two entries. The houses had been built to accommodate the workers who had flooded into the area with the arrival of the railway almost sixty years before. The Morans' two-up, two-down was very different to the Kirks' three storeyed home, which had once been a lodging house.

Knowing she could never tell her mother what had just taken place, nevertheless Hannah wanted to be close to her. The girl peered through the kitchen window; the austerity of the Morans' house always made her feel uncomfortable. Unlike the Kirks' house there were no ornaments, spare cushions or antimacassars; only a small rag rug covered the bare floor in front of the fireplace.

Alice was seated on a straight-backed chair, lank strands of auburn hair dangled either side of her small thin face, flushed and tear-stained. Hannah's mother was in the act of dropping a bloodied rag on the fire.

Hannah knocked on the window and both looked up. Susannah Kirk was a plain woman, of Welsh descent, with greying dark hair and almost black eyes. She looked weary to the bone; her lined face dragged down with grief. The spotless white apron she had donned that morning was stained with blood. As for Alice, great sobs wracked her slender body.

'What is it you're wanting, Hanny?' Susannah's voice was filled with a powerful music and sometimes the girl marvelled that such a sound could come from her diminutive frame. Yet there was strength in her tiny mother that the girl admired and envied. She controlled her six-footer husband, Jock, who handed his wage packet to her unopened just as Hannah did, with the power of that voice and a will of iron. Yet even her strong mother had her Achilles' heel.

Hannah took several deep breaths to calm her nerves and putting aside her own troubles she entered the house. 'I came to see how things were and if I could help? Is... is Mrs Moran OK?'

Her mother shook her head and a deep sigh escaped her. 'I've known Florrie all my life. She grew up in a lodging house similar to ours and only came to live here after the money her aunt left was all gone. Everything she had, Mal spent. She was a fool to marry him... but then even your dah and I were taken in by him those early days when he first came from Scotland, newly widowed, poor mute Kenny was only an infant...' Her voice drifted away at the memory.

Hannah moved over to the armchair where Alice sat and rested her hands on her shoulders, sharing her grief, wondering how she would fare if she were to lose her mother. Her friend glanced up at her from red swollen eyes and her throat moved but no words came out. Hannah rested her cheek against her hair. 'I'm so sorry, Alice.' They stayed like that a moment and then Hannah looked at her mother. 'Where is Mr Moran?'

Susannah poked the fire. 'Took himself off, didn't he! As soon as Granny and I walked through the door first thing this morning, after Kenny came running for me. With a bit of luck he might never return but I've little hope of that.' Her lips pressed together a moment and then she looked at Alice. 'Do you know what Kenny did with that scruffy mongrel he brought here last night? I could tell he was really affected by its death.'

'He went off with it wrapped in sacking when he went out to work, Mrs Kirk, after you went up to Mam. Probably he'll bury it when he gets a chance. I thought he might have been home by now. I just hope to God he... he comes back. I couldn't bear to be alone here w... with Father.' Her voice sounded thin as stretched elastic, as if all the strength had been sucked out of her.

Hannah felt tears spring to her eyes, remembering last evening when she had followed her dah round here. If the sight of Mrs Moran's bruised and battered, crooked body had not been enough to make her weep, then Alice cowering in a corner and Kenny huddled against the kitchen wall, nursing the dead dog, would have done so. The young man was such a gentle soul that her heart had gone out to him.

'Kenny'll be back,' said Susannah with a sigh. 'He should have known better than to bring an animal into this house but I can understand why he wanted to help the beast.'

So did Hannah, but how she wished he could stand up to his father. Yet, who was she to talk about courage? She felt a chill just thinking about Bert, scared of what he might do next if he caught her alone. At least Florrie had loved the mute, motherless boy that Mal had brought to the marriage. He would be deeply affected by her death, but then, so would Alice.

Hannah felt despair. It was all wrong men having such power over women and children. Great Britain was supposed to be a civilized country, exerting influence all over the world. Only earlier that year Edward VII had been declared Emperor of India – yet of what use was that to those struggling to survive in these British Isles? Her spirits lifted a little, because at least two promising events had taken place that year. First, Mrs Emmeline Pankhurst had founded the Women's Socialist and Political Union and a Labour man called Henderson had won a by-election in Barnard Castle, a town up in the North East of England. Both were dedicated to fight the cause of the suppressed.

'What about the baby?' she asked, suddenly remembering the child.

'Out of Mal's reach,' said Susannah, smiling faintly, and keeping to herself what Granny Popo (who had been born in Liverpool) had said about letting the baby die. The tiny girl had been scarcely breathing when she was born. 'Be berra off. What kind of life is it going to have living in this dump?' Part of her understood the old woman's reasoning to put a hand over its tiny mouth but Susannah had decided the child had to be given a fighting chance.

'You mean… it's dead?' Hannah glanced down at her friend.

'No!' Alice's face looked almost beautiful as she spoke and gazed at Susannah. 'Granny Popo's taken her to safety.'

'Florrie gave her life for the child,' said Susannah, her expression grim.

'So where is the baby?' asked Hannah, smiling.

Her mother said, 'I wrapped her in flannel and Granny's taken her home to her granddaughter. Dolly gave birth just a few days ago and lost the child, but her milk has come in, so pray God that she might be able to save Alice and Kenny's sister. She's only a tiny scrap but the fact that she came out alive must say something about her fighting spirit.' She paused a moment. 'And heed me now, you girls,' she said, her dark eyes fierce. 'Not a word about the baby being born alive to anyone. Especially Mal.'

'Not a word, Mother,' said Hannah swiftly, praying the child would survive but not really holding out much hope.

'If only Mam hadn't defied Father and taken us to listen to Pastor Wise in Liverpool the other night.' Alice sighed heavily.

'You're right, girlie,' said Susannah with a shake of her head. 'But Florrie was in such a fatalistic mood lately that I could see trouble coming.'

'She never had much going for her, did she?' murmured Hannah.

Susannah could only agree. Florrie's curvature of the spine had meant she could not walk upright and had scurried along like a crab. Her widowed mother had owned a lodging house but then died when her daughter was only ten. Her spinster aunt, a schoolteacher, had raised her, frightening off any boy who might have showed an interest because her niece had a pretty face, a trusting nature and would come into her nest egg. Florrie had always looked for the good in people and somehow had seen something in Mal. But then Susannah and her husband had taken Mal at face value when he had turned up at their lodging house. He was a charmer, didn't seem short of money and was willing to work hard. Many had said Florrie was lucky to catch him. But as the years went by, with only Alice being born alive, he had changed and the family had seen little of his wages. What had he spent the money on? God only knew. Mal was no drinker, smoker or gambler. Why he felt such a need to beat the living daylights out of his wife and terrify his son and daughter, Susannah had never understood. As a tiny lad, Kenny had lost control of his bladder whenever his father was in one of his black moods, such a shaming thing. He was eighteen now, the same age as her Bert, but the two were very different. Her son was strong, handsome, smart, admired and had nerves of steel. Kenny was a loner, sensitive, his spirit cowed by his father's violence. God only knew what was going to happen to him and Alice, now. A girl needed a mother at her age.

Hannah looked at Florrie's daughter and wished she could do more for her but the law wouldn't let her take her away from her father, even if Mal would have allowed it. Well, she could help her at least right now by giving her a break and suggested she come back to their house and have a cup of tea. Hopefully Hannah had brought some leftover cakes from Bannister's bakery where she worked; they could have those with it.

Subdued and grief-stricken, Alice agreed to accompany her neighbours. When they entered the kitchen it was to find Bert sitting in an armchair. He had changed into a blue shirt and grey trousers with a knife-sharp crease in them, and had a bandage tied round the hand holding the Bible he was reading. Only for a second did he allow his eyes to fix on his eldest sister's face. Due to her mother's presence she could meet his gaze squarely and show no fear but she could read in his expression that the last thing he intended was that she would escape punishment for that scratch.

He bounded to his feet and said to Susannah, 'Come and sit down, Mother! You look worn out.'

Her round face lit up. 'I am. It's good of you to notice but then I should expect that. But what have you done to yourself, son?' She reached out and touched the bandage.

He smiled down at her. 'It's just a graze. I did it when I knocked the bails from the wicket and put their last man out. I scored a hundred runs… won the game for them.'

'You did give it a good wash?' He nodded. 'My talented boy,' she said proudly.

He helped her into the chair he had vacated. 'Everything OK?'

She shook her head and said sadly, 'Florrie died.'

'That's a shame! You'd been friends for so long.' He turned to Alice. 'I'm so sorry about your mother.'

The girl's cheeks burned and she whispered her thanks. She had always been in awe of her friend's big brother, but fancied him all the same.

Susannah said soberly, 'We'd been friends most of our lives. Like you she loved her church, Bert. I wonder what'll be done about her funeral? Mal didn't approve of her attending chapel as you know.'

'Never mind that now, Mother.' He looked at her with concern, his hands resting on the arms of the chair either side of her. 'What you need is a revitalising cup of tea.' He glanced at his sister and smiling, said, 'Hanny, get on with it… there's a good girl.'

'I don't need telling,' she said stiffly, irritated by the interplay between mother and son. How she wished she had the gumption to tell her mother the truth about the oh so perfect Bert!

Alice was still standing on the rag rug, looking ill at ease. Hannah told her friend to sit down and hurried into the scullery, wondering how someone who was supposed to be a Christian could be so two-faced.

Her elder brother was a member of the young men's Bible class at St Bartholomew's in Sibell Street and was so conversant with the Scriptures that he never failed to win a prize each year. It was not fair! Hannah knew she was as clever as he was but she was expected to look after the younger ones on a Sunday afternoon and take them to Sunday school, so her parents could have a rest for an hour or so. It wasn't that she begrudged her mother that time but when she arrived at the mission hall, she helped with the children. A task that she enjoyed but, even so, her mother didn't regard telling Bible stories to infants as of equal value to Bert's endeavours. When she had told her parents that she would like to be a teacher, Susannah had said that it was a waste of time… she was bound to marry… and, besides, they couldn't spare the money with Bert doing his apprenticeship. Instead, Susannah had found Hannah a job at Bannister's bakery on Foregate Street in the ancient city centre. At least it meant she was away from the house, meeting people and the job had its perks. There were the free leftover cakes and bread and the fact that she could allow her mind to wander and think her own thoughts.

Hannah had no sooner put the kettle on, than the lobby door opened and her younger sisters, with three-year-old Freddie, entered. He stopped suddenly, held his legs apart and wet himself. 'Wee wee,' he said, sticking his finger in the puddle. 'Sor-ee!' He beamed up at Hannah.

'What are you, Freddie?' She could not prevent a smile. Her youngest brother looked like a cherub, despite having dark curls instead of the customary gold of the winged creatures, but he did have the angelic big blue eyes.

'He's a nuisance,' said Grace, who still resented not being the baby of the family. She was ten years old, with light brown hair down to her waist and a squat figure clad in a plain blue frock covered by a white pinafore.

'He's been holding that in,' said Joy, tall for her twelve years but with her mother's dark hair and eyes. She wore identical clothes to Grace but was already developing curves.

Bert told his younger siblings to sit down and be quiet, so that their mother could rest and he would read them the story of David and Goliath.

Hannah pondered on how her brother loved the sound of his own voice. For a long time she, too, had been deceived by Bert but, during a trip to visit her mother's cousin at Moreton by the sea, Hannah came to realise that her brother wasn't the perfect being she had always believed him to be. She wondered, only afterwards, if his intention had been to drown her, but, of course, they would never know now. Fortunately old cousin Joan had been on hand and a few sharp words had concluded the incident but her mother had been unprepared to listen to her side of the story.

Hannah glanced at her friend. Poor Alice, she was one of those that considered Bert God's gift to the female race. She was ready now to hang on to his every word.

Susannah said, 'Get a floor cloth, Hanny, and mop that mess up.'

Hannah obeyed her instantly and, after that, she made tea and placed jam tarts onto a plate. She wondered how long before her dah would be in. He had gone straight from work to visit a workmate who had been injured in an accident. She thought about how different the two Scotsmen were. Jock would not have dreamed of lifting a hand against his wife. Mal Moran wouldn't hesitate. Jock had got his son an apprenticeship; Mal had left it to Florrie to find Kenny work with a coal merchant. Mal would probably be home soon, repentant as usual, but this time he was going to get his eye wiped because there would be no Florrie to forgive him. He was going to be in a right mood when he found out his wife was free of him at last and was safe in the arms of her Jesus.

Chapter Two

Mal Moran marched along with all the appearance of a man with a mission. Strong shoulders, used to working machinery and lifting containers of the lead mined in Wales since the time of the Romans, were pulled back and his head was held high. Rusty hair straggled from beneath a cloth cap and his full-lipped mouth protruded slightly as he rehearsed the words of apology over again. He was feeling better, as he always did, after visiting Eudora Black. She had healing in her hands and knew just what a man needed to rid himself of the filth inside his soul. What need did he have of a god who had hung on a cross? Florrie would forgive him. She always did because that's what her faith taught her. Aye! They'd be fine as long as that bitch from the back had skedaddled.

He walked onto the Queen's Park suspension footbridge, erected in 1852 and now suffering some wear and tear, planning on cutting through Grosvenor Park, the other side of the river, and heading up towards home along City Road towards the General Railway Station. The happy voices of trippers, who were making the most of the long summer evening, came up from the shining waters of the Dee below and there were still people promenading along the tree-lined Groves on the far bank. He frowned, resenting those who could afford to take a holiday in one of the most popular of North West England's holiday destinations, very different from the flamboyant Blackpool with its more working class clientele. Today he couldn't stand the men in pale flannel trousers and striped blazers; straw boaters on their arrogant heads. As for the women with their whale-boned, corseted figures, feathered and beribboned hats atop fancy hairdos, some carrying parasols protecting their complexions, they irritated him. He couldn't bear the posh English accents that grated on his ears. How he hated them! Sometimes he felt the same about the Welsh with their sing-song voices, jabbering in their foreign tongue. He didn't mind the Irish, despite their religion. He felt a kinship with them for having suffered hundreds of years at the oppressor heel of the English, like his own race, the Scots.

He reached the other side of the bridge and headed up towards home, unaware of his son's hazel eyes on him. And, even if he had been, Mal would have taken no notice of Kenny.

–

Being ignored by his father suited that young man down to the ground. Kenny knew from long experience that the only way to survive was not to draw attention to what he was doing. But last night had been scary, almost too much to bear. He had felt saliva welling up inside his mouth, drenching his tonsils, tongue and teeth. There had been a fire inside his chest that had threatened to burst out but he had managed to control it, held back by his stepmother. Despite her disability, she was a strong, spiritual woman with a will of steel. Even so, it was time she stopped taking what he thought of as blows meant for him, though he never knew what he had done wrong.

He dragged out the back of his shirt and his fingers explored the puckered skin of the silvery scar on his back. It had been there as long as he could remember. Definitely before he and his father had come to Chester. Something terrible had happened in Scotland, too horrible for him to remember. Just like he would prefer to be able to forget last night.

Shame caused the hot tears to prickle the inside of his eyelids as he rested his chin in his hands. Coal dust begrimed fingernails dug into his cheeks as he remembered how his father had choked the life out of the dog he had found down in the streets inside the city walls that Kenny loved to explore. The area was a world away from where he lived.

There, he was at one with the tourists who came to admire Chester's medieval buildings and enjoyed shopping in the city's famous covered Rows. Like them, he was free to gaze with interest and wonder at the Roman remains and walk the walls. But some places were not what they seemed: he knew about the small area of back alleys and courts of the city. Slums that had been there a lot longer than those condemned buildings in the sprawling seaport of Liverpool. Due to the silting up of the River Dee, Liverpool had replaced Chester as the premier port in the north west of England. Now it was on its way to gaining city status, and only the other week, the foundation stone for a great Anglican cathedral had been laid by King Edward and Queen Alexandra on St James' Mount. Still, Liverpool was a very different place from his beloved city.

Kenny's thoughts were wandering and he brought them back to the remembrance of yesterday and the sight of the dog's nose hidden in a crumbled greasy newspaper, its thin shanks quivering as he touched it gently. He had pitied it so much that he had given in to impulse and jumped down from the coal wagon and fed it some of his carryout. It had licked his fingers and he had been unable to resist taking it home. He knew his stepmother would understand, just as Alice and Hannah would, and they had.

Hannah: Kenny loved her but knew he could never speak of that love. She wasn't for the likes of him. She was kind and clever and needed someone who would be her match, not a weakling. He wiped his eyes with the darned cuff of his jacket sleeve and forced his thoughts away from the picture of her holding him in her arms, kissing all his pain away, talking, laughing, being together always. Sometimes he felt that he might have talked once, had dreams of doing so, but then he told himself it was all in his imagination. Occasionally, after being in Hanny's company, he would open his mouth and try to speak but, somehow, the words in his head just couldn't get past whatever was blocking his throat. His stepmother had taken him to a healing service once to see if a visiting preacher, said to have special God-given power, could unstop his tongue. He had put a hand on his head and fingers in his mouth, prayed fervently, but to no avail.

He thought of his stepmother and her kindness to him. Unlike his father, Kenny understood her desire to believe in a God of justice and a better world than this one, although his taste ran to a more ritual, flamboyant form of worship than hers did. Not wanting to upset her, it was only on a weekday that he followed his own inclination and attended Evensong in the Cathedral.

He took a deep breath, knowing he could delay no longer, and threw the shovel into the back of the coal wagon. It landed with a thud on a heap of empty sacks and raised a cloud of coal dust. He thought about the newly dug grave, along the Dee, where he had buried the dog and hoped it would not be disturbed by foxes. He hoisted himself up into the driving seat, picked up the reins and clicked his tongue. The horse walked on in the direction of the ancient multi-arched, Old Dee stone bridge, Kenny praying that the baby was born and his stepmother had survived the birth.

–

'I'd best get home,' said Alice, dusting pastry crumbs from her fingers and squaring her shoulders. She had been hanging on, not wanting to go home, hoping that maybe Granny would come with news of her baby sister. She hadn't and Alice dared delay no longer; if her father arrived home and she was not there, then his mood could be even more terrible than she cared to think about.

'Hang on, girlie!' Susannah placed three jam tarts on a plate with a screwed up scrap of newspaper containing tea and condensed milk, thinking that the gesture might soften Mal's heart towards his children. She knew her husband wouldn't mind if she went with the girl. Besides, she wanted to clean up Florrie's body. She would cook supper when Jock returned. He was late but then he was on an errand of mercy. The injured man might never see again.

She smiled encouragingly at Alice. 'I'll come with you, lovey.'

Alice whispered her thanks.

Suddenly Bert smiled at her and said, 'If there's anything I can do, Alice, do let me know.'

She blushed, wondering what he thought when he looked at her. That she was a mess, probably. 'Thanks,' she said in a low voice. What would Bert say if she asked him to beat her father into pulp for her?

He was big for his age but then her father was massive. She couldn't risk Bert being hurt for her sake.

She watched Susannah pick up a clean nightdress, towel, flannel and block of soap from the table. The girl felt a rush of warmth. 'It really is kind of you to do so much for us, Mrs Kirk, when you've got your own family to see to.'

'What have we been put on God's earth for but to help each other, Alice dear?' Yet suddenly Susannah felt anger against the Almighty. How could He allow one of His faithful servants to suffer the way Florrie had at her husband's hands? Thank God she was fortunate in her husband.

As she followed Alice out of the house, Susannah remembered how Jock had knocked at her mother's door in search of lodgings. It was the day the old queen had been proclaimed Empress of India; the same week Susannah had seen her first steam-driven vehicle on the road. Jock had been a well-set up youth, with a broad Scottish accent, newly arrived from the north. An orphan with no family, he had come south in search of work and security.

Her widowed mother had taken him in. Soon he proved his usefulness and had stayed on, painting and repairing things when needed, mending shoes and boots, never putting a foot wrong. His accent had moderated and, knowing which side his bread was buttered on as mother and daughter cosseted him, he was polite and thoughtful. When the old woman died, he asked Susannah to marry him, despite her being eight years his senior. She had trained him in her ways and the marriage had worked out well.

They entered the Morans' kitchen via the back way. The room was deserted and they thought themselves safe. Then they heard the sound of boots on the bare wooden floor overhead and a peculiar groaning. Alice's eyes dilated and she reached out a hand to the woman.

'Get a grip on yourself, girl. There isn't anything to be frightened of,' said Susannah despite her heart beating uncomfortably fast. She led the way up the bare wooden stairs, calling, 'Is that you, Mr Moran?' Silence.

Neither of them was prepared for the sight that met their eyes. The man was bent over the bed. His large hands gripped the arched body of his dead wife top and bottom, pulling, pulling. Even as they watched there was a crack as if a bone had broken.

Alice gasped. If she had been RC she would have crossed herself as some kind of protection against evil. Susannah cried, 'Didn't Florrie suffer enough without you desecrating her body? Leave her alone!' Both rushed forward. He turned, his face ugly, yet tear-stained. He brushed Alice aside with a sweep of his arm and she fell against the wall. Susannah went for him. 'My God! What kind of man are you?'

'Don't mention God in this house,' he roared and hit her in the face with his clenched fist.

Susannah toppled backwards. Blood trickled through her fingers as she clutched her nose. Trembling, Alice tried to force herself away from the wall to go to her aid but was too frightened to move.

Mal dragged Susannah up and shoved her out of the bedroom with the flat of his hand. 'Out of here, yer interfering old biddy!' Alice found the courage to follow, even though she was trembling with fear.

Susannah made a grab for the banister rail but missed, lost her footing and fell downstairs. Alice screamed but was unable to move or think straight for a moment. Then at last she said in a shaking voice, 'Yer… yer've really done it this time, Dad!' She forced her way past him, her feet hardly touching the treads as she made her way downstairs and bent over Susannah. Immediately the girl realised she must have banged her head because she was unconscious. She probably had other injuries because she lay awkwardly.

At that moment the door opened and Kenny stood there. Alice glanced up at him and then indicated with a jerk of her head their father's position at the top of the stairs. He looked up, his hazel eyes wide with shock and fear.

'Quick! Fetch help from the Kirks!' she hissed.

Before Kenny could move, Mal thundered down the stairs and grabbed his son's shoulders and rammed him against the wall. 'You'll stay where you bloody are. We've got to get out of here!' The man's face was chalk white.

'We… we can't l-leave M-Mrs Kirk?' stammered Alice.

He glared at her. 'Don't argue with me, lassie!' he hissed, as he hit her across the mouth with his free hand.

Kenny fought down his fear and swung a blow at him. Mal smacked him across the side of the head and sent him sprawling onto the stairs. 'You try that again, laddie, and I'll bloody knock you into next week,' he snarled.

Kenny's head was ringing and he felt sick with fear as he attempted to free his feet from where they had become entangled with those of the unconscious Susannah.

Alice looked at him, amazed that he had risked getting hurt for her sake. He had never tried to fight back before! Despite the pain in her face, she attempted a smile.

Mal let his arm drop, took a deep breath and eased his jaw. 'No time to lose,' he muttered. 'We've got to get out of here but I'll need money. Don't either of you move!'

Terror instilled over many years made them obey his command. Both gazed helplessly at Susannah's round and pale face, wishing they could do otherwise. It seemed terribly, terribly wrong to them both that this indomitable little woman might die. Suddenly Kenny staggered to his feet and took off his jacket and folded it. Alice realised what he was about and gently lifted the woman's head while he placed his jacket beneath it. With tears in both their eyes, Alice whispered a prayer that she wouldn't die. Then they heard the sound of their father's feet on the stairs and both hurriedly stood up.

'Come on!' Mal seized hold of an arm of each and kicked Susannah's feet out of the way. Alice opened her mouth to protest but the expression in Mal's eyes silenced her. Then suddenly he surprised her by saying, 'Where's the baby? What's happened to it?'

'Dead!' she lied, determined that at least her sister would have the chance of a better life than either she or Kenny.

He fixed her with his bloodshot eyes. 'Are you telling me the truth? What was it? Where's its body?'

'Gr-Granny took it… to be b-buried. It was a – t-tiny, tiny girl.'

'A girl!' he said huskily and, to her amazement, his eyes filled with tears. At this astonishing sign of weakness she said, 'We don't have to run away, Dad! We could get help for Mrs Kirk. She's still alive!'

Mal stilled and then his face twisted and he blinked rapidly. 'D'yer think I'm a bloody loony! She looks like she's going to die. I've no bloody intention of swinging for her. She had too much to say for herself. She had it comin'!'

He must be mad, thought Alice, mad to blame this dear woman who had helped them so much in the past. But taking his anger out on the innocent was nothing new. She felt a choking sensation in her chest thinking of her brave mother, who had so often dared to stand up to him. 'Th-then you… you go and l-let us stay with h-her. Besides wh-what about M-Mam upstairs.'

He threw back his head and his laugh sent a chill through them both. When he sobered he said., 'Ye'd be round at the Kirks' in a flash and Jock'd be after me. Besides yer my own flesh and blood! Where I go, ye go. Now not another word! Do yer hear me, lass? Don't make me want to hurt either of yer again.'

He opened the door and glancing about, dragged the pair of them out onto the pavement. Kenny and Alice stumbled outside. Next door, a curtain twitched before dropping into place again. The girl wanted to scream that there was a woman in need of help behind their front door but Mal's fingers dug into her arm, warning her.

Despite the churning inside his stomach and the hammers beating a tattoo inside his head, he knew he had to keep calm but Alice was suddenly refusing to move. A shove in the back caused her to lose her footing. 'We've got no time for ye to be standing there like a bloody statue!' he growled.

Kenny dragged his arm free and helped Alice to her feet, avoiding looking at his father. Mal hustled both of them down the street in the direction of the Shropshire Union canal.

Alice was past crying. Her face throbbed and her knees hurt. She had heard her mother say Susannah Kirk ran her household like a well-oiled machine. Alice felt as if her heart would break. Not only had she lost her mother and didn't know if her baby sister would survive but, surely if Mrs Kirk died, then her whole family would hate the name of Moran forever. Oh, why, why, why couldn't she have been born to that family instead?

Her father travelled at a fair lick, forcing them into a run through Newtown and across the canal via Cow Lane Bridge, past the warehouses and bonding stores of the Shropshire Union Railway and Canal

Company, and through an archway in the city walls. They went down Frodsham Street, and Alice spared only a fleeting glance for the beautiful façade of the eighteenth century Friends' Meeting House where she, Kenny and her mother had listened to speakers advocating non-violence. She felt that choking sensation in her chest again and longed to put back the clock and for her mam to be alive.

They crossed Foregate Street where there were more black and white half-timbered buildings. Kenny thought of Hannah as they passed Bannister's bakery. His heart was heavy at the thought that he might never see her again. God only knew where his father was taking them and what lay at the end of their journey. As the majority of the shops were closed, there were few people about now and those who were around would most likely have their minds on their supper, looking forward to their day of rest tomorrow. Dear God, why don't you punish my father? But no thunderbolt came from the sky to strike Mal down – and really Kenny did not expect one. The side of his head throbbed and he accepted that there was evil in this world and the struggle against it was not so easily won.

Mal hurried them along St John's Street and plunged down Souters Lane where, in the Middle Ages, the shoemakers had dwelt. Kenny recalled how Hannah had painted a picture in words for him, describing how the craftsmen had sat cross-legged in front of their open shop fronts with soft leather shoes on their lasts, sewing soles onto uppers. She was mad about finding out all sorts of things about the past and had filled him with the same passion. She had a head like a ragbag, collecting and storing all sorts of information, which she talked to him about. He felt wretched thinking about how she would feel if her mother died and hated himself for not being there and having the courage to prevent it.

They passed the Ursuline Convent and, below that, the red-bricked Georgian house that was the Bishop of Chester's Palace. Both buildings had views over the river and Kenny wondered if their father would take them across the bridge and head for Wales.

Once down on the Groves, Mal, still keeping a tight hold on his children, stopped to draw breath. There were few people about now and, as he looked about him, he found himself remembering walking along here with the scuttling Florrie. Her deformity was what had attracted him; he had wanted to look after her in those days; he hadn't married her for her money. He remembered her enthusiasm for Alderman Charles Brown, one of the Browns of Chester, who was responsible for laying out the promenade with refreshment kiosks, a bandstand, the landing stages from which pleasure boats departed to cruise up the Dee and rowing boats which could be hired. She hadn't been so bloody religious in those early days, but when she turned into a Holy Josephine that had finished them.

Anger, grief and fear swelled up inside him and he hurried with his children to the footbridge that he had crossed earlier and led up to Queen's Park, an area of select villas built for the prosperous during the last century.

Once on the other side, Alice could keep silent no longer. Who did her father know who was wealthy enough to live here? 'Where are we going, Dad?'

'You'll bloody find out soon enough,' he grunted.

Despite the time of evening, a youth and an old man were still working in one of the front gardens. The former was not wearing a cap and she noticed that his hair was dark and rampantly curly. He glanced up as they passed, and Alice thought *I like his face.* Her steps slowed without her being conscious of it. Her father swore and cuffed her across the head, dragging her on.

He stopped at the gate of a house with a maroon-painted door. Then, taking a deep breath, he opened the gate and hurried them up the path. He tugged the brass bell pull and they heard it jangle inside.

Alice's gaze strayed towards the youthful gardener a couple of gardens away. He had paused in his hoeing and was looking their way, a frown puckering his dark brows. She thought, if only he could help her.

'Stop making eyes at that bloody lad. I don't want him remembering what we look like!' Mal grabbed a handful of her hair and forced her head round. His hand shook and spittle oozed at the corners of his mouth.

She was terrified.

Footsteps were heard approaching the door from the other side and Mal released his hold on her. A maid opened the front door but, just behind her, stood a woman. Only by the slightest twitch of her heavy eyelids did she express surprise. 'You can leave this to me, Mary,' she said in well-modulated tones.

The maid moved out of the way and walked down the hall.

Alice stared at the woman. Who was she? She could have been of any age between forty and sixty. She had good skin and eyes of an indeterminate colour. Her grey hair was pulled away from her face and pinned up into a neat bun. She wore a navy blue skirt with a kick pleat and a plain white blouse with a high collar fastened with a cameo brooch.

'Malcolm dear, back already?' she said.

No one ever called her father by his full name, thought Alice. What was this woman to him that he should come to her when he was on the run?

'I need yer help, Eudora. Can I come in?' Not waiting for her answer, he almost fell over the brass threshold in his eagerness to get inside.

The woman rested a hand on his back a moment and he winced. She stared at Alice and Kenny. 'Are these your–'

'Aye! I had to bring them with me.' Mal wiped his sweaty face with the back of a hand covered with wiry dark red hairs. 'I'll explain once we're alone.'

'It had better be good and quick. I'm expecting… a client.' She smiled at Alice and Kenny. 'I'm Mrs Black. Come in, dears. You look done in. Your father upset you, has he? Never mind, I'll sort him out.'

Alice, who hated being called 'dear', especially by people she did not know, made no move to do what the woman said. The familiarity between the two adults angered her. Was this woman a high-class tart? She had heard of the sort who sold their bodies for money in the milliner's where she worked. Her employers made hats for what they called the *inbetweeners* as well as the more respectable working class women and social climbers. Had the money he should have spent on his family gone on her? Alice thought of her mother's broken body and was filled with anguish. Whoever this woman was, Alice was certain Florrie would not have wanted her to enter her house. The girl summoned up a vestige of courage and, hoisting her skirts up at one side, she leaped the steps and tore off in the direction they had come.

Mal swore and bellowed, 'Come back here or I'll kill ye!'

'Malcolm really! You're bringing down the whole tone of the neighbourhood.' Mrs Black's tone was furious.

For once he ignored her and leapt over the threshold, storming after his daughter. Kenny would have followed but the woman seized his wrist and her fingernails dug in like talons. Her eyes bored into his. 'Now take it easy, no need for you to worry. Do you hear me, Kenny? Relax, dear. One troublesome offspring is enough. Do you want your father tanning your hide so hard you won't be able to walk? Relax!' Kenny felt himself doing exactly what she said. He could smell the strong scent of roses and the evening sky seemed to have taken on a strange hue. 'He'll catch her. I've never known a man so fit and strong. There's nothing for you to worry about. What a sensible young man you are,' she said soothingly, her grip on his wrist unrelenting.

Alice fled past the drive where the young gardener stood in the gateway, gently swinging his hoe. As her father drew level with him, the hoe slipped from his grasp, and Mal tripped over it. He fell heavily but was on his feet in no time and turned on him.

'Sorry, sir,' said the youth, and bent to pick up the hoe.

'Yer bloody did that on purpose,' snarled Mal, kicking the hoe out of his reach before hoisting him up by the back of his jacket and heaving him through the air. He landed on the road, the breath knocked out of him. Mal bent over him but, before he could strike, the gasping youth grasped his nose between a thumb and a finger. Mal snorted and his eyes watered as the hold on his nose tightened. His hands slid on the surface of the road as he tried to get a grip and his boots sought a foothold. At last he managed to dig in his toes and knock that hand away. He seized hold of his tormentor's head and would have banged it on the ground if he hadn't felt a hand on his arm.

'Hey, hey! You leave Sebastian alone,' bellowed the wizened old gardener.

Alice glanced over her shoulder at the sound of his voice and saw her father send the old man sprawling against a garden wall. The youth was trying to get up but Mal knocked him down. Only a moment did she hesitate, her thin body trembling with apprehension, then she ran and jumped on her father's back, putting her arms about his neck. She heaved with all her might but he flung her off as if she weighed no more than a kitten. She landed on the road on her bottom beside Sebastian. It really hurt.

'Stop this immediately! I've never heard such a commotion. It's a disgrace.' The voice was female.

They all froze. Alice's eyes met Sebastian's treacle toffee brown ones. The skin beneath the left eye was already swelling. 'I'm really sorry,' she said, mortified.

'I'm glad to hear it but don't think that excuses your shocking behaviour,' said the little old lady dressed in a silver grey silk gown. It was obvious, not only from her tone, she was not about to stand any nonsense. She clutched a poker and, in her other hand, she held a whistle. 'Get up and away from here before I summon a bobby.'

Recognising the voice of authority, Alice stood up. Immediately, her father grabbed her arm and forced her in the direction of Mrs Black's house. The girl could hear the old lady tearing a strip off the youth for brawling like a common Liverpool slummy. 'Now go round the back and tidy yourself up. I don't know what Gabrielle or my son will think.'

Alice wished she could have explained to the lady that it was probably her father who had started the fight but it was too late now. They were only feet from Mrs Black's gate when the door of the house slammed. Mal broke into a run dragging Alice after him. He tugged on the bell pull again and again but the door remained firmly shut.

The expression in his eyes when he turned towards Alice caused her blood to chill and she felt that choking sensation once more. He was going to kill her. He dragged her down the steps. If he hadn't had hold of her then she would have sunk to the ground; her legs felt like blancmange. If he believed Hannah's mother dead then she was the only witness to the crime and, daughter or not, she felt certain that would not count with him. He might want to shut her mouth for good. If only that youth could have saved her. But he had tried and that thought somehow gave her courage. Then suddenly she remembered her half-brother. Where was Kenny? Dear God, had that scarlet woman seized him for her own wicked ends, or had he managed to escape? She could only pray for the latter and that he would get help for Mrs Kirk before it was too late.

–

Kenny sat on a hard leather sofa gazing at Mrs Black who was playing with one of those kids' metal clickers that could drive you mad with the noise if they go on too long. She was obviously vexed but, at least, she didn't appear to be blaming him for not answering her questions. It had obviously not occurred to her until now that he was mute.

'I should have remembered you couldn't speak but it's something Malcolm doesn't talk about often.' She sighed. 'You're no use to me, I might as well let you go. Stand up.' She clicked the clicker again and, whether it was a nervous reaction or not, Kenny found himself on his feet and following her out of the room on the first floor and down a carpeted flight of stairs. The room upstairs had thick carpets, fancy curtains and tea served in delicate china cups. Where had his father met her and what was between them? What was he doing in this house with this woman? Where was his father? Where was Alice? He felt a rising panic. He had to find her. Mrs Black opened the front door and, waving him out, closed it firmly behind him.

For a moment Kenny just stood on the step, not knowing what to do. He had no idea where his father had taken Alice and soon it would be dark. The sun was sinking in the west and, from the stillness of the evening, the birds had gone to rest. Had his father gone off to walk to Wales or would he take a train? He must have had some kind of journey in mind for he mentioned needing money. The memory of Mrs Kirk lying in an awkward heap at the bottom of the stairs filled his head and he knew he had no choice but to make for home and get help for her first. He, too, was going to need money and knew where his stepmother had hidden some. At the thought of Florrie, he felt a deep ache inside him. Without any more delay, he broke into a run and headed for the river.

Chapter Three

Jock Kirk entered the kitchen and his gaze swept the room, resting a moment on each of his children. Grace had scissors in hand and was cutting dollies from newspaper on the table, already set with an embroidered tablecloth, cutlery and condiments. Joy was flat on her stomach on the rug, talking about the pictures in a cloth book to Freddie. Bert's face couldn't be seen, hidden behind the *Chester Chronicle.* He sat in his father's armchair one side of the black-leaded fireplace. Hannah was sewing, pulling needle and thread through the flounce of a floral skirt. She glanced up and met his serious blue eyes. 'Hello, Dah!'

'Mother not back yet from delivering Florrie?' he asked, the slightest of Scottish burrs in his deep baritone.

'Mrs Moran died.' There was a tremor in Hannah's voice as she looked at him. He was a tall man, lean and rangy, with a craggy face and large mouth. He was wearing the clothes he went to work in, khaki corduroy trousers, grey cotton shirt and tweed jacket. On his feet were heavy black boots.

'Now that is bad news.' He removed his cap, revealing neatly trimmed fair hair, and turned it between his fingers in a restless movement. 'How's Mal taken it?'

She could tell he was upset. 'Don't know yet. Mother went back with Alice a short while ago. Maybe he's not in yet and she's staying around till he turns up. She's probably seeing to Mrs Moran's body, too.' Bert lowered his newspaper. 'It was half an hour ago, Dah. I think it's time someone went round there and brought her back. You know her devotion to all the lame ducks in the area – how she's not scared of anyone. I think there's times when she needs rescuing from herself. She looked tired out and in no fit state to be bandying words with Mr Moran.'

'Perhaps I should go round there,' said Jock, after a moment's hesitation.

'No, Dah!' said Hannah swiftly, thinking he looked worn out himself. She placed her sewing on the footstool to one side of the sofa and stood up. 'I'll go. You sit down.' She turned to Joy. 'Put the book down and make Dah a cup of tea, there's a love.'

'No trouble,' said Joy, handing the cloth book to Freddie and getting to her feet.

Hannah went down the yard and across the entry into the Morans' back yard. She glanced through the kitchen window but the room was empty. Her mother must still be upstairs seeing to Florrie and poor Alice with her. Perhaps Mal Moran wasn't home yet, or Kenny. She opened the back door and paused a moment to listen for any sound but all was deathly quiet. A sensation similar to an icy finger traced a path down her spine. Something was wrong! She moved further into the room.

Her legs turned to jelly and her hand reached for the wall as she saw her mother at the foot of the stairs. Her heart pumped blood so fast, she thought she would faint and sank to her knees besides Susannah's unconscious body. She recognised Kenny's jacket beneath her head. What had happened here? Whatever it was, Kenny must have seen it. How could he have left her mother like this?

She felt confused, angry and frightened as she searched for her mother's pulse. At first she could not feel anything, so conscious was she of the hammering of her own heart. She forced herself to calm down and concentrate on a spot on her mother's wrist. She felt a faint beat and then another.

She stumbled to her feet and, brushing away tears, hurried out of the house, scared to death that, while she was gone, her mother might die.

The family looked up, as a white-faced Hannah entered the kitchen.

'Where's Mother?' asked Grace, pausing in making the line of paper dollies dance, and looking past her sister.

Hannah opened her mouth but no words came out. Jock pushed himself up from his chair, his expression concerned. 'What is it, lass?'

Only then did she manage to say, 'Mother's lying unconscious at the bottom of the Morans' stairs; I think she must have fallen. I didn't go upstairs but I'm sure the house is empty.'

Jock's face registered shock and then he rushed out of the room. Bert stared at Hannah only a moment, before following his father. Grace and Joy exchanged frightened looks and went only as far as the yard, staring up at the back of the Morans' house in the fading light.

Hannah began to shake and hurriedly sat down. Tears rolled down her cheeks. She looked at Freddie who should have long been in bed but, in her mother's absence, he had been allowed to stay up late. His chubby face puckered. Then suddenly he got up and scrambled onto her knee. 'Don't tie!' he said, attempting to wipe her tears away with a grubby hand.

She cuddled him, trying to untangle her thoughts. Where was Alice? Had she seen what happened? Surely she must have been there when her mother fell down the stairs? Surely she wouldn't have left her lying there and not come to them for help if it had been an accident? Suddenly, she was convinced that Mal Moran had to have something to do with it. He hated her mother; could have been really mad because his wife was dead. For all of the Morans to be missing at such a time must surely mean there was something fishy about her mother's fall. Could he have pushed her down the stairs before forcing Alice and Kenny to go with him? They were that scared silly of him they would have gone.

Hannah could no longer sit still and struggled to her feet. She told Freddie to stay where he was, to be a good boy and that she would be back soon. But, before she could leave the house, Bert entered via the back way, followed by Joy and Grace, who were clinging to his hands, their faces pale.

'Mother's still alive, isn't she?' Hannah's voice shook.

'Yes!' Even Bert looked pinched and white about mouth and nose. 'Dah wants a screwdriver. He's going to take their kitchen door off the hinges and bring Mother over here.' He paused, and there was a strange light in his eyes. 'You didn't go upstairs, did you?'

'No! Why?'

'I've never seen such a sight. It's a right bloody mess and Mrs Kirk's body appeared a different shape. I went up to check the house was empty.' Bert opened the dresser drawer as he spoke, rummaged around for a screwdriver and slammed the drawer back into place, leaving Hannah staring after him as he went out.

How could Florrie's body look different? It must be because she was dead. Hannah made herself hurry upstairs to prepare her parents' bed for her mother, her thoughts and emotions in turmoil.

Between them, Jock and Bert managed to manoeuvre the door with the unconscious Susannah laid out on it upstairs, round awkward corners and into the front bedroom on the first floor. Hannah, with Joy's help, eased her onto the bed and removed her shoes.

'Best not undress her, Hanny,' said Jock, breathing heavily as he placed the door against the wall. His craggy face was flushed with exertion but he, too, looked pinched about the nose and mouth. 'Just cover her up. You'll sit with her, lass. Bert, you run round to the doctor's house.'

'C-can we afford a doctor?' asked Grace, who had now squeezed into the room, followed by Freddie. There were tearstains on her cheeks and she looked frightened.

'He's a nice doctor,' murmured Hannah, her eyes not moving from her mother's face. 'I've heard he sees some people for free. I'm certain that when he knows what's happened to Mother, he'll come because he appreciates the work she does for the poor.'

She glanced up at her father. 'What about Mrs Moran? We can't just leave her body in that house. Shouldn't the bobbies be informed?'

Jock gazed down at Susannah and, at first, didn't appear to have heard his eldest daughter because he did not answer. When he lifted his head, there was such an expression on his face, that Hannah suddenly felt scared for him. 'I'll take the door back and lock up and see if the neighbours heard or saw anything before I go for the police.' His eyes wandered again to his wife's blanched face; he bent and kissed her with quivering lips, before squeezing past his children and out of the room. Bert followed him.

Hannah pulled the covers up to her mother's chest, then perched on her father's side of the bed and took one of Susannah's limp, work-worn hands in her own. Her sisters and Freddie sat alongside her, gazing at their mother's face. 'I hope Dah and Bert ar-aren't going to-to be long,' stammered Grace.

Joy, who had been swallowing audibly since they had laid Susannah on the bed, suddenly knelt beside it. 'I'm going to say a prayer to God to make her wake up,' she said.

Hannah and Grace scrambled quickly down beside her, put their hands together and closed their eyes. Freddie followed suit.

'*Dear God, please make our mother wake up and be better,*' prayed Joy.

'*Make the doctor come quickly,*' said Grace.

'*Help us to do the right things to help her, in the name of Jesus Christ our Lord, Amen,*' murmured Hannah.

Freddie echoed *Amen*.

The four of them got up and gazed down at their mother hopefully but she lay as still as the *Sleeping Beauty*, as if she mightn't wake up for a hundred years.

-

Jock hammered on the Morans' neighbour's door. A curtain twitched in the downstairs window and he breathed a sigh of relief. He was shivering with nerves and a peculiar excitement that he couldn't understand.

The front door opened and a woman stood there in a nightgown with a coat draped over her shoulders. *Not the kind of sensible night attire Mother wore*, thought Jock, part of his mind seeming detached from the rest. She had a towel round her long, wrinkle-free neck and her damp brown hair hung each side of her smooth-skinned face, covering her shoulders.

'It's Mr Kirk, isn't it?' she said.

'Aye, that's me.' He flushed. 'I'm sorry to disturb yer but I wonder if yer've seen anything of Mal and his kids. Only...'

Her brown eyes widened and she clutched the edges of her coat together. 'I thought there was something up! The screams coming out of there have been something chronic. You know what he's like because you've been round there often enough. Did he kill her? I saw him hurrying off with Kenny and Alice... ooo... just over an hour ago.'

'I'm not here about Florrie, although she is dead – but my wife,' interrupted Jock. 'My lass Hanny found her at the bottom of the Morans' stairs. She's out for the count and I reckon he's to blame for it.' Jock's voice trembled and he had trouble controlling his chin which had gone all wobbly. He took a deep breath. 'If ye could tell me which way they went, I'd appreciate it, lass!'

'Shouldn't you go for the constable?' She looked concerned. 'I can see that you want to get your hands on him yourself and you're a big strong bloke, but are you wise?'

That last comment angered him. He had been sensible all his life and probably he wasn't being wise in wanting to do just what she said and get his hands on Mal. But the sight of his wife's shuttered face and the fact that she wasn't there telling him what to do and that he hadn't been able to prevent poor Florrie's death, made him feel as if his insides had been caught up in a whirlpool. 'Just tell me which way they went,' he said harshly.

She placed a hand on his shoulder and a strand of damp hair brushed his cheek as, leaning down, she pointed a finger in the direction Mal and his children had taken. 'They went towards the canal.'

'Thanks!' Feeling slightly uncomfortable at the intimacy of her hand on his shoulder, Jock hurried away. Although he wanted desperately to get his hands on Mal, part of him longed to rush back home to check that Mother was still alive. His head felt peculiar, thick and aching. He couldn't imagine life without her. But if he delayed looking for Mal, the bastard might get away. He'd taken his bairns with him and they could be in danger. Where the hell could he have gone? It would have made more sense if he had headed towards the General Railway Station rather than the canal – but he might have friends in town or, if he believed Susannah was dying or dead, he could be planning on crossing the river and making for Wales. Mal was a beast and he had to find him.

–

Hannah came downstairs after putting Freddie to bed and checking up on her mother again but there was no change. As she entered the kitchen, Bert pushed his plate away and resting his chin on his elbow, said, 'I know you've done your best, Hanny, but I can see if Mother doesn't recover we could all die of starvation or food poisoning.' Hannah felt like emptying the contents of the plate on his head. How could he speak in such a way when their mother could be dying? Her nerves were as taut as violin strings and she was in no mood for such comments. And where was her dah with the bobbies? Had Jock gone after Mal himself? It was the only reason she could think of for his being missing so long. The doctor had called but there appeared to be nothing he could do. All he had said was that the next forty-eight hours were critical and that if they believed in prayer then they should pray their mother would gain consciousness soon. Hannah would not have left her alone but Bert had made the decision that she cook them all something to eat. She would have argued with him but hadn't wanted to upset her siblings. Maybe he was right in saying they needed to keep their strength up, but she hadn't been able to eat a thing. Oh, if only her dah would come home! Where could he be? What if he had found Mal Moran and there'd been a fight? Maybe right now their dah was lying in a pool of blood, unconscious or dead. She felt a shiver go right through her.

'What's wrong with you?' Bert frowned at her.

'Why can't you go and look for Dah?' she burst out. 'You're sitting there doing nothing!'

'You're making a mistake speaking to me like that,' he said softly. 'Haven't you heard Mother say *You're not to give cheek to your elders and betters?* So keep a hold on your tongue. There's a limit to my patience. Now pour me a cup of tea out. There's a good girl.' He picked up the newspaper and began to read.

I thought you loved Mother, Hannah thought, *And I'm not your good girl*. She longed to snatch the newspaper from his grasp and rant at him. Instead she turned her attention to her younger sisters, who were still at the table. 'Eat your supper, Grace. It's time you were in bed.'

The girl pushed her plate away, saying, 'I don't want to eat it. It's horrible.' She glanced at Bert for approval.

'Copycat!' said Joy, frowning at her. 'But if you're not going to eat it then I will. It'll stoke the engine as Dah says.' She emptied her sister's plate onto hers.

Grace looked up at Hannah. 'Mother'll get better, won't she?' Her voice trembled.

'Of course she will. We've prayed, haven't we?' Hannah's tone was reassuring, but she crossed her fingers behind her back.

Grace relaxed and watched Joy shovel liver, as tough as old boot leather, into her mouth. 'You've got a stomach like a pig's.'

'Don't you be cheeky to your elders and betters,' mumbled Joy.

'Now who's the copycat?' said Grace, sticking out her tongue.

'Quiet, you two!' Bert folded the newspaper and dropped it on the floor. 'Hanny's right. It is time you were in bed or I'll take a slipper to you.' He stood up.

'You wouldn't, would you, Bert?' said Grace astonished. Then she laughed. 'I know, you're joking.'

He smiled. 'Maybe I am, maybe I'm not. You be a good little girl and do as you're told. I know we're all worried about Mother but you need your beauty sleep.'

Grace got off her chair. 'OK! I do want to be beautiful when I grow up.'

Hannah could not believe the way he was behaving. 'How can you speak about slippering them tonight of all nights? It's not your place to punish them, even if they'd done something to deserve it.'

Bert's pale blue eyes fixed on her pale tense face. 'Don't interfere, Hanny. Mother and Dah aren't here so I'm in charge. It's well past the girls' bedtime.'

'I'm scared to go to bed. I'm scared Mother might die and Mr Moran might come and get me,' said Grace, shivering.

'If Mal Moran's got any sense he'll be miles away by now. Anyway, he won't touch you while I'm here,' said Bert confidently, throwing out his chest.

Grace went over to Hannah, put her hand in hers. 'Will you come to the lav with me?' Hannah nodded and the two sisters went out, followed by Joy.

It was dark in the yard and Grace kept squeezing her eldest sister's hand. 'I wish it was still light,' she said, as Hannah opened the lavatory door. 'Things seem better in the light.'

'We've only got a few hours before the sun rises and it'll be Sunday. Better the day, better the deed! I remember Mrs Moran saying that,' said Joy, resting against the whitewashed wall and gazing up at the Morans' rear bedroom window.

Hannah made to close the lavatory door but Grace put a hand against the inside. 'I want to be able to see the pair of you.' She pulled down her drawers and sat on the wooden seat, scrubbed almost white.

Hannah leaned against the open door and looked up at the stars, bright as diamonds in a navy-blue velvet sky. Her heart felt like lead and she was fit to drop. She knew that if her mother didn't wake up in the next day or so, then she'd go downhill quickly without food or drink. And even if she came round, her brain might have been damaged by the fall. Maybe she had been knocked silly. She had known that happen to a boy when she was at school. The idea of her mother not being all there in her head was terrible. How would they manage without her hand on the reins, controlling the household?

She felt a tug on her sleeve and looked down at Grace. Her sister rested her head against Hannah's hip. She put an arm about her. Joy went into the lavatory, sitting down and swinging her legs and singing *Jesus wants me for a sunbeam*. Her tone was mournful. Hannah smoothed Grace's hair with an unsteady hand, thinking each minute seemed an age and she wanted to sleep the next twenty-four hours away and to wake up and her mother to be her normal self.

She went upstairs with her sisters and watched them dive under the covers of the double bed the three of them shared, heard them say another lot of prayers for their mother and then went into her parents' bedroom. Susannah had not moved at all.

Hannah sat on the bed and smoothed back her hair with an unsteady hand. 'Please wake up, Mother,' she whispered with tears in her eyes, but there was no response.

Hannah sat for a while, gnawing on her lip, willing her to open her eyes and flash her familiar smile. At the same time her ears were straining for the sound of her dah's footsteps in the street below. After a while, when neither happened, she rose with a sigh and went downstairs. The dishes needed washing, and the porridge oats and the salt fish needed putting into soak for breakfast. Perhaps Bert would come up and sit with Mother while she performed her tasks.

When she suggested that he sit with their mother, he shook his head. 'It upsets me seeing her like that.'

It upset her but she knew it would be a waste of time saying that to him. She washed the dishes and then put coal on the fire, aware of Bert watching her every move. Had she been a fool to come downstairs? She believed that not even Bert would think of trying it on when their mother could be dying. When he threw the newspaper on the floor, she almost jumped out of her skin.

'Why can't you sit still,' he said, leaning back in the chair, his hands clasped behind his head. 'Talk to me! You must have some idea where the Morans have gone.'

'W-Why? I'm n-not M-Mal Moran's shadow,' stuttered Hannah. 'I have no idea w-where they are.'

'Alice and Kenny are your shadows, though!'

'No, they're not! An-and even if they were, I still wouldn't know where Mr Moran would run to.'

'OK! OK! I believe you,' he said, yawning and closing his eyes.

Oh, the relief! Maybe he would go to sleep in the chair. She remembered how her brother had teased her when she was much younger, pulling her hair and tickling her unmercifully, until her laughter turned to tears not just of frustration but pain. She had accepted it because some of the other girls of her age had said their brothers were just the same. A year ago, though, *the Curse* had started and her mother had put a stop to such behaviour. Hannah had overheard her speaking to Bert about how he had to treat her differently. She was no longer a child but had started to grow into a woman. Hannah had known, from the tone of his voice, that he had not been happy at what had been said, although he had said the right things to their mother. However his behaviour towards Hannah had altered so subtly at first, that she thought that she was imagining it. He had started touching her in passing: A pat on her hip, her shoulder, her bottom, brushing suddenly against her bosom. Putting his hand up her drawers, as he had done in the yard, had been something new and had almost frightened her to death. She could not stand being in the room with him any longer and decided she would go the lav and then sit with her mother.

She went down the yard and shot the bolt on the lavatory door. Part of her didn't really believe Bert would follow her there but, a few minutes later, she heard his footsteps approaching.

'What are you doing in there? Are you going to be there all night?' He rattled the latch.

'I've an upset stomach,' she gasped.

He made no response but she could hear him breathing. Then, thankfully, his footsteps retreated and her whole body sagged with relief. Even so she stayed another five minutes or so before sliding the bolt back slowly and stepping outside. Fortunately there was no sign of Bert.

She stood a moment, thinking about Alice and Kenny, wondering where they were as she gazed up at the silent house across the entry. She remembered the scream that had caused the pigeons to fly. She felt the breath catch in her throat and, at that moment, she heard the tinkle of breaking glass. She froze. It came again. She hesitated only a moment before climbing up the door onto the lavatory roof where she could see into the Morans' yard.

Her heart seemed to miss a beat as she caught sight of Kenny climbing through the lower window and she remembered her dah taking the door back. He must have locked up. She wasted no time watching him but was off the roof and into the opposite yard. She tiptoed up to the open window.

Kenny was kneeling in front of an armchair. On the floor was its cushion. She heard the sound of material being ripped. A minute or so passed and then he stood up and turned in her direction. She heard the hiss of his breath as he saw her.

'What are you doing? Where have you been?' she said in an angry whisper. 'Did your father push my mother down the stairs? You can just come out. I'm not going to do you any harm but Dah will want to speak to you. Where's your dad? Is Alice with him? Mother's unconscious with head injuries.' Hannah's voice trembled. 'You've got to write down what happened for me, Kenny. Justice has to be done if your dad's responsible.'

Kenny longed to answer her. He could not make out her features clearly but he could picture the little crease of worry between her eyes and that shake in her voice meant her mouth was quivering. He had watched her turn from a dimpled toddler into a girl who had played at house with Alice. Sometimes he had been included in the game of Mothers and Fathers, with Hannah treating him as if he was the same age as her. He hadn't really minded, happy that she wanted his company. The last person he wanted to imitate, though, was his own father, so he had done his best with hers. The trouble was Jock Kirk could answer back, although he seldom did as far as he knew. As for Hannah, she was a dab hand at taking off her mother and telling Kenny exactly what to do. But, one day, she had got real mad at him, wanting an answer. In frustration she had given him a pencil and a scrap of paper and told him to write how he felt. He had stared at the paper and then thrown the pencil down and stalked off, feeling stiff with shame and embarrassment. Only then had she discovered that he could neither read nor write; his father having decided it was a waste of time paying the few pence that would have enabled his mute son to have some kind of education. Kenny had been amazed and touched when she set about teaching him, making a game of it, calling it School. She'd had such patience going over and over the letters and words with him, as well as passing on things she learnt at elementary school. She had told him he was a quick learner considering his disability. She had also told him that she would like to be a teacher but there was little hope of getting her way. He had written down that she would make a good teacher and she had hugged him. He remembered his stepmother's surprise, as well as Alice's, when he began copying verses from the Bible, decorating them with borders of flowers and birds, and bringing books home from the library. Hannah hadn't been the least bit surprised, she was proud of him.

'Will you stop standing there like a lump of wood and come on out!' she said exasperated. 'Come round to our house and you can write down all you know.'

There was a lot Kenny wished to get out of his system, and he wanted to please her. When he had found the house locked up and Mrs Kirk's body gone, he had been scared to go round to the Kirks'; besides he needed to find out where Alice and his father had gone and he didn't want to waste time. He thought that maybe they had caught a train out of the city. Perhaps., if he went the station, someone might remember seeing them and know their destination. He had money now – money that his stepmother had hidden for the baby. How she had managed to salt it away without his father knowing, he could only guess at, but the money couldn't help her or the baby now. His plan had been to write out a description of his half-sister and their father, and show it to the tellers and porters at the railway station. Maybe Hannah would help him do that, although right now she sounded really fed up with him, and he didn't blame her.

Slowly he walked over to the window and was about to climb out when a voice said, 'So the dummy's come home to roost! I wondered who you were talking to, Hanny.' Bert's bulky outline made an appearance just behind Hannah. He elbowed her aside. 'If my mother dies, Kenny, your father and you will swing for it. You mightn't have pushed her but you're an accessory after the fact.' Bert lunged at him.

Kenny shot back from the window. Bert was inches taller and twice his weight. Kenny knew lots of people thought Bert a lovely bloke but Hannah's brother had never been nice to him, so now he expected no mercy at his hands. Kenny stared at Hannah in desperation and then ran out of the room.

She turned on her brother, furious. 'Why did you have to do that? He was just about to come out.'

'Shut up!' Bert caught her a clip over the ear and then swung a leg over the sill. He was about to bring the other one over, when she grabbed his foot. He twisted and hit her hand with his clenched fist and dragged his foot free. 'You shouldn't have done that, Hanny. I won't forget it,' he said in a silky tone and shook his head as if more in sorrow than anger. Then he picked himself up from the floor and went after Kenny.

Hannah rubbed her ear and sucked her bruised knuckles but wasted no time hanging around and raced out the yard and down the short length of entry into Francis Street. She was just in time to see her brother turn the corner into Brook Street. She wanted to prevent Bert from beating Kenny but knew she would have trouble catching them and, even if she did, how would she be able to stop Bert? He was so much stronger than she was. Besides she must think of her mother and her younger sisters and brother alone in the house. She had to go back and could only hope that Kenny, who could run like the wind, would avoid capture.

She made her way back home, hoping Kenny would eventually come to their house under his own steam. All was quiet as she pulled the key on the string through the letterbox but, when she entered the kitchen, it was to find it empty. She went upstairs and there found her father slumped in a chair beside the bed in her parents' room, his hand clasping her mother's, his eyes closed. By the light of the gas lamp, she could see that even in repose the strain showed in his face but he was not asleep because, as she approached the bed, his eyes opened.

'Where've ye been, lass? Where's Bert?'

'You met with no luck, Dah?' She knew that he wasn't going to be pleased when she told him about what had happened at the Morans'. Placing a hand on his shoulder, she realised he was cold and rested her cheek on his hair for a moment in way of comfort.

'I've searched everywhere but couldn't find Mal. I went to the police station in the end and told them about Mother and Florrie. They're going to put out a description of Mal, Alice and Kenny. I'm to inform them as soon as Mother comes round.' He sounded weary to the bone.

'Don't be angry with me, Dah, but Kenny came home. He would have been here with me now, I'm sure, if it hadn't been for our Bert interfering and frightening him off. I didn't want Bert hurting him, so I tried to stop him, and Kenny managed to get out of the house. Bert's gone after him.'

Jock lifted his head and she stepped back. He swore softly. Something he would never have done if his wife had been awake. 'You shouldn't have done that, lass. Bert wouldn't hurt him.'

'He might. He was angry.'

Jock nodded, frowning. 'He loves Mother! Mal must have sent Kenny for something. Let's hope we can get his whereabouts out of him.'

'Bert mightn't catch him. Kenny can't half fly.'

Jock's face looked as if set in granite. 'If he doesn't, he'll have me to answer to. Now make me a cup of tea, there's a good lass.'

'What about your supper?' Her slender face was concerned.

'I don't feel like eating.' He gazed down at the prone figure of his wife.

'You've got to eat, Dah,' she urged.

He nodded. 'I will when I'm ready.' He sighed, hoping his son would soon be home with Mal's lad in tow.

Half an hour later Bert arrived back at the house.

Jock had come downstairs and was sitting in front of the fire, having a warm and drinking tea. He put down his cup and got to his feet. 'Well?'

'He gave me the slip. I would have caught him if it hadn't been for…' Bert stopped, wiped the sweat from his brow and stared at Hannah.

'I know about that,' said Jock, his blue eyes sharp as they slid from his son's flushed face to his daughter's pale one.

Bert heaved a sigh. 'I could have cracked my head open on the floor when she grabbed my foot.'

'You shouldn't have threatened Kenny, making out he might hang if Mother dies,' retorted Hannah.

'So you care more about *him* than your own family!' Bert darted a look at his father. 'She needs to know whose side she's on – is she a Kirk or is she a Moran? Anyway, I sure as hell frightened the life out of the dummy.'

Jock groaned and put his head in his hands. 'I know ye thought you were doing the right thing, Bert, but it might have been better if you hadn't said that to him about hanging,' he said in a muffled voice.

Bert glared at Hannah. 'Just you wait,' he mouthed silently, before saying in a loud voice. 'I'm sorry, Dah. My mistake! I only wanted to give Kenny something to think about. Hopefully he'll come back here tomorrow and write down what he knows. If he doesn't, then I reckon we should take a stroll down town. He was heading in that direction.'

'Maybe, maybe,' said Jock, lifting his head and staring at his daughter. 'You scoot off to bed, lass. Let's hope tomorrow brings good news.'

She went over to him and put her arms about his waist and rested her head on his chest. 'Goodnight, Dah. I'm sure Mother'll wake up tomorrow.' He patted her shoulder and kissed the top of her head.

To Hannah's relief, her sisters were asleep and so was Freddie in the tiny box room next to theirs. Bert slept on the next floor, which had housed the lodgers in the past. She went into her parents' room and gazed, once more, at the unconscious Susannah. 'Come on, Mother,' she urged, taking her hand once again. 'Please, wake up!'

But Susannah made no sign of having heard her.

Slowly and sadly Hannah left the room. She undressed and slid beneath the bedclothes, easing Grace over with a push of her bottom. She lay on her back, gazing up at the ceiling, worrying about what the next forty-eight hours might bring. She prayed again for her mother and Alice and Kenny, as well as for the baby, hoping she was still alive. Turning onto her side, she buried her face in the edge of the pillow, seeking oblivion so she could forget, for a short while, the terrible happenings of the day.

Chapter Four

'Stop that, Freddie!' Hannah lightly slapped her younger brother's hand away from his willy and pulled down his nightshirt. Her head ached and she felt other-worldly. It was the next morning and there was still no change in her mother's condition and she was starting to believe that she wasn't going to wake up and this dreadfully nightmarish sensation wouldn't pass. She thought about the policeman who had turned up and questioned her an hour ago at nine o'clock; he'd also spoken to her father and looked in on her still unconscious mother.

'Hurry up with that fish, Hanny, luv.' Jock gazed into the mirror over the fireplace from eyes that seemed sunken in his head as he shaved. 'And don't forget the bread and butter.'

'Excuse me, Dah!' She reached round him for the pan then gasped as the heat from the handle burnt her fingers. The pan slipped and would have spilt water onto the fire had he not grabbed the handle with the towel and moved the pan onto the hob.

'Be careful, lass.' He sounded weary.

'Sorry!' She clutched her hand, thinking that her dah looked as if he had not slept at all, either. Probably he had lain there, willing her mother to wake up just as she had. Maybe he had placed his arm across her, thinking that way he would keep her anchored to this life. It was what Hannah would have done. She would have been worried sick in case she died right beside her. What would happen to them all if she did die? The thought made her want to weep. How would they manage?

'Have ye burnt yer hand, lass?' Jock looked down at her from worried blue eyes.

Hannah grimaced. 'I'll be OK, Dah. I'll put some butter on it later.'

'Yer a good lass.' He rested a hand on her shoulder. 'Do it now. I'll put out the fish. Do you think you'll be able to cope without me for a while? The police said Mal bought a train ticket to Birkenhead and Alice was with him. So I've got to have a go at finding Kenny and see what he knows. Besides, Mother'll give me down the banks, when she wakes up, if I'm not doing something.' He gave a lopsided smile as he wiped the last of the soap from an earlobe.

'You've done your bit trying to find Mal, Dah. Leave it to the police. I'm sure she'd rather you were here when she woke up,' said Hannah, smearing butter on her burn.

'I know why yer saying that, lass,' replied Jock gravely, as he divided the fish and placed it on two plain white plates. 'But I just can't bear sitting up there, waiting for her to come round.' His voice shook. 'And you do know I won't harm Kenny.'

Hannah said in a whisper, 'But what if she were to die, Dah, while you weren't here? What would I do?'

He stood perfectly still, gazing down at her, tears shining in his eyes. 'You'd rather I stayed?'

'Yes!'

'OK, lass.' He sat down and picked up his knife and fork.

She was so relieved that she kissed him on his ruddy cheek, just as Bert entered the kitchen. He smirked, 'What's she been up to, Dah, that she's trying to get round you?'

'I'm not doing anything of the sort,' said Hannah tartly. She left her father's side and was about to put out the porridge for Freddie and herself, when there was a knock on the front door. She and her father exchanged glances and Hannah was about to go and answer it when Jock stopped her, placing a hand on her shoulder. 'I'll go. It could be the police again with news of Mal.' The caller was the Morans' neighbour, whom Jock had spoken to last evening. She was wearing white cap, apron and black dress, as she worked as a waitress at the General Railway station. She looked all agog. 'Good morning, Mr Kirk,' she said, a breathless catch in her voice.

'What is it?' he said, surprised but alert for news.

'I thought you might like to know,' she said, 'that Kenny Moran is in the ticket queue for Birkenhead. If you're quick you might catch him. It's a long queue.'

Before Jock could even thank her, Bert's excited voice came from behind him. 'We'd best go right away, Dah.'

'Aye! You're right,' said Jock, avoiding his daughter's eyes as she stared at him from the kitchen doorway: 'Hold the breakfast, lass. We won't be long.' He and Bert were out of the house before Hannah could even reach the front door. They left their informant behind in their haste and before Hannah could speak to her the woman was hurrying after them.

Hannah wished she could have gone too but, at that moment, she heard the sound of feet on the stairs and, turning, saw her sisters.

'Mother's not awake yet,' said Grace, her thin face pinched with worry.

'I know! But she will wake up. I'm sure of that,' lied Hannah.

'How can you be so sure?' Joy pushed past her younger sister and she stood gazing up at Hannah, twisting part of her nightgown round her right hand.

'Because I am, that's why.' She placed a hand on each of the girls' shoulders and urged them gently into the kitchen.

'I want a wee wee,' said Freddie, clutching his crotch and doing a little dance on the linoleum.

'Right!' She grabbed his hand and said, 'Joy, you can put out yours and Grace's porridge. Be back in a minute.'

She hurried Freddie down the yard and lifted him up, holding his nightshirt out of the way while he aimed for the hole in the wooden seat. She thought absently-mindedly that it would need scrubbing soon to stop it stinking. With the other part of her mind, she thought of Kenny and whether Jock and Bert would get to him before he got on the train to Birkenhead. He must know where his father and Alice had gone after all! She wondered what her mother would make of everything if she knew that Jock was depending on mute Kenny to give him answers. Suddenly, she felt an overwhelming need to be upstairs with her mother, urging her to wake up.

'Finished!' said Freddie, giving his willy a little shake. 'Get down now.' He wriggled in her arms and she backed out of the lav before putting him down. He ran up the yard, and she wondered just how much he understood about their mother's condition.

Immediately she set foot in the house, she hurried upstairs but her mother lay in exactly the same position. Downstairs again, Hannah knew that it was going to be left to her to prepare their Sunday lunch, something she had never done before in her life. Her mother had told her food cost money and she couldn't afford her to waste it while teaching her to cook. She could wait until she had a husband. Susannah could make a Sunday joint feed the family for four days. Hannah could not see herself performing the same miracle. Her mother was a marvel and there was no way that she could match up to her ability and standards.

She remembered playing at houses, pretending to eat mud pies and putting her rag doll on a potty. She and Alice had giggled and thought it fun but, of course, it was nothing like the real thing. Would she ever see poor Alice again? Hannah yearned for those childhood days when life had seemed so straightforward and secure.

Her heart was heavy in her breast when she explained to her sisters about the visit from the police and then about Mrs Taylor, calling to say Kenny was at the station and how Jock and Bert had gone after him.

'D'you think they'll catch Kenny?' said Joy, plucking at her nightgown with nervous fingers.

Hannah shrugged. In one way she hoped they would but she didn't want poor Kenny being hurt.

After they had finished breakfast and Joy, Grace and Freddie were washed and dressed, and Hannah had been upstairs again to check up on Mother, she set the girls to peeling the vegetables. Grace moaned but Hannah was firm with her.

'But I've never done it before,' wailed her younger sister, kicking the table leg. 'Mother or you always done it.'

'Shut up and get on with it,' said Joy with a scowl, placing newspaper over the table and setting to with the special sharp little knife her mother used for the job of peeling potatoes.

'Yes, do as you're told, and mind you don't cut yourself,' said Hannah, taking the mutton from the meat safe and placing it in the cooking tin with a chunk of dripping. She was in the act of putting it into the oven of the black-leaded range when Freddie tugged at her skirt. 'Mudder! Wan' Mudder!'

'Yer can't have her,' said Grace, who was making a pig's ear of peeling a potato. 'She's hurt her head and—'

'Shut up, Grace!' said Joy, nudging her with an elbow. 'He's not going to understand. She'll be better soon, Freddie. She's tired and needs to sleep.'

At that moment, there was a banging on the door. The three sisters froze and glanced at each other. Was it Jock and Bert back with Kenny or had the police come to say they had traced Mal and Alice's whereabouts?

Hannah rushed to the door.

'What's going on, girl?' Granny Popo stood on the step looking very put out. She wore a long black skirt, a frilly, cream blouse under a black waistcoat and a black bonnet that had been fashionable in 1887 when she had lost her son, Dolly's father. 'I thought your mam might have been round by now to see how Florrie's babby is, and mebbe give our Dolly a couple of coppers a day for giving the child of her best.'

Hannah sagged against the doorjamb. 'She's still alive then?'

'She's hangin' on. Can't make no promises, mind, whether she'll still be alive by the end of the week.' Granny's wrinkled face was pulled as if by a drawstring as she sucked on a clay pipe.

'Mother's upstairs unconscious. I thought you might have been the police saying they've caught Mal Moran.'

Granny Popo's eyes almost popped out of her head. 'What'd that devil do? I knew I shouldn't have left her on her own with Alice.'

'Come in and I'll tell you,' said Hannah, flinging the door wide. Suddenly she was glad to have the old woman to talk to.

Granny stepped over the threshold and hobbled up the lobby in Hannah's wake. The three younger Kirks gazed at her with fascinated eyes because she looked like a character out of a book in her old fashioned clothes. Although the old woman knew their mother well, they'd had little to do with her. She settled herself in a chair next to the fire and bent to unfasten her laces, then she eased off her shoes and rubbed her bunions. 'That's better.' She smiled at the children. 'Yous just pray to God that you never end up with feet like mine. Now what's this about your mother, girl? And what's that child doing with that spud? There'll be none of it left the way she's going about it.'

'I can't do it!' said Grace sulkily, throwing down the knife and folding her arms.

'Less of the temper,' said Granny, and pursed her lips in disapproval. 'Pick that knife up and give it to me! Quick as a flash or you'll be feeling the back of me hand.'

Grace glanced up at her big sister. 'You heard,' said Hannah.

Scowling, Grace picked up the knife and warily approached the old woman. She grabbed the girl's wrist. 'If your mother's sick, your sister needs all the help she can get. She doesn't need sulky pusses being a pain in the backside. I'll show you how to peel a spud.'

She felt the edge of the blade with her thumb and proceeded to peel most of the potatoes with a minimum of waste, while Hannah explained in a low voice what had happened to her mother. Granny clucked her tongue several times and called Mal rude names under her breath. When Hannah had finished, the old woman said, 'It could be that you'll have to think of putting the babby in an orphanage if she surprises me and survives, me duck.'

Hannah bit her lip. 'You think so? Mother wouldn't want that, I'm sure,' she said, tucking a curl, that had come loose from the pile pinned on top of her head, behind her ear.

Granny stared at her a moment, then said, 'Well, we'll see. Our Dolly's really taken with her and's doing her best to get the mite to feed. Although she looks like a skinned rat at the moment – not the least bit attractive.'

'Poor little thing,' said Hannah with a sigh, wondering what Alice would think of what Granny had said about her little sister. She hoped her friend was safe. God only knew what Mal might do to her if he was in one of his black moods.

'Now perhaps I could have a peek at your mam?' said Granny, heaving herself to her feet.

'Of course!' Hannah led the way upstairs and into her parents' bedroom. Granny tutted several times, felt the unconscious woman's forehead, lifted her hand and read her pulse. Susannah's eyes were still shut, although – Hannah could have sworn that her right hand had been on the coverlet when last she looked in and now it lay on the pillow. Her heart leapt. 'Mother!'

No answer.

Granny flashed her a keen glance. 'What is it, me duck?'

'I-I thought her other hand had moved.' The old woman nodded. 'Perhaps it did. If so then it'll move again.' She smoothed back Susannah's greying hair with an unsteady hand. 'We've been through a lot together, Susie, me dear friend. I hope there's more lives we can have an effect on in the future.' She stepped back and stared a moment longer at the unconscious figure, before bustling outside and downstairs.

Hannah followed her to the kitchen, where Granny pleased her by helping her two younger sisters peel the rest of the vegetables and place them in salted water. 'Thanks! You are kind,' she said to the old woman.

Granny brushed her gratitude aside, put on her shoes and said, 'I'll hope to see yous termorra and there's better news.'

'I hope so, too,' said Hannah in heartfelt tones, and saw the old woman out.

When she returned to the kitchen, Joy said hesitantly, 'Do you think it would be OK for us to take Freddie to the park? Or do you think we should go and sit with Mother?'

'You could go and have a look at her and stay with her for five minutes and then go the park,' said Hannah gravely. 'Perhaps she'll wake up while you're there and give you one of her best smiles.'

'I'd like that,' said Joy, and calling Grace and Freddie, they went upstairs. Ten minutes or so later, the three of them were down again. Joy had a smile on her face. 'She's still asleep but Freddie almost sat on her hand and it moved.' She added hastily, 'That's good, isn't it?'

Hannah's face lit up. 'I'm sure it is.'

'Should we stay in and wait to see if she wakes?' said Grace.

'If you want.' Hannah's smile embraced the three of them. 'But maybe the fresh air will do you good and when you come back she'll be really glad to see you.'

Grace and Joy looked pleased with her answer and, fetching their coats and a ball, went out.

Hannah was upstairs in seconds, determined to stay with her mother until she woke up. As she held one of her mother's hands and chatted about the visit from Granny Popo, she could not help her thoughts wandering a little to what might be happening to Kenny, and whether her dah and Bert had caught up with him. They had been out for quite some time. Surely they must have seen him but what had happened when they had?

-

Kenny felt done in after worrying all night about Alice's safety and what Hannah must be thinking about him. He had spent most of the night in the vicinity of the Northgate locks. The three locks had a total fall of thirty-three feet and had been excavated out of the sandstone rock over a hundred years before. Kenny was friendly with the lock-keeper and several of the families who lived on the barges working the canals. His lack of talk did not seem to bother them and they were grateful for his help unloading coal and materials for the factories or working the lock gates. In exchange they shared their brew, bread and crumbly Cheshire cheese, allowing him to warm himself by their stove. It wasn't the first time he had taken refuge with them.

He did have another refuge, if he felt in need of one, and that was with his employer, Mr Bushell. But, right at that moment, he was on his own, knowing there were some things he had to do himself.

The queue shuffled forward and he glanced about the huge General Station. Trains came and went from here to Wales, the Midlands, London, Birkenhead and Warrington. For Manchester, one had to go to Northgate Station. Passengers were milling about, so he had no choice but to wait and, all the time, he was keeping his eyes open for anyone he knew. It came as a shock when he saw Bert and Jock Kirk and he quickly ducked his head. The queue moved and he went with it. The woman in front stopped abruptly and the toe of his boot scrapped her heel.

She yelped and turned on him. 'That hurt, young fellow melad! What have you to say for yourself?' Kenny stared at her wordlessly. 'Well?' she demanded. His lips moved but no sound came out. She turned to the man at her side. 'Make him say sorry.'

Kenny took one look at the short, burly bloke with shoulders like those of a bull, and got himself out of there. It was just bad luck that Bert, closely followed by his father, was coming towards him. Bert yelled something that Kenny did not catch but it was enough to make him run. He slipped like an eel through the crowds. Several heads turned as Bert shouted, 'Stop thief!'

Desperation caused Kenny to elbow several people out of his way and he headed for the overhead footbridge and tore up it. Bert belted after him. Kenny dodged several hands that reached out for him and made it down the other side. Then his luck ran out and he felt a hand on his shoulder and was swung round. Kenny struggled but the man was strong and kept hold of him until Bert arrived.

Grinning he said, 'Thank you, sir! He's a right little sneak. I'll take over now.' Bert twisted Kenny's arm up his back and pressed his forehead against the back of Kenny's head. 'You shouldn't have run like that, Dummy. I don't like being put to all this extra trouble. I'm upset enough as it is with what your father's done to my mother. You do know what your father is?' Kenny struggled to free himself. Bert sighed. 'Dear me! I'm forgetting you don't know what your tongue's for but I wonder if I hit you hard enough I might get a squeak.'

Kenny panicked and brought his head forward and then jumped and flung it back. He knew he had hit Bert right on the nose by the sound he made and the curse that followed. He was allowed no time to crow but was soon wishing he had kept still, as Bert proceeded to try and beat him into pulp. Watched by several people, some proclaimed it was a disgrace, but Kenny was soon on his knees, one of his eyes half-closed, his nose bloodied, his jaw grazed, his ribs feeling as if they were broken.

'What's going on here?' bellowed a voice.

Most of their audience melted away but some murmured approval as the huge bobby yanked Kenny to his feet and seized Bert by the back of his collar with a hand the size of a plate. 'He started it, Constable,' cried Bert in a strangled voice.

'I don't care who started it.' He banged their heads together. 'The pair of you can cool off in the cells. You're giving our fair city a bad name.'

Kenny's ears were ringing and Bert wasn't feeling too good either. When a panting Jock hovered into view, he was glad to see him. 'Dah, will you tell the constable that I had just cause for what I've done to Kenny.'

A stunned Jock stared at the bloodied features of Kenny. 'Yer did that, son?'

Bert touched his nose gingerly. 'He struck the first blow. After that I just lost my temper. I knew I shouldn't have but I was thinking of Mother.'

Jock understood exactly how his son felt but, even so, he was shocked. Bert had made a right mess of the poor sod. But at least he had the chance now to talk to Kenny and, hopefully, get the whereabouts of Mal out of him. It would ease some of the ache inside him if he could have a go at Mal. So he managed to smile at the constable as he placed a hand on Bert's arm. 'I'm sorry about this, officer, but if ye could hand my son over to me, I'll deal with him. I'll take the other one, too, if you like. He's a neighbour's lad and I need to have a word with him.'

The policeman, his bushy brows and beard bristling, growled, 'Would you now? And how am I to know that you wouldn't give him a hiding either? What's this all about? You'd better come along to the police station with me. They've both disturbed the peace and I'm taking them in.' He turned away, forcing Kenny and Bert to walk in front of him towards the station exit.

'Dad, tell him about Mother and how Kenny's wanted for questioning to do with an attempted murder,' yelled Bert over his shoulder.

The policeman stopped and fixed Kenny with a stare. 'Is this true, lad?'

Kenny shook his head and winced. He longed for nothing more than to lie down and pass out, so he couldn't feel the pain.

'It's no use expecting an answer from him. He's a mute,' said Jock, realising he was going to have to come clean and let the police question Kenny. 'But he's not deaf and he can write answers down for you. I've already reported the crime.'

The policeman fixed Jock with a stare. 'Is that right now? Then we'll go along to the station. But I'm telling you now, your son's still going in a cell. I'll not have anyone taking the law into their own hands on my patch.'

Bert opened his mouth to protest but Jock ordered him to shut up and told the policeman that he had every intention of sticking to the law.

–

Hannah gazed at the clock on the mantelpiece, worried and near to screaming point.

Not only had her mother not gained consciousness, but the Sunday dinner was going to be ruined if her father and brother didn't come in soon. Where were they? Should she wait, shouldn't she wait? She gnawed on her lip. Ten minutes more she decided. The minutes dragged but at last she decided that to waste food was a sin and proceeded dishing the food out for her siblings. A couple of minutes later she heard the key being pulled through the letterbox. She dropped the spoon and flew to the door.

'Thank God! What took you so long, Dah? Did you find Mal?' She stared at her father, then realised her brother wasn't with him. 'Where's Bert?'

'I'll tell you later, lass. How's your mother?' He brushed past her and headed for the stairs.

She followed him, her grey-blue eyes shining with tears. 'She moved, Dah! Twice her hands have been in different places, but she still hasn't opened her eyes or said anything.'

Jock paused, turned and kissed his daughter on the top of her head. 'You stay here. I'll go up alone.' He took the stairs two at a time.

He entered the room and, taking a deep, calming breath, sat at the side of the bed gazing, for the umpteenth time, at his wife's lined face, which now showed bruising. More often than not in their nineteen years of marriage, he had been able to forget she was eight years older than he was. She had always been so energetic and full of life. In his mind's eye, he could see her little figure bustling about the kitchen, cleaning, baking, and doing so many other tasks for him and the children. She had knelt in front of him every evening when he came in from work, without even being asked, and unfastened his laces and eased his boots from his aching feet.

He cradled her limp, gnarled, work-worn hand between his hands and squeezed it gently. Shutting off outside distractions he concentrated, willing her to wake up before saying, 'Come on, time to open yer eyes. I need ye! The bairns need ye! Ye've had a rest, now wake up and speak to me, Mother.'

Her eyelids flickered. A tingle raced through Jock's body. Had he really seen that movement? 'Come on, lass! Let's have yer do it again,' he urged. 'Open yer eyes wide!'

There was no response but he was determined not to give up. He squeezed her hand again. 'Hanny's done the Sunday dinner. It won't be as good as what you cook but she's a good girl and a trier. She's sick with worry about you.' He paused. But there was no movement. He continued. 'Bert and I went after Kenny. We were hoping he would lead us to Mal. I tell you, I want to tear Mal's head from his shoulders but we still don't know where he is. Bert's made a bit of a mess of Kenny's face. They're both in jail.' He squeezed her hand again and, this time, felt the slightest quiver of a finger against the edge of his left palm. Tears pricked the back of his eyelids and he felt as if a marble had stuck in his throat. He swallowed and said huskily, 'That's it! Ye're going to be fine.'

Susannah's eyes opened and fixed on his craggy, ruddy features. She frowned. Her head felt as if it had been mashed and her nose! Oh, her nose! She wanted to put up a hand to touch it but, when she tried, her arm felt too heavy to lift. She also had an enormous ache in her side and back. She winced.

Jock brought his head close to hers and asked anxiously. 'Are yer hurting bad? I should never have let this happen to you!'

She did not answer, wondering who this man was; her eyes slowly roamed the bedroom and returned to his face. She had no idea where she was or who she was.

Jock saw the bewilderment in her eyes and knew he needed help with this. 'The bairns! I'll get the bairns and then the doctor.' He kissed her on the lips and then hurried out of the bedroom.

Hannah looked up as Jock came into the kitchen. She knew from his expression that what they had been praying for had happened. 'She's awake?' There was joy in her voice.

He beamed and putting his arms round his eldest daughter, he waltzed her round the room. 'She hasn't spoken yet and I can tell she's confused and in pain but that's not surprising, is it? But she will get better.' He sounded suddenly unsure of himself. 'I'm going for the doctor – Sunday or no Sunday, payment or no payment.'

Hannah hurried after him to the front door. 'He did say to tell him when Mother woke. So I'm sure he'll come out,' she called with a lilt in her voice.

Jock raised his hand and then ran like an athlete down the street despite the fact that just a few hours ago, he'd felt like a very old man.

Hannah left the remains of her dinner on the table and took the stairs in a rush, followed by her younger siblings; her heart was singing.

Susannah lay in the same, prone position but now her gaze fixed on Hannah's face as she entered the room. The girl sat on the side of the bed. 'Don't look so worried. You're going to be all right!' she said happily.

'Yes, you're going to be OK,' said Joy, sitting on the other side of the bed and lifting Freddie on to her knee. Grace stood at the bottom, gazing at her mother with a big smile.

Susannah did not speak and Hannah noticed the uncertainty and fear in her eyes. The girl reached out a hand to her but her mother drew her arms in close to her body.

Hannah was surprised. 'What is it? There's nothing to be scared of! You're safe in your own bed. Dah's gone for the doctor. He thinks you're in pain. That wouldn't be surprising, would it? Considering I found you at the bottom of the stairs.'

Susannah's lips quivered and her eyes filled with tears. With difficulty, she lifted a trembling hand and brushed them away.

Hannah was at a loss at what to do, but then remembered the remedy for all ills. She went downstairs and made a pot of tea. Hastily the younger children followed her.

'What's wrong with Mother? Why doesn't she answer us?' asked Joy, her dark eyes resting on Hannah's strained face.

'Shock, maybe. Not surprising if she fell downstairs and is in pain. Imagine what it must do to your head and body when you fall all that way. She's all shook up,' murmured Hannah, spooning tea into the pot.

Freddie suddenly said, '*Jack an' Jill went up de hill to fetch a pail of wa-er. Jack fell down and broked his crown—*' He rubbed his head and beamed. 'Mudder needs vin'ger and brown paper.'

His sisters laughed. 'You could be right, Freddie,' said Hannah, ruffling his curls. 'Joy, cut some bread and butter and I'll take it up to Mother with a nice cup of tea.' Hannah climbed the stairs, hoping that this time her mother would speak to her. 'Tea and bread and butter.' She adopted a cheerful tone. 'I'd best help you to sit up.' She placed the cup and saucer on a chair along with the plate of bread and butter.

Susannah watched her but, as her daughter would have placed her arms round her to lift her into a sitting position, she pushed the girl's hands away.

Hannah was taken aback and gazed at her mother with worried eyes. 'You've got to sit up to drink your tea. You've had nothing to eat or drink since tea yesterday.'

Susannah didn't want tea. She wanted to be left alone. A picture of an angry man flashed into her mind. She could smell blood! Then the image was gone. Terror seized her and she began to tremble.

'It's OK, Mother! I'm not angry.' Hannah's hand covered one of Susannah's. 'If you want to stay lying down then you do. We'll just have to work out a way for you to drink your tea.' She attempted a smile. 'A cup with a spout, that's what we'll have to get.'

So this girl was her daughter, thought Susannah, and presumably the other children were hers, too. Why didn't she know them? The man, who had come into this room – was he their father? If he was, then that meant he was her husband. Why couldn't she remember?

There was the sudden sound of feet on the stairs and men's voices. Susannah held Hannah's hand limply; the fear inside her refused to go away.

Her husband entered the room with another man dressed in a frock coat and trousers.

Hannah quickly removed the tea and bread and butter and stepped out of the way. 'She doesn't seem to be able to speak,' she said in a worried voice.

The man acknowledged her words with a slightly raised hand.

'The doctor's come to see ye, Mother.' Jock smiled down at her.

He was her son. No! Impossible! He was her husband. Then why did he call her Mother? Susannah felt terribly confused and panic threatened to overwhelm her. She tried to move but ached all over.

'Hurts does it, Mrs Kirk?' The doctor took hold of her wrist and smiled kindly.

If she had felt in the mood to talk, she would have said she didn't need him to tell her that. What she needed was to be left in peace, but that was the last thing the doctor was going to allow. He set about prodding and poking, asking questions which she did not answer, ordering her to wriggle her toes and fingers and move her head.

'Don't want to talk? That's all right with me.' The doctor turned his head towards Jock. 'A fall is a shock to the whole system. It's possible your wife has damaged her spine. But there's slight movement in her toes and fingers so…' He paused and there was a gleam in his eyes. 'I don't know how you feel about your wife having the opportunity of being one of the first women in the north to have her bones photographed by a marvellous new machine. It sends rays through the body and takes pictures so we can see if a bone is fractured. They call it an X-ray machine.'

Jock looked interested. 'At Chester Infirmary, you mean?'

The doctor nodded. 'Tomorrow I'll have the horse ambulance call round to take her there. Once we know what the damage is, then I'll know what to do about it. We'll have her skull photographed, as well.'

Jock did not argue. He wanted the best for his wife. 'Hanny, you're going to have to stay home until Mother's on her feet again,' he said firmly, and left her to see the doctor out.

It was no more than Hannah had expected but she did hope it wouldn't be for long. When Jock came back upstairs, he stood smiling down at his wife. 'So what do ye think, Mother, about being a pioneer of medical science? An X-ray machine that'll take a photograph of yer bones. It's a wonder!'

'Will I be going with her, Dah?' asked Hannah, knowing he couldn't afford to take time off work.

'Course, lass. Who else?' He beamed at her. 'Now about my dinner? I'm starving! Joy can come up and sit with Mother.' With a backward glance at Susannah, who was lying with her eyes closed, he said, 'See you soon, Mother.'

Hannah kissed her cheek before following him downstairs, thinking she must get Joy to make more tea and take some up for their mother in the small teapot.

Soon Jock was seated at the table, eating his dinner as if starved. Between mouthfuls, he told Hannah about Bert and Kenny being in the police cells.

Hannah's eyes widened and, if Bert had been the only prisoner, she would have been completely delighted by the news. 'What happened?'

'They'll probably let Bert out in a few hours but they'll be keeping poor Kenny in. They've had a doctor out to look at him and...'

Immediately Hannah's mood changed and she couldn't disguise her anger and concern as she rested both hands on the table and glared at her father. 'Why? What did our Bert do to him? Why didn't you stop him? You said you wouldn't let him hurt him.'

Jock adjusted his necktie and cleared his throat. 'He lost his temper for once and beat him up. Don't look like that, Hanny!' he pleaded. 'Ye know how much he loves Mother. As soon as I've had my dinner, I'll be off again to see if they've got anything out of Kenny.'

Hanny's eyes darkened. Hadn't she known her brother would hurt Kenny if he got hold of him? For the constable to get a doctor out to look at him showed how badly he must have been beaten. She wished she could go and see him. It might give him some comfort. Had he been able to write down information about Alice and Mal Moran's whereabouts? She would have to wait for her father to return before finding that out. In the meantime her mother's needs had to come first. She wondered what Alice would say if she knew that 'oh so perfect' Bert had beaten her brother to a pulp. Then she began to worry about her friend, wondering what had been happening to her since last they had heard of her.

Chapter Five

'Move, move! And not a word from you, girl, or I'll do to ye what I did to yer mam,' growled Mal, his fingernails biting into Alice's arm as he hurried her down an unknown street. Terrified, she almost fell over her feet in her eagerness to comply with his order. She believed him; how could she not when for most of her life she had been witness to his changes of mood: with a swipe of his arm or his clenched fist, he would work out his demons on her mam. She had stopped concerning herself with their eventual destination, although she could smell the sea and that did make her wonder where on earth they were going… but her main thought was concentrating on getting there in one piece. Not for one moment did she believe that she could escape from her father a second time. She shuddered, wanting to weep as she remembered how he had flung the youth, who had tried to protect her, like a rag doll, and, even worse, her mother's crooked body, which surely he had cracked in half the way he had handled it. She hated him for that but she had no intention of giving him any trouble and, maybe that way, she'd stay alive.

They were in Liverpool, having travelled on the new electric train under the Mersey from Birkenhead. A marvel of ingenuity, Kenny had showed her an article in the newspaper about it. The old steam operated trains had been closed down because the smoke from the engines had almost choked people to death in the tunnel beneath the riverbed. If she hadn't been so scared of her father, then she might have been worried at the thought of the restless water bursting through the rock just above the roof of the train. But they had arrived safely and, from the little she knew of this sprawling port, they must be heading for the Mersey.

Where was he taking her at this time of night? Surely he wouldn't have tickets or know what ships were sailing? Unless he planned on throwing her in one of the docks? Panic seized her by the throat and, for a moment, she froze and couldn't move.

Her father was jerked to a halt. 'What the hell's the matter with you?' He brought his head down so it was level with hers and she could smell his foul breath. 'We've got to hurry or we'll miss the boat!'

Thank God for that! 'What... what boat?'

'The Isle of Man boat. Now run!' He almost wrenched her arm out of its socket as he began to jog and, after an initial stumble, her feet were forced into moving so swiftly to keep up with him that she thought she might take off and fly. She could see the river gleaming in the moonlight and ships displaying lights. They passed under the overhead railway, another marvellous engineering feat and a first in the country for Liverpool. In no time at all they were on the landing stage and joining a bustling, excited throng of people streaming up the gang plank of the *Mona's Isle.* Her father had shown two tickets but she had no idea where he had purchased them.

He did not hang around on deck, which was a relief because the thought had now occurred to Alice that he might be planning to drop her overboard in mid-river and she had become weak with terror again. But then he surprised her by asking a steward where his cabin was and they were directed to it. Alice was amazed that her father would spend money on such a luxury. But once inside the tiny lamplit wood-lined space, with its two bunk beds and modest furnishings, Mal locked the door and turned and stared at her. 'Now you can't escape me,' he said, his left eyelid twitching.

She tried to speak but could not get the words out because her mouth was so dry – that twitch was always a dangerous sign.

'Ye have nothing to say?' he demanded.

She shook her head.

'Then get up on that top bunk and I don't want a move out of ye, lass, or yer dead.' Alice found the strength to climb onto the top bunk and watched her father remove his cap and run a shaking hand through his thatch of dark red hair. Then he held his head in his hands and groaned. 'Oh, ma bleeding head.'

Hastily Alice lay flat, thinking that if he was going to go on about his head, then his next move might be a punch in the face for her. His headaches over the past few years had been her mam's excuse for his behaviour, yet he never went near a doctor to see if anything could be done about them. Reminded of her mam, Alice's eyes filled with tears. She was going to miss her so much. Her mam had been her rock, her bulwark against her father's violence. What was going to happen to her now? At least Kenny was beyond his reach. She had to be thankful for that. He had been even more terrified of their father than she was. Hopefully he had escaped that Black woman, although, thinking about her appearance, she hadn't looked like a tart; more like a piano teacher. Even so, looks could be deceptive and poor Kenny wouldn't know what to do with his bits and pieces if she was a seducer of innocent young men.

Alice wiped her eyes with the back of her hand and removed her thin-soled shoes and slid beneath the bedcovers. She hadn't had time to pick up her jacket when they left the house and was cold. She tried to lie as still as she could, but her nerves were in such a state that she couldn't stop shaking. Her father was muttering, going on about sin and forgiveness, swinging from a rope and it being all *her* fault. Who was the *her* he was going on about? Herself? Her poor brave mam? Or maybe it could even be Mrs Kirk? Alice just hoped, as he wandered in his mind, that he would forget about her and she could survive the night. Sleep was impossible.

Nevertheless Alice was so tired that, eventually, she did doze off. She woke suddenly and fumbled for the wood either side of the top bunk as the one beneath creaked. She could feel the bruises on her arm where her father had gripped her and her mouth still hurt from the smack in the face. Her eyes felt full of grit and her stomach rumbled. She had not had anything to eat since the jam tarts at the Kirks' and was desperate for a wee. She shook as the lower bunk creaked again but was also aware of other sounds, of people hurrying past their cabin, the shouts of the crew, engines reversing and the slap of waves against the hull.

Her father's face hovered into view. She shrank back, gripping the wooden crossbeam with one hand. He brought his face close to her small strained one as he braced himself on the swaying floor. 'Now listen, lass, there's nothing for ye to fear if yer do as ye're told. We're both in this up to our necks so we've got to stick together.'

She nodded her head vigorously, 'Anything you say, Dad! It was an accident wasn't it? You didn't mean for Mrs Kirk to fall downstairs! I'd swear on the Bible to that if I...' She pulled herself up short because his expression had changed. What an idiot she was forgetting his moods could change like the weather, especially when anything to do with religion was mentioned.

He put a heavy hand over hers. 'I don't care about *her*! They can't prove a thing if ye keep yer mouth shut real tight. I'm really sorry, though, that Florrie's dead. I didn't mean to hurt yer mammy but she defied me and was teaching you to go down the same road. I couldn't allow that. I played by her rules, that sin has to be punished.'

'But... But f-forgiveness? It mentions forgiveness too, Dad.'

'Aye! And she always did forgive me,' he said eagerly. Then his expression darkened. 'Although I wouldn't have needed forgiving if she'd done as told in the first place. A wife must obey her husband.' He smoothed back Alice's tangled auburn hair with a shaking hand before patting her left cheek lightly. 'Bairns are to do the same. Just remember that, lass, and don't go behind ma back telling tales and we'll get on fine without our Kenny. But when I get ma hands on him I'll...' He took a deep breath and clenched his fists.

She didn't like the way the conversation was leading, terrified he might put those big hands of his about her neck and press on her windpipe until she couldn't breathe. 'Dad, I need the lavatory. You must need it, too. Can we get out of here?' she squeaked.

Mal's expression lightened. 'Aye! Enough gabbin'! Let's go before we leave the ship. We don't want to be the last off, more likely to get noticed that way. Got to be part of the crowd. It's Scots week in the Isle of Man. I bet ye didn't know that.' He helped her down and unlocked the door, keeping hold of her thin arm as they swayed along the corridor.

It was a relief to get out of the cabin and to find the lavatories. She longed to linger, to stay on the boat and hide away where her father could not find her but she knew that was only a pipe dream. He would come in and drag her out if need be. She needed a knight in shining armour but where was he when a girl needed one? She thought of the young gardener and felt sorry that she would never have a chance to get better acquainted with him.

Her father seized hold of her again as soon as she appeared outside. He drew her into the line of passengers shuffling towards the gangway. They were a jolly, well-dressed crowd and some looked askance at Alice's bruised face and thin figure in the well-worn, high-necked blouse and soiled skirt. She felt ashamed of her appearance and wished she were only two inches high, so no one could see her. That inner trembling started up again and she took deep breaths of the fresh sea air, as she remembered the last sight of her mam; she could almost smell the blood and urine and felt sick and dizzy. She tried to comfort herself with the thought that at least the baby had survived and that her mother was in heaven now, but oh, dear God, how she wanted her father punished. None of this 'forgiveness' he went on about for him.

Seagulls screeched and swooped overhead. Alice thought of the Groves where seagulls and pigeons competed for the scraps from the trippers' picnics and she longed for home. Her father dragged her along the busy pier in the direction of grey stone buildings and she wondered why they had come here. At last they reached the promenade and people began to go in several directions. Her father forced her on in grim silence and she lost all sense of direction, too tired to care. She was aware her feet were sore: the cardboard inner soles she had cut from a porridge packet were crumbling to pieces and she could feel the cobbles through the holes in her shoes. Eventually, they arrived at a railway station where all was hustle and bustle.

As they stood in a queue for tickets, she felt dreamlike and the voices with different dialects of those about her seemed to be coming from a distance. She was reminded of market days in Chester, when so many farmers and their wives came in from Wales, the Midlands, Lancashire and Cheshire. Was she going to faint? She was grieving, hungry, tired and frightened. Her father dragged her forward and she almost fell as she tried to keep up with him.

They just made it into a crowded carriage before doors slammed and the guard blew his whistle. Douglas was left behind in no time and the train was passing through countryside. The hypnotic click-clack, click-clack of the wheels on the rails lulled her and she found herself nodding off.

'Move yourself! We're there!' Mal almost lifted her from the carriage. She gazed about her, blurry-eyed, as her father hurried her on. She had but a fleeting impression of Peel, but it appeared much smaller than the port of Douglas, as Mal hurried her through the streets to the outskirts of town.

He stopped in front of a long low house with a gable at one end containing an upstairs window. He did not bother with the front door but led her round the side of the building to the rear. Hens clucked and scattered before them. A woman was hoeing among rows of vegetables and appeared not to have heard them. 'Don't move!' ordered Mal, and strolled over to her.

Alice noticed a wooden bench and sat down, too weary and hungry to go anywhere, too tired even to fear or think. She held her face up to the sun. On the breeze came the sound of her father's voice but she could not make out what he was saying. She frowned and opened her eyes; instantly she was aware of the woman's scrutiny. It was not a friendly look. Who was she? Was she, after all these years, finding something out about her father that she had never known – that he was an adulterous womaniser?

Alice could see now that the dumpy female wore a sacking apron over a plain black skirt and pink blouse; her face was weather-beaten despite the white calico sun-bonnet she wore over mousy hair. Well, he certainly didn't go in for attractive women, she thought, remembering Mrs Black.

The woman beckoned to Alice and led the way into the house. The girl was interested in houses, had delivered hats to some fine ones in Chester on several occasions. She wasn't like Hannah, who loved the medieval, all black and white timber framed with uneven floors and lead-paned windows, instead Alice preferred those large houses with gardens, built outside the city walls during the last century for the growing middle-classes. Of course, she knew that dreams of having such a house were probably all that she would ever have.

Her gaze swept the long room. At one end was a fireplace where a bowl covered with a cloth stood on the hearth. She could smell yeast, so presumably it was dough rising. Her spirits lifted a little. Perhaps she would get something to eat at last.

The woman spread a cloth over a table. Yes! They were going to be fed. Alice continued her survey of the room. At the other end was a ladder that went up to an opening in the ceiling. She presumed that led to the only room upstairs. Would they stay the night here? Where would her father sleep? Was there any way she could seek help from this woman so she could escape him? Unlikely in the circumstances because, if she was someone from her father's past and cared for him, then she would definitely be on his side.

Alice gave the furniture a quick once over; a well-worn sofa, a bench close to the table and a dresser containing crockery. A large sink was situated beneath a window that looked out onto fields. The room felt light and airy but there was no evidence of children living here or a man.

Alice's stomach rumbled and she watched the woman place a dish of soused herrings, a pat of butter and a plate of soda scones on the table. Mal told Alice to sit down. So she sat on the bench and was handed a mug of buttermilk. She would have preferred a cup of tea but drank the liquid gratefully. The woman served Mal, piling food onto his plate, talking rapidly as she did so in a language which, to Alice's dismay, she could not understand. She presumed it was Manx, and that her father must have spent time on the Isle of Man – but when had that been? She knew so little about her father's past.

She waited to be told to help herself but the woman rattled on while Mal stuffed himself. Alice could stand it no longer and took a scone from a plate and buttered it. Nobody rebuked her, so she took another. She helped herself to some herring and felt strength flowing into her. She glanced at her father, who was yammering away in that foreign tongue again. What were they talking about? Whatever it was, it seemed to please her father because his expression relaxed and, when he next spoke, he sounded less intense. Perhaps they were talking about her? Was her father going to dump her here and go off on his own? That would suit her down to the ground; somehow she would manage to get onto a ship that would take her back to Liverpool and then home. She grimaced, doubting the reality of her father leaving her having brought her this far. Why couldn't they speak the King's English? It struck her, suddenly, that they could be planning her death! A chill went through her and she started to her feet.

'Sit down!' ordered Mal.

Hurriedly she did as told. Cut off from all normality, she wanted to weep, longed for her mother not to be dead, wanted to go home, however humble, wanted to know if Kenny and the baby were all right and that Mrs Kirk was still alive. A huge lump filled her throat and she couldn't eat anymore.

That night she was sent up to bed with the woman. Her father had told her that she was his cousin and there was no use trying to speak to her because Catrina spoke no English, only the Gaelic. So there was definitely no help to be had from her.

Alice quaked as she listened to the sounds of the house settling down for the night. The wind whistled about the eaves and she pictured the waves lashing against rocks. How she would have loved to have come here with her mam and Kenny and sit on the sand, watching people and maybe having a paddle, but that could never happen now.

Alice thrust her head beneath the pillow, her eyes wet with tears, trying to shut out the sound of her father's cousin snoring, longing for the peace that sleep would bring but she could not relax. So she slid out of the bed and tiptoed downstairs, thinking to attempt to escape. She got far as the door but the scraping of the bolt roused her father, who was sleeping on the sofa.

He was up in a trice and seized her by the hair and thrust his face into hers. 'Where the hell d'yer think ye're going?'

'The lavatory, Dad!' she cried, reaching up with her hands to take the strain from the roots of her hair. 'You're hurting me!'

He lifted her off her feet and muffled her scream with his palm. 'Ye know lying is a sin! If you try that malarky again, I'll beat ye till your black and blue.'

She almost wet herself with fear and scuttled back to bed with a need to use the chamber pot. Catrina woke and let forth a string of incomprehensible words. Alice didn't have the nerve to climb in beside her and instead lay on the rug beside the bed, shivering in her chemise; only when she was convinced the woman was asleep once more did Alice creep under the bedcovers.

The next day she was given breakfast and afterwards told to sweep the floor. Glad of something to do, she made a thorough job of it. From the way her father was watching her she knew there was going to be no chance to get away from him. Even when he turned his back on her, she was convinced he had eyes in the back of his head because, when she made for the door in her search for a shovel, he whirled round and told her that he would get it when she stammered what she wanted. Once she had finished sweeping, a duster and polish was handed to her. She polished the table, bench and dresser. After that she was told to keep still and not be a nuisance. The minutes dragged and the day seemed ten times as long as a normal one at home. She wondered what her employers had made of her not turning up for work and felt terrible about it, having enjoyed her job. She thought if Mrs Kirk died, it would get a mention in the *Chester Chronicle*, and most likely her father would be named as a murderer. Maybe, because of her disappearance, they might think she was dead and no one would try and find her. She felt a rising panic, remembering how he had said that they were in it together. Maybe if they didn't think she was dead then she would be branded as a murderess, too! She began to believe she was going off her head and rose to her feet and began to pace the floor.

'Keep bloody still!' ordered her father, looking up from a map on the table in front of him.

'I need some fresh air!' she cried, wringing her hands. 'And I could do with a change of clothes so I could wash these I've got on.'

'Later,' he said.

She had to be satisfied with that and sat down, wondering where his cousin had gone, wishing she could have gone out with her.

Later her father did take Alice for a walk, showing her the large sweeping bay, to the side of which was situated the small Peel Island with a castle on it. The sands were dotted with people despite the windy weather. He muttered something about the Vikings but that was the only thing he said and it wasn't long before they were heading back to the house.

Catrina was there and preparing a meal. She and Mal started talking again in the Gaelic and he took a newspaper from her. Alice would have liked to get a look at it but the opportunity did not arise. After their meal Catrina went upstairs and when she came down it was with a bundle of clothing. She handed a well-worn brown skirt and a cheese cloth blouse to Alice, but provided no underwear. Alice decided she would just have to go without while her own were washed. She watched as Catrina gave a clean shirt and underwear to Mal, and wondered if her father's cousin was a widow, who had kept her husband's clothes for sentimental reasons. Or did she have a husband, or a brother, who worked away from home? But she was afraid to ask Mal anything more about his relation.

The next morning Alice changed into the clean clothes, which fitted perfectly; she decided that they had once belonged to a younger and slimmer Catrina. Later Alice washed her soiled clothes in the sink, letting her imagination take wing, dreaming that the man, whoever he was, would arrive home and be furious when he found Mal in his house. He would think the worse and beat him into pulp and help her escape.

After hanging out the washing, she went indoors to search for last night's newspaper but could not find it. She presumed there was something in it they didn't want her to see or, perhaps, it had simply been used to light the fire.

The following day passed with no change. Alice felt so sad and lonely, wondering what was being done about her mam's body. Would Kenny have been able to arrange a funeral?

Then on the Thursday she was taken to the harbour, a woman having brought a message that the fishing boats were coming in. Only then was Alice told that Catrina had a Manx husband who had been out with the fishing fleet. While Mal talked to him, Catrina joined other Scottish women intent on helping their menfolk with the catch; as well as salting the fish in barrels, Peel had its share of kippering houses. Alice guessed the husband was not going to help her escape, so she had to do it alone. Trying to look casual, Alice wandered off, eyeing up the boats, looking for one likely to go further than the fishing grounds, so she could stow away.

'I hope ye're not thinking what I think you're thinking?' Mal's voice startled her so much that she tripped over a rope and would have fallen into the sea if he had not grabbed her by the back of her own clean blouse. He thrust his face into hers. 'Back to the house! We're not going travelling just yet.'

'Does that mean we will be leaving here?' she said in relief.

'We'll be leaving for Scotland on Monday evening.'

'Scotland!'

'Aye!' A nerve twitched beneath his left eye and he laughed mirthlessly, and then thrust a hand against her spine and sent her flying along the pier. She picked herself up and decided she would think twice before opening her mouth in future. The last thing she wanted was to go to Scotland and she despaired because surely her father would keep an even closer eye on her once they were on the Malnland.

Exactly a week and a day after their arrival on the Isle of Man, Alice and her father boarded a ship to Ardrossan. Despite the sea being rough, the voyage was accomplished without much discomfort. She and Mal joined the crowds of returning holidaymakers on an express train to St Enoch's, Glasgow. Alice could only understand half of what was said in the conversations going on round her because the Glaswegian accents were so strong. How could she possibly get them to understand her if an opportunity arose for her to make a run for it? She was aware of a familiar despair as she looked at her father. His eyelids were twitching and he looked so ugly, she wondered how her mother had ever fallen in love with him. She grieved that she would never see her again this side of the veil and began to fret that, perhaps, her body had been placed in a pauper's grave.

Suddenly she noticed passengers starting to gather their baggage together but her father still sat unmoving. She glanced out of the window and half-rose in her seat as a sign saying St Enoch flashed by. 'Dad, I think we're nearly there.'

Mal said, 'There's no rush. We've not slowed down yet.'

'But the name of the station just…' Alice got no further. A hideous grating noise drowned her words. The carriage tilted. She lost her balance and landed in the lap of a man sitting in the seat opposite. The carriage reared higher. She struggled, trying to get a grip on something, anything, as she was flung from the man's knee. She glanced about wildly for her father and saw him slumped against the side of the carriage, blood running down the side of his head, his eyes closed. Her heart was pounding but, before she could try and do something, someone collided into her, then another person. She felt herself sliding, but was cushioned by a further body. She could hear screams, sobs, breaking glass, splintering wood and screeching metal as the carriage tilted even higher. She was being smothered by bodies, could not breathe. The pain in her elbow was really bad. She could not move her arms, her legs. She was frightened, she did not want to die but tried to comfort herself with the thought that she was going to her mam. As she felt herself slipping into darkness, she wondered how Kenny would feel when he discovered she and their father were dead.

Chapter Six

Kenny stepped out of the side entrance of the police station into Princess Street and took a deep breath of fresh air. He strolled along into Northgate Street and stood on the corner, near the town hall, watching people going freely about their business. Some, probably sightseers, were going into the cathedral, which had gone through several alterations since medieval times. Maybe he would go and say a few prayers some time today but not right now. His hands clenched in his jacket pocket. He had to find Alice. His strapped ribs might hurt and the bruising to his face still showed, but he was able to move his jaw without it hurting and, most importantly, he was free.

Nine days they had kept him in prison and, even if he could talk, he wouldn't have been able to with the mess Bert had made of his jaw. Kenny had written down the little he knew about what had happened to Mrs Kirk but had made no mention of Mrs Black. Kenny frowned, wondering if he had made a mistake there, but he didn't really want the police going after his father. Mal might panic and do something terrible to Alice. The police had been good to him and, although it had chaffed him not to be able to get out in the fresh air, he'd been grateful for the roof over his head and food in his stomach. Today the police had returned his money to him along with his notebook and pencil. They had even given him a secondhand suit of clothes which was much better than the one he had been wearing. They had called on his employer, Mr Bushell, and he had apparently given Kenny a good character reference, saying he was hardworking, meticulous and honest as the day was long. Hadn't he trained the lad himself? He wanted him back and would have put him up until Alice was found if the sister, who had looked after him since his wife died, hadn't been against it.

It had been a relief to Kenny that the coal merchant had promised to take responsibility for Florrie's funeral, mourning her passing as they had attended the same church.

Kenny grieved for her and wished he could have been there to pay his respects. He would have to see his employer sometime soon because he must not risk losing his job by taking more than a couple of days off. If he could find Alice and get her away from their father, he would have to support her and himself. But one step at a time. He frowned, considering how his father had a good head start on him. The police had traced him to Liverpool but so far had not discovered whether he was still there or moved on somewhere else. Kenny decided that he would go to Liverpool later that day, not that there was any certainty that he would do any better than the police at trying to trace his remaining relatives.

First though, he planned on calling on Mrs Black. Kenny'd had plenty of time to think in prison and had come to the conclusion that she might be able to cast a light on his father's whereabouts. If she'd read the newspaper, like he had the one the sergeant had given to him, she would know that Mal was missing and wanted for assault and battery.

The paper had also reported that Mrs Kirk had regained consciousness but was still confined to bed, having sustained head and back injuries. It was possible that she might never walk again – and she had yet to speak about the incident in the Moran house which had led to her injuries. It also appeared that she didn't recognise her husband or her children.

Poor Mrs Kirk! Poor Hanny! Kenny's heart ached for them both. He was convinced that the girl he loved must now hate the name of Moran and anyone connected to it. Bert certainly did, having threatened him with another beating if he came near any member of his family. As it was, Kenny had no intention of returning to the area. His old home had already been let, according to Mr Bushell and, even if it hadn't been, Kenny wouldn't have wanted to return to the house that held so many unhappy memories.

His eyes smarted as he remembered how his stepmother had suffered years of abuse. How she had borne such suffering for so long and gone on forgiving his father, he couldn't understand. Only her faith could have helped her do that. Whoever said women were the weaker sex had it wrong. He owed his stepmother a great deal and was wracked with guilt for his own cowardice. He should have been protecting her, not the other way round, but at least he could try and make amends by finding Alice. What he could do to get her away from their father he didn't know; the thought of facing Mal filled him with dread but he had to do his best. Without any more delay, he set off in the direction of the Dee, and Mrs Black's house.

–

Sebastian gave a final sweeping polish to the automobile that was his employer, Mr Waters', pride and joy, and cast a glance in the direction of a young man going up the path to Mrs Black's house. 'She's not in!' he shouted.

Kenny turned and looked his way.

Sebastian flung the chammy leather into the wooden carrying box, a scowl on his face. 'Weren't you here the other week with the redhead and the bloke who picked a fight with me?' He strolled towards him. 'A lot of bloody help you were!'

Kenny remembered, to his shame, that it was this youth who had tried to aid Alice in her escape. Scarlet with embarrassment, he reached into his pocket and withdrew his notebook and pencil and wrote on a sheet of paper. He tore it out and handed it to him.

Sebastian read it and then looked up with a grim smile. 'So you're her half-brother and mute. Perhaps that explains your behaviour a little but not much. I haven't seen them since you and they were here last. That's not to say they haven't been to Mrs Black's place. I'm not always around. But Ma might know something. She talks to most of those in service around here. Come round the back and we'll ask her.' Sebastian unrolled his sleeves and buttoned the cuffs before shrugging on his jacket. He picked up the carrying box and led the way round the side of the house to the kitchen where a woman was making sandwiches.

Kenny gazed at her with undisguised interest. She was more handsome than beautiful, and had the same raven black hair and brown eyes as Sebastian. She had smooth olive skin and there was an air about her that was compelling.

'Ma, have you seen a girl and an older man, both redheads, go into Mrs Black's house? Remember I told you about them. The man who picked me up like I was a baby and threw me.'

'Who is this wanting to know?' She regarded Kenny with a haughty expression that made him doubly aware of his secondhand clothes and bruised face.

'He's mute, Ma,' said Sebastian quietly.

Kenny reddened and hastened to write down his name, adding that the man was his father and the girl his half-sister and he was particularly worried about her safety. He tore the page out and showed it to Sebastian's mother.

She wiped her hands on a dishcloth and dried them on a towel before smoothing down a spotlessly clean apron and taking the sheet of paper from him. She read swiftly before handing it back to him. 'I am sorry. I cannot help you. I would if I could. What business has your father with Mrs Black? It's not good I think. That woman, I do not trust her. She has men, lots of men coming to her house. I do not like that. This is a respectable neighbourhood.' Her dark eyes flashed with disapproval.

'I don't think they're after what you think, Ma.' Sebastian's voice was amused.

She fixed him with a stare and said haughtily, 'And what would you know about such things, little man? You keep your nose clean or I chop it off!' She brought a knife down on a cucumber.

Sebastian turned to Kenny. 'They all wear the same clothes – shabby pin-striped suits and felt hats.'

His mother said, 'That is true! It is a mystery. But then she is new to the area and I have yet to make the acquaintance of her maid but I will find out.' She waggled a finger at him. 'Now you must go. Miss Victoria's train will be arriving and you should be there to collect her and her friends. If Mr Waters were here you would have been on your way by now, so out of my kitchen.' She shooed him.

Hastily Kenny left with Sebastian, who said as soon as they were outside. 'Tough luck, mate! But if I hear anything, where can I get in touch with you?' He was thinking that if this mute half-brother was the only person Alice had to depend on to rescue her from their father, she needed all the help she could get.

Kenny scribbled in his notebook *I don't have an address but we'll hopefully meet again. If you're going to the General Station, could you give me a ride?*

Sebastian did not hesitate. 'Sure. But wait for me by the Old Bridge. I don't want Mrs Waters seeing you get in the motor. She'd tear a strip off me and she can really make a bloke feel small,' he said, scratching the back of his neck and looking rueful.

Kenny smiled his thanks and hurried in the direction of the old mill building where once wheat had been ground into flour but now was occupied by a tobacco and snuff company. He appreciated what Seb was doing for him, even though he felt uncomfortable in his company, knowing that he probably despised him for not going to Alice's rescue last time they had seen each other.

True to his word, Sebastian picked Kenny up near the old stone bridge. Too narrow for vehicles to pass each other with any comfort, they had to wait a while until several horse-drawn vehicles, a bicycle and a motor van had crossed from the other side. Soon they were on their way again with the roar of the weir on their right drowning the noise of the engine. Kenny, detecting concern and not just nosiness from Sebastian earlier, had written down a few details about Alice, himself and their father. He hoped that the more Sebastian knew about the kind of life they'd led, the more understanding and willing he would be to help him trace her.

They motored up Lower Bridge Street where some of the houses had their main entrance on the first floor, and certain shops could only be reached by going down steps. The street had character and Kenny loved the way so many buildings were different from others. The Tudor House, a three-storey black and white house, just a little above St Olave's church, was said to be the oldest building in Chester. Further up in Bridge Street were covered Rows, walkways along the first floor of houses, cut back by a full bay, the second floors were held up by pillars. These had been given plenty of attention during the restoration in the 1800s, and were unique to the city.

The Rows were crowded with shoppers and the road was busy with horse-drawn private carriages, waiting for their owners to appear with their purchases; there were a couple of beer drays, a tram and more than the odd motor van and bicycle. The policeman on traffic duty was doing his best to keep the traffic moving but he had a job on his hands, and Sebastian's automobile's progress was slow. The smell of manure and fumes was so overpowering that Kenny decided it would be quicker and more pleasant to get out at the top of Watergate Street, where the old High Cross was situated at the junction of the four main medieval streets near St Peter's church. He slipped the folded sheet of paper into Sebastian's jacket pocket, smiled his thanks and vaulted over the door before vanishing amongst the crowds, thinking to walk the rest of the way. He would take the train to Birkenhead where he would then catch the ferry to Liverpool.

On the train he did a sketch drawing of his father and Alice and, when he got off the ferry at the Pierhead, he showed it to as many seafarers and ticket booth tellers as possible. He was still there when the Isle of Man boat came in, loaded with people with Scots accents. Listening to their conversations as they streamed in the direction of transport, he felt a memory stir. He took his sketch and showed it to as many of the crew as he could but without any success. Yet, somehow, he'd had a strong feeling that it was to the Isle of Man that his father had taken Alice. Should he buy a ticket and go there? It would take a fair amount of the money he had. He stood on the landing stage, gazing at the steamer, wondering what was best to do.

–

Alice sat huddled in a blanket, a shaking hand gripping the handle of a mug. Her teeth chattered against its rim and some of the hot liquid spilt and trickled down the front of her blouse. She took several deep breaths and avoided looking at the shattered railway carriage with its crunched nose in the air. That she had survived the accident seemed a miracle to her. She had been fortunate in being rescued quickly and, except for what a doctor thought might be a chipped elbow that throbbed like hell, had escaped lightly compared to many others.

Passengers were sitting or lying in various degrees of injury or shock. Rescuers were still at work dragging people from the wreckage. Some of the seriously injured had been taken to hospital. Several people were dead. A few feet away a man lay still on the platform. Until someone had covered him with a blanket she had been able to see part of his head caved in. Two hours ago, that man, who'd also been in the same carriage as Alice and her father, was laughing at some holiday memory. Tears trickled down her cheeks. She felt such pity for him, but not so much for her father.

She could scarcely believe her good fortune. He was seriously injured. Unconscious! There seemed a rough kind of justice in that. He had been taken to hospital but not before she had emptied his pockets. She had astounded herself by seizing the opportunity. Now she felt sick and a little ashamed, knowing her mam would have disapproved heartily. Yet what choice had she? How was she to get home without money? What she had done made sense. Without any form of identification it would be difficult for her father to be traced and, without money, it would be hard for him to trace her if he recovered from his injuries. Besides she had a right to some of his money. She'd had to hand over her wage packet unopened to him every week of her working life. And all of them, except for Mal, had gone without for the past few years.

Alice would have been on her way by now, if a woman had not insisted that she sat quietly drinking hot sweet tea. The trouble with sitting quietly was it gave her more time to think about what she had done. Never had she seen her father lying so still and pale and a long forgotten memory had popped into her mind. One of the few times he had played with her. He had taken her to the park and pushed her on the swings. He had laughed as she laughed and kissed her before placing her up on his shoulders and taking her home. She was certain he had enjoyed that time as much as she had but it was a long time ago and so many other dark memories had overlaid it. So why did she have to think of it now? Maybe blood was thicker than water after all.

'Och! Yer all on yer own. How are yer doin', hen?'

Alice looked up at the middle-aged woman and pinned on a smile. 'I'm OK, thanks! Just glad to be alive.'

'Ye're no Scottish.'

'No. I'm from Chester in the South.'

'Then ye'll want to be getting back there.' The woman's eyes were kind. 'Were yer with a relative?'

Something about the woman's face reminded her of her dead mother and hatred suddenly filled Alice's soul. How could she feel sympathy for a father who had done what he had done to her mother? But she didn't want this woman hanging around her, offering assistance, so she lied glibly saying that her father was about somewhere and they'd be leaving soon and that seemed to satisfy her.

Alice felt so weary, thinking of getting herself home. Her parents had always been there, making decisions for her. Most likely she would have to get a Manchester train and change for Chester, or perhaps one going to Crewe, or even Liverpool. She hoped there was one or the other leaving that day. She gnawed on her bottom lip. What if Mrs Kirk was dead and the story of her father being on the run was in the national newspapers with a description of them both? Someone might recognise him in the hospital and then they might come looking for her. She must leave now.

Alice was in luck. There was an overnight express to Manchester. She would have to wait a while and it wouldn't leave from where she was now but that did not bother her too much. So she bought her ticket and found her way to the right place. Then, tired out by the events of the day, she sat down. Suddenly, she started to shake and tears rolled down her cheeks. She had come so near to being dead. A woman stopped a couple of feet away from her and stared at her. Not wanting to draw any more attention to herself, Alice got up and walked away, wiping her tears with the back of her hand.

She bought a cup of tea and a slice of Dundee cake and told herself that everything was going to be all right. So what if her description had been circulated in the newspapers? How many redheaded men and girls lived in Britain? It wasn't as if the police had a photograph of her. So what if she had to take another train! What were the odds against her being involved in another crash on the same day? She squared her shoulders, knowing she must be sensible and brave. She had to think of the future. She had to find Kenny.

It was raining when she arrived in Chester; weary but overjoyed to be in her own city again. Then she saw a billboard advertising that morning's Wirral edition of the *Daily Post*. It said that fifteen people had been killed in a Glasgow train crash and the driver arrested. Her knees trembled and she thought she would faint but, after taking several deep breaths, she managed to pull herself together and walk calmly out of the station. If her father was dead then she and Kenny were free of him at last. She had to find her half-brother but first she needed food and a hot drink. She headed for the nearest cocoa house on Brook Street and ordered bacon, eggs, fried bread and a steaming mug of the finest cocoa in the place.

The waitress raised her eyebrows. 'Let's see your money first, Miss?'

Alice knew she must look a mess. After all she had been in an accident and had dirt and blood on her clothing. She dug into a pocket and withdrew a half crown. 'A toff at the station gave it me – said I looked half-starved.'

'Lucky you,' drawled the waitress. 'I'll expect a tip.'

Alice grinned and when the girl brought the food, gave her tuppence. On the train she had counted the money she had taken from her father. Twenty-three pounds, sixteen shillings and tuppence, three farthings! It was a small fortune to someone in her position.

While she ate, her thoughts were of her dead mother and the baby she had died giving birth to. Had her baby sister survived these last ten days? Hannah would be able to answer both those questions because she would know something that Alice didn't, and that was where Granny Popo and her granddaughter lived. But did she dare go near the Kirks' house? What if Mrs Kirk was dead? Hannah might not want to see her. Might hate her for leaving her mother lying at the bottom of the stairs unconscious. Hannah was a very understanding person and had been her greatest friend but such a thing could surely destroy even the longest friendship. Having been through so much during the past few hours, Alice knew that she couldn't cope with seeing the hate and pain in Hannah's eyes and decided, then and there, that the Kirks' house would not be her first port of call.

She had to find Kenny! And it was here that Alice's fertile imagination began to run away with her. That Mrs Black might have him prisoner. When the girl remembered how eager her father had been to get inside that woman's house, she thought it possible that he was in her power somehow. Alice's green eyes narrowed like a cat's. Hannah would have said she was being over-dramatic but then her friend hadn't had her life. She had a father who was good and kind and respectable. She had no real idea of how evil the human race could be. Alice decided that her starting place to find Kenny would be Mrs Black's. She would not allow that woman to frighten her. Anyway, with a bit of luck she might bump into the young gardener. What had the old man called him? Sebastian. It was an uncommon name but she liked the sound of it. As soon as her meal was finished, she would make her way to Queen's Park.

Alice sighed: there was no sign of the young gardener anywhere and, on top of that disappointment, it was still raining. She wiped droplets of the drenching stuff from her face and sighed again. It's supposed to be summer, Lord! The roses blooming in the garden proved it and a beautiful scarlet they were but what use were roses if there was no beau to give them to you?

She switched her gaze to Mrs Black's front door and, summoning her courage and saying a prayer, pushed open the gate. She got no further. A hand gripped her elbow. She yelped with pain and spun round, her heart thumping, the thought in her head that her father had somehow made a miraculous recovery and come to get her. It was such a relief to see her half-brother that she clutched the front of his jacket with both hands.

'Kenny!' she cried. He looked incredibly clean for once; no sign of coal dust anywhere but he had bruising on his face. Had that bitch inside done that? He hoisted her up in his arms and kissed her on both cheeks. That surprised her. He wasn't usually one for showing affection. She hugged him. 'I had a feeling I'd find you here but I thought you might be inside, that she had taken you prisoner.'

He grinned and touched her chin lightly with his knuckles.

She blushed. 'Oh, never mind! I know what you're thinking: that I'm letting my imagination run away with me as usual. You're here and that's the main thing.' She placed the tip of a finger on the bruise beneath his eye. 'How did this happen? It's not the one that Dad gave you?'

Kenny shook his head and lowered her to the ground. Taking one of her hands, he drew her away from the house.

'Who did do it? And how's Mrs Kirk? Is she still alive?'

Kenny nodded and began to walk. He had decided yesterday to give Mrs Black one last try, thinking that it would be foolish to go to the Isle of Man without having some idea of where his father might stay. He had hoped she might be able to come up with an address. As it turned out he had made the right decision. He hadn't got to see Mrs Black but finding Alice here was like picking all winners in the Chester races. How she came to be here alone was something he couldn't wait to hear.

'I'm so glad Mrs Kirk's alive,' said Alice, a delighted smile on her face. 'It means that we can ask her about the baby.'

Kenny stared at her, startled. 'What baby?' he mouthed silently.

She looked at him in surprise, thinking he scarcely ever mouthed words. 'Mam's baby!

'Although…' Alice paused, 'it's possible she mightn't have survived. She was so tiny you wouldn't have given tuppence for her chances.' Kenny stopped abruptly, his hazel eyes concerned. He cleared his throat but Alice rushed in with a, 'I know you must be feeling like I do – hoping that she's survived but worried how we're going to cope with a baby. I'm probably out of a job, I don't know about you. And we could be orphans! Dad's probably dead. I took all his money. That's how I got here.'

His eyes widened and he put an arm about her shoulders. There was so much he needed to know, but the rain had become a downpour and they were getting soaked. He took her to the Little Nag's Head Cocoa House on Foregate Street. The room was steamy and smelled of cigarette smoke, sweat, damp wool and mackintoshes. They managed to find a table, squeezed between two others, occupied on one side by a pair of buxom women with rosy cheeks talking in Welsh and on the other by a man, who looked like a farmer, and his wife.

The waitress apologised for the price of the cocoa. 'I don't know if you read about it but the government's put a tax on it.'

Alice shrugged, thinking they had other things on their minds than the price of cocoa. She continued to talk while they waited for the steaming cups to appear; pouring out her feelings, not giving Kenny a chance to interrupt, although she did take notice when he scribbled in his notebook and responded to his written messages and his responses. The one that made her feel better was *If Dad's dead, your mother's death has been avenged. Now we can start our lives over again.*

Alice smiled. 'I've got over twenty pounds! I'll give half to you.' He dug into his pockets and produced two pounds, six shillings and thru-pence. She stared at the money, her mouth slightly open. 'Where did you get that?' She did not wait for him to write down his answer. 'With that and Dad's money we should be OK for a while. Although…' she remembered something that she'd worried about all the time she had been away. 'Did Mam have a funeral?'

Kenny replaced the money in his pocket and wrote in his pad, *Mr Bushell arranged it. She's buried in her aunt's grave. We can put flowers on it.*

For a moment emotion had her by the throat; she could not speak and tears rolled down her thin cheeks. Then she dabbed at her damp face with her sleeve and said, 'Of course we can.' She sipped at her cocoa. 'Mrs Kirk! Hannah! Have you seen them at all?'

No. Mrs Kirk's flat on her back. She might never walk again. And she hasn't spoken about what happened yet. It must be the shock. Bert beat me up and says he'll do it again if I go near any member of the family.

'Bert!' Alice was filled with dismay but then decided she could not believe he would do such a thing. 'Are you sure it was Bert? Was it dark? Could you have made a mistake?'

Kenny shook his head and wrote briefly what had happened. Then added *He despises me. Thinks me a dummy.*

Alice shook her tangled auburn curls vigorously. 'How can you believe that? He's a lovely bloke.'

You don't know him. He said I was an accessory after the fact. I could hardly walk after the beating and spent over a week in jail but the police were kind to me. We're going to have to find somewhere else to live and build up a new life.

Alice was really upset about Bert and covered the hand holding the pencil. 'I see why you want to stay away but he probably just saw red because he loves his mother so much. It was wrong of him but some people hit out when they are hurt or angry.'

Like our dad?

Alice was silent, shocked by the thought that her brother could compare Bert with their father. She didn't want to believe what Kenny was telling her. It had to be a misunderstanding. He had to be wrong. She took a deep breath. 'You wouldn't try to see Hanny?'

Kenny sighed and removed her hand.

What's the point? She only ever felt sorry for me – probably despises me now. She must hate the name of Moran.

'You don't know that.' Alice leaned across the table. 'Wouldn't you like to find out how she's really feeling?'

He hesitated and then shook his head. *We've got to forget about the Kirks altogether. They've got no role to play in our lives anymore.*

She was utterly dismayed but it suddenly occurred to her that Hannah might feel exactly the same about her for having left Mrs Kirk unconscious at the bottom of the stairs. How terrified they had both been of their father! She still was, though she could scarcely believe that she was free of his suffocating presence and able to begin the new life Kenny was suggesting. She desperately wanted to see Hannah but maybe Kenny was right. When tragedy hit people's lives it could change them for better or for worse. Having one's mother end up a silent, bedridden cripple was a terrible thing to have to cope with; particularly when there might be no end to it. Sadly, Alice decided she had no choice but to go along with Kenny's instinct and join him in leaving their previous life behind.

Chapter Seven

Hannah entered the bedroom and gazed down at her mother. Why couldn't she speak? Sometimes the girl despaired and at others she felt filled with anger. It was two months now since that terrible day when she had found Susannah at the bottom of the Morans' stairs; summer was over, and yet still there was no sign of recognition from her mother despite all that was done for her.

Granny Popo had assisted her in the past weeks, washing her mother's hair and giving her bed-baths. She'd also helped feed her, give her a drink and slid the potty beneath her pale white buttocks while Hannah and Joy lifted her. Then last week the doctor had suggested another X-ray and so off to the Infirmary they had gone in the horse ambulance and more photographs had been taken of Susannah's spine and skull. They had shown that the crack in her backbone was knitting and the one in her skull had healed, which had delighted the family – and one would have thought would have given her mother some pleasure if she'd understood what was being said. And there was the real difficulty, how much did she understand?

If Jock spoke to her, she shrank away as if she couldn't bear him near her and the hurt in his expression caused Hannah's heart to ache for him. She could only hazard a guess what it must be like for the pair of them sleeping together, still. The doctor said that the shock to her system must have gone deeper than he had initially thought. Even so he had told them that her mobility should start to improve soon, and she could have a pillow so her head and shoulders were raised higher. This meant it was easier for her to feed herself, and she had a better view of people and the room.

Yet, not a smile did Hannah get from her mother, and she was not the only one. Even Bert's presence failed to bring a glow to her eyes, despite the fact that he would sit with her for half an hour at a time, reading the newspaper aloud. That she did not show any appreciation of his filial devotion irked him no end.

Hannah had hoped that the sight of the younger children might cause some reaction and it had; Susannah had frowned at the noise they made, so Hannah had shooed them out of the bedroom and it was obvious that they were hurt at their mother's inability to respond to them.

Hannah's next hope for a positive reaction had been when Granny brought Florrie's baby with her for the first time. The child now bore little resemblance to the 'skinned rat' the old woman had called her at birth. Although she was still only tiny, she was at least holding her own. Hannah was aware that a number of childish illnesses could carry her off in no time at all and knew she really shouldn't get too fond of her, but even so she was enchanted with the child. Her red-gold hair swirled in tiny waves on her delicate skull and her eyes would follow Hannah's finger as she moved it in front of her heart-shaped face. The plain white nightgown she wore, originally intended for Dolly's baby, was still much too large, and the nappy swamped her, but she kicked her legs about and gurgled.

Yet the child seemed to create no pleasure in Susannah and even the mention that this was her friend Florrie's child only caused a tiny pucker between her thick dark eyebrows.

Hannah sat on the bed, wondering what next she could do to stimulate her mother. The doctor had said from the beginning that they must talk to her but she had run through so many subjects, including that of Mal, Kenny and Alice, wondering where they could possibly be. She missed her friends and wished she had made the time to visit Kenny when he had been in the police cells. She could only guess why he had not called on her when he was released, and that was he must believe himself unwelcome at their house. She had visited Mr Bushell, his previous employer, hoping he might be able to help her, but he couldn't tell her where Kenny was living. She became convinced he had gone in search of his father and Alice, wherever that might be. Perhaps he had lied about not knowing where they were. That thought hurt. She had believed she could trust Kenny to be completely honest with her. She sighed, wishing he was there for her to talk to… he had been such a good listener, never interrupting and taking over the conversation like her brother.

Her expression clouded. She was careful not to be alone with Bert. Fortunately when her dah finished work it meant that he came home the same time as Bert, although that did not prevent her brother watching and criticising in his so called *I'm only joking* voice, as she tried to fill her mother's shoes. It was such hard work and housework was so tedious.

She had to chivvy her sisters to help her when they came home from school. As for Freddie, it maddened her that he had been almost dry before her mother's fall but was now wetting his bedding most nights. She hated the smell of wee when she had to dry the sheets as quickly as she could. Hannah didn't want to moan but she never got to the library in St John's Street these days and even if she could when did she have the time to read or just walk for the pleasure of it? She missed her job, especially her work mate, Agnes, the younger shop girl, who was part of a big family with a carping father, whom she never let get her down. Agnes was always game for a laugh.

Money! There was another thing. Hannah had never been taught to manage money and keep house and was finding it difficult, although she was convinced she was being kept short. There definitely wouldn't be much in the kids' stockings when Christmas came this year, unless she bought groceries on tick at the corner shop and used the housekeeping to buy the younger ones a few little things. Is that what her mother did?

She gazed at Susannah, looking for some sign of recognition but her mother only stared at her and then closed her eyes. From below, came the sound of Freddie crying. Suddenly near to tears herself, Hannah rushed out the room, only to collide into Bert.

He shoved his newspaper under his arm and steadied her, gripping both her arms so that part of his wrists brushed the sides of her breasts.

'What's the matter, Hanny? You're not still trying to get her to talk? It's a waste of time. I've tried. If she doesn't answer to me, she won't answer to anybody.'

'Let me go!' She tried to free herself but his hold on her tightened and his fingers stroked her breasts. She felt a rising panic. 'Let me go! Where's Dah?'

He sneered. 'Down the yard. He's coming to pieces like those knitted garments you buy second-hand and unravel to knit into something else.'

She paled. 'It's not true!'

He laughed. 'If you want to pretend that everything's going to be fine in this house, especially between him and Mother, then you're dreaming, dear sister.'

Her insides seemed to turn to ice. 'What d'you mean? Of course, things will be all right once Mother is able to walk and talk again.'

'And when's that going to be? Never if you ask me.'

'I'm not asking you.' She managed to wrench herself out of his grasp and pushed her way past him and down the stairs.

As soon as Freddie saw her he held up his arms. His chubby face was tear-stained. Then she saw the mess of horsehair on the rag rug and the cushion from her father's chair on the floor. The scissors were on the table and there were no sign of her sisters, whom she had left cutting out paper dollies. 'Oh, Freddie, what have you done?'

'Cut, snip, snip – animal,' he said in a jerky voice, pointing at the cushion.

'No, Freddie, no animal. It was naughty of you to cut the cushion.' She groaned.

It was a real job to pick up the stuffing and ram it back into the cushion and, all the time Freddie was clinging to her skirt and trying to get on her knee. She felt like screaming, but, in the end, she lifted him into her arms. It was then he showed her his hands. There were red weals on the palms of both. 'Bert,' he said. 'Sore!' He held them up for her to kiss.

She kissed both gently and rubbed butter on them. Then put him down and finished sewing the cushion. By the time she had finished, it struck her that her father had still not come in from down the yard. She thought about Bert's earlier comment about him 'going to pieces'. Bert couldn't be right, could he? She knew Jock was suffering. He snapped occasionally at the children and that wasn't like him at all. If only her mother would speak. Hannah was certain that then everything would get back to normal, but it didn't take place that day.

-

Jock lifted the bedcovers and shifted across the mattress nearer to his wife. It was four months now since she had regained consciousness and, although she could now walk, there was still not a word out of her. It was the doctor and Hannah who had got her up out of the bed and forced her on to her feet but she wouldn't go far and it hadn't been the beginning of a miraculous change in their circumstances. Susannah kept to the bedroom except for trips to the lavatory, and another visit to the Infirmary in St Martin's in the Field; where the doctor, keen as mustard, insisted on her having another one of them X-rays done. Old Granny Popo had voiced her uneasiness about *them there X-rays*, saying it was perhaps that first one that had done something to her head. Jock didn't want to believe that. He was an engineer and believed in progress. The doctor said that what was wrong with her now was all in the mind and no amount of X-rays were going to cure that but at least they knew her bones had healed.

The doctor had been kindness itself, never asking for a penny, saying he was interested in her case. He said they just had to be patient, kind, talk to her and try and get her to have some exercise. Then if that didn't work, perhaps they could try something else. Jock had asked 'What?' and the doctor had surprised him by saying he had seen something similar to his wife's condition before, and that, sometimes, another shock could do the trick.

Jock sighed, feeling down in the dumps. Every evening, as soon as he came in from work, he came up here and sat with his wife. He forced her to hold his hand and asked how she was feeling, but she just looked at him with loathing, as if he was a monster. When he came to bed like now, and would have cuddled her, she shrank away.

Her rejection was inexplicable to him and painfully so. It was Saturday night and he worked hard to keep his family. The last few weeks had been more exhausting than usual, getting up in the dark and going downstairs and having to light the fire. Hannah was a good girl, she generally got up as soon as she heard him move and would make his carry-out. Then after a cup of tea and a few rounds of toast it was out into a freezing, dark, often foggy day.

The customary cuddle with his wife every night had been a comfort and, even more so, having his marital rights on the rug in front of the fire on Sunday afternoons when the youngsters were at the mission hall. For a couple of hours he and Mother had time to themselves without worrying about the bairns wondering what they were up to. But everything was different now with her up in this bedroom wearing an air that said *Don't come near me.* And all the time he had to put a good face on things for his children's sake. Hanny was doing her best to look after all of them, keep the house, clean and tidy, and do the shopping and cooking, but she wasn't a patch on her mother. What kind of life was it for a girl of her age, but what could he do about it?

He yearned for the familiarity and security of the old days, of Sunday, that day of rest, as he had known it. It had helped him get through the week. His loins ached and he longed for release. One of his hands strayed downwards but then he drew it back. It was sinful. He reached out for Susannah but, as soon as he touched her, she crossed her arms across her chest and hunched up her knees. Suddenly he felt so angry he wanted to strike her. What had he ever done to her to make her behave towards him in such a way? Just as quickly the anger drained out of him. It was all down to bloody Mal Moran! If he had him in front of him right now he'd... dear God, he'd smash him to smithereens with a hammer. He had changed the woman Jock respected and cared for into a silent stranger. He had never experienced those feelings that songs, poetry and novels tell you about being in love: that walking on air or the sensation that his blood was turning into liquid fire with desire. But Susannah was essential to his wellbeing. The warmth he had felt towards her in the early days had deepened and her need for him had been just as strong and had made him feel her happiness depended on his being around. They were a team, working well in harness, having faced so many challenges together. Despair gripped him. Why couldn't God do something? Jock's hands clenched into fists. He wanted justice. But Mal and his children seemed to have vanished from the face of the earth.

-

Alice linked her arm through Kenny's and smiled up at him as they ran up the steps of the lodging house in Garden Lane. Their breath formed clouds in front of them. It was that cold, but so sunny and the air was so crisp, she felt she could almost take bites out of it. It was lovely to think that upstairs in their apartment the fire would be in, red and glowing, waiting to welcome them. Now that they lived on the opposite side of town, they had been regularly attending the Wesleyan Mission Chapel on the corner of Plum Terrace. Alice was keeping faith with her mam's beliefs and Kenny came with her every other week. On the alternate Sunday, he went to the service at the Cathedral. Alice was ready for her Sunday dinner and knew Kenny would be, too. She had stuffed lamb's hearts and placed them in gravy with sliced potatoes, onions and carrots. She had partially stewed them in a saucepan on the fire earlier that morning.

Shopping with her mam in the past, watching and helping her in the house, meant Alice knew that offal was cheap and tasty if cooked in the right way. It was a pity they didn't have the use of an oven, but they got by. Last night they'd had liver, which had been as tender as you could want it. The secret was to slice the liver thin and quick fry it, with onion gravy, fried potatoes and peas. King Eddie couldn't have enjoyed better.

She and Kenny clattered upstairs to the attic room on the third floor. Mr Bushell had been party to them getting it because the landlady had been a childhood friend of his wife. And although Mrs Bushell had died some years before, he still saw Glenys Secombe at meetings on the Methodist circuit. A seamstress by trade, she lived on the ground floor and collected rents from the other tenants for the owner of the property. He knew Kenny's desire to build a new life so was keeping quiet about his whereabouts.

Kenny and Alice had furnished the room simply with second-hand stuff. A sofa served as a bed for Alice but Kenny slept in a proper bed. He would have given it up for his sister but she said that he brought more money in than she did and worked harder. Alice hadn't even tried to get her old job back but had instead managed to find employment as a sweeper-upper in Denson's drapers, milliners and dressmakers in Northgate Street Row. She hoped that within the year they would allow her to resume her training as a milliner, so she was keeping her hand in by practicing at home.

With Kenny's permission she had bought several millinery items; something she had not been able to do in the past, due to their father taking everything they earned. She had Kenny measure her head from the tip of one ear to the other and from her forehead at her hairline to the nape of her neck. Then she purchased a crown block a half inch larger than her own small head, as well as a brim block, needles, berry pins, wires, thread, stiffening solution and adhesive. The first hat she made was green to match her eyes and, having taken note of what her previous employer had told her about balancing the crown with the proportion of a woman's figure, age and facial features, she made sure the crown was small and the brim upturned. She trimmed the hat with dark green ribbon and a daisy she made with stiffened white cotton and wire. The hat was much admired and, when Alice said that she had made it herself and quoted a price that she knew was lower than anything paid in the shops, a couple of requests had been forthcoming from Miss Secombe and one of the other tenants. Alice hoped that this sideline might prove to be a good little earner in the months to come.

She and Kenny had also purchased a drop-leafed table and two dining chairs, some shelving for dishes, pans and food, a couple of chamber pots, a jug, a washbasin, and bedding. She had made a rug out of sacking and rags bought in the market. To ensure privacy when washing, and at bedtime, they strung a thin rope across the room and placed a blanket and their coats over it. Clothes had been something else for which they'd had to fork out, but again they'd bought used clothes from the market.

Her life was so different now that sometimes Alice had to pinch herself to reassure herself she was not dreaming. As it was she did dream. The images that haunted her sleep were the stuff of nightmares. She would wake trembling and crying and go to Kenny for comfort.

Kenny, too, had nightmares, but of course, he never spoke of them. In his waking hours he tried to forget the horror that petrified the child inside him. Since his father had gone from his life he'd had the same dream on several occasions. He was in pain and hiding under a table. In the background he could hear a woman screeching, while all around him was the stench of burning flesh.

'Doesn't it look cosy?' Alice shrugged off her coat and hung it on the hook on the back of the door. The table had been set before they went out and the fire really was red at its heart. For a moment she held out her frozen fingers to its warmth, then rubbed them to help the circulation get going. Then with the poker she opened up the fire and wiggled the pan on the coals to make sure it was secure.

Kenny took a writing pad from a drawer and began to write his latest letter to Hannah. Not that he had ever sent any of them but somehow it helped him to keep the memory of her fresh in his mind and got his frustrations off his chest. Having told Alice that they had to put the past behind them, he knew what a hypocrite he was but, somehow, he couldn't break the habit.

He smiled as Alice sang *For all the Saints who from their labours rest.* She loved to sing hymns. It was a way of cocking a snook at their father, dead or alive. She would never have dared to do so with him in the house.

'I'm really looking forward to Christmas. Aren't you, Kenny?' she called over her shoulder. The festive season would be upon them in two weeks' time.

He nodded, even though he knew that she was putting on her bright side for him. Last week she had, again, brought up the subject of seeking out their baby sister. They had heard the news that the child was still alive from Mr Bushell, who had made enquiries for them via one of his other coal delivery men. Kenny understood that Alice found it hard to be satisfied with this information alone, although she did accept that it would be difficult for them to manage, financially, if she gave up work to care for the baby. They had also heard that Mrs Kirk had gained the use of her legs but neighbours reported that she'd 'gone a bit queer in the head', never speaking and still keeping to her bedroom. There was a lot of sympathy in the neighbourhood for Mr Kirk and his children.

Oh, how Kenny wished he could do something to make Hannah's lot easier. How he longed to see her. Yet he realised that Christmas was definitely not the time to suggest they meet. She must be mourning all those happy Christmases the family had spent together in the past, which were now at an end.

Alice interrupted his thoughts and he looked up. 'We could make some paper chains and decorate this room,' she said eagerly. 'And I'll get us a rabbit and make a lovely stew for Christmas dinner.'

He nodded and signed his letter with a certain amount of frustration. It would be great to know that, having written it, he would get an answer.

Alice sat across the table from him. 'It would have made my Christmas Day even better if I could have looked forward to seeing the baby. You realise we still don't know her name,' she said wistfully. 'Imagine seeing her here in our own wee home.' The girl gazed about her with pride. She loved this little haven under the eaves and enjoyed the job of keeping it clean and tidy. There was a damp stain in the corner of the ceiling where a slate was loose but that was only a tiny flaw.

Kenny reached out a hand to her. She took it and brushed it against her cheek. 'I know,' she said, trying to sound cheerful. 'I have to carry on being sensible. We know she is being cared for and I must be content with that. But I do feel guilty, Kenny; we don't pay anything towards her keep.'

Kenny knew how she felt, although, to him, the baby didn't seem real because he had never set eyes on her. Even so, he suddenly came to a decision: he would place some money in an envelope and post it after dark through Granny Popo's door. Just a few words, no name, no address, *For the baby with our best wishes – thank you and a very happy Christmas.*

Chapter Eight

Hannah felt near to tears as she gazed down at the note in Kenny's handwriting. Then she looked at the baby as she suckled Dolly's breast. 'So how much was it?'

'Two florins! Yer could have knocked me down with a feather!' Dolly rocked gently in the old rocker. Small and curvaceous, she was untidily dressed, her blouse hanging outside a brown skirt which dipped where the hem had come unstitched. Her thick chestnut hair was twisted in a knot on top of her head but tendrils of hair had come loose and hung over her ears. 'But if they think they're going to get her away from me for two florins they're much mistaken. Aren't they, me lovely?' She kissed the baby's red-gold curls.

'Now, Dolly me duck, don't yous be talking like that. She's not yer babby, and yer've got to think about what your fella's going to say when he comes back from India with the army,' said Granny, from the other side of the fireplace. The old woman looked worried as she drew on her clay pipe, her wrinkled face reminding Hannah of a spider's web as her mouth pursed. 'I'd like to know where Mal is in all this,' continued the old woman. 'It's a mystery to me. I can't see him being behind putting thank you notes with money through my front door. Has Kenny done this off his own bat? If so, how can he afford it? Does Alice have any part in it? One thing's for sure, in my opinion, there's no intention at the moment to take the babby away from us yet, otherwise they'd be here in person.'

'It is a mystery. You're right!' said Hannah, slamming one fist into the open hand that held the note, creasing it. 'But if Kenny could write this to you, then why can't he write to me? I helped him to learn to write. We were close. He must know something of what's happening in our house. Someone must have told him. Surely he can't be far away if this note was delivered by hand.' Her grey-blue eyes were bewildered and angry.

'You're right there,' said Dolly with a sniff.

Granny removed the pipe from her mouth and scowled. 'Someone else could have delivered it and the pair of yer are forgettin' what he's bin through. Lost his stepmother, doesn't know where Alice is, and's recovering from a bullyin' violent father and being beaten up by Bert.'

Hannah stared at her, then nodded and said slowly, 'You're right. Alice must have told him about the baby before they got split up. We were especially careful to keep it from Mr Moran, so I doubt he knows. He's gone to ground somewhere – maybe Liverpool, who knows – and he could still be frightening Alice to death.'

Granny nodded. 'Difficult to find anyone in Liverpool if they want to lose themselves.'

'If only she could write to me and let me know how she's going on,' sighed Hannah.

'Well, it seems she can't,' said Dolly, gently removing her nipple from the baby's mouth, and putting the child over her shoulder and patting her small back. 'So yer'll just have to hope that Kenny is still looking for her… and if he writes again, that he'll tell us any news he has.'

Granny nodded. 'I think he will write again now he's broken the ice. Likely send us more money… as for this money…' She beamed at her granddaughter and the baby, 'we use it to make our Christmas and the babby's a merry one.'

Hannah agreed, while hoping that Kenny would think again and write to her next.

But a whole week passed and no letter had arrived for Hannah. It was Sunday morning in the Kirk household and Bert was reading aloud from the newspaper. Apparently in America, one of two brothers called Wright had managed to get a heavier than air powered flying machine, carrying a man, to fly a distance of eight hundred and fifty feet in fifty-nine seconds. 'That's some engineering feat, Dah,' he said, looking across at his father, who was gazing moodily into the fire.

'A Yorkshire man flew before the Americans did,' said Hannah, placing the flat iron on the fire to heat up. 'I remember Dah telling us years ago that he was a baronet,' she added, her face screwed up with concentration.

'That's right, lass,' said Jock, glancing up with sudden interest. 'Sir George Cayley. He started with models of whalebone, string and feathers and went on to make toy gliders, tackling the problems of forward propulsion and lift before planning an internal combustion engine to provide power. It was his coachman, who actually made the first manned flight... Sir George being seventy-nine by the time he developed his ideas. It flew two hundred yards right across Brompton Vale and the coachman climbed out the wreckage and gave notice.'

'I don't blame him,' said Joy, looking up from the stocking she was darning. 'If we were meant to fly, Dah, God would have given us wings.'

'I don't agree,' said Hannah firmly. 'What I love about history is the way you can see how mankind's developed. Machines have made life easier for people. Just think of the train and how it brings the tourists in and the farmers and their wives to market.'

'I'd like a puffer engine for Christmas,' said Freddie, glancing up from the wooden blocks his father had made him last year.

'You'll be lucky,' murmured Hannah, taking a scorched rag and lifting the iron from the fire. 'There's no money in the kitty for engines.'

Jock looked at her, cleared his throat and said gruffly, 'I'll give ye an extra ten shillings, lass.'

Hannah smiled her thanks, thinking she could buy a little toy for each of the younger ones, and it meant she wouldn't run up too much of a bill at the corner shop. She knew that she wouldn't be able to get a wooden engine. Freddie would just have to make do with something else, a couple of lead soldiers perhaps, and a couple of skipping ropes for the girls. There wasn't going to be anything in her own stocking but the best present she could have would be for her mother to be her old self again.

On Christmas Day, Hannah was feeling in an optimistic mood. Late last night, Agnes from the bakery had called round with a bun-loaf and mince pies, as well as a shilling; these were gifts from Mrs Bannister, her previous boss, who said she would be happy to have her back any time. Hannah was truly grateful and determined to go in person and thank her after Christmas.

She suggested that Jock and Bert help Susannah downstairs, so she could join them in the breast of lamb hotpot dinner she had made. 'If she can sit and eat her dinner up there then surely she can eat it down here?' she said firmly, having thought long and hard about the idea. 'There's nothing wrong with her back now. Just because she's not right in her head, it doesn't mean that she has to stay in that room. She's going to lose the use of her legs if she doesn't start moving herself.'

'Hold on, lass,' said Jock, running a hand through his hair and frowning. 'It's not me stopping her. I've tried to persuade her to do things but she just looks through me or turns away.'

'I think you're best leaving her where she is for dinner,' said Bert. 'She'll find it noisy down here with the kids.' He fingered his fledgling moustache. 'Perhaps later in the day when the kids go out to play, we could try it. I think she's got used to the peace and quiet in the bedroom. It's restful with the fire glowing and nobody else disturbing you.'

'Nice to have nothing else to do but read the newspaper when you're up there with Mother,' said Hannah tartly. 'And having a second fire in the house costs money.'

Bert looked pained. 'It's hard work reading aloud. You want to try it.'

'There's nothing I'd like better.' Her hands went to her hips and her eyes sparkled. 'But it's me that has the job of helping her wash her hair, carrying up trays and keeping the fire going, as well as a hundred other things in this house.'

'Leave off!' said Jock, his fists clenching. 'Don't let's argue on Christmas Day. I'll carry her down if she's not up to walking. Noise or not, it just might be the right thing to get her going again.'

So the decision was made and, an hour later, Jock went upstairs and entered the bedroom. Susannah was sitting up against the pillows, that faraway expression in her eyes that so disturbed him. He felt nervous.

Where did she go in her head when she looked like that? He took several deep breaths, and glanced about the room, wondering how his elder son could find it so peaceful with his mother the way she was. Jock wished he could find some peace of mind but it was getting so that he couldn't sleep nights. He just couldn't understand why his wife turned away from him the way she did. It wasn't as if he had ever been violent towards her.

He went over to the bed. 'Mother, I'm going to take yer downstairs. It's Christmas day and ye should be with me and the children.' He did not look her in the face but drew back the bedcovers to reveal her small, round body in an off-white flannelette nightgown. She looked like a little dumpling, having put on weight with lying in bed so long and eating well.

He reached down for her. One muscular arm going about her shoulders, the other beneath her buttocks. He had her attention. Her expression was startled, frightened. 'No need to look like that,' he muttered, hoisting her into his arms. With one hand she clung to his shirt but with the other she hit out at him, catching him a blow on the chin. He tried to ignore her action but then she lashed out at him with both hands, slashing his face with her fingernails. His face stung like billyo!

For a minute or so he took the blows and then something snapped inside him. He flung her onto the bed. 'Yer bitch!' he yelled. 'Bloody stay there if that's what yer want. But yer'll be spending yer nights alone in future. I've had enough! Yer can rot for all I care.' He took hold of the bedcovers and dragged them up so that they covered her completely, before leaving her alone.

He stormed downstairs, took his coat from the hook in the lobby and left the house. He walked swiftly, having no idea where he was going, but with the intention of putting as much space between him and the house as he could. At the bottom of Brook Street, he crossed Cow Lane Bridge and headed towards the city centre. He went along Frodsham Street and turned in the direction of the Eastgate, now a favourite meeting place for young lovers since the clock on top of the wall had been erected to celebrate the old queen's Diamond Jubilee. As he looked up at it he collided with a woman.

'Look where you're going,' she said, clutching her hat.

He looked down and recognised the widow Taylor, the Morans' former neighbour. 'Sorry!' His voice was gruff.

She lifted her face to him and before he could carry on walking, took hold of his sleeve. 'Mr Kirk! Your face is bleeding and you look upset. Is something wrong?'

'Bloody everything!' he said, then begged her pardon.

'That's all right.' She squeezed his arm, her expression sympathetic. 'Mrs Kirk no better?' He shook his head. 'It must be terrible for you, especially at Christmas-time.' He nodded, still unable to speak. Then she said hesitantly, 'At any other time I wouldn't suggest this but, with it being Christmas day – I wonder if you'd like to join me in a drink?' Jock was so taken aback that his mouth fell open. A delicate pink coloured her cheeks. 'I shouldn't have asked,' she said in a low voice. 'It's not a very lady-like thing to do, asking a gentleman out for a drink.'

A gentleman! She thought him a gentleman! She didn't look at him like he was a monster. The tightness in his throat eased. Jock only ever drank on special occasions such as Hogmanay. But wasn't Christmas such an occasion? 'I'd like that. Thanks.'

Her smile dazzled him. 'It's me that should thank you. Christmas is a very lonely time for me since my husband passed over.'

'Ye don't have to live on yer own to be lonely.'

She stared at him fixedly and then surprised him by saying, 'Let me wipe away that blood.'

The feather in her hat tickled his chin as she bent her head and opened her bag. She took out a handkerchief and dampened a corner of it with her tongue. Then she took hold of his jaw and dabbed the dried blood with the linen. The swell of her breasts brushed against his chest. He felt a rippling sensation in the pit of his stomach. He had been a faithful husband for a long time. That wasn't to say he had never looked at another woman and let his imagination run riot, but that was as far as it went. Yet here he was thinking things about this lonely widow. Not that he would do anything, he assured himself. Even so, when he remembered his wife attacking him, there was nothing more he wanted at that moment than to try and forget all about her.

She replaced the handkerchief inside her bag and slipped her hand in the crook of his arm. 'The name's Nora. Shall we go? I know a very nice place not so far away that's open for a few select customers.'

For an instant he felt uncomfortable with her suggestion, then he thought, What the Hell! Didn't he deserve some fun after working bloody hard for months on end, not to mention handing over his wage packet for more bloody years than he cared to think about? Very few men did that. He would make it up to Hannah and the kids another day.

–

The raised voice, the thunderous sound of their father's boots on the stairs, and the slamming of the front door, sent Hannah and Bert dashing upstairs. They found their mother struggling with the bedclothes. Hannah helped her sort them out and then the pair of them hoisted her up against the pillow.

'Are you all right, Mother?' they chorused.

She sighed and closed her eyes. Bert sat on the edge of the bed and took her hand, squeezing it. Hannah willed her to speak and tell them what had happened to set their dah shouting and dashing out of the house. But her mother just carried on lying there with her eyes closed, freeing little sighs.

There was a scuffling sound outside the bedroom door that caused Hannah to whirl round, hoping her father had returned. 'Is Mother going to get up?' asked Grace.

'It doesn't look like it to me,' said Joy, giving Susannah a sad glance. 'Perhaps we'd best go ahead and have dinner without the pair of them. It's not like Dah to lose his temper but he can eat when he gets back.'

Hannah nodded. She was frustrated that her plan hadn't worked and upset that it was the first time that the whole family had not sat down together for Christmas dinner. But she decided there was nothing for it but to do as Joy suggested. So they all went downstairs.

It just didn't feel like Christmas, thought Hannah, as she gazed at her brothers and sisters gathered around the table. Bert suggested they say grace and pray for their parents, which they did, before the younger ones fell on the food. He took his mother's dinner up but did not linger. As soon as the meal was over, the girls asked if they could go out and play with the skipping ropes. Hannah said that they would have to help her with the dishes first. Bert, however, went out.

Jock and Bert were both back in time for tea, which consisted of the mince pies and sliced bun-loaf. Immediately he entered the kitchen, Hannah could smell the alcohol on her father's breath, although he wasn't staggering about as if worse for drink.

'Where've you been, Dah?' she asked, taking his dinner out of the oven.

'Ask no questions and ye get told no lies.'

The words were only slightly slurred. He pulled out a chair and lowered himself onto it, reached for his knife and fork, and beamed round the table at his children.

'You all right, Dah?' asked Joy.

'Mother not joining us?' asked Jock.

Hannah stared at her father. Had he forgotten? His mind wasn't going, too, was it? 'Not today,' she murmured.

'Not any bloody day if ye ask me,' said Jock mildly. 'But that's her loss. We'll just have to carry on as we have been. I never thought we'd manage but we're not doing too badly, are we, me wee bairns?'

'No, Dah!' chorused his younger daughters, and reached for more cake.

Hannah glanced at Bert. A faint smile played about his lips as he returned her look and, suddenly, she felt extremely uneasy. If their father was going to take to drink, what would happen to them?

–

Christmas and New Year were over and January had passed with no change in Susannah. In the February newspapers, the Irish Nationalist leader, Redmond, was calling for Home Rule. There had been another form sent to Dolly for the baby, who had now been given a name – Matilda – as suggested in the letter from Kenny. Why couldn't he write to her? wondered Hannah as she ladled out the porridge and avoided looking at her elder brother.

Last night Bert had come into their bedroom. Grace and Joy were asleep but Hannah had too much on her mind. Still, some inner voice had told her to pretend to be asleep as she sensed him looming over the bed. It had seemed an eternity before he left the room. She wanted to plead with her father to open his eyes and see that Bert was trying to usurp his position, but Jock wasn't the one for conversation at the breakfast table these days.

Most nights he went out after supper, coming in well after she had gone to bed. Hannah had found a blanket and pillow downstairs on the sofa yesterday morning, so obviously he was no longer sleeping with Mother. Hannah had asked him a week or so ago where he was going and he told that it was just for a walk, but who in their right minds would do such a thing these cold, foggy February evenings?

He was holding back money, too. She guessed he was drinking of a Saturday, because Sunday mornings he had a bad head. She was going to have to get him to listen to her, though, because they were in debt to the corner shop. Mrs Jones had taken pity on her at first but now she wanted the bill paid in full.

Hannah had no idea how she had run up such an amount and had been too scared to tell her father; now she had no choice. Besides, she needed extra money to buy more coal. If only she had someone she could confide in about Bert and money. She could talk to Granny Popo about her sisters and how they were getting hard to handle but that was all. Still, the old woman did come and sit with Susannah and talk to her as if she was taking in every word. She told her how the baby was coming along and it was obvious the old woman loved the bones of the child.

At first Hannah had felt embarrassed by the way Granny Popo provided Susannah's answers when she talked to her. On those occasions Hannah would hold her breath and pray for her mother to speak up and say that wasn't what she thought at all. The thought popped into Hannah's head that, perhaps, she should be taking a leaf out of the old woman's book by at least talking to her mother more. She had got out of the habit in the last few months, feeling that it was a waste of time.

So now she sat sideways on the bed and took Susannah's hand in hers. 'Mother, I just hate it when you lie there and say nothing. I want you to get up and be your old self. I've got myself into debt and need your advice. I can't handle things the way you could.'

Susannah stared at her daughter but remained silent.

Hannah wanted to weep. What's wrong with her, God? What good is it to you or anyone her being like this? Do something if you're up there! She tried again with her mother. 'I get the housework and cooking done with no trouble now and since Freddie turned four, suddenly he seems to be dry most nights. He no longer cries for you and, although that's good in one way, in another it saddens me. I need you back. Dah needs you. He's changing and it scares me. Please, come back to us! Please!'

No response.

Hannah got up, resisting the urge to shake and yell at her mother to pull herself together. Her patience was fraying and she knew she had to get out of the room.

That evening, as soon as Jock and Bert came in from work, Hannah brought up the subject of money. She was glad the younger ones were playing in the street. A whole gang of kids had gathered under a lamp-post; having thrown a rope over one of the bars, they were now using it as a swing.

She took a deep breath, 'Dah, I need more housekeeping money. I have to buy extra coal because of the two fires and Freddie needs new boots. Bert doesn't give me anything. He must get some money, although I know he doesn't get much, him still being an apprentice, but I'm not a miracle worker who can turn thin air into money. I owe the corner shop and Mrs Jones wants her money. Speak to him.'

Bert frowned. 'Just because I had a birthday not so long ago and had a rise it doesn't mean I have to hand that over to you. We know you're doing your best but if it isn't good enough then don't be blaming me.'

Her cheeks flamed. 'It's not my fault! You always were no good at adding up.' She turned to her father, her arms folded across her chest. 'Dah, you know Mother had all your wages and mine. It is true I can't manage as well as her but then it was her job. I haven't had her to teach me and am having to learn as I go along and on less money. And as I said, it takes more coal with her stuck up there in the bedroom.'

Jock sighed heavily and got up from the chair. 'I'll give ye another half a crown. Bert, yer'll give Hanny your rise.'

Bert's handsome face mirrored his dismay. 'Good God, Dah! I'll never manage. I buy Mother little treats with that money, I don't want to stop doing that.'

For a moment Jock was lost for words. There were times when an overwhelming guilt dragged him down and he told himself he had to end the affair with Nora. He wriggled his shoulders. 'It's either that or she has no fire up there,' he muttered. 'She needs that comfort.'

'We all need some comfort, Dah. But I'll do what you say.' Bert smiled at Hannah, reached into his pocket and took out tuppence and handed it to her. She thanked him. He bowed slightly before sitting at the table and spreading out that evening's newspaper and began to read aloud about the possibility of fighting breaking out between Russia and Japan because both wanted control of trade in Korea and Manchuria.

Jock pressed half a crown onto Hannah's palm and then went down the yard. He was avoiding going upstairs as much as possible. The less he saw of his wife, the easier it was to deaden that voice in his head that told him he was behaving very badly.

As Hannah fried fish to go with the potatoes and peas for their supper, she felt a victory had been gained. She still had the worry of paying off the debt but was hoping Mrs Jones would accept the half crown on account and agree the same payment for the next few weeks. But she didn't know what to do about boots for Freddie, and tuppence wouldn't go far to pay for the extra coal. She had no idea if her mother had been in a boot club. She had heard such a thing mentioned in the queue at the fishmonger's the other day. If her mother didn't have money in that, perhaps she had some rainy day money hidden away? She had always managed to produce boots and coats when it was an absolute necessity.

As soon as Bert and Jock went out after supper and her younger siblings were in bed, Hannah went into her parents' bedroom. She gazed at the silent humped shape in the bed, silhouetted in the firelight. Feeling guilty about what she planned, Hannah hoped her mother was asleep. She knew it would be more sensible to search the room in daylight but she did not want to wait. Systematically she went through the chest of drawers and the old fashioned wardrobe that had belonged to her grandmother, feeling for coins. She did not bother with the linen in the cupboard at the side of the fireplace because that was washed and ironed regularly. On the shelves on the other side she found a box of letters, cards and faded sepia photographs that she vaguely remembered her mother showing her when she was younger, but there was no money there. She felt inside the matching flower-painted vases on the fireplace and in the glass powder bowl on the chest of drawers. Not a farthing!

Hannah straightened up, depressed. Then as from nowhere, she remembered Kenny slitting the chair cushion that dreadful day when everything had gone wrong in their lives and wondered whether he had been searching for money for his father. Where were they all? She felt that overwhelming sense of hurt and anger that he could send money to Dolly in a letter, but not write to her. She wished she could forget him.

She carried on with her search, double checking places until, much to her relief, she found money sewn in the hem of an old skirt, belonging to her mother, right at the back of the wardrobe. As she undid the stitching and counted the coins she had a sense of being watched. She whirled round but her mother was still curled up in the bed, eyes closed. Perhaps it was guilt that made her feel the way she did but it was stupid to feel guilty and she had to suppress it. Every worker needed the tools to do a job properly, she reasoned. She finished counting and hid the money in her underwear. She did not wait for her father and brother to come home but went to bed. Immediately she fell into a deep sleep.

At first she thought it was a dream when a voice whispered, 'Time for you to earn that money, Hanny.'

She thought of her mother's rainy day nest egg. 'No!' she said sleepily.

'Oh yes!'

'No. She'd understand.' Hannah struggled to wake up but it was as if there was a weight on top of her keeping her down. She couldn't breathe, was suffocating. She fought her way out of the darkness, woke, gasping. Her legs were spread-eagled and her nightdress was up round her thighs. Terrified, she would have cried out but a hand covered her mouth.

'Shush now, Hanny! You don't want to wake the girls. Best we keep this to ourselves, luv.' She recognised her brother's coaxing tone, could smell his hair cream and feel the rough flannelette of his nightshirt against her midriff. And oh, my God, she could feel something else as well.

'Oh, let me go, please let me go, Bert! I'll give you the money back,' she babbled against his hand, and attempted to push him off.

'Don't do that, Hanny!' he whispered, his apology for a moustache brushing her ear. 'I don't want to get angry and hurt you – and, honestly, to tell you the truth this is well worth the money – at least I know no one else has had you.'

Panicking utterly, she fought him but it was no use. He smothered her scream with his hand. The smell of the peppermint drops he liked to suck filled her nostrils as his breath came in gasps. Then he sighed and collapsed in a heap, almost squashing the breath out of her.

She did not want to believe what had happened had taken place. How could Bert do such a thing to her? He knew it was wrong. Scared silly her sisters might wake and remembering what her mother had told her when she had started with the curse, she thumped him on the shoulder and kicked at his legs. He groaned and slid off her. She pushed him onto the floor where he lay in his nightshirt. She wanted to kick him and kick him where he lay but she knew she had to act quickly.

Dragging her nightgown between her legs and clutching it there, she managed to get downstairs without falling. She prayed her father would not wake up. Feeling dreadful, she threw up in the sink and then sluiced the mess away and washed herself underneath repeatedly. Tears ran down her cheeks. She wanted to kill her brother. He had committed a terrible sin. How could you let this happen to me, God? What are you playing at? What is it you've got against our family?

She wanted her mother to hold her and tell her everything would be all right but there was no comfort to be had from that silent figure upstairs. And how could she tell her father what had happened? She couldn't stay here, but what if Bert was still in her bedroom? He might do it again. The horror engendered by what had taken place chilled her from top to toe. Then she remembered her sisters and, scared that Bert might do something to them, knew that she had to go back upstairs. As Hannah went past the sofa, she peered through the gloom, holding her breath, hoping Jock had not heard her. Then she realised he was not there. She picked up the blanket and pillow but no one lay there. Perhaps he had gone the lavatory. No! She wasn't thinking straight. He would have had to pass her. Maybe he had heard something upstairs and gone to see what it was.

He was not in their mother's room. The door was ajar to the girls' bedroom but, thank God, there was no sign of Bert. Shivering, she climbed into bed, worrying over her father's whereabouts. She could not sleep for thinking about what Bert had done and wondering where Jock could be. So it was, she heard the clock downstairs strike six and someone enter the house.

How she was able to behave normally when she got up, Hannah had no idea. It was as if she was watching another self perform her tasks. Maybe it was the same for her father, she thought, watching him eat his salt fish. Where had he been last night? And how was she to face her brother? Her insides quivered just thinking of him.

When Bert finally got up, Jock had already left the house, saying as it was Sunday, he was going for a walk. Hannah did her best to avoid meeting her elder brother's eyes. He was humming a hymn tune. How could he be such a hypocrite? She tried to concentrate on listening to her sisters' chattering while she washed and dressed Freddie but, even so, she sensed Bert watching her. What was going on in his mind? He had said about knowing no one else had ever been with her, did that mean he had been with girls of easy virtue? She was frightened to be alone with him in the house. Her mother did not count. She came to a decision, placed the meat in the oven and went out with her sisters and Freddie to the park.

The fresh air made Hannah feel better but her thoughts were in confusion and she felt icy when she thought about what men and women did to have a child. Bert had ruined such a relation for her. She felt soiled, unclean. She would never marry. If her mother remained the way she was, it was doubtful she would anyway. As the eldest daughter, Hannah knew where her duty lay.

That night she could not sleep, fearful Bert would sneak into the bedroom again and force himself upon her. She wanted to move the chest of drawers against the door but could not manage that alone and besides her sisters would ask questions and what answers could she give them? She slid out of bed and put a chair there, and thought of placing one of her mother's hatpins under the pillow. She did not expect to be rescued by her father. He was up to something. Maybe he had joined a card game. She did not want to think he might be out spending his money on a woman of ill repute. No! She was wicked even to consider such a thing.

She could not sleep, starting at every sound, but Bert did not come that night. Jock crept into the house just before dawn and at last she fell asleep. It was only when she woke that she remembered it was her seventeenth birthday. Well, there would be no cards or cake. They had all depended on her mother to make a fuss of such events.

Later that morning Hannah went into the corner shop, which her mother had always called a 'jangling shop'. At least she found pleasure in placing a heap of coins on the counter. 'I think you'll find there's three pounds, two shillings and ninepence, farthing, Mrs Jones.'

The small, thin woman with sharp features turned from weighing out sugar into a blue bag and smiled. 'There now, girlie, I knew you'd manage it if you had to.' She scooped up the money. 'And how's your mam?'

'The same. And I'd like a receipt, please, and to see you crossing our name off your book. Then I'd like–' she rattled off a list which included jam and semolina and a packet of jelly crystals.

She was scrubbing the front step when the postman stopped and held out an envelope to her. 'Feels like a card, Hanny,' he smiled.

She dropped the scrubbing brush into the bucket and wiped her hands on the sacking apron and took the envelope from him. She recognised the handwriting immediately. Kenny! Dear God! At last! She tore the envelope in her haste. It was a birthday card. Fancy him remembering, she thought, as she gazed at the red roses and the black lettering wishing *A Happy Birthday to a Very Special Person*. There was a message.

Dear Hanny,

We'd love you to have a happy birthday and we'd like nothing more than to give our best wishes in person today but this card will have to do. It's now almost eight months since that terrible day when our mam died and we hope your mother might be a bit better. If you'd like to meet us – how about this Sunday in Grosvenor Park in the ornamental gardens at three o'clock?

Love Alice and Kenny.

'Oh!' gasped Hannah, pressing the card to her bosom and then placing it down the front of her apron. Alice and Kenny! Her eyes shone with tears.

'Nice message, is it?' called the postman.

'Yes! Just what the doctor ordered.' She got up off her knees, picked up the bucket and emptied it down the grid in the gutter. Then stepping over the wet step, she wiped her feet on the coconut mat and ran upstairs to place the card in her underwear drawer.

That afternoon Hannah sang in a tremulous voice as she prepared a hot pot, made a jelly, and a dish of semolina which she placed in the bottom of the oven. It would be lovely with a big spoonful of jam in it. She was not going to think about what Bert had done to her. He wouldn't get the chance again. She must remember to place the chair under the handle every night. As she set the table, she thought about what to wear on Sunday. After taking a cup of tea to her mother, she and Freddie went for a walk with the intention of meeting the girls from school on the way back.

'What's this in aid of?' asked Bert, letting the semolina drip from his spoon back into his dish. He smiled at her and said in a teasing voice, 'I hope you're not wasting that extra money me and Dah gave you.'

She ignored him, gazing at Jock, wondering where he went nights. 'It's me birthday, Dah. I thought a little treat for us all would be nice.'

He stared at her, a flush on his cheeks. 'Bloody hell, lass! Why didn't yer say earlier? Mother always made a fuss of birthdays.'

Hannah felt uncomfortable. 'I didn't want to bother you. You have enough to think about.'

He did not deny that but looked anguished. He dug into his trouser pocket and produced a shilling and reaching across the table, placing it next to her plate. 'Get yerself a little treat. Ye deserve it. Yer a good lass. I know how difficult it must have been for ye giving up yer work to stay at home with Mother the way she is.'

Hannah thanked him in a husky voice and pocketed her shilling. She would buy a pair of stockings with it because even her best pair had darns in them. Joy suggested they sing Happy Birthday and the two girls and Freddie did. After that the jelly was greeted with rapture by the young ones. Bert even thanked her for allowing them to join in her special day and placed tuppence by her plate. She ignored it.

That evening when she went to bed, her mind full of the card from Kenny and Alice, wondering when they had found each other and what had happened to Mal. Alice had obviously managed to escape him but how had she found Kenny? Well, she would find out soon. She let her mind drift, imagining the moment when she saw them both for the first time in months.

'So it's your birthday!' Bert's whisper reached her from the bedroom doorway.

Hannah's heart jerked like a puppet on a string and the blood pounded through her veins. Stupid, stupid, stupid! She had forgotten to place the chair under the doorknob. 'Go away!' She attempted to strengthen her voice but it shook.

'Don't be like that, Hanny! I've got a present for you.' He moved towards her, his figure dark, bulky and threatening.

'Don't come any closer,' she hissed in a trembling voice, feeling for the hatpin beneath the pillow. She was shaking so much she almost dropped it. As he wrenched the bedcovers from her grasp, she lunged at him with the hatpin. It went through the shirt fabric and into the fleshy part of his upper arm. He yelped. 'What the hell was that?' Reaching up he pulled the hatpin out, felt its sharp point with the edge of his thumb. 'Naughty, naughty! I'm going to have to punish you for that, Hanny luv.'

'I'll scream. Dad'll c-come.' She was so terrified that she could hardly get the words out.

'Dad's not here. He's got himself a fancy piece. He can't live without it, you see. Us men are different from you females. He's taken up with the widow woman who lives next to the Morans' old house. I followed him one night.'

Hannah did not want to believe it and would have screamed that he was lying, that Dah wouldn't do such a thing, but Bert must have read her mind. He clapped a hand over her mouth and dragged down the bedcovers, despite his younger sisters' sleepy protests. Hannah fought him but he hit her across the head so hard her ears rang.

'What's going on?' muttered Grace, attempting to seize her share of the sheet and blankets, yawning and blinking as she did so.

'Go to sleep, Grace, you're having a dream,' said Bert in a gentle voice. 'Shush now, luv.' He put his mouth against Hannah's ear. 'One word, Hanny, and I'll do the same to them.' She believed him.

He removed his hand from her mouth and forced up her nightgown. Then he drew the bedclothes up so they covered them, heads and all. 'Isn't this cosy, Hanny?' he said in a friendly voice.

The sickening scent of hair cream, peppermint and sweat filled Hannah's nostrils and she wanted to throw up but Bert was pressing down on her and, all the while, humming *Happy birthday to you*.

–

Hannah felt as if she was living in a nightmare: only her brother's threat, that he would do the same to their sisters, was preventing her from throwing herself into the canal, that and the thought of keeping the appointment with Kenny and Alice. She hated her brother, hated him but who was there to stop him? Not her dah certainly. Her brother's words had shocked her. How could her father have got so close to that widow? She had always kept herself to herself and looked a right prude. Hannah had always considered her father someone special and felt betrayed, as though she had lost something valuable.

Hannah carried a tray into her mother's room and gazed down at her with a sense of helplessness. Her hair resembled a bird's nest. It was weeks since she had washed it. She looked like a very old woman instead of middle-aged. If only she could be herself again.

'Well, here's your dinner!' said Hannah brightly. 'Pea soup I made with a ham bone just like you used to.' She placed the tray on the chair next to the bed. 'It'll be Easter in a few weeks and I don't know whether to get a piece of ham or a couple of rabbits. I wonder if Dah will be spending the holiday with us, or the widow in the next street? I'd rather it was with us but the atmosphere in this house is so bloody horrible now I can understand him wanting to get out of here but that's no excuse for him.' She sank onto the side of the bed and brushed back her mother's hair. 'Oh, Mother, please come back to us? I don't think I can bear much more.' Her voice broke on a sob.

The woman in the bed stilled and, for a moment, Hannah thought she would speak and held her breath. Then her mother reached for the spoon and began to sup the soup.

Chapter Nine

Alice sang softly as she waited for Kenny. Normally he did not take this long to get ready. It was peculiar how he had suddenly decided to send Hannah a birthday card and suggest they meet in Grosvenor Park. He had written in his pad for her that he'd had a strong feeling that she was in trouble and needed them. *A Feeling!* Men weren't supposed to have a sixth sense like women. But she hadn't been about to argue with him, delighted that he had changed his mind about having nothing to do with the Kirks.

Although, what if he had been right all along and Hannah didn't want anything to do with them? They might get to the meeting place and she wouldn't be there. What then... would Kenny not accept that as a rebuff and go to the Kirks' house? Alice's face clouded. She just didn't know with him at the moment. He was changing and she couldn't judge how he'd react to events and suggestions as she used to. Mr Bushell had given him a rise on his nineteenth birthday and, since his sister's sudden death, he had Kenny helping him with his book-keeping; a job which had been done by his wife first and then the sister. Mr Bushell having had no formal education and his eyes being none too good for close paperwork.

Alice twitched the blanket that hung from the cord looped across the room. 'Hurry up! We're going to be late if you don't get a move on.' That wasn't true. They had plenty of time but she couldn't wait any longer to find out if Hannah would be at the meeting place. She wondered if her old friend had heard the rumour that Mr Kirk was carrying on with Mrs Taylor, who'd lived next door to them. She didn't want to believe it; in fact she refused to believe it. Jock Kirk was a nice man for whom she had great respect. He wouldn't do such a thing.

Alice thought of her own father and the nightmares she had of him rising out of a coffin with his hands curled, ready to choke the life out of her. She felt a familiar sense of dread and shuddered. He not only haunted her dreams but, occasionally in her waking moments, she visualised him turning up out of the blue, seeking vengeance for taking his money and leaving him for dead.

Kenny pushed aside the blanket and smiled self-consciously. He was wearing a navy blue worsted suit, a pale blue shirt and a silver grey muffler. His brown hair was still damp from his attempts to make it lie flat.

His hazel eyes had lost their haunted expression and he had put on flesh. He tilted his head to one side and spread his hands as if to say, *Well, what d'you think?*

She smiled. 'Smart! You look respectable. Nobody would believe you were a coal man during the week. There's some good stuff to be had in the market. But your hair's still damp.' She went over to him and touched it, frowning. 'You could get a chill in this weather and we can't afford for it to get onto your chest and you have to take to your bed.' He mouthed *That'll be the day. I've never had a day in bed in my life.* 'I wish spring would hurry up and come,' she murmured, still gazing at him. 'You're best wearing your cap.'

He frowned as if to say *Don't fuss!* Then he patted his inside pocket to make sure he had the brooch he had bought Hannah, for her birthday, before heading for the door. He had saved the rise that Mr Bushell had given him, certain that Alice would understand his need to show Hannah that he still thought a lot of her. He and Alice still had to be very careful with their money if they were to keep out of debt.

As they left the house Alice was glad the sky was a clear pale blue and the air crisp. She didn't want her latest millinery creation getting wet.

They were both in such a rush to get to the meeting place that they reached Grosvenor Park much quicker than they had estimated. The land on which the park was situated had been presented to Chester Corporation in 1867 by the second Marquess of Westminster. When it was originally laid out, a long line of Roman earthenware water pipes had been discovered, creating great excitement for those interested in such things. Kenny remembered Hannah mentioning it to him once, long ago, when they'd played Hide and Seek in the Nunnery ruins. Suddenly, he wondered what he would do if she didn't turn up.

Kenny's heart was thudding in his chest, as the ornamental gardens came in to view. Instantly he caught sight of a slim figure wearing a brown coat, she was bruising the leaves of a dead looking lavender plant. A blue and red plaid tammy covered most of her flaxen hair. Her face was in profile and the corners of her mouth drooped. She carried an air of deep sadness and Kenny's heart seemed to twist inside him.

Alice called her name. Immediately Hannah faced them and her expression lightened. Alice ran and flung herself at her, hugging her tightly. Hannah returned her hug, too choked to speak for a moment. Then she held Alice off so she could get a proper look at her and said in a puzzled voice, 'You look so well!'

'You don't.' Alice's eyes were concerned as they scanned her friend's face. 'I'm sorry your mother's still not right. You do know I didn't want to leave her?'

'Of course! Kenny said so in his report to the police. How did he manage to find you?' Hannah turned to him and her eyes widened. 'Bloody hell, Kenny! You haven't half changed, too. I swear you've put on pounds and...' She found herself hesitating to say that his face was far more attractive than she remembered. Instead she said with a scowl, 'Why the hell didn't you write to me? You sent little notes and money to Dolly but not one line to me to say that you were OK?' Kenny mouthed *Sorry!* And moving Alice aside, he took hold of Hannah's hands and held them so tightly that she thought he would break her bones. 'Go easy,' she said with a light laugh. A blush deepened along the line of his cheekbones and he loosened his grip. His eyes glowed with warmth as he gazed down at her. She felt some of her pain ease. 'OK! I know you really are pleased to see me and had your reasons for not writing for so long. But didn't you think that I'd be worried about the pair of you?'

'No,' said Alice promptly. Surprised by a sudden sense of possessiveness towards him, she dragged down on Kenny's left arm, so he had to drop one of Hannah's hands. 'He thought you might hate us.'

'Hate you!' Hannah's voice went up an octave and her expression was incredulous. 'Never in a million years! Although I admit I was angry, as well as relieved, when Dolly told me about the note with the money for Matilda.'

'There, I told you,' said Alice in a triumphant voice, hugging Kenny's arm. 'Nothing you worried about was true. We could have been in touch with Hannah months ago if you hadn't been such a coward.'

Kenny looked embarrassed.

'Don't call him a coward,' said Hannah, frowning. 'If his feelings had anything to do with what our Bert did to him, I don't blame Kenny being careful. Dah said Bert made a real mess of him.' She squeezed Kenny's hand. 'He was a swine towards you.'

Alice intervened swiftly, 'Bert loves your mother. He probably didn't intend to hurt Kenny the way he did.'

Hannah looked disbelieving but only said, 'Have it your way, Alice. You always did think the sun shone out of our Bert. I know different. But he's the last person I want us to fall out over.' There was a tremor in her voice. 'I'd rather forget him and talk instead about what's happened to you both in the last months. But what I want to know, first off, is where's your father?'

Alice said in a hard voice, 'Dead, we hope!'

Hannah's eyes widened, 'Dead!'

'Rough justice… that's what Kenny said. Although… we're not absolutely sure he is dead.' Alice shivered as a cold wind blew up from the river. At least that's what she put the icy feeling down her spine to.

'Make up your mind!' exclaimed Hannah. Kenny's gaze went from one to the other and he drew both their hands through his arms, and then urged them in the direction of the Groves. The two girls did not resist but obeyed his sudden show of strength.

He took them to Ainsworth's refreshment rooms overlooking the river; open because Sundays always brought some people down to the Groves even out of season. A few boats still wintered on the river and the remains of the floating swimming pool, now closed, could be seen. He led them to a table and to a chair each.

Hannah felt his warmth towards her wrap round her like a comfy blanket and she smiled up at him. 'What a good idea! The only thing is that I haven't any money.'

'He has,' said Alice dryly. 'Mr Bushell gave him a rise recently.' She paused to give the order to the waitress for three teas, as well as a plate of buttered scones, and then continued with what she felt compelled to say. 'Before you tell us that you went to see him and he told you he didn't know our address, that was true. Kenny still works for him but he didn't want our whereabouts being known.' Her smile faded as she rested her elbows on the table. 'I've already explained why, so I don't have to mention your Bert's name again.'

'No, you don't,' said Hannah, aware of Kenny's eyes on her face. She realised with a deep sadness and anger, that she could never, never speak to him about Bert's terrible violation: he'd taken her innocence and virginity, making her feel dirty and unworthy of a decent bloke. She took a deep breath and forced a smile. 'Tell me instead what happened to your father.'

So Alice told her everything that happened from the moment she had witnessed Hannah's mother's fall down the stairs, pausing only when the waitress brought their tea and scones, and resuming her story once they'd all consumed a scone and drunk some tea. Hannah listened intently to every detail. At a couple of points in the narrative she interrupted with a, 'You amaze me, Alice. I never thought you had it in you.'

At last she finished speaking. 'So you see what I mean when I said we're not sure he's dead.'

Hannah nodded, her eyes were dark with emotion.

'So what about you?' said Alice, leaning towards her across the table. 'Tell us how things are with you?'

Hannah pressed her lips together and crumbled the remains of a scone on her plate with unsteady fingers. 'Terrible!' she blurted out.

Her voice was passionate when she added, 'I hope your father is dead! It's what he deserves for what he's put our family through. I-I don't know where it's going to end. Mother might as well be dead for all the good she is to us.' She stopped abruptly, her eyes tragic, and put a hand to her trembling mouth. 'I'm sorry, I didn't mean that. I love her really… and at least I still have her with me. You've lost your mother and must be missing her terribly. I'm ashamed.'

Kenny reached out and pulled her hand away from her mouth and held it firmly in his own, longing to take her in his arms and soothe away her hurt. He glanced at his half-sister meaningfully.

Almost immediately Alice said, 'We understand.' She bit her bottom lip hard, wishing Kenny didn't feel he had to hold Hannah's hand and comfort her all the time.

Hannah brushed away a tear and gave a watery smile. 'Thanks! It's stupid of me getting worked up. Does no good.'

Kenny decided that it was time to brighten up the atmosphere. He took from his pocket the small package he had brought for Hannah and presented it to her.

'What's this?' she said, her eyes widening.

Alice said, 'He bought it for your birthday.'

Hannah's cheeks turned pink with pleasure. 'You shouldn't have!' But she couldn't wait to remove the brown paper and open the box. She gazed at the brooch with its artificial green and red stones representing leaves and flowers. 'It's beautiful!' She lifted shining eyes to Kenny's. 'I'm touched. It's really nice of you. Here! Fasten it onto my coat.' She stood up.

Delighted by her reaction Kenny was all fingers and thumbs as he undid the clasp and pinned the brooch onto her lapel. He was aware of the smell of her skin and the scent of hair, the curve of her breast so close to his hand and wished he had the nerve to hug her close to him. Instead he kissed her cheek and stepped back.

Hannah caressed the brooch with a finger, smiling up at him. 'Thanks. You've made my day.' She sat down, and reached out for another buttered scone. There was a silence. Then she said thoughtfully, 'Have you considered going back to that Mrs Black's house, just in case your dad did survive his injuries and got in touch with her?'

Alice shook her auburn head and her green eyes suddenly glowed. 'I wouldn't mind going there. We haven't thought about it nor had the time, to be truthful. When work's finished, what with having to cook our evening meal, the apartment to keep clean and shopping and making hats, I'm too tired. To be honest I've been trying to forget about Dad. But, as it is I can't really. I have nightmares about him finding me and choking the life out of me.'

Hannah could understand that. 'It would be best if you knew for sure whether he was dead or not. If he's still alive, maybe he's already been in touch with Mrs Black. He might even be at her house now. Maybe someone living in the same road might have noticed him. That "gardener" bloke for instance.'

'I suppose you're right,' said Alice casually. She suddenly remembered something that she had clean forgotten, hadn't even mentioned to Kenny that she could recall.

'What is it?' said Hannah, recognising the look on her face. 'You've thought of something.' Her fingers strayed to the brooch on her lapel and she caressed it.

'I never asked Dad why we were going to Scotland. He must have had his reasons,' said Alice, and glanced at Kenny. 'Did he have any family there? I don't remember him mentioning them and you were only an infant when you left but try and think… do you remember any aunts, uncles or other cousins?'

A face flashed into Kenny's mind and to his astonishment his hands began to shake so much he had to put his cup down.

'What is it?' asked Alice, her eyes brightening. 'Have you remembered something?'

Hannah stared at him, recognising horror when she saw it. 'Leave him alone,' she said roughly. 'What does it matter about your father's Scottish relatives? If there are any, they've never bothered to get in touch or come looking for him. I think Mrs Black's your best bet if you want to find out if your dad's alive or not.'

Kenny nodded agreement, his hands were still trembling and his mouth felt dry. He knew that sooner or later he was going to have to face up to whatever it was that lay hidden deep in the recesses of his mind.

'When would you go?' asked Hannah, curious to see Mrs Black. Was she really Mal Moran's fancy woman? She felt the pain of disillusionment, thinking of her father and the Taylor widow.

'Next Sunday,' said Alice, thinking about the gardener's lovely brown eyes and black curly hair.

'I'll come too,' said Hannah firmly, adding hastily, 'That's if you don't mind?'

Kenny smiled and shook his head.

'That's settled then,' said Alice happily. 'In the meantime, do you think we could go along today and see our sister? She's still well, I hope? That's if you've got the time?'

'I'll make time. As for how well Matilda is, she was fine last time I saw her,' said Hannah, and hesitated a moment before adding, 'But be prepared – Dolly's possessive of her.'

Immediately Alice rounded on Kenny. 'I knew we should have gone earlier – just knew we should have had her with us.' She jumped to her feet and without a word to either of them walked out of the refreshment rooms, her expression tight with annoyance.

Kenny grimaced at Hannah and stood up. She took his arm and they hurried outside but already Alice was out of sight. 'I shouldn't have told her,' said Hannah, biting her lip. 'Sorry. But I just thought she'd best know.'

He shrugged and they walked on in silence.

Alice hammered on the front door of the house in Seller Street, only a few yards from Canal Side. She was impatient to see her sister, determined to have her live with them, even if it did mean that she'd have to give up her job and they'd have to go without.

A sleepy-eyed Granny opened the door. Minus her bonnet, her clay pipe dangled from the corner of her mouth. Before she could speak, Alice said loudly, 'I've come for my sister. I appreciate your looking after her all this time but it's time she was with her family, where she belongs.'

A voice from within called, 'Over my dead body!'

Alice stiffened and glared at Granny. 'Was that your Dolly?'

Granny took out her pipe and sighed, looked up and down the street and saw Hannah and Kenny approaching in the distance. Luckily, except for a boy playing with a dog and a couple of girls with hoops, no one else was in sight. 'You'd best come in, duck, although I must say I don't like yer tone. Sunday afternoon is hardly the right time to come looking for an argument. Your mam was a real Christian and she wouldn't approve of yous disturbing the Sabbath.'

Alice flushed and gripped her hands tightly in front of her. 'I'm not looking for an argument. I just want my sister. You can't blame me for that.'

'I'm not one for blaming anyone. Why don't you come in and let's talk about what's best for the babby?' Granny hobbled into the kitchen.

Alice's colour was high as she stepped straight from the pavement into the house. She pushed aside a curtain that served to keep out the draughts and immediately her eyes lighted on Dolly sitting in the rocking chair with a baby at her breast. 'Matilda!' she cried.

'Yeah!' exclaimed Dolly, a fierce light in her eyes. 'We call her Tilly. I ask you, Miss Moran, could you do this for her?' she said, a hand thrusting the breast, with the suckling baby attached, higher.

Alice's colour deepened. 'Don't be daft!'

'Enough of that,' rumbled Granny, pointing the stem of her pipe at her granddaughter. 'Behave yourself. Miss Moran is Tilly's sister and you've known from the beginning the day would come when her family came to claim her. I think it's a bit early mind, but let's be sensible about this.' She paused, a sharp eye still on her granddaughter. 'We've appreciated them sending the money, haven't we, Dolly?'

'Yes, Gran,' said Dolly with assumed meekness.

At that moment, Hannah and Kenny entered the room, the old woman having left the door open for them. Both looked from Alice to Dolly and the baby. 'Well?' asked Hannah, attempting to assess the situation.

Dolly was staring at Kenny. 'You must be Mr Moran. We really are grateful for the sums you've been sending us. I do hope you're satisfied with how I've looked after Tilly. I have to say. she's not a ha'porth of trouble to me. She does so enjoy the breast.'

Kenny could not help but stare at her ample bosom. Hannah nudged him. Immediately he looked away, having assured himself that his younger half-sister was being well looked after.

Granny Popo tutted, shook her head at her granddaughter and her tone was severe when she said, 'You're embarrassing the young man.'

Dolly replied with a hint of laughter. 'I'm sure he knows I didn't mean to.' She took the baby gently off the breast and covered herself up. 'Would you like to hold her, Mr Moran?' She offered the child up to Kenny.

He smiled faintly into her amused eyes as he took the baby from her. Alice drew in her breath with a hiss. 'He doesn't know how to handle babies.'

Kenny raised his eyebrows as if to say *That's all you know* and cradled the little one in the crook of his arm, thinking he had seen enough women with babies on the streets to know how to do it. The baby sucked her fist and gazed up at him from hazel eyes. An expression of wonderment crossed his face. *She had his eyes!*

'She recognises you,' said Dolly smoothly, struggling out of the rocking chair and resting a hand on his arm. 'I'd say, too, that you definitely know how to handle a girl.'

Alice and Hannah glanced at each other, startled expressions on both their faces. Instinctively they drew closer together and scowled at Dolly. 'Haven't you got a husband in India?' snapped Alice.

'Yeah! What's that to do with anything?' Dolly challenged Alice, folding her arms across her bosom. 'Want to write to him, do you?'

'Enough!' thundered Granny, hitting the drop-leaf table with her fist. 'This babby! This babby,' she repeated, 'has not been weaned yet.'

'You're saying,' said Hannah, deciding it was probably better to try and soothe the hostile atmosphere, 'that it wouldn't be sensible to take her away from Dolly just yet.'

'I am,' said the old woman, jerking her head like a marionette several times. 'I suggest that she's left here, Mr Moran carrying on sending a small sum for her upkeep and that he and his sister visit whenever they can.'

Kenny nodded agreement, without even looking at Alice.

Alice frowned, thinking that she should have had some say in the decision made for her sister. What had got into Kenny, nursing her with that dopey expression on his face? 'Can I hold her?' she said abruptly.

He lifted his head and almost reluctantly handed over Tilly. Alice gazed intently down at the baby, looking for a likeness to herself or her mother in the tiny, triangle-shaped face, but to her surprise, she could only see Kenny, and horror of horrors she thought she saw her father, as well. She definitely had his eyelashes and his nose, as for her hair… it was carrot red! At that moment she felt something wet trickle through her hands. Oh Lord! She hadn't given any thought to all the nappies a baby might go through in a day. 'I agree,' she said, and hastily thrust her sister at Dolly.

Granny lowered herself into a sagging armchair the other side of the fire from the rocking chair with a grin. 'You could take her out Sunday afternoons in the pram if you like.'

'You have a pram?' Alice was surprised because one had to pay out a fair amount of money for a pram. Then she noticed the wooden one set against a far wall. It looked battered, was painted brown and only had a makeshift hood that didn't seem to match. She'd have loved a new one to wheel her sister out in but beggars couldn't be choosers. 'I'd like that,' she said. 'Wouldn't we, Kenny?'

He nodded agreement. From his pocket he took a shilling and handed it to Dolly. She thanked him with the boldest of smiles that brought a flush to his face.

Hannah frowned and suggested that she collect Tilly in her pram the following Sunday afternoon and meet Kenny and Alice outside the Falcon Inn on Lower Bridge Street to save them a walk. From there they would cross the old bridge to the leafy suburb of Queen's Park to Mrs Black's house. So it was settled.

Hannah was delighted to have the outing to look forward to. Yet, as soon as she set foot in her own home, she felt as if a hundred-weight of coal had descended on her. She had a whole week to wait before she would see Kenny and Alice again. In the meantime she had to keep her brother at a distance but at least she knew how to do that now.

But that evening when she went up to look in on her mother and then checked the younger ones to bed, she noticed that the chair from their bedroom had been removed. She went downstairs to see if it was in the kitchen, which it was, and she was about to take it upstairs when Bert entered the house and caught her in the act. She tried to get it through the kitchen doorway in a hurry but he stopped her.

'No, Hanny love!' He wrenched the chair out of her grasp.

She wanted to tell him to go to hell, to leave her alone, but the words wouldn't come. She wanted to run but fear anchored her to the spot.

He shook his head slowly from side to side, and reached out for her.

She managed to jerk herself out of his reach, then turned and ran up the stairs. He was after her like a rocket, laughing. She never got the chance to open the girls' bedroom door. He seized her on the landing and forced her down onto the floor. The linoleum was cold beneath her back and she tried to push him away but he was too heavy. 'No! Mother might bloody hear! And what if I was to have a baby?' she gasped.

'Tut, tut! Girls shouldn't swear,' he said in a mocking whisper. 'As for Mother hearing us – even if she did, do you really think she's going to do anything? She's lost her marbles.'

'Don't say that!' Hannah was trying to hold on to the hope that her mother would recover and be herself again, her dah would then stop what he was doing and she would be safe from her brother's assaults. 'Please, let me go. It's wrong. It's a sin. You know that from going to church.'

For a moment he stilled and she pushed with all her might, hoping he was having second thoughts about his actions. But the next moment she knew he was unrepentant. 'No, Hanny. It's not a sin. If you knew your Bible, you'd know that Lot slept with his daughters, and Sarah was Abraham's half sister. So it's OK for relatives to do it.' He forced her arms down again and crushed her with his body. 'Now be a good girl and shut your mouth or you'll wake the kids, never mind Mother.'

The familiar scents of his hair cream, peppermint and his sweat made her stomach heave. The hardness of the floor and the buttons on his trousers made the act all the more painful and her back felt as if it would break. At one point her head banged against her parents' bedroom door and she cried out, but her mother did not come to help her. Then thankfully it was over and he got off her, humming, '*Thine be the glory, risen, conquering Son*.'

'Blasphemer!' she whispered, feeling utterly brutalised.

He kicked her prone body and his voice was harsh when he said, 'Enough of that! By the way, if you do start having a baby, you'd best find yourself a boyfriend quick and play the whore.'

Hannah struggled to her feet and was halfway down the stairs when a door opened upstairs and Grace's sleepy voice said, 'What's a whore?'

Hannah felt as if she would die of shame and shrieked, 'Go to sleep! Forget what you heard. You don't want to know.' She hurried downstairs to try and wash all trace of him away and to huddle on the sofa, stony-faced, railing silently against the hand fate had dealt her.

Only slowly did she become aware of footsteps overhead and then Grace's voice droning on and on. Then she heard Bert yelling something incomprehensible but it was enough to get her to her feet and run upstairs. Joy was out of bed and Freddie was crying for Hannah. Bert was dragging Grace by the arm from their mother's room.

'Let her go, you cruel sod!' shouted Hannah, and went for him, clawing at his face. He released Grace and smashed Hannah's hand against the wall. Grace stood shivering in the doorway, her teeth chattering, watching them. Hannah clutched her hand and called Bert a bloody bully. Then suddenly a husky voice said, 'You woke me up! What's going on? Where's Jock?'

They all stared at the shadowy figure in the doorway of their parents' bedroom. Hannah and Bert drew away from each other.

'Y-You s-spoke, Mother,' stammered Hannah. 'Y-You spoke!'

'I had to. You were making such a racket.' Her voice sounded like a rusty hinge. 'It's not Christmas morning, is it?'

'Christmas has gone. It'll be Easter soon.' Hannah's voice wobbled. 'Oh Mother, Mother!' She stumbled towards her and put her arms round her. Then her sisters were each side, huddling as close as they could get.

Bert watched them, his mouth a hard line as he felt the scratches on his face. Then he said, 'I'll go and get Dah. He's probably fallen asleep downstairs. He's going to be over the moon you've come to your senses, Mother.' He put a hand on her shoulder and kissed her cheek, then hurried downstairs.

Susannah, normally undemonstrative, kissed the top of her daughters' heads before gently pushing them away. 'I don't understand, why are you all up when it's dark? And someone had best shut that child up.'

'It's Freddie, Mother, it's your youngest son, Freddie!' Hannah stared as if through a misty window, her eyes drowning in tears. 'You haven't spoken to us in over seven months. You didn't seem to know us.'

'I didn't know who I was,' said Susannah, resting her back against the wall, her eyes peering through the dimness at the faces of her children. 'I thought that if I kept quiet, I wouldn't get hurt. I was scared.'

Hannah was shocked. 'Why should you think we'd hurt you?'

'You said I was pushed downstairs.'

'That was Mr Moran,' cried Joy, her eyes wide in her pale face. 'And he's not here, Mother.' She clutched at her arm.

'Mr Moran! I couldn't remember… don't remember falling. I thought… Jock was responsible for my fall.' Suddenly Susannah wailed, making them all jump. 'What must Jock think of me? How will he ever forgive me?' She buried her head in her hands.

'Mother, Mother, what are you talking about?' said Hannah, hugging her against her with strong young arms, but wondering even as she spoke, would her mother forgive him if she was ever to find out what he'd been up to?

Susannah pulled herself together, lifting a tear-stained face to her eldest daughter, and clutched a handful of her blouse. 'It doesn't matter. I've probably got things confused.'

'He loves you, Mother,' she said, determined to convince Susannah of the truth of that. 'He loves you!'

'Yes. Of course he does!' Susannah's voice was unsteady but sounded brighter, and her hand felt for that of her eldest daughter. 'Let's go downstairs. Goodness me,' she said, stumbling forward. 'My legs feel really strange… and my throat that feels odd, too.' She laughed, gripping the banister rail, as well as Hannah, as she searched for the next stair with her bed-socked foot. 'I feel like I'm a child starting all over again. How have you managed? Did you pay off the debt?'

Hannah almost fell downstairs in her fright. 'Y-You remember me telling you about that?'

'Yes! Don't stop on the stairs, Hanny, you'll have the girls and the other… the boy falling.'

With a feeling of dread, Hannah kept silent until they entered the kitchen. The room was empty, although the gaslight was on and Bert must have thrown coal on the fire before going in search of Jock. With a sinking heart Hannah went into the scullery with the kettle and filled it. She found the back door ajar. She felt relief that her mother had come to her senses but was scared silly that she was going to remember what she had said to her about her dah and the widow at the back.

Back in the kitchen she placed the kettle on the fire, forcing a smile at her mother, who was sitting in an armchair with Grace on her lap and Joy kneeling on the rug in front of the chair; Freddie, though, was keeping his distance. Hannah thought of Bert telling her dah about Mother. It was going to be a helluva shock to him. Hannah's eyes glinted. Serve him right! For better, for worse, that's what it said in the marriage service and he had broken his vows. He ought to be thoroughly ashamed of himself.

'Mother, do you remember everything I told you?' she asked, hoping that despite her dah's fall from grace that she couldn't, and needing to know for her peace of mind.

Susannah screwed up her fat little face and for a moment a scared expression showed in her dark eyes. 'Don't know! So much said… some went in one ear and out the other, I suppose. I remember a baby.' She stared at Freddie. 'Was it him?'

'No.' Hannah said no more, deciding that perhaps it was best if she said little about most things until she had more time to think. Who was to say that a question might not trigger a memory? The mind was a strange thing. It had a habit of making unexpected connections. Best if she got on with making tea.

By the time her older brother reappeared with a strained looking Jock in tow, Susannah and the rest of the family had had some tea and toast and Joy was telling her mother how she was getting on at school.

'I was ju-just down the yard, Mother,' said Jock, smoothing his hair with a trembling hand. 'I had the runs – must have been our Hanny's cooking.' He bent over and kissed his wife's soft wrinkled cheek. She smiled up at him, placing a hand on the side of his face. 'My boy Jock,' she said with a break in her voice. 'Just as good-looking as ever. I'm sorry for being out of it for so long. I forgot who you were, thought you were one of these wife-beaters and had pushed me down the stairs.'

Jock swallowed. 'No, lass,' he said huskily. 'I would never do that.'

'Do you remember me, Mother?' Bert pushed himself forward, so he and Jock juggled for a position in front of her, almost falling over the kneeling Joy.

Her face lit up and with her other hand she stroked Bert's handsome face. 'I remember you reading to me. You had a nice voice, although I can't remember all you said.' Her brow suddenly knitted as she seemed to be searching her thoughts.

'It doesn't matter, Mother,' he said, smiling down at her. 'You remember me and that's all I care about.'

There was a silence.

'Will you be getting up in the morning from now on?' asked Joy, struggling to her feet, by dint of using her father's legs as aids.

'I hope so. My head feels strange and… I suppose it'll take some time before I can do all the things I used to.' Her face crumpled and she looked like a little girl lost.

'Yer'll have to take it easy,' said Jock hastily. 'Stick to just looking after the family and the house.' He squeezed her shoulder. 'Yer always did do too much running around after other people, Mother.'

A tremulous smile came over Susannah's face and she covered his hand with her own. 'If you say so, Jock. I know you just want the best for me. But you'll have to tell me all that's been happening.'

Hannah saw a vein in his throat jerk and then throb. She glanced at Bert, wondering how her father had felt when he had turned up at the widow's house. Shocked that his son knew that he was there? She read a warning in Bert's eyes and she felt despair, wishing she could tell her parents of the violence and the shame he had inflicted on her but knowing she couldn't.

Susannah smiled at the circle of faces about her. 'Time for bed for you young ones I think.'

Joy and Grace kissed their mother but Freddie still kept his distance even though he could not take his eyes off her. He scurried out in their wake with a wave and a 'Night, night!'

Hannah took the cups and saucers into the scullery, thinking to take her time washing them in the hope of overhearing her parents' conversation but a call from the kitchen told her that was not on the cards and, reluctantly, she was forced to follow Bert upstairs.

He stopped on the landing and reaching out a hand, before she could escape into the bedroom, seized her chin. 'One word to Mother, my lovely little sister, and you'll regret it. Not that for one second she'd ever believe you. I'll let it drop that I've seen you with a fella.' He kissed her forehead and went upstairs to his bedroom.

If Hannah had had the poker in her hand she might have hit him with it then. The warning made her so angry. As soon as he was out of sight, she crept downstairs and sat on the bottom step, hugging herself in an attempt to keep warm. The kitchen door was firmly closed and, although she caught the murmur of her parents' voices, she could not make out a word they were saying. She turned and made her way upstairs, hoping all would be well between them.

She slid into bed besides her sisters, wondering what the future would hold for her now that her mother was hopefully well on the road to recovery. She hoped to God that it wasn't disgrace. One thing was for sure, there was no going back; but she prayed she and her mother would be spared anything else going wrong in their lives.

Chapter Ten

Hannah entered Bannister's bakery with her mother on her arm and breathed in the lovely aroma of freshly baked bread and fruitcake baking. It was three days since Susannah had got up from her bed and spoken. Hannah was delighted to have her mother up and about, giving the odd order and asking questions, but she had found the hours spent with her exhausting in a way. Maybe that was because she was tense, praying for the *curse* to come but also worried that what she had said about her dah and the widow Taylor was one of those tidbits of information that Susannah might remember.

'Hello! How lovely to see *you* here, Mrs Kirk,' said Agnes, the shop girl, resting her hands on the counter and beaming at her. 'Feeling much better, are yer?'

'Yes, thank you.' Susannah clutched Hannah's arm tightly and sent her a sidelong glance as if to say *Who is this?*

'Hello, Agnes,' said Hannah, smiling. 'This is Mother's first outing into town, so I thought we'd come and see you and buy a couple of lovely fresh Viennas and a bag of buns.'

'Coming up straight away!' Agnes beamed at them, almost shot to attention and saluted. She was small and had a pert bosom that not even the large, thick white apron could disguise. Her hair was russet coloured and her eyes brown. She flittered over to the shelf behind her and took two loaves and wrapped them in a sheet of greaseproof paper. She placed them on the counter and said to Hannah, 'So will you be coming back to work here?'

Hannah glanced at her mother. 'I'd like to if there's a vacancy but maybe I'll have to wait a couple of weeks or so until Mother's feeling more herself.'

'She looks well and we could do with you here.' Agnes reached for a pair of tongs and took seven buns from a plate in the window.

'I thought Miss Whittaker would be helping you,' said Hannah, watching her put the buns in paper bags.

'She's helping in the back. Mrs Bannister hasn't been too well lately. Poor ol' soul.' Agnes wrote the price of bread and buns on a piece of paper and pushed it across the counter.

'I'm sorry to hear that,' said Hannah, watching her mother fumble for her purse in the pocket of her long black coat. She sorted through the coins once she had it open. Hannah had to resist taking the purse from her and sorting the money out for her.

The doctor had told her that she must not be doing everything for her mother when she was a bit slow, but must allow her to do things in her own time, otherwise she just might not bother. At last Susannah handed the money over to Agnes and smiled at the girl. 'There now. I hope I've got it right.'

Agnes counted it and grinned at her. 'To the last farthing, Mrs Kirk. Well done!'

'Thank you, lovey.' Susannah nodded at her and picked up the bags of buns.

Hannah took the bread. 'See you again, Agnes.'

'Soon I hope,' said the girl, resting her arms on the counter. 'As I said, we could do with you here.'

Hannah's tiny dimples appeared at the corner of her mouth. 'I'll have a word with my dah and see what he says.' Placing the loaves in the shopping bag along with the bags of buns, she waved to Agnes as she and her mother left the shop.

'She seems a nice girl,' said Susannah, as they waited for a break in the traffic before crossing Foregate Street. 'Should I have recognised her?'

'You have seen her in the shop before, Mother, but you don't know her… not like you knew Florrie Moran.' Hannah held her firmly by the arm and hurried her across the road.

'Florrie! I wonder…' The woman's voice trailed off.

Hannah looked at her anxiously. Her mother was always starting a sentence and then breaking off before it went anywhere. Also she seemed unable to remember anything that had happened the day of her fall. She wouldn't have known she had delivered Florrie's baby if Hannah hadn't reminded her. She showed no interest at all in where it was or what had happened to Alice or Kenny or even Mal. Hannah wondered if that was down to her mother being unable to cope with too much information at the moment. But at least if she carried on like this it did mean that she was unlikely to ask too many questions about those nights when her husband had been missing from her bed.

The next day Hannah decided her mother might enjoy an outing to Moreton to visit her cousin Joan. At the station she had a fright when she caught sight of Mrs Taylor through the window of the tearoom where she was a waitress. The woman noticed her staring because a flush rose in her cheeks. Then with a toss of her head she looked away. Hannah glanced at her mother to see if she had noticed anything amiss but she seemed oblivious to the widow's existence. They had a nice day walking on the sands before catching the train home. On the return journey Hannah started with stomach cramps and by the time she had arrived home the *curse* had come. She felt like singing.

Her mother insisted that she lie down with the stone hot water bottle. 'You've done so much for me in the last months, Hanny lovey, that it's time you took a little rest.' She tucked a hand-crocheted blanket about her daughter. Hannah felt a warm glow at her mother's actions. It was a very long time since her mother had tucked a blanket round her. From that moment she began to believe that some good might come out of the terrible time they had both been through.

But the next evening Jock was two hours later than his normal time for coming in from work. Hannah watched him as he apologised to her mother, hoping that it wasn't just an excuse when he said he'd been to visit an injured workmate. His lateness made her anxious but she knew there was nothing she could do about it except hope he was telling the truth.

The week could not go fast enough for her and it was such a relief knowing that Bert would never attempt to come into their bedroom now his mother was fully aware of things and their father staying home nights.

–

Hannah pushed the pram and then ran to catch the handle. She did it again. Tilly chuckled, clutching the sides as the game was repeated. It was drizzling but the baby was well wrapped up, so Hannah was not going to allow the weather to worry her. She was on her way to meet her friends, blessed by the thought that Bert would never again force himself upon her. She told herself that she must try and forget what he had done and look forward to returning to the bakery in a fortnight. By that time, hopefully, her father would have finished with that woman if he hadn't already and her mother would be able to cope without her in the running of the household.

It had felt so strange letting go of the reins and being told what to do. Hannah knew exactly what to do, but it had been a delight obeying her mother when she had almost given up hope of her ever making a full recovery. She doubted still whether her mother could do all the things she had been able to once. She had aged and seemed to need to take life much slower. Still, the world was a better place than it had been a week ago.

She skipped past the ancient Rows, where quite a number of people were gazing in shop windows, sheltered from the rain. Alice and Kenny were waiting for her in a doorway, near the medieval black and white pub, The Falcon, on the corner of Lower Bridge Street and Grosvenor Street. Kenny was clad in his Sunday suit and Alice wore a dark green coat with a floppy brimmed black velveteen hat on her auburn hair misted by the drizzle.

Kenny smiled when he caught sight of her but Alice was frowning. Hannah splashed through a large puddle in her gumboots, conscious that her macintosh was far too big for her slender figure, but her mother had always believed in buying larger sizes. She wondered if they would notice the change in her today.

'Hello!' said Alice, and looked down at her baby sister with a slight pucker between her brows. 'I wasn't sure if you'd bring her with it raining.'

Hannah shrugged. 'I thought you'd want to see her.'

Kenny bent and tickled his half-sister under the chin. She gurgled, gazing up at him with wide hazel eyes and then seized part of the blanket and sucked it.

'She's teething, the little love,' said Hannah fondly. 'Granny Popo reckons once she's got a couple of teeth Dolly will soon start weaning her.'

Alice mumbled, 'Does that mean we'll have to take her then?'

Hannah looked at her with a knowing expression in her eyes. 'Changed your tune, have you? Realised that babies are hard work?'

Alice flushed. 'It's not that I'm scared of hard work. It's just that I'm not sure if I can cope. Mam never had a baby for me to learn on, unlike you with your mother. I'd rather wait until she's a proper little girl and Kenny's twenty-one and earning better money.' Hannah looked at Kenny, who was staring at the pair of them. He raised his eyebrows.

'It's okay' said Hannah laughing, 'I think you're being very sensible. Babies aren't everybody's cup of tea. As long as Kenny can carry on paying for the privilege and Dolly's husband stays in India, let her do it. After all, her husband might not care for her looking after another man's baby once he's home. Now, are you going to wheel the pram?'

Alice nodded and took the handle. Kenny fell into step at Hannah's side. His arm brushed hers as they began to walk down to the river. 'I've got some good news,' she said.

'We've heard on the grapevine,' said Alice and shot a smiling glance at Hannah. 'We're really glad – relieved is the word! No wonder you're looking as if you'd been given the crown jewels.'

'Things are so different I keep having to pinch myself.' Hannah's face glowed.

'I've felt like that. It's great.' Alice's eyes were suddenly damp.

Kenny seized Hannah's hand and squeezed it. She returned that squeeze and did not withdraw her hand immediately but was content to let it lay snugly in his grasp for a little longer before casually letting go.

'She'll never be able to do all the things she used to,' continued Hannah. 'Dah's told her that she's just to look after us, and the house.

He's also agreed to my going back to work in a fortnight. You can't imagine how glad I am about that. It's not that I hate housework and looking after the family, but I can't say I enjoyed the task.'

'You might if you were doing it just for a husband,' said Alice, her face serious. 'I love taking care of our apartment. But it's enough for me having one room and just Kenny and myself to see to.'

Hannah smiled. 'I'd like to see your apartment.'

Alice nodded. 'You can one day but, there won't be time today. Let's get a move on across the bridge and let's hope this drizzle doesn't turn into a downpour.'

Hannah and Kenny didn't need telling twice and hurried onward.

When they reached the other side of the Dee, they walked up to the crescent where Mrs Black lived. From there they could see the river shrouded in mist.

'Doesn't it look mysterious,' murmured Hannah. 'You can almost imagine the ghosts of the Romans rising out of it.'

'Oh, don't start on history,' said Alice in a teasing voice. 'That's something I haven't missed about you.'

She glanced about her, remembering the last time she was here it had been raining. The roses had been in bloom but now it was the time of year for the daffodils to start making their appearance. Suddenly her pulses leapt as she noticed a figure in a macintosh and cap tying up some drooping plants. She wanted it to be Sebastian. Was almost certain it was the same garden that he had worked in last time. Would he remember her if she went up to him and said hello? Oh, Lord, she didn't have the nerve.

As it was she did not need to because, to her surprise and delight, Kenny went and tapped him on the shoulder. Sebastian looked up, pushing his cap to the back of his head; the damp weather had caused his black hair to curl tightly. His dark eyes widened in surprise and he pocketed a ball of twine. 'Well, look who's here! I'd bloody given up on you, mate. You could have had the decency to come and tell me how you got on with the search for your sister.'

Kenny looked apologetic and then jerked his head in the girls' direction. Sebastian saw them then and his sensuous mouth curled into a smile as his eyes met Alice's. 'Hiya!' He lifted a hand in greeting.

'He's a good-looking bloke,' whispered Hannah.

'Isn't he just.' Alice felt a rush of pleasure and thrust the pram handle at Hannah and took a step forward as Sebastian strolled towards them with an easy grace.

He gazed down at Alice's smiling face. 'So he found you then.'

'It looks like it. I'm really sorry for what my father did to you.'

'You said so at the time. But it was my own fault. I tripped him up on purpose.' There was warmth in his eyes that she had never seen in a man's before.

'Honest?' She was touched that he should do such a thing for her and her whole body felt as if it was aglow.

'Honest to God!'

'He… he might have killed you.' Her voice was low and deep with concern.

'But he didn't. How did you manage to get away from him?'

Hannah was getting wet and, though happy for her friend to fall in love with this good-looking young man, she decided that the conversation might go on for some time and would be better taking place indoors after they found out what they wanted. 'Ask him about Mrs Black, Alice?'

Sebastian glanced at the tall slender figure in a green macintosh in surprise. 'She's a widow – and a rich one. She owns property in Liverpool, would you believe?'

'Why is she living over here then?' said Alice, despite her annoyance at being interrupted at such a lovely moment by Hannah.

Sebastian shrugged. 'Could be that she has good taste. She has men visiting her. Rent men bringing her the books so the maid says. Ma reckons she was something else before becoming a rich widow but won't soil her lips with the word.' He grinned. 'Ma's prone to flights of fancy. Anyway she has no proof of that – just a feeling. Ma has lots of feelings. It's the mixture of Irish, Spanish and French blood in her.'

Alice was astonished. 'She's a foreigner?'

He said solemnly, 'Aren't the British a mongrel race?'

Alice glanced at Kenny, who nodded. 'I suppose so,' she said with a shrug.

Sebastian thrust his hands in his pockets. 'Anyway, what d'you want with Mrs Black?'

'To find out if she knows anything about my dad's whereabouts,' said Alice without hesitation. 'Believe it or not we're now looking for him.'

Sebastian's dark brows drew together and he scratched the back of his neck. 'You amaze me. He hasn't been here. Seen little of Mrs Black lately. She's sacked her gardener and live-in maid and just has a woman going in daily. Unfortunately, she's not one for gossip according to Ma.' He blinked rain out of his eyes and wiped his face with the back of his hand. 'That's all I know but I'll keep my eyes open if you like?'

'Thanks,' said Alice, and fearing he might now walk away, added, 'We think he's dead but…'

'Dead?' His expression showed incredulity. 'Then why are you looking for him?'

She bit her lip. 'There was an accident. It's a long story. We've seen and heard nothing from him since. He was still alive last time I saw him but unconscious, near death I'm sure.'

'But you didn't stay around to find out.'

She blushed but fortunately for her, Sebastian asked no further questions. She was grateful but wondered what he made of what she'd told him. 'As I said it's a long story.'

He smiled. 'I don't blame you for running, luv. I'd need to know where you're living if I find out anything.'

Alice read in his words a desire to keep in touch with her. 'Kenny!' She snapped her fingers and turned to her half-brother. He was already ahead of her and writing down their address.

Kenny tore out the page and handed it to Sebastian. He pocketed the paper and said warmly, 'My friends call me Seb, by the way.'

Alice said softly, 'Thanks, Seb. You do know I'm Alice. This – is my friend, Hanny. Hannah Kirk, that is.'

Hannah twinkled up at Sebastian and held out a hand. 'Nice to meet you, Seb.' They shook hands.

He turned back to Alice. 'See you soon then.' He walked away and she watched him bend to his work.

'He shouldn't be working on a Sunday,' she said seriously. 'I wonder when he has his day off?'

'He's in service. They have to work when they're told – but I'm sure you'll get to know when his time off is,' murmured Hannah with a faint smile. 'Did you notice his accent? I'd swear he's from Liverpool.'

'I like the way he speaks,' said Alice, her expression dreamy as she continued to gaze after Sebastian, having forgotten about Tilly.

Hannah looked at Kenny. 'Remind her it's raining and let's get going,' she said. He didn't have to. Alice heard her, put out her tongue and gripped the other end of the handle of the pram. The three of them walked swiftly back down towards the river.

–

Alice could not stop thinking about Sebastian. His dark eyes haunted her dreams and, even as she swept up bits of cotton thread, fabric and trimmings, she could not get him out of her mind. What would her mam have thought of him? She would have wanted to know his religion before job or anything else. Alice gnawed on her lip. Irish, French and Spanish blood – he had to be a Catholic. Florrie Moran might have sung in church *Red and yellow, black and white all are precious in His sight* but that would not have included the Papists. She had believed people should stick with their own kind. Oh dear, what would she do if he were to ask her out? The question was to plague her in the weeks to come.

A couple of Sundays later Alice and Kenny returned from church to find Sebastian waiting outside the house. He detached himself from a lamp post and walked towards them. She was delighted to see him but, for a moment, she thought her father might have turned up and that was why he was here. She went pale and said, 'Don't say that you're here because you've seen our father!'

He shook his dark curly head and removed his hands from his pockets to grasp one of hers. 'No. Don't look so worried. I thought I'd just come and see you.'

Relief flooded through her and she allowed herself to show her pleasure at seeing him. 'Come inside! We'll be having dinner soon. Share it with us.'

He shook his head, a smile softening his refusal. 'I can't. I've got to be back soon. My boss, Mr Waters' ship's due to dock in Liverpool tomorrow and I've got to take his daughter home this afternoon, so she's there to welcome him. She's been staying with her grandmother. It's her garden I was working in. Ma's her housekeeper and cook but I work for Mr Waters in Liverpool.'

That news came as an unpleasant shock. 'Hannah said you had a Liverpool accent.'

He said ruefully, 'I didn't know it was that noticeable.'

'Oh, it isn't!' said Alice hastily. 'I like the way you speak.'

Sebastian said softly, 'That's good because I'd like us to get to talk often. I'm over here quite a lot.'

She smiled and realised he was still holding her hand. 'Have you time for a cup of tea?'

'Glad you asked.'

Alice led the way into the house. In no time at all, the three of them were sitting in front of the fire with steaming cups in their hands. 'Tell us about your mother, Seb?'

A faint smile lurked in the depths of his dark eyes. 'If Ma has a fault it's that she's inclined to embroider a story. You want to hear the one about how she survived on the streets of New Orleans?' He paused. They looked at him expectantly. 'She never knew her mother. She died when Ma was born; her father was a Spanish/French musician who got caught up in the American Civil War. He died in her arms from his wounds, or so Ma says. She barely survived. Old Mrs Waters heard her singing outside a theatre after the war ended. Ma was in rags, shivering with the cold, so she took pity on her and brought her back to England.' He grinned, showing even, strong teeth.

Alice was fascinated. 'That's what I call a story. Much better than the real ones about the past that Hannah and Kenny love.'

Sebastian threw back his head and laughed. Alice blushed. 'I didn't mean to say your mam made it up.'

'Of course you didn't!' His eyes teased her wickedly. 'Just that she could write a fiction and sell it for a penny a sheet.'

Kenny decided to take part in the conversation and mouthed, *Is Mr Waters in the cotton business?*

Sebastian smiled. 'Smart alec! But there's also the farm that he rents from the Duke of Westminster; Mr Waters' younger brother's looking after it at the moment.'

'So what's the family's connection with Chester?' asked Alice, interested in how the other half lived.

'Old Mrs Waters married a second time, a cousin of old Mr Waters. He had pots of money. When he retired from business in Manchester he bought the house in Chester, saying the climate was better for his health. He died six years ago. Ma's been with the old lady through thick and thin, takes care of her and her granddaughter when she comes to stay. Miss Victoria had rheumatic fever recently and it's damaged her heart.' His expression was suddenly grim. 'She's been told that she's got to take it easy, but she's stubborn like her father.'

'You're fond of her,' said Alice, a wistful expression on her small face.

'I'm fond of the whole family. They've been good to Ma and me.'

'Is she spoilt?'

'You bet she is, but she's got nice ways about her and she cares about people,' he said, smiling. 'She was really interested in you and your friend; she saw us talking and she'd like to help you. She's in favour of a better education for the working class girl, as well as higher wages for them.' He drained his cup and stood up.

Alice got to her feet quickly, determined to spend even an extra minute in his company. She felt slightly envious of Miss Victoria, who could see him every day and whom he thought so much of. 'She wants the vote for herself, does she?'

'Too right, she does! Not that the master knows about it, which is just as well because he'd put his foot down there.' He shrugged on his jacket. 'I'll have to get going. If I were you I'd forget your father and Mrs Black. I know the past is all round you here in Chester but you're only young, you've the future to look forward to.'

'Oh, I agree with you,' said Alice hastily.

She had quite decided that Seb was the kind of bloke she was looking for and was determined that he would come and see her again. She couldn't wait to tell Hannah about his visit.

–

She didn't get the chance until a week later, on a fine spring day. 'Well that was some story!' said Hannah with a twinkle in her eye after Alice had finished telling her all that Sebastian had said.

Alice said defensively, 'He did say his ma could tell a good tale.'

Hannah was thinking, Aye, but what happened when she came to England and where does Sebastian's father figure in the continuing tale?

'Well, what are you thinking now?' asked Alice, as Hannah pushed the empty pram while she and Kenny walked Tilly between them, along the Groves in the sunshine. Tilly was keen to gain her independence and it took all their attention to skirt round people to avoid bumping into them, as there was so many strolling by the river. From the surface of the water came the sound of trippers enjoying themselves, boating. Soon there would be the odd preacher on a soapbox and a band would strike up.

Alice was hoping she might bump into Sebastian, and was dressed in a new frock of primrose cheesecloth; Tilly wore a matching outfit with smocking on the bodice. Alice liked dressing her up and had enjoyed sewing every stitch.

'He didn't tell you anything more about Mrs Black, though,' said Hannah, wondering what Alice would think if she were to voice her thoughts about Sebastian's paternity.

'No, but I'm not going to bother my head about her and Dad anymore. He's out of my life and that suits me fine. Don't you agree, Kenny?' Alice glanced at her half-brother, who was gazing at Hannah. He nodded absently.

'So what about this picnic we're supposed to be having? Are we going to go on the other side and find a nice quiet spot away from the crowds? Or shall we stay this side and listen to the band when it strikes up?' said Hannah.

Alice said promptly, 'I'm for the band and watching people.' But she thought, if there was just me and Sebastian, then I'd definitely feel different about getting away from the crowds.

They found a grassy spot beneath a tree, not far from the bandstand, and ate cheese sandwiches and scones washed down with sarsaparilla bought from a herb shop; their bad experiences put aside, if not completely forgotten.

Chapter Eleven

Alice glanced up as her half-brother entered the room. 'I've had a letter from Seb,' she said excitedly.

Kenny noted her flushed face and shining eyes and was worried. He knew how to balance Mr Bushell's books but had no experience of how to handle a girl of sixteen who was in love. He felt ill-equipped when it came to making the proper responses.

'He says there's no news on the Mrs Black front and asks if I want to go to the musical comedy showing at the Music Hall off Northgate Street. The Waters are going to be over here for the races. Is that OK with you?'

He hesitated before removing his jacket and pouring water into a flower sprigged china bowl, then began to wash his hands, face and neck.

'You don't want me to go?' Her face fell and she dropped the letter on to the table and came over to him. 'Please, Kenny, say I can go?'

He sighed and sluiced away the dirty soapsuds from his neck and face, wondering why romance was in the air for Alice and Sebastian but not for him and Hannah. He knew he mustn't expect anything from her just because he had bought her the brooch for her birthday but, secretly, he'd hoped it might foster a deeper affection between them. Still, Alice had to figure first in his thoughts. She was his responsibility. He remembered his stepmother and the way she had cared for him. What would she want him to do for her daughter? He liked what he knew of Sebastian but, convinced he was a Catholic, he knew such matches didn't make for an easy life if it came to marriage. Should he warn Alice about that or was he making too much of what might just be a one off visit to the music hall? Perhaps he should invite himself along.

When Kenny wrote that he thought that he should go with them, Alice flushed and said, 'Don't you trust him? You're prejudiced because he's from Liverpool. You think the truth about him is that his ma's really a slummy and all that talk about America and her father dying in her arms was made up.'

Kenny looked incredulous and wrote *Don't be stupid! What have I to be snobby about? Besides I've met his ma and she's definitely foreign. She looked down on me! The thing is, he's probably Catholic and what would your mam think of that? Not that it makes any difference to me because I like bells and smells but I thought you were keeping faith with her faith. I just don't want you getting hurt.*

She took a pace away from him, her expression unhappy. 'Don't you think I haven't thought about religion? But it's only an outing to the Music Hall. I'm hardly going to rush off and marry him. But if you want to play gooseberry, come along. I'm sure Seb'll understand.'

Being a gooseberry was the last thing Kenny wanted, so he decided he had to trust Sebastian to treat his half-sister with respect, and that she, too, would behave sensibly. She was delighted when he wrote that down and kissed the top of his head before ladling stew with dumplings into a bowl for him and telling him to eat up.

The Orchid could not be bettered in Alice's opinion but then she had never seen a musical comedy before.

'I'm glad you enjoyed it,' said Sebastian, his mouth curling into a smile. They came out of the building, which Hannah and Kenny could have told them began life as a medieval chapel, and had become a theatre in the eighteenth century. Fifty years ago it had been converted into a concert hall and Charles Dickens had given readings there. He took Alice's hand and squeezed it as they left the alley and walked up Northgate Street, past the Cathedral. 'Don't you think some of the songs were daft, though?'

'I didn't care. It took me out of myself.' Her eyes sparkled and she was very aware of the feel of his hand in hers. 'If it was good enough for the King and Queen it's good enough for me.'

He grinned. 'You believed what the posters said?'

'Why shouldn't I?' she challenged him. 'Why shouldn't the King and Queen come to Chester and see the play?'

'Because they were in the audience on its opening night, that's why. It was at the new Gaiety Theatre in London last year when Gabrielle Ray, the postcard queen, played Liza Ann the mill girl. Miss Victoria's godmother, who lives in London, took her to see it and she told me all about it.'

'OK! So the posters are just pretend. But I could easily imagine myself that mill girl marrying into the aristocracy,' said Alice with a tiny smile as they headed for the Northgate. 'It must be lovely to have no money worries.' She glanced sidelong at Sebastian. 'How was your Easter? I forgot to ask. We were really busy at work with so many women wanting their Easter bonnets to show off in church and at the races this week.'

'I was busy too. Had hardly any time off.'

'They work you too hard,' she said indignantly.

'I enjoyed it. I like being down at the docks in Liverpool and watching the ships come in and unload.'

'So you didn't have to ferry Miss Victoria around much?'

'No.'

'Is she pretty?'

He smiled. 'Not as pretty as you, but she's a nice face; she's tall and has a mass of dark hair.'

Alice was pleased with the compliment. 'I bet she wears nice clothes.'

'She dresses well – but looks no nicer than you do in what you're wearing now.'

Alice was twice as pleased. He certainly knew how to make a girl feel good. The green coat was from the second-hand stall in the market but it had been cleaned and she had trimmed it with some black braiding. The black hat, which sat at a jaunty angle on her auburn hair, she had, of course, made herself.

His brown eyes were warm as they gazed down into hers. 'Will you come out with me next Monday evening? The Waters' are staying over until the Tuesday. They've bought tickets for Buffalo Bill's Wild West Show. You must have seen the posters?'

Had she seen the posters! They were everywhere! There wasn't anything Alice would enjoy more than to see the Sioux Indians dressed in their feather headdresses, war paint and beaded costumes, re-enacting *The Battle of The Little Big Horn*, along with men dressed in the uniform of the American Cavalry. But that wasn't all! There were cowboys riding bucking broncos and Buffalo Bill, himself, showing off his shooting skills from the back of a galloping horse. She had thought there was no chance of her being able to go because even the cheapest tickets were a shilling and that could buy food for two meals for her and Kenny.

'Mr Waters has bought the best seats for them, of course,' continued Sebastian. 'But he's also got tickets for the cheaper seats for the servants. Ma doesn't want to go and I wondered if you'd like to come in her stead?'

'Of course, I'd love to go with you.' She swung on his hand, wanting to dance with joy.

'Then it's settled,' he said, and hugged her.

She drew away from him slowly, her eyes downcast, remembering how Kenny had put his trust in her to be sensible. 'I do appreciate you wanting me to go with you.'

'And I appreciate you accepting,' said Sebastian, a slight quiver in his voice.

She glanced up at him and knew he understood.

When she told Kenny Sebastian had asked her to go to the Buffalo Bill Wild West Show with him, he could not conceal his envy. *You lucky duck! But don't get too fond of him. It mightn't work out and you'll get hurt. Think what your mam would have said.* He had this urge to keep on warning her to be sensible.

Alice's bottom lip quivered and, for a moment she did not speak. Then she said, 'I haven't forgotten! Don't spoil things for me.' She put her arms round him. 'I'm so happy, Kenny. I feel like I'm making up for lost time – for all those years we suffered with Dad being the way he was.'

He understood and felt ashamed of himself. He returned her hug and determinedly suppressed his jealousy of her good fortune in not only going to the Wild West Show but also being able to walk out with someone she was in love with.

Alice knew she was going to have a lovely time at the Show, which, for one day only, was at the Roodee, a huge area where the Chester races and annual fair took place, down by the river not far from the castle. The next day it would move on into Wales. The performances took place in a huge pavilion lit by a special electric light plant.

Alice clutched Sebastian's hand tightly as the historical spectacle unfurled before her eyes; performances from the Cowboy cyclist, the rope tricks and daring horseback riding of the Mexican soldiers, cowboys and Indians, had her closing her eyes several times, fearing for their lives. It was so thrilling and Sebastian's hand was so warm and strong in hers, that she did not want the evening to finish. But all good things came to an end and, although a kiss would have concluded the evening beautifully, Sebastian refrained from overstepping the mark.

The following weekend when Alice told Hannah all about it, her friend said the same as Kenny, that she was a lucky duck. She was in no way jealous of her going out with Sebastian. She wanted her friend to be happy, although she wondered what would happen to Kenny if the outings became more frequent and serious. She had settled back at work happily and all seemed well between her parents. Her mother appeared to be coping with the housework, shopping and taking care of their needs without too much difficulty. Granny Popo had visited but hadn't brought Tilly with her and seemed not to have mentioned Alice or Kenny, either. Surely her mother would have said something if she had? Bert was, once again, his polished self to Hannah and his mother. Hannah felt like smacking his smiling face. As for her dah, he was home on time most nights and the evenings he was a little late, her mother seemed unsuspicious. Hannah wanted to believe that the excuses he made were genuine.

–

Alice continued to see Sebastian in the following weeks whenever she could, which wasn't as often as she would have liked because he spent more time in Liverpool than Chester. But each time she saw him, she fell deeper in love with him. He was kind and thoughtful, always asking how Kenny was as well as complimenting her on her appearance. She asked him more about the Waters' and about his mother and whether he was content to carry on being in service for the rest of his life. It was certainly not the kind of life Alice envisaged for herself.

As soon as she had discovered that he drove Mr Waters' automobile and knew something about the internal combustion engine, it occurred to her that maybe there could be a future for him in one of the new motor engineering workshops in the city. She suggested it to him.

It was obvious from his expression that it was something he had never considered. 'I've been with the Waters' all my life. They're like family to me... and I don't know as much about engines as you think I do,' he responded with a characteristic openness.

'But you'd probably make more money if you learnt, Seb,' said Alice as they walked along the Dee, hand in hand.

'So you seem to think.'

He changed the subject, telling her that Mr Waters would be off to America again soon.

'Will Miss Victoria go with him?'

He smiled faintly. 'She'd like to go but she's coming over here to stay with her grandmother instead.'

Alice smiled happily, that meant he would be staying over here, too, and she squeezed his hand tightly. 'That's nice.'

For a moment he just gazed down at her, then he caught her to him and glanced left and right before kissing her. His lips were warm and slightly moist. It was their first kiss and all that she imagined a kiss should be. Her insides felt as if they were melting and that she could float off like a balloon. Then his mouth lifted from hers and she opened her eyes and looked up at him. Whatever he saw in their depths caused him to lower his mouth and kiss her again. She clung to him, returning his kiss with passion. When they finally drew apart, because they heard someone coming, Alice knew that their relationship had taken a big step forward. At that moment no words were necessary but, sooner or later, Alice was sure he would ask her to marry him.

However seeing more of Sebastian meant that Alice saw less and less of Hannah, Kenny and their toddler sister. All Alice's thoughts were concentrated on being in love. When she was not with Sebastian it was as if she was only half-alive and, when they were together, they wanted to be alone. They would cross the Dee and walk along the river, past men fishing on the bank and pleasure boats steaming up the river, cows in fields, talking about this and that, until they had left all sign of habitation behind. Then they would allow themselves to be seduced away from the path into meadows where the grass grew high and they could wander unseen, with the intoxicating smell of meadowsweet around them, in a world that seemed all their own. She would complain that she was a little tired and he'd remove his jacket and place it on the ground. They would sit a few inches apart, drinking in each other with thirsty looks; then his arm would go round her waist and she would lean against him, lifting her face to his. He would tease her sometimes, pressing a kiss on her brow, her cheek, her chin, then against the column of her throat, before covering her mouth with his in a deeply satisfying way. They would continue to kiss while his hands caressed her shoulders and moved down her arms. She would capture his hands and place them about her waist so that he could bring her close to him, breast to chest. Then he would lower her onto his jacket and their kisses would become more passionate, which meant she had to be strong to resist the tantalising urges inside her that would overrule her head and so allow their bodies to have their way. To lower the flame between them she would cough and go on coughing and reluctantly he would pull back, a faint smile in his dark eyes, get to his feet and hold down a hand to her. She would rise and, her clinging to his hand, they walked back to the path and proceeded home.

Kenny got angry with her. Not only did he feel neglected and envious of her relationship with Sebastian but he was annoyed that she was spending no time at all with Tilly. One Sunday afternoon, he visited Granny Popo's and found Hannah there. He was relieved to see that Dolly was out because she wasn't averse to flirting with him, and sometimes he found her boldness embarrassing.

Immediately Hannah rose from the rocking chair where she had been sitting with Tilly on her knee, a slate and chalk in her hand. 'What no Alice again?' she said, her expression piqued. 'She's not being fair to you or me.'

Kenny nodded, hoping she was not so annoyed that she would go back home straightaway. She was wearing a cotton frock of the deepest blue with tiny yellow flowers sprinkled all over it. There were two frills running down from her shoulders to her waist, which took in the sweet curves of her breasts. He wanted to seize hold of her and press her against him, to feel the lovely warmth of her body against his, to find comfort in her embrace and kiss her red lips, to unfasten her flaxen hair and bury his face for a moment in its silk. He moistened lips that felt suddenly dry, then became aware of Granny's eyes on him.

'Listen, ducks!' said the old woman abruptly. 'Why don't the pair of yer leave Tilly with me and go for a walk by yerselves?'

His heart lifted, and he looked for Hannah's reaction to that idea and was pleased to see that she was smiling. 'Why not? We could walk the wall, take in the view from there. It's ages since we've done that.'

Relieved, he freed an enormous breath and smiled his thanks at Granny. She rose from her chair, where she had been enjoying a pipe of tobacco and saw the pair of them out, patting Kenny on the shoulder at the door and saying, 'Make the most of it, lad, 'cos yer going to have to take that sister of yours in hand. Don't be too soft on her just because she's had a bad time in the past.'

He nodded, knowing that she was right.

Hannah was silent as they made for the canal, both had trodden this path before and knew, without needing to communicate, exactly where the other would wish to start the walk. He itched to reach and take her hand but was scared that she would reject him. He glanced sidelong at her, noting with a catch in his throat that sometimes her mouth still had that sad droop to it and wondering what worries she still might have now that her mother was back in charge again. Mr

Bushell had told him that the affair between Jock Kirk and their old neighbour was said to be over. He only hoped that was true and wished that it was in his power to lift every worry from Hannah's shoulders.

Suddenly she became aware of his stare and her eyes quizzed him. 'What is it, Kenny? Have I got a spot on my nose amongst all the freckles that have come out? I have tried getting rid of them with lemon juice but it hasn't worked,' she said ruefully.

He shook his head, smiling, and wished he could say that he would still love her if she had a thousand freckles. Suddenly a bloke holding a horse by a leading rein came lumbering towards them. Hannah seized Kenny's arm and pressed against him to allow the horse to pass. Afterwards, she slipped her slender hand through his arm and, in companionable silence, they continued their walk alongside the canal with him imagining them having many such walks as husband and wife. At the same time he knew it could never happen unless he took the initiative and made a move towards her.

They came to the Phoenix Tower, so-called because it had a phoenix, the emblem of the Painters' and Stationers' Company, carved into its wall. He was sorry that she had to release his arm for them to climb to the top of the tower but they couldn't have done it otherwise. Once on the top, they stood side by side, gazing out over the outlying parts of Chester in one direction and the countryside in another.

'Just think,' said Hannah, her voice dreamy, her elbows resting on the ancient stone, 'that just over two hundred and fifty years ago Charles the First stood on this very spot, watching his army being defeated by the Roundheads at Rowton Heath.' Kenny knew that already but he was content to listen to her talk and shifted his elbow so that it rested against one of hers. 'Imagine how the women must have felt, knowing that their men were being killed or routed by Cromwell's army. Imagine what it must have been like months later when Cromwell's forces came and Chester was under seige and cannon damaged the Northgate and part of the wall.' Her brow furrowed. 'If men took more notice of women there wouldn't be wars.' She changed the subject abruptly. 'What d'you think of the Suffrage Movement, Kenny?'

The suddenness of the question took him by surprise but he reached for his pad and pencil. *I'm all for women having the vote, for those who have no men to support them, to be paid a living wage, but working class men need their wages going up, too. We need Labour MPs in parliament and that wouldn't be popular in Chester, so here we need more Liberals.*

She nodded and her blue eyes were thoughtful. 'You're right! But I'd go one step further, we need women in parliament.' He raised his finely defined eyebrows. She laughed and poked him in the chest. 'Now there's a revolutionary thought!' She changed the subject again and her expression was moody. 'I had some bad news this week. Mrs Bannister died. She was lovely was Mrs Bannister. Her son, who does most of the baking, has taken over and he's not a bit like her. Already he's on at Agnes and me in the shop. We scarcely dare speak a word to each other without him telling us to get on with our work.'

Kenny put the news down as the reason for her looking miserable earlier. He mouthed. *Perhaps you should change your job.*

'Perhaps! But it has its perks.' She squeezed his arm. 'You're so peaceful to be with, Kenny. No shouting from you – no snide remarks with hidden meanings.' He presumed she was talking about Mr Bannister. She changed the subject yet once again. 'So what are you going to do about Alice and Seb? She could be riding for a fall. He seems a good bloke but she's an innocent. You really shouldn't be letting her go off on her own with him so much.'

What can I do? She's crazy about him.

Hannah's mouth set firm and she slipped her arm through his. 'You're her older brother and responsible for her. Perhaps you could suggest that you and I could go with them sometimes. We could be a foursome.' Her eyes teased him. 'That's if you can put up with more of my company?' His face lit up and if only he had the courage, he would have kissed her on the spot. Instead he comforted himself with the thought that this could be the first step to bringing them closer.

Once home, he waited for Alice to come in and then he wrote down his feelings about her behaviour, especially about her neglect of her sister and friend. He suggested that she and Sebastian make up a foursome with him and Hannah in future.

When she read his words, Alice flushed and her lips tightened. 'I thought you trusted me? I'm sorry if you feel you can't.' Kenny felt a spurt of anger and wrote down *Stop thinking of JUST yourself! Didn't you take in what I wrote? Have you no remorse for neglecting Tilly and Hannah?*

Alice's throat moved and she lowered her head and toyed with the sheet of paper. 'Of course I'm sorry that I haven't been able to see them. I'll go with you next Sunday and see them. Write to Hannah and tell her to meet us at Granny Popo's.'

Kenny nodded. Alice made to move away but he seized her arm and jerked her round and tapped the pencil on the paper where it suggested that she and Sebastian make up a foursome with he and Hannah. 'OK! I read it. I'll see what he says.' With that, Kenny had to be satisfied.

–

Hannah saw Bert pick up the letter as she came downstairs. 'Who's that for?' she asked.

He glanced at her name on the envelope, 'Wouldn't you like to know?' he said softly, rubbing it against his chin, his eyes smiling as they rested on her rosy morning face.

'Give it to me!' She tried to snatch it from him but he held it up in the air.

'Try harder.'

She was furious but resisted playing his game. Instead she called to her father. 'Dah! Bert's got a letter that's mine and won't give it to me.'

Jock came running: it was seldom that his eldest daughter asked anything of him these days. 'Give it to her, Bert.'

He tossed the letter to Hannah and shook his fair head. 'You didn't have to go crying to him,' he sneered. 'I would have given you it if you'd asked nicely.' He glanced at his father. 'Wouldn't you like to know, Dah, who's writing to your daughter? Has she a secret admirer, I ask myself?'

Hannah had recognised Kenny's handwriting and hoped that Bert had not, unlikely though that would be. She flicked the blonde hair that reached down to her waist over her shoulders. 'Don't be silly. It's from Agnes at the shop. She's been off with a septic finger and said she'd let me know if she could meet me, so we could go and listen to the band down by the river.'

'Pretty, is she?' said Bert, leaning against the lobby wall.

Hannah ignored him, thanked her father, and hurried upstairs. The early morning sun flooded into the bedroom and, thankful that her sisters had gone downstairs, she sat on the bed and slit open the envelope.

Dear Hanny,

Will you be at Granny Popo's on Sunday? I've spoken to Alice and she's remembered there are other people in the world than Sebastian. We are well. Hope you are, too? How's work going? Hope to see you on Sunday.

Yours, Kenny.

She smiled, and folding the letter neatly, placed it in the pocket of her skirt. Of course he would see her on Sunday. She was looking forward to it, already. She had missed girl talk with Alice, although she had enjoyed Kenny's company last Sunday much more than she'd have dreamed. He was just the male company she needed right now. She could trust him never to deceive or betray her.

As Hannah walked to work, she thought about Mr Bannister and his harassment – naturally she hadn't told Kenny everything. While Mrs Bannister had been alive there had been no trouble of that sort. He had worked in the bake-house to the rear of the premises and pretty well kept himself to himself, having little to do with the shop staff. But now he was often in the shop, telling them he was just making sure they weren't slacking. They had little time for that as they could have done with an extra girl to help them. Miss Whittaker, who had worked for the family since she left school in the 1870s and was now in her late forties, was spending more time in the back making cakes and pies instead of being in the shop. This meant more work for Hannah and Agnes. If he had any sense, she thought, he'd have taken on another baker and left the older woman to run the shop in his mother's place.

She knew it was going to be busy that morning because farmers and their wives, from the surrounding counties, were in town for the cattle market. It was sometimes difficult to understand what they were saying because of their different dialects.

She addressed a customer, 'Can I help you, madam?'

The woman answered her in broad Lancashire. She asked for a Sally Lunn and pointed at an oblong iced currant bun in the window.

Hannah smiled. 'We call them nutty twists.'

'Eee! Fancy that!' The woman's jowls wobbled. She asked the price, and counted out money along the glass counter, coin by coin.

Hannah hurried to pick the money up, because already another woman was flourishing a sixpence. 'I'll have a cottage loaf, please.'

Hannah dealt with her, then turned to a little girl, whose head barely reached the counter. 'Any custards?' she said in a loud voice. 'Only Mum's been sick in bed, but now she's fancying a custard.'

So it went on for most of the morning with little time in which to take a break. Hannah's feet ached. Mr Bannister came in several times with trays of fresh bread, currant buns, iced fairy cakes and jam tarts, ordering the girls to display them in the window or on the shelves to the rear of the counter. 'Come on, come on, move yourselves! I want them empty trays in the back in five minutes.' His sharp eyes went to the till and noticed the drawer was open. 'What's this!' He slammed it shut and then looked hard at Hannah. 'If there's any money missing it'll be docked out of your wages.'

Hannah opened her mouth to protest but he had gone through into the back again.

'He's awful,' said Agnes. A strand of her russet hair had come loose from her cap and her eyes gleamed with annoyance as she tucked it back into place. 'I wish it was him that had dropped dead instead of his mam.'

'Me too!' muttered Hannah, and placed a couple of fresh doilies on a large oval plate before putting iced fairy cakes onto it.

'It's not that I don't like the opposite sex.'

Of course not, thought Hannah, thinking of how Agnes flirted with the men who delivered the sacks of flour, bags of sugar, dried fruit, tins of jam, treacle and syrup, as well as yeast, butter, cream and lard.

'It's just that give a man a tiny bit of power and they become tyrants. My dad for instance. I'd much rather work for a woman.' Hannah agreed, but there was no time to pursue the discussion as a couple of customers entered the shop.

Mr Bannister bustled in just as she turned the CLOSED sign on the door for lunch. He was a short, fat man, and wore a large white apron over his trousers and shirt, on his balding head was a starched white cap. 'Well, has Miss Griffiths worked well, today, Miss Kirk?'

Hannah looked at him, startled. He'd never asked her that before. 'We both have. We could do with extra help on market days.'

'Maybe you're right, we'll see how things go.' He clapped his hands together. 'Well, off to your lunch then, but be back here at two sharp.'

Hannah had brought a packed lunch, so walked with Agnes down to the river. Agnes eyed up every man that passed and made comments about each that took her fancy. 'Now, I like his moustache, not too big. I bet it tickles when he kisses yer.' She giggled.

Reminded of Bert's moustache, Hannah found it hard to share the joke. She sat down on a bench and fed a pair of swans and their growing cygnets with bits of her sandwich, looking forward to the weekend when she would see Kenny and Alice.

Agnes giggled again and said, 'What about them? They'd do us. I'll have the tall, dark and handsome one, you can have the other. Neither look short of a bob or two.'

Hannah glanced at the two men in question, whom she estimated were in their thirties, and rolled her eyes and played up to her. 'Past it, don't you think? I like them a bit younger, so I can mould them into shape.'

'Oh, I like older men. They have more money,' said Agnes. 'But perhaps you're right,' she added with a chuckle. 'I'd want a bit of life in them, want them to dance to my tune.'

On the way back to the shop, Agnes popped into the indoor market, telling Hannah to walk on. 'It's my brother's birthday soon, so I want to get him a card. I'll need to send it early as he's abroad with the army.'

So it was Hannah got back to work a few minutes earlier than the others. Mr Bannister was just opening up. 'Starting work early to impress me, are you?' he said, partly blocking the doorway, so she had to brush past him. She did not like that at all. Nor did she like it that, when she took off her jacket, he commented on her figure, adding, 'Can tell you aren't scoffing the wares when I'm not here.' He sniggered.

Irritated and nervous, she reached for her apron and pulled it over her head. 'Here, let me help you!' He seized the ties and jerked her against him.

'Please, I can manage.' She pulled them out of his grasp, and would have moved to the other side of the counter, but he blocked her way.

'That wasn't friendly.' He pressed against her.

'Please, Mr Bannister, I've work to do.'

'How about a kiss?' he whispered against her cheek.

'No, I—'

The doorbell jangled. Cheeks aflame, Hannah turned, hoping it was her customer. To her dismay it was Bert and she could tell from his expression that he had seen her employer standing so close, his head almost touching hers. Swiftly she put a large space between herself and her employer and whispered to her brother, 'It's not what you think?'

'I should hope not.' Bert's expression was disparaging as he eyed Mr Bannister up and down. 'I'm Hannah's brother.'

The man looked at the size of Bert and nodded briefly, before exiting to the back of the shop in a hurry. Hannah was relieved to see him go, but the last thing she wanted was to be beholden to her brother. 'What can I do for you, Bert?'

He smiled. 'Just called in, Hanny, to remind you that Mother wanted two cottage loaves.'

She nodded and said coldly, 'I hadn't forgotten.'

'I didn't think you had.' He reached across the counter and pinched her cheek. 'If you have any more trouble with him, tell me.' She pulled away from him. The doorbell jangled again, and Agnes slid round the door, eyeing up Bert. 'Hello! Who's this?'

'He's my brother and he's on his way out,' said Hannah firmly.

Agnes beamed at him and held out a hand. 'I'm Agnes. How'd you do?'

'Charmed, I'm sure.' Bert took her hand and quizzed her with his eyes. A nice little armful, he thought. 'Fancy a stroll along the river this evening?'

'You're a fast worker,' said Agnes, smirking.

'Leave her alone, Bert. She's too young for you,' said Hannah, alarmed.

Both of them ignored her, and set a time and a place to meet.

'Why didn't you tell me you had a brother like that?' said Agnes, her eyes glowing, as soon as Bert had gone.

'Because he's smarmy and two-faced.'

Agnes looked shocked. 'What a thing to say about your own brother!'

Hannah flushed. 'I'm just warning you. Anyway, here's Miss Whittaker and a couple of customers.'

The younger girl hurried to remove her jacket and put on her apron before the older woman could report her to Mr Bannister for wasting time.

When Hannah arrived home that evening, her mother was standing on the doorstep, leaning on the yard brush, talking to their next door neighbour. 'Hello, Hanny!' The woman smiled. 'Had a hard day?'

'It was OK.' She returned the woman's smile before turning to her mother. 'I've brought your bread, Mother. What's for tea?'

'I've made a fish pie. Pop it in the oven for me. It'll be ready for when Bert comes in.' Susannah's face softened as she added to her neighbour, 'He's such a good lad. Bought me a bag of sherbert lemons at the weekend, he knows they're my favourite. He said I looked like I needed cheering up.'

The woman agreed that Bert was a lovely young man. 'Never walks past you in the street. Always stops and passes the time of day.'

Hannah wanted to shriek *You don't know him!* But instead she just walked into the house and put the fish pie into the oven. If she and her father were united in one thing, it was their dislike of fish pie. It was glorified mashed potato with bits of fish the fishmonger sold for people's cats. The only ingredient that made it palatable was the melted Cheshire cheese on top. She wondered whether her mother would be so keen to please Bert if she knew the truth. She also wondered what she'd make of his date with Agnes. She felt certain no girl was going to be good enough for her son in Susannah's eyes.

Hannah placed the bread in the crock. She washed her hands and face, and then tidied her hair, before setting the table. Her mother entered the house along with Bert and Jock some half an hour later.

'Something smells good,' said Bert, a rapt expression on his face as he breathed in deeply. 'Is it your fish pie, Mother?'

Susannah touched his sleeve, and smiled. 'I know it's not Friday, but the fishmonger's had bags of bits going cheap, so I thought, fish is good for us, and I know you like it.'

'Meow!' murmured Hannah. 'Meow, meow!'

Her mother frowned at her. 'There's no need for that, Hanny. It's perfectly good fish.'

Hannah caught her father's eye. He was smiling. She looked away, not wanting him to think that, just because they shared the same sense of humour, she had forgiven him for going with that woman thus allowing Bert to rape her.

The children were called in and the family sat down at the table. Almost immediately Grace said, 'Yeuk! Fish pie! I hate fish pie!'

'Fish is good for you,' said Bert, watching his mother ladle out a large helping onto his plate with satisfaction. 'It's good for the brain.'

'Then I'll have some,' said Grace promptly, smiling eagerly at him for his approval.

'Yeah, you need it,' said Joy, reaching for a slice of bread and butter from the plate in the middle of the table. 'Mary in her class told me she got most of her sums wrong today, Mother.'

'That's enough of that,' said Jock, glancing across at her, fork poised halfway to his mouth. 'Don't tell tales. Your sister's got plenty of brains.'

'If only she'd use them,' said Joy in an undertone to Hannah. 'You know what she did when we were playing out before? She went and tossed up against the wall because one of the other girls was doing it, but our Grace forgot to tuck her skirts in her drawers. If I hadn't have been there, then she'd have ended up in a right mess. Someone said that she was just like that Mrs Taylor. What do you think they meant?'

Hannah stiffened and shot an uneasy glance across the table at her father but he seemed unaware of what had been said, although her mother had looked at Joy, then glanced away. Hannah said quietly, 'I've no idea. Now shut up and let me eat in peace.' Joy fell silent. Hannah ate, although the fish and potato might as well have been wood shavings. Thinking of her dah sneaking out to Mrs Taylor had reminded her of Bert sneaking into their bedroom. She wondered if her sisters had any remembrance of his doing so. Had they been at all aware of what he had done to her beneath the bedcovers? She felt sick, thinking about it.

'Freddie, don't just use your fork! You've a knife here,' said Susannah, interrupting Hannah's thoughts. She watched her mother give the knife to him before addressing Bert. 'How was your day, son?'

'Worked hard as usual. There was a nasty accident with a wrench. One of the other apprentices hit another across the knuckles. It made a right mess of his hand. Isn't that true, Dah?'

Jock nodded. 'Broke a couple of bones.'

Bert said, 'Did Hanny tell you I called in at the shop, Mother?'

'No.' Susannah looked surprised. 'Why did you do that?'

Hanny glared at him.

Bert said gravely, 'She looked as if she was in trouble. I went to her rescue.'

Six pairs of eyes turned towards Hannah. 'What's this, Hanny?' said Jock.

'Yes, what's this, Hanny?' echoed her mother, her dark eyes concerned.

'I could have got myself out of it,' said Hannah, with a touch of defiance.

Bert shook his head in mock reproof. 'There's no need to be ashamed, Hanny. We all know there's men prepared to take advantage of a nice looking girl like you.' She thought, *You've got a bloody nerve, you swine!* Her hands curled into fists on her lap.

'You mean – a man tried it on with Hanny?' Jock's face was thunderous, and he half-rose in his seat.

'It was nothing, Dah!' said Hannah hastily. 'I don't want to lose my job. He was just messing about.'

Bert smiled across the table at his father. 'It's all right, Dah! I scared him off. No need for you to worry. He knows Hanny's got a big brother watching out for her now.' Susannah's anxious expression faded.

'That's good. Thank your brother, Hanny.' Hannah refused to do so. She felt furious with him, would have liked to strangle him. He always had to make himself look good. She could not bear sitting at the same table with him. Instead she stood and began to collect the dirty dishes.

'I don't expect thanks,' murmured Bert. 'I was just doing what I thought was right.' His words made Hannah want to puke; she wished she had the nerve to tell her parents what kind of person their eldest son was. She put on the kettle for the dishes, imagining their reaction. Would they believe her? She felt depressed, thinking how Bert always managed to make it look as if it was she who was in the wrong. As she waited for the kettle to boil, she imagined pouring the water on his private parts. That would make him bloody scream and never go near another girl again, she thought grimly.

As she washed the dishes, she thought of the coming meeting with Kenny and Alice and relaxed a little. That, at least, was a bright spot on the horizon.

For the rest of the week Hannah made sure she was not alone with her boss, but as it was, he seemed to be keeping his distance. Agnes prattled on about having met Bert and how she was seeing him again. Hannah stopped listening. She'd issued her warning and could do no more.

Bert came into the shop on Saturday. Agnes, besotted, slipped him an iced bun for free. He whispered to his sister on his way out, 'So how's the sugar daddy?'

'That's not funny!'

He laughed, and went out, whistling.

Hannah told Alice and Kenny about Bert's antics in the shop when she walked with them in the park that Sunday. Alice appeared to be only half-listening, possibly because Tilly, who had passed her first birthday and could walk unaided, was proving a handful. It seemed incredible to Hannah that the tiny baby, who Granny said looked like a skinned rat, had grown into this lively child in such a relatively short time.

Hannah said loudly, 'Alice, did you hear me? I'm wanting sympathy.'

'I heard. Bert's only teasing you. He knows you wouldn't have a sugar daddy. And at least he's warned off Mr Bannister.'

'I'm lucky not to have lost my job.'

'You're a good worker.' Alice changed the subject and began to talk about Sebastian, and how there had been a sighting of Mrs Black but none of her father.

'It's over a year since the accident. He must be dead,' said Hannah.

Kenny nodded his agreement.

Alice said, 'I want to believe that because it would make me feel safer. But at the same time...' She paused.

'What?' said Hannah, rolling her eyes. 'You still think he's alive and he's going to come after you for his money?'

Alice bit on her bottom lip. 'I know it's stupid. I even feel guilty occasionally. He was my dad.'

'You're daft! Besides you managed to forget that when you took his money. I'd try reminding yourself what a bully he was.'

Alice decided that she *was* being daft. These days there was someone far more important to fill her thoughts.

Sebastian continued to do just that. As summer turned to autumn and the tourists thinned out, he'd agreed that a foursome to the music hall or theatre was an acceptable way of spending the time when he was in Chester. So Kenny got his way, but it didn't turn him and Hanny into a courting couple.

On the anniversary of Alice's mother's birthday in November, just as Theodore Roosevelt was winning the United States presidential election, Alice and Kenny visited Florrie's grave to place flowers on it. Hannah accompanied them and listened as Alice said softly, 'Our lives have changed so much, Mam. I wish you could have shared the last sixteen months with us.'

Hannah's eyes were damp. Since the rape, she had developed a reluctant admiration for the dead woman. To have lived her Christian belief, and forgiven her husband again and again, took some doing. Hannah knew she could never forget what Bert had done to her, to forgive him really stuck in her throat. She couldn't do it. She was also worried about Agnes, who appeared less cheerful than usual. Hannah wondered if Bert had finished with her but didn't like to interfere. At least at home things seemed fine. Her mother was starting to make preparations for Christmas. She had already made the pudding, and was talking about this year's celebrations being the best ever for the family. Hannah could only hope that she wouldn't be proved wrong.

Chapter Twelve

Thursday before Christmas was frosty and the air was filled with talk of a white Christmas. In the Market Square vendors could be seen disposing of boughs of red berried holly and mistletoe. Butchers' windows displayed pigs shaved and grinning: outside poulterers' shops hung plump turkeys and geese, and braces of pheasant. Come Saturday, Christmas Eve, the weather changed, becoming damp and misty.

In the bakery Hannah and Agnes were rushed off their feet as housewives bought plum pudding, mince pies, Christmas cakes, bun-loaves and bread. For the past few weeks the smells coming from the bake-house had been overwhelmingly mouthwatering. She pondered on how Mr Bannister was making lots of money; although his takings could never match Bollands on Eastgate Row, who could boast of having supplied wedding cake to the King, as well as his mother Queen Victoria.

Hopefully there would be a bonus at the end of the day for her and Agnes. Mrs Bannister had always been generous at the end of the busiest time of their year, giving them half a crown each and a bun-loaf. Agnes had been in a strange mood, hardly speaking and her small face looked pinched and her mouth set in a straight line.

'Anything wrong?' Hannah asked her.

Agnes shrugged. 'What could be wrong? It's Christmas, isn't it? Good news and peace to all men and that!' Her lips quivered.

'There is something wrong! Is it your family?' Hannah could not help but be concerned, unable to remember if there were eight or ten of the Griffiths'. She knew the father worked on the railway, there was a brother Chris, who was in the army, and a sister, Emma, who had just started as a domestic, but the rest were only children and took some clothing and feeding.

Agnes's eyes filled with tears and she opened her mouth to speak. Then the shop bell tinkled and several customers entered. The moment was lost and did not come again during that long day.

At seven in the evening, a queue had already formed of those wanting to use the bakery ovens to roast their Christmas fowl or flesh. Susannah had slipped in earlier with their goose and given it to Hannah.

By eleven thirty, Hannah was almost asleep on her feet; Agnes appeared to have vanished but she had no time to worry about her now. At last Mr Bannister said she could go. Her mother's goose had been one of those that had gone into the ovens first and was cooked to a turn. 'You've worked well,' said her employer gruffly, handing her an envelope and a bun-loaf wrapped in greaseproof paper. Then, as her father knocked on the shop window, he turned and went into the back premises.

Hannah felt the envelope and pocketed it, smiling wearily up at Jock as she opened the door. 'The goose is on the counter, Dah.'

'You alright, lass?' His eyes searched the dim recesses of the shop.

She nodded. 'Fine! But I could sleep for a week.'

He hugged her against him, then released her and lifted the baking tin with the still steaming goose, being careful not to splash the fat. Father and daughter left the shop to the sound of church bells calling people to the midnight service.

Christmas Day arrived in the Kirk household well before dawn with Grace and Joy waking a bemused Freddie, as well as Hannah. Not that she really minded. Her sisters' cries of delight were something she could share in, even when they brought Freddie and his stocking into their bed and she had to put up with cold feet and sharp elbows and having a slice of tangerine almost stuffed up her nose. And, as she laughed along with her younger siblings, she remembered how she had worried that the joys of Christmas would be missing this year.

She had helped the younger ones make paper chains, cutting coloured paper into strips and glueing them together. The glue wasn't very good and the chains fluttered down onto Jock's head several times but he laughed saying it was just part of the fun.

The goose was succulent. The fat was strained and saved to rub on chests if any of them should get bronchial coughs in the winter months still to come. The Christmas pudding was delicious, although Bert chipped a tooth on one of the thrupenny bits. 'It's a daft custom,' he said, allowing himself to sound cross for once.

'I think it's smashing,' said Joy, winking at Hannah across the table. 'I know exactly what I'm going to buy with mine.'

Bert forced a smile. 'Of course, it's great for kids, but a chipped tooth'll spoil my good looks.'

'Nothing could spoil your good looks,' said Susannah, touching his hair as she got up to make a fresh pot of tea.

'You're biased, Mother,' he said, placing an arm about her waist, and hugging her to him.

Afterwards, he went out and the rest of the family played Snap for Dolly Mixtures and toffees, Hannah helping Freddie when it was his turn. The day flashed by all too quickly.

On Boxing Day, Jock had a treat in store for the family and took them to see the pantomime at the Royalty Theatre. They all loved it, even Bert joined in shouting *Look! He's behind you!* Here again was that side of him that people loved. Oh, how Hannah wished she could forget what he'd done to her but she couldn't. At least her parents appeared genuinely happy in each other's company. Hannah wished every day could be like Christmas and Boxing Day when people made the effort to be extra thoughtful to others.

On New Year's Eve, Hannah arrived home to find her mother had done an enormous baking and that, as usual, her father was going to go first-footing despite the fact that he was fair-haired and luck was supposed to lie with a tall, dark stranger.

The younger ones were in bed by eight o'clock but Hannah was told she could stay up to help her mother finish cleaning the house from top to bottom and see in 1905. Bert slipped out of the house about nine. Jock fell asleep in the chair and not until Susannah woke him, did he put on his boots and outdoor clothes. Then with his pockets weighed down with bread, coal, salt and several shiny, new pennies, he set out.

As church bells pealed, Susannah kissed her daughter's cheek and wished her a happy New Year.

'The same to you.' She returned her mother's kiss, thinking that it had to be better than the start of 1904 when life had seemed so dark.

Susannah poured two small measures of sherry into glasses and handed one to her daughter. 'Good health, Hanny!' She drank the sherry in one go and then began to pour small measures of whisky into several glasses.

Hannah sipped her very first sherry slowly to make it last. It tasted sweet and rich and reminded her of the fruit cake she had cut into slices earlier.

Within the hour, they had provided hospitality for several visitors. As Susannah chattered to the callers, Hannah handed round sandwiches and cake. Someone had brought a fiddle and several people began to jiggle about.

One o'clock struck. Bert and Jock were still out. Hannah felt the tension building up inside her. Where were they? She watched one of the neighbours, who they had never been that friendly with, whispering in her mother's ear. Her mother's expression changed and suddenly Hannah felt a chill run down her spine. What was she saying? Her mother glanced across at her, and suddenly the girl hoped it wasn't what had come into her mind. *Dear God, make it not be so. Please don't let Dad be at the widow's house. Make that woman not be raking up the past. Make it be that he's only talking with friends or neighbours, and help him to prove that he isn't with that woman. Make him come home now!*

She didn't care about Bert. He could be dead in a ditch for all she cared. He had turned twenty a month ago and thought himself a real man.

The kitchen door opened ten minutes later and Jock stood swaying in the doorway, a grin splitting his face. He staggered forward and clapped a hand on his wife's shoulder and sang, 'O my luv's like a red, red rose, That—'

'You're drunk!' Susannah's expression was cold and she would have pulled away from him but he grabbed her arm and squinted down at her.

'It's Hogmanay, woman! What do ye expect? Haven't I remained sober for most of the past few years? If a man can't get drunk tonight, when can he?'

Her expression was uncompromising. 'Where the hell have you been?'

He rested a hand on the back of a chair and stared at her. 'I'm not telling ye. A wife should trust her husband.'

Susannah turned to their guests; before she could say a word, they hurriedly made their excuses and vanished. By the time the door had slammed on the last of them, she was calling Jock an adulterer and shrieking that Nora Taylor was a whore, so loudly that it was a wonder the window did not shatter and the gas mantle break. Hannah began to shake. The moment she had dreaded had arrived.

'M-Mother! C-Calm down! You'll wake the girls and Fr-Freddie!' She seized her arm.

Susannah removed it with a look of disdain. 'You knew! You told me when I lay in that bed upstairs but I'd forgotten. Something twigged when Joy mentioned that woman's name months ago but I couldn't remember what I knew. Only tonight when that woman said how brave she thought I'd been over the Taylor woman did your words come back to me. Now get out and leave me and your father alone.'

'But it's o-over.' Hannah glanced at Jock. 'I-Isn't it, Dah?'

He stared at her as pale as a bucket of whitewash, speechless with shock. She could not bear to see them like this and ran from the room and escaped down the yard. She stood there, trembling, listening to her mother's raised voice, accusing him of being with *that woman*. He denied it. She screamed that she didn't believe him. He let out a roar that stunned Hannah, because he had always been a controlled man. He called her a *cold-hearted bitch, who had bullied him for years.* Hannah covered her ears. She wanted to rush in and tell them to stop it. That bloody widow! Was her dah telling the truth when he said that he hadn't been there? She wanted to believe him.

She looked up at Nora's back bedroom window. Anger surged inside her. She found a chunk of mortar, left over from when her father had pointed part of the brick wall, and climbed onto the lavatory roof. She eyed up the distance to the window and flung the mortar. There was the sound of breaking glass. Then she heard footsteps and scrambled off the roof.

Just as her feet touched the ground, the door to the entry opened. Her heart jerked as there came the sound of heavy breathing and she could smell bay rum hair lotion and peppermint drops mingling with beer fumes. The large dark shape of her brother stumbled into the yard. The beating of her heart accelerated and she tried to get out of his way by pressing herself against the lavatory door.

He heard her and turned slowly and peering into the darkness. 'If it isn't our Hanny!' The words were slurred.

'Go away!' She had rushed out without a coat and was shivering with cold and fright.

He seized hold of her feeling her roughly all over. 'Ahh! What a figure you have, Hanny. Much better than that stupid Agnes; she wasn't a patch on you. Too easy!' Hannah struggled, tried to scream but terror had frozen the muscles of her throat. 'You're shivering, love. Don't worry, I'll warm you up.' He was pulling up her skirts, loosening her drawers. One of his trouser buttons dug into her groin. 'Happy New Year, Hanny!' he whispered against her neck as he thrust himself into her.

She wanted to die.

–

Alice groaned and dragged the bedcovers over her head trying to shut out the banging. One of the tenants had either forgotten their key or Miss Austin, their landlady, had locked the door on any New Year revellers staying out past one o'clock. She heard movement on the other side of the blanket and then the sound of feet on the linoleum. Good old Kenny! She settled down to sleep again trying to recapture her dream and was just drifting off in Sebastian's arms when the flare of a match and the pop of the gaslight jerked her awake. 'Kenny, what are you doing?' she moaned.

'It's me! I'm sorry for waking you,' said a trembling voice.

'Hanny!' Alice stared at her friend clinging to the hanging blanket. 'What are you doing here? What's happened? You look terrible.'

'I feel terrible!' Hannah had been holding back the tears but now she sank onto the sofa and broke down.

Kenny stood watching, pain in his eyes. Alice scrambled from beneath the covers and put an arm around Hannah. 'Gosh! You're freezing! Where's your coat?' She pulled the bedclothes over them both. 'Kenny, wake up the fire.' He hurried to do so. Alice patted Hannah's back. 'There now. It's OK.' Her words only made Hannah cry all the more. 'Is it your mam?' asked Alice.

Hannah managed to sniff back her tears. 'Yes! No!' How could she tell them the truth about her mother finding out about Mrs Taylor, never mind the truth of what Bert had done to *her?*

'Then what are you doing here at–' Alice looked at the clock on the mantelpiece, 'half past two in the morning?' She paled. 'It's not Tilly is it?'

Hannah's ravaged face quivered. 'She's fine as far as I know.'

'Your sisters, Freddie, Bert?'

Hannah stiffened and swallowed with difficulty. 'They're OK.' With a trembling hand she wiped her damp face. 'I shouldn't have come. It was stupid of me because what can *you* do, after all.' Tears welled in her eyes once more.

Alice wiped them away with the edge of the sheet. 'But you did come, so you might as well tell me what's wrong,' she said firmly.

'I can't talk about it. It's too horrible.'

Kenny stood away from the fire and wiped coal dust from his hands. He glanced at Alice, who took a deep breath and said, 'OK. You don't have to talk about it. You're welcome to stay here as long as you like but when your mam wakes up and finds you missing, she's going to be worried.'

Hannah put a trembling hand to her mouth and bit on a finger. 'You're right. I'll go home. I'll go now,' she mumbled.

'I didn't mean you had to go right now,' said Alice hastily. 'Have a cup of tea.'

Hannah shook her head and, getting to her feet, rushed to the door.

'Come back!' cried Alice, scrambling out of bed. 'You'll get a chill. Bunk down here till it gets light.'

'Got to go to work.' Hannah had the door open before they could stop her. She raced down the stairs.

'Go after her,' cried Alice, staring at Kenny.

He did not need any urging and was pulling on his boots. Having dragged on some clothes to answer the door he was already half dressed. He lifted his overcoat from its hook and hurried out. He paused, only a moment, on the step outside to fasten his laces and then set off at a run. Hannah was travelling at a fair lick because she was well down the lane. He was unsure how she would react when he caught up with her. She was in such a state, she might get hysterical. The last thing he wanted to do was to put pressure on her to tell him what was wrong. He knew what putting pressure on people could do to them. He just wanted to make sure she got home safely because there were still drunks about.

For a moment he lost her and then realised she must have taken a short cut up Chichester Street into Upper Northgate Street, but he did not backtrack knowing he could catch up with her at the canal.

The cold air was catching in his throat when at last he spotted Hannah. She had stopped on the bank of the canal and was gazing into the water, swaying slightly. Suddenly he just knew what she was about to do. Oh, my God! He was filled with horror. What had happened that she should come to this? He wanted to shout, felt certain that if he really tried, the words might come, but he was all out of breath and when he made the attempt her name came out as if he was being strangled. It was no good, he'd forgotten how to speak. He ran like crazy.

Hannah shivered uncontrollably wanting to be rid of the misery and shame that was weighing her down. She gazed into the dark silky waters steeling her will to throw herself in. Then she almost choked as she was grabbed from behind. She struggled, hitting out and kicking backwards.

Kenny gasped with pain and then spun her round. Her face expressed shock. 'You!'

He was so angry with her that he shook her hard and she almost fell into the water. She grabbed hold of his coat and begged him to stop. 'I'm sorry! I'm sorry! I didn't want to do it. Please don't be angry with me!'

All the fury seeped out of him. He could feel how cold she was through the fabric of her frock. He released her and removing his coat he thrust her arms in the sleeves and buttoned her into it. He took her icy hands and chaffed them until she begged for mercy. Then he kept tight hold of one of them and forced her in the direction of her parents' home.

Hannah did not say a word, ashamed for even thinking of doing away with herself. How would her mother have felt, what with already having to cope with learning about her dah carrying on with Mrs Taylor? It could have pushed her over the edge. And what about the girls and Freddie and her dah, as well, they'd have been really upset.

They came to the house. She watched as Kenny reached a hand through the letterbox and drew out the key. He opened the front door and pushed her inside. All was quiet. He was about to walk away when she put a hand on his shoulder. 'Your coat,' she whispered, unbuttoning it and handing it to him.

'Thanks. You saved me life.' She brushed his cheek with her lips.

He wanted to catch her to him and kiss her passionately, to tell her that she could depend on him, that he would look after her if she would give him that right, but how could he? He could only think that perhaps there was some fella she was involved with that he knew nothing about; someone who had hurt her badly. He shrugged on his coat and then from his pocket drew out his pad and pencil. Hesitating before writing swiftly, he tore out the page and gave it to her. He did not stay to see her read it. His courage had failed him but he had done the best he could.

NEVER SAY DIE! WE ALL HAVE OUR SECRETS AND YOU CAN TRUST ME WITH YOURS IF

YOU WANT TO TELL ME ABOUT IT, ALL MY LOVE KENNY.

She read the words several times, tears rolling down her cheeks, before folding the paper into smaller and smaller squares. She curled her fingers on it, watching Kenny until he was out of sight, knowing that she could never tell him what Bert had done. She dared not risk destroying his respect and love; she wanted him to believe that she was the same person he had always known.

Wearily she climbed the stairs and crept into the bedroom. She placed the note beneath her pillow and then undressed and curled up next to her sisters. She ached all over. Footsore and exhausted, she no longer felt quite so desperate, comforting herself with the thought that at least Kenny cared enough to come after her and save her. The memory of him giving her his coat warmed her and she tried not to think of what Bert had done to her – but could not help doing so. If there really was a hell, she hoped her brother would burn for all eternity. She held that picture in her mind for several seconds. Then Kenny filled her thoughts once more and she could almost feel him placing her arms in his coat sleeves and buttoning it up. She knew that at least if she needed help at any time, he was there for her.

She drifted into an uneasy sleep to be wakened a couple of hours later by the voices of her sisters and her mother telling her she had overslept and would be late for work if she didn't shift herself. Immediately Hannah remembered all that had happened prior to that wild run to Alice's and Kenny's apartment, and the misery returned. She felt under the pillow for Kenny's note, read it again, and when she went to the lavatory, she flushed it away, knowing that if anyone was to find it there would be too many questions to answer.

It was a relief to realise that Bert and Jock had already left for work. Hannah went out without any breakfast and, when she entered the shop, it was to find Miss Whittaker and Mr Bannister with their heads together. 'You're late,' said her boss, frowning.

'I'm sorry. But my parents had a bit of a party last night, it being Hogmanay.' Hannah hastened to fasten her apron and put on her cap.

'Understood. But don't let it happen again. Half an hour's money will be docked from your wages,' said Mr Bannister, fiddling with the till. 'Carry on both of you – and don't forget, Miss Whittaker, to put that notice in the window.'

Damn! Hannah knew there was no point in arguing. 'Where's Agnes?' she asked as soon as their employer had disappeared into the back.

Miss Whittaker sniffed. 'You might as well know now that Agnes has been sacked.'

'What!' Hannah was stunned. It was one bad thing on top of another. She wondered if Agnes had been caught giving cakes away.

Miss Whittaker opened the till and placed some change in it. 'I caught her with her hand in the till on New Year's Eve. I didn't make a fuss about it at the time because we were busy, but I kept my eye on her.'

Oh, the fool! Hannah felt so sorry for Agnes. But why steal? They'd been given their bonus. Had she done it to help her parents out? They had probably got into debt because of Christmas, and the bonus might not have been enough to get them out of trouble. Hannah gazed at the older woman with worried eyes. 'Will she go to prison?'

'No. As she didn't get away with the money and broke down in tears, Mr Bannister decided to be lenient with her. Of course, he couldn't give her a reference. We're going to have to train a new girl. Here's a customer. Now get on with your work.'

Poor, poor Agnes, she truly was having a bad time of it, too. Not only would she have trouble getting another job, but Bert obviously wanted to be rid of her from the way he spoke about her. A spurt of anger welled up inside Hannah. The swine! Agnes was best shut of him. She decided to visit Agnes on her way home from work.

But when Hannah arrived at the house, it was to be told in a gruff voice by one of her younger brothers that she wasn't home. That dad had thrown her out. 'He said that she's brought disgrace on the family.'

'Where's she gone?'

'Dunno.' He shuffled his feet as if uncomfortable talking about it.

Hannah could have wept for her workmate, having no choice but to tell her parents that she'd been sacked for stealing. She went home, feeling depressed. She was glad that Bert had eaten his tea, and gone out again. Her father was absent from the tea table, too, but her mother was presiding over the teapot, her face strained and white.

'You might as well know now, Hanny, I'm planning on staying with cousin Joan in Moreton this coming Saturday night,' she said without any preamble. 'I'm taking the young ones and I want you to come, too.'

Hannah's heart sank. 'You're leaving Dah?'

Susannah gave a mirthless laugh. 'And what would I do for money? Besides there's no way I'd allow him to feel free to go to that floosie whenever he liked. Not on your nellie! I'm just teaching him a lesson. I've asked Bert to come, but he said he didn't want to miss church and that I'm not to worry. He'll manage to cook himself something. He's a good son.'

The two-faced swine! Hannah thought. She placed her hand over her mother's where it rested on the table. 'I'm sorry, Mother, for everything. When will we be going?'

'Not until after you've finished work on Saturday. Your dah's got to realise that I'm worth ten of that woman.' Susannah's dark eyes glinted.

'But, Mother, he isn't seeing Mrs Taylor anymore.'

Susannah ground her teeth. 'Don't mention that woman's name in this house. We'll be away next weekend, too, and the next. I'll put it about that Joan's getting on and isn't feeling too well. I'll not have the neighbours making a meal of our business. She'll probably welcome some help with the cockling, so'll be happy to have us.'

Cockling at Moreton – at this time of year! Hannah shivered at the thought. The wind really whipped in from the Irish Sea across the Wirral Penisular at that point. Her mother wasn't thinking straight but Hannah guessed there would be no changing her mind. Still, hopefully it would only be for a few weeks if her dah grovelled. The only trouble with her mother's plan was it just might push him back into the arms of Nora Taylor.

She sighed, knowing that she would miss seeing Kenny and Alice weekends but her mother obviously wanted her to go with her, and her needs must come first. She would have to write to Kenny and explain the situation.

–

Alice glanced up as Kenny entered the room. 'There's a letter for you. It's on the table. I'm sure it's from Hannah.' She added with a smile, 'I've one from Seb. I told you he spent Christmas with the family on the farm?'

He nodded, picking up the envelope. His grimy face was tense as he slit it open with a finger.

Dear Kenny,

It was stupid what I thought of doing. Cross my heart I won't act so crazy again. Don't worry if you don't see me for a while.

His face fell as he read on.

These dark evenings, I don't feel like making the effort to go anywhere and Mother decided me and the kids are to go with her to visit her cousin this Saturday evening and we'll be staying through to Sunday evening. It looks like we'll be doing the same for the next few weekends to come. I'll be in touch.

Thanks again, Hannah.

Kenny folded the letter and placed it in his pocket. Did she really mean she would be in touch, or was she just being polite? Maybe deep inside she was embarrassed by what she had done and couldn't face him, nor had she liked him suggesting she share her secret with him.

'Is Hannah OK?'

He nodded.

'Is it that private?' asked Alice, surprised by his not offering her a glimpse of the note.

Irritated, he mouthed, *Are you going to tell me what's in Seb's letter?* Alice blushed. 'That's different. Hannah's not going to be writing you love letters, is she?'

No, more's the pity! He sighed inwardly, and poured water into a bowl, and began the job of washing away that day's coal dust.

'I'm sorry,' said Alice softly, kissing the back of his neck. 'That was cruel when I know how much you like her.' She sat down. 'I'll read a bit of Seb's letter to you.' She cleared her throat, and began to read a little self-consciously, *I took Miss Victoria to Delemere Forest in the motor, and she picked a Christmas tree. Then when we got it back to the farm, which her uncle manages for her father, we decorated it with baubles and little parcels, sticks of barley sugar and bags of chocolate money.* Alice paused. 'I felt really jealous when I read that bit.'

Kenny could understand that. He wished it could have been him and Hannah, choosing a Christmas tree and taking it to their own little home to decorate it.

'They had candles, as well,' murmured Alice, tapping the letter against her teeth. 'Corkscrew shaped ones. Miss Victoria was all starry-eyed, but her uncle said they were a fire hazard and wanted them removed. He didn't get his way, though, because Miss Victoria has something wrong with her heart, as we know.' She smiled faintly at Kenny. 'Seb writes the children of the farm-labourers were starry-eyed, too. They all got presents and there was a party.' She added wistfully, 'I've never had a party.'

Kenny reached for his pencil. *Your day will come.*

She smiled and said cheerfully, 'Of course it will. I'm not really jealous of Miss Victoria. She deserves our sympathy. Even so…' She fell silent.

Kenny wondered what Alice had been going to say. Perhaps she was worrying about whether the future she had in mind with Sebastian would really happen? He sluiced the dirty soapsuds from off his neck and face, wondering what he should write in his reply to Hannah, wishing he could read their future, sad that the foursome with Alice and Seb had not lasted longer. Still, if he was not going to see her for several weeks he could write and keep her informed about what they were doing.

-

Hannah was in shock. She had gone into work on the Monday, after a windy, freezing Sunday at Moreton, to be greeted by the news that Agnes' body had been fished out of the canal.

'I can scarcely believe it,' said Miss Whittaker, as she placed the still hot bread on greaseproof paper on the shelves. 'To kill herself just because she got the sack was a stupid thing to do.'

Of course it was. But was it as simple as that? Hannah's head was in a whirl. She was remembering not only what Bert had said about Agnes being easy, but what the girl's little brother had said about her being thrown out of the house for bringing disgrace on the family. Could she have been pregnant? Could that have been why she had killed herself? Hannah could not forget how terrible she had felt on New Year's Eve.

Did Agnes' family know of their daughter's association with Bert? Surely they couldn't because if Agnes had been in that kind of trouble with her parents knowing about it, then surely her father would have been round at their house demanding Bert marry their daughter. Suddenly fear and trepidation shot through Hannah like a warm knife through butter. What if Bert had got her pregnant? Dear God, what would *she* do?

Chapter Thirteen

Hannah bent over the lavatory bowl and retched but there was nothing more to bring up so she pulled the chain and went outside, trembling and filled with despair because the *curse* had not come and this was the sixth time she had been sick in the last week. She stood leaning against the lavatory door. Dear God, what was she to do? She didn't know how she was going to tell her mother. Maybe if she had gone with her and the younger ones yesterday evening to Moreton then she might have found a way. Instead she had cried off because she had felt so dreadful, saying she was seeing a friend. Is this how poor Agnes had felt? How she wished she had come to her! But sadly it was too late for Agnes and she had to think of herself.

She had been too worried to give thought to the possibility that her dah really had taken up with Mrs Taylor again. But what she had feared might happen must have done, because he had gone out after supper and not come back. So Hannah had ended up alone in the house. Fortunately Bert had been out when she had gone to bed, so she'd taken the poker with her and placed a chair beneath the doorknob.

He had come in just before midnight and, rat-tatted on her bedroom door, saying, 'Little pig little pig, let me in! Or I'll huff and I'll puff and I'll blow your door in!'

He was a big bad wolf, all right, and there was no way she was going to play his game. 'Go away, Bert! I – I've got the poker here,' she'd said.

'There's no need to be like that, Hanny. I thought we were friends, as well as brother and sister.' His voice held an injured note.

'Friends?' She choked on the words. 'You don't know the meaning of the word. Just go away! When I think what happened to poor Agnes! If Mother knew–'

'Now, Hanny, don't talk like that. You'll only end up in trouble if you say anything to her. She won't believe you. Agnes could have said no, you know? But she so wanted to hang on to me that she flung herself at me. I'm only human. How could I resist?' Trust him to lay all the blame on Agnes, thought Hannah, feeling so upset she wanted to weep. 'You could have married her.'

Bert laughed. 'Come off it, Hanny, I deserve better than her.' He hammered on the door. 'Let me in. You know you really want it. With no one else in the house we could do it a couple of times.'

She was astonished. How could he believe that was what she wanted? He had to be sick in the head. 'Go away! If you carry on like that I'll put my head out of the window and scream. I'll scream so loud Dah might hear, if he's at Mrs Taylor's, and then you'll be sorry!'

'You haven't before.'

'That's because I didn't want to frighten the girls – and besides you were in the room and wouldn't have let me get to the window – and I was so ashamed of what you did to me. You made me feel dirty!'

There was a long silence. Then she heard him sigh. 'You've really hurt me saying that, Hanny. It's not that I'm scared of Dah, but I wouldn't like Mother upset. I'll call it a day, but don't think I'll forget this.'

She heard him moving away upstairs and then the slam of his bedroom door. Even so Hannah had been unable to sleep after that. She was hurt and angry, not only with Bert, but her dah, too. He should have been there to protect her. Of course none of the dreadful happenings of the past eighteen months or so would have happened if it were not for Mal Moran but her father had to take his share of the blame. In the end she had given up trying to sleep and had got up, just as dawn was streaking the sky, lit the fire and made herself a cup of tea.

Hannah wiped a trembling hand across her sweaty face. She did not want to go back into the house until her mother returned with the kids. Bert was most likely still in bed and, so far, there was no sign of her father coming home. She would go to Alice and Kenny. They were long due a visit from her anyway and she owed Kenny a couple of letters. She had really appreciated his. Fortunately, she had put on her coat to come down the yard. All she had to do was go out of the back door and walk along the canal and up to Garden Lane and they would take her in.

When Hannah arrived at the lodging house, the man who answered the door said Alice and Kenny had gone out a while ago. Deeply disappointed and near to tears, she descended the steps wondering what to do. She thought a moment. Could they be in church still? Or could they possibly have gone straight from there to see Sebastian? Kenny had mentioned something about him being back in Chester soon. Hannah decided to head across the river to Queen's Park.

As she walked, she knew that she still could not tell them about her troubles. She just needed their company. She considered how they had matured since having to fend for themselves. They had shown they could cope on their own without their parents. How they would react if their father came back into their lives was something she had not thought about. She despaired of her own dah. How could he carry on the way he did? One thing was for sure and that was that he was in no position to preach morality to her. But what would she say if her parents asked her who the father of the baby was? Dear God! How could she tell them it was Bert? It would destroy her mother – if she could accept that her white-as-the-driven-snow son could do such a thing. Bert would probably persuade her that it was Hannah's fault, that she had led him astray. Or he would deny it, calling her a liar and cite someone else as responsible.

By the time Hannah reached the crescent where Mrs Waters lived, she was feeling tightly wound up as a clock spring. To her disappointment, there was no sign of the automobile that Sebastian drove and he certainly wasn't doing any gardening. Perhaps he hadn't come this weekend. She didn't have the nerve to knock on the door of Mrs Waters' house and ask. It seemed she had wasted time and energy coming here and could have screamed. Slowly she walked along the crescent and then paused when she came to the house that Alice had pointed out as belonging to Mrs Black.

Curiously, Hannah gazed at the house and suddenly the door opened and a woman stood in the doorway. Was she Mrs Black? It puzzled Hannah why a woman who owned property in Liverpool and lived in such a house would have anything to do with Mal Moran. Surely she could have chosen someone better to have an affair with? Although love was an unpredictable emotion and no respecter of looks or commonsense. The woman's grey hair hung loose about her face and she was wearing a dressing gown of pink satin. She seemed to notice Hannah and beckoned her.

Surprised but as curious as the proverbial cat, Hannah pushed open the gate and hurried up the path. The woman watched her, no emotion showing on her face. Her skin was sallow and she had bags under her eyes. 'What is it you want, dear?' she asked.

'Mrs Black?'

'Yes. Who are you?' She watched Hannah's face closely.

'Hannah Kirk! You won't have heard of me but my family live in the next street to where the Morans did. I believe you knew Mr Moran – Mr Mal Moran?'

For a moment Hannah thought the woman had not taken in what she said and was about to repeat it when her arm was seized. 'You have news of him?'

'Well...' Hannah hesitated. It was obvious Mrs Black hadn't heard from Mal Moran, so what would be the point of speaking to her?

Mrs Black smiled. 'Don't be shy, dear. Come on in and have a cup of tea.'

Hannah was desperate for a cup of tea. She was also hungry. Maybe she would get a biscuit with her tea. She stepped over the threshold.

'You know where Malcolm is?' asked Mrs Black, her mud-coloured eyes alight as she led Hannah towards the stairs.

'No, frankly,' said Hannah, following close on her heels. 'I was wondering if you might. I was told he visited you eighteen months ago. He killed his wife, you know, and nearly did for my mother.'

The woman gazed blindly at the newel post. 'So that's why he was here,' she whispered. 'I knew there was something dark in his mind.

It's been closed to me since last I saw him.' There was a short silence then her eyes focused on Hannah's face once more. 'Why didn't the police come? What took you so long? Are you a friend of his daughter? Where is she?'

Hannah chose to ignore the questions. 'We think he might be dead.'

'Dead! Malcolm dead! Why should you think that? No. I'd have known, surely?' Mrs Black's face was pale. 'Please, explain yourself. I'll not be ungrateful.' She squeezed Hannah's hand. 'A cup of tea, we'll have a cup of tea. I've cake.' She beamed at the girl. 'Do you like Madeira?'

'I like any cake but you don't have to hold my hand. I'm not going to run away.' Hannah returned her smile, thinking the woman was definitely a bit weird. That was probably why Alice had taken against her.

'Unlike his daughter,' said Mrs Black, as if she had read Hannah's mind, laughing lightly. 'Come upstairs, and make yourself comfortable, my dear. It's a long time since I've entertained what I'd call a proper visitor.' She led the way, calling over her shoulder. 'You can't know how I've worried about Malcolm. He was such a troubled man, and I was doing my best to make him better.'

Mal, troubled? Hannah found it easier to believe that it was his wife and children who were troubled... and what was it she had been doing to help him? She followed Mrs Black into a large room with windows that reached from the floor to the ceiling. Crimson velvet curtains were drawn back and fastened with silken cords. On a windowsill stood a bowl of early flowering hyacinths. The view was magnificent, the late morning sun sparkling on the Dee.

'You know that song?' said Mrs Black, and not waiting for an answer began to sing, '*There was a jolly Miller once lived on the river Dee, He worked and sang from morn till night...*'

Hannah grinned. She knew few people who would burst into song at the drop of a hat. 'You've got a nice voice.'

Mrs Black's eyes sparkled. 'Thank you, dear. I often think about those words when I sit here.' She waved Hannah to an easy chair. 'I've been so concerned about Malcolm. I hate to lose anyone before I've finished sorting out their problems, and he was in such a mess.'

What did she mean lose? And as for problems, Hannah wished she could sort out hers. Sitting down she noticed the china teapot, a cup and saucer and a plate of cake on the occasional table. 'I'll fetch another cup and then you can tell me everything,' said Mrs Black, gazing into Hannah's eyes. 'You look peaky. Are you all right?' She sounded like she really cared.

Hannah was tempted to tell her the truth, then had second thoughts. 'I'm fine.'

'Hmmm!' She didn't look convinced. 'You need someone to talk to, don't you, dear? Such a pretty young woman you are. Have plenty of beaux, do you? I'm sure you do.' Mrs Black stared straight into Hannah's eyes.

If she only knew the truth, thought the girl, her eyelids drooping. She began to feel relaxed, almost languid. The scent of the hyacinths was overpowering. The woman's soft voice seemed to be coming from a distance. 'So tell me everything about Malcolm and his daughter, Alice, isn't it? Tell me about yourself too?'

Between bites of cake and sips of tea Hannah told her as much as she wanted to know, of Florrie's death and how Mal had pushed her mother downstairs and how terrible everything had been at home. She even told her about Alice and the train accident in Scotland.

When she finished Mrs Black murmured, 'My, my, what a naughty girl Alice was stealing from her father! Resourceful, though. He was fond of her, would you believe? I do so appreciate you coming and telling me all this. There's almost nothing worse than not knowing. I would like to help you. Your life's been so hard lately. What is the trouble that's worrying you so deeply, dear, that you still feel unable to mention it to me? You really do look peaky. I've helped out many a girl in trouble. You can tell me, you know? I can be trusted with secrets.'

The room felt hot, or maybe she was feeling so warm, thought Hannah, because she felt embarrassed, and yet she wanted so much to get her trouble off her chest. She really did feel she could trust this woman. 'I'm having a baby.' The words came out slowly. 'It's my brother's and I don't want it. He forced himself on me.'

'Oh my dear! That is bad.' Mrs Black sounded distressed and leaned towards her. 'Best do something about it now before you're too far gone. I have some powder that might help you. I'll get it and you can take it in your tea. I've used it myself, so I know it works, but the less said about that the better.'

Mrs Black left the room and re-appeared a few minutes later. She unfolded a greaseproof paper and poured a small amount of white powder into Hannah's cup and then re-filled it with tea. 'Now drink that up, dear. I'll give you the rest in case one dose doesn't do the trick.' She placed the small greaseproof paper sachet inside Hannah's pocket. Obediently the girl drank the tea.

'I really do appreciate you coming and telling me all that you have,' said Mrs Black. 'When you get outside you'll go straight home, won't you? Now eat your cake and then I'll let you out.'

Hannah ate her cake and then followed Mrs Black downstairs. The woman went outside with her onto the pavement. 'I hope everything works out for you, dear. And I'd stay away from that brother if I were you.' She smoothed back Hannah's hair from her face. 'Does your little brother have toys? Does he have one like this?' She showed Hannah a metal clicker. 'When you hear it click you'll forget having been in my house and speaking to me.' She clicked it twice, then hurried back up the garden path to her front door.

Hannah blinked. Now where had she been going? She looked about her and recognised the crescent. What was she doing here? She was supposed to be going home. She began to walk, past an automobile. In the front passenger seat sat a young woman wearing a hat of which Hannah was immediately terribly jealous. It was made of chip straw in green and blue, trimmed with soft bronzy plumes. She wore a russet velvet jacket and pinned to her lapel was a brooch of topaz and silver.

Hannah smiled as the girl caught her eye and then she looked away quickly, thinking she looked like she had money and most likely would consider Hannah beneath her. She hurried on but had not gone far when her name was called. She hesitated. Was that Sebastian's voice? Should she turn round? No, she had to get home, so carried on walking.

There's something wrong with my eyes thought Hannah as she stumbled along Egerton Street, past the engineering works where Jock and Bert worked. Her head was pounding and everything looked blurred and she was so tired. She prayed that her mother would change her routine and arrive home with the kids earlier than usual so she could rest and be safe. But when she arrived at the house only the strong smell of burning and Bert were there to greet her.

He frowned at her. 'Where the hell have you been? I thought the least you could do was make some dinner for us. I know when to take no for an answer.' Ha! That'll be the day! Hannah sank into an armchair and put her head in her hands. 'What are you sitting like that for?' Bert knocked down one of her arms and dragged her to her feet.

She could not bear him to touch her. 'Let me go!' she screamed. 'I'm having a baby and now I feel like I'm dying and it's your fault!'

He shook her by the shoulders. 'Now you know that's not true, Hanny. I haven't done it to you since Mother got better.'

'New Year!' she gasped.

He frowned. 'No. You're blaming me for someone else. Your boss at work perhaps.'

'That's a lie!' She glared at him. 'You did it to me outside the lavatory. You'd been drinking. And last night you would have done it again if I hadn't put the chair under the knob. You're nothing but a filthy bastard!'

He hit her. 'It's not nice to hear such language from you.' She gasped and put a hand to her face but before she could say anything, their father entered the room. 'I could hear the bloody pair of yer down the yard! Have ye no thought for the neighbours?'

Hannah reached for a chair and clung to it. 'He hit me, Dah!' She stared at him, seeing two of him. Both faces wore a tense expression and she was terrified. Perhaps she was about to go blind!

Bert blurted out, 'That's because she asked for it, Dah. Was accusing me of filthy behaviour to cover up her own shameful act. Remember me telling you about that boss of hers?'

Jock clouted him across the face. 'I heard it all. Shut your mouth, and let me think.' Bert took a step back, his hand gripping his jaw.

'You shouldn't have done that, Dah. You've no right to talk? Carrying on with her at the back again!'

Jock's expression was anguished, and his hands curled into fists. 'But we're talking here about yer doing it to your own sister and that's terribly wrong.'

Bert's eyes narrowed and he lowered his hand. 'You're making a mistake, Dah.'

'Am I?' Jock turned to his daughter. 'Well, Hanny?'

She reached out a hand to him. 'Help me, Dah!'

He took her hand and squeezed it. 'How? You want me to tell Mother? She's not taking my word for anything these days.' Hannah clung to that strong, work roughened hand. She guessed that was true. She felt so ill that it was difficult to think straight or stand upright. Mother might not believe him. She would believe her so-called perfect son first. Her blue-eyed boy! Hannah would be utterly out in the cold, along with her father. She made a decision. 'Give me some money, Dah. I'll go to Granny Popo. She'll help me to get rid of it.'

Jock stared at her, white about the mouth. 'I don't know about that, Hanny. Your mother's told me tales that would make your toes curl. What if you were to...'

Hannah felt cold with fear but she inserted steel in her backbone and stood ramrod straight. 'I'll take a chance. Mother's been hurt enough. Give me the money and expect me when you see me. Don't tell her anything about this, and get rid of that widow. She's done as much harm to this family as Mal Moran.'

'I wouldn't have gone back to her if it hadn't been for your mother being so cold during the week and going to Joan's and staying there every Saturday night and Sunday. I work hard, lass, and what thanks do I get?'

Oh, he was weak, thought Hannah, as she watched him dig into his pocket, take out a handful of change and give her the lot. She was scornful of his excuses but said nothing. She took the money and, ignoring Bert, she hurried out of the room. She could only pray that her brother would get his comeuppance some day. Despite feeling so ill she might drop dead any minute, she knew that she would need a few things from upstairs. If Granny succeeded in aborting the baby then she had to have rags for when she started bleeding. Maybe she had better take another dress and unmentionables. She placed them in a pillowcase. Then, with her head still feeling as if it was about to explode, she went downstairs. Her father held her tightly for a moment and surprised her by saying he loved her. Not enough, she thought as tears filled her eyes, not enough. And she left without a backward glance.

Hannah felt so dreadful that she could think no further than one step at a time, as she headed in the direction of Granny's house. She made it across the canal and then collapsed.

When she came round, she was being carried. Astonished, she clutched one of the arms that held her and gazed up into Kenny's anxious face. Thank God it was him. But he was not alone.

'She's awake!' Dolly looked relieved. 'Are you feeling better, Hanny? You collected quite a crowd. We didn't half got a shock when we realised it was you. It was a worse shock when we couldn't wake you.'

'Thanks, Dolly.' Hannah's voice was just a thread of sound, and she would much rather not have her company. She had stopped liking Dolly when she had flashed her bosom at Kenny. 'Where are you taking me?'

'Home.'

'No!' Hannah could not have that and gripped Kenny's lapels and tried to pull herself up. 'I don't want to go home. You'll understand, Kenny. Bert's there and you don't want to see him, do you?'

His eyes scanned her agitated features and he nodded.

'This is daft,' said Dolly, hands on hips, looking exasperated. 'You can't not go home just because you say Kenny can't stand your brother.'

'You don't understand,' said Hannah fiercely, and hesitated before adding, 'I've got to see Granny.'

Dolly's eyes narrowed. 'What for? What's so important?'

The last thing Hannah wanted was for Dolly to know she was in trouble. 'It's private! None of your business.'

Dolly's eyes flashed with annoyance. 'We'll take you home.'

'No! Take me to Alice, Kenny.'

Dolly bristled. 'She's at our house. You've got to go home.'

'Shut up!' Hannah couldn't stand much more. She gazed up at Kenny. 'Please.'

He turned and began to carry her in the direction of Granny Popo's.

Dolly gasped and hurried after them, her breasts bobbing and strands of her hair blowing in her face. 'You've got a bloody cheek. D'you know that, Hanny? A mam and a dad you've got! I'm a bloody orphan. So why should I shut up and you not tell me why you want my gran?'

'You've got a husband,' countered Hannah, then groaned as waves of pain struck her.

Kenny's arms tightened about her and he shook his head at Dolly, scowling at her. She pressed her lips tightly together and her expression was stony. Hannah sagged in Kenny's arms and closed her eyes.

When they arrived at the house, Alice was kneeling on the rug playing with her sister. She looked up in surprise. 'Hannah! I didn't expect to see you today.'

Dolly said grimly, 'We found her out for the count on Canal Side.'

Granny Popo's sharp eyes fixed on Hannah's peaky face. 'What's up, duck?' Hannah did not want to say the words aloud in front of Kenny, or Dolly either. Although she might have guessed what was wrong with her. 'I think I must have ate something that disagreed with me and Mother's not home,' she whispered.

'What an excuse!' said Dolly, dropping the stuffed pillowcase on the floor. 'I think she's running away myself. Been up to something if you ask me.' She looked meaningfully at her grandmother. 'People don't go fainting for nothing.'

'Hush, girl,' muttered Granny Popo, heaving herself up from her chair. 'Put Hanny down, lad. If something's upset her then what she needs is a good dose of castor oil to purge her.'

Hannah looked at her in alarm. As if she wasn't suffering enough! But perhaps the old woman was right and a purge would do her good. It would be horrible while it was happening but, hopefully, afterwards she'd be better. She watched Granny Popo open the cupboard door next to the fireplace, take out a bottle and steeled herself to take her medicine like a man.

'If you're going to give her that,' said Alice, her eyes fixed on the bottle with distaste, 'she'd be better going home. She won't be off the lav for ages.'

Hannah looked up at Kenny and shook her head. 'I want to go with you,' she whispered.

Dolly heard her. 'Listen to her! She's playing up to him, Gran. She's going to use him.' She glared at Hannah, hands on hips.

'Shut up! Just remember, girl, you've got a husband.' Granny Popo poured castor oil into a dessert spoon. She gazed kindly into Hannah's pinched, sallow face. 'Get this down you, duck, and if it doesn't do the trick, we'll try something else.'

Hannah reached for the spoon but her hand was shaking so much Kenny held it for her. She baulked as she tasted the oil and nearly threw up but the old woman acted swiftly and held her mouth shut. 'Swallow it down, girl.' Hannah struggled, feeling as if she was choking but by a sheer effort of will, she swallowed the horrible stuff down.

Within ten minutes she was down the yard. She felt dreadful, as if her end had come and lost all track of time. She was convinced she would die there as the waves of pain kept coming. Her head throbbed and the cold was getting to her.

'Hanny.' It was Alice's voice. 'Are you OK?'

'Don't ask such a daft question!' she gasped crossly. 'Are you having to go home?'

'Kenny's refusing to go.'

Good old Kenny, thought Hannah, and she decided to be selfish, and not insist that they went and must not worry about her. They were her friends and she wanted them close. She knew that Dolly had guessed what was up with her and hoped she could keep her mouth shut. Hannah did not doubt Granny Popo would.

Alice leaned against the wall opposite the lavatory. 'Is it something really bad that's wrong with you, Hanny?'

Hannah did not answer. She did not want to voice her predicament. She wanted it to go away. Prayed it would go away.

'I'll take that for a yes,' said Alice. 'Is it why you don't want to go home? Whose is it?'

Still Hannah remained silent.

Alice asked her again but when her friend still did not answer, she gave up and went back inside the house.

It was an age before Hannah felt confident she could leave the lavatory and not have to rush back there but what she hoped would happen had not happened and she could not face another dose of castor oil that night. Her head still throbbed and every muscle and bone seemed on fire.

Granny Popo waved her to a seat in front of the grate. Hannah held out her cold hands to the blaze. Dolly must have taken Tilly to bed because both were missing, as was Alice. Kenny had stood up as Hannah came in and now, at Granny Popo's bidding, he made a pot of tea and poured a cup for Hannah, carrying it over to her. She sipped it gratefully.

'Any luck, girl?' said the old woman.

Hannah hugged her stomach and winced.

'Well, if it hasn't done the trick then you're best telling your mother. But for now you go with Kenny. He'll look after you. There's talk doing the rounds about your dad and mother falling out; that your mother's away at her cousin's most weekends with the kids. Is it true?'

'True, both true,' said Hannah miserably. 'I'm just hoping they'll come to their senses.' She drained her cup and stood up.

The pain was bad but she tried not to show it. Going over to Granny Popo, she pressed her cheek against that of the old woman and thanked her. Then, with Kenny carrying her pillowcase, she left the house.

As soon as they were outside Hannah linked her arm through Kenny's and leaned against him. 'I don't know how far I'll be able to walk,' she gasped. 'But I don't expect you to carry me. Perhaps we could take a cab, I've got some cash.' She patted the pocket where she had put her father's money. 'Although I'd rather hang on to it for emergencies.'

He touched her pale cheek with a gentle hand then indicated that she stay where she was and vanished. He returned five minutes later with a handcart. She stared at it in astonishment and then laughed weakly. 'OK! I'm willing if you are.'

He held the handles while she climbed in, glad it was getting on towards dusk and prayed that no one she knew would see them.

By the time they reached the apartment, Hannah was doubled up with pain. Alice opened the door to them. She was looking worried but said nothing only helping Hannah over towards Kenny's bed. He placed the pillowcase on the floor and went out again.

'How did you get here?' said Alice, helping Hannah to lie down and removing her shoes.

'Handcart.' She made a noise halfway between a giggle and a groan.

'Whose?'

'Don't know.'

Alice sat on the side of the bed and chaffed Hannah's hand, her face concerned. 'Do you want to talk about it now?'

Hannah shook her head and pressed her lips together, forcing back a cry of pain.

'OK,' said Alice, frowning. 'I won't ask any questions, only what about your mam? She's going to be worried if she doesn't know where you are.'

'Dah knows some of it. We don't want her knowing. I asked him for money so he gave me all that he had. Remember me coming here in the early hours of New Year?'

Enlightenment dawned in Alice's eyes. 'You were in a right state! It happened then?'

Hannah was tempted to tell her the truth about the Bert Alice thought so wonderful, but she just could not bring herself to speak his name. 'I was raped by a-a stranger by our back gate,' she whispered. 'But I couldn't tell my mother or Dah. They'd had this terrible row. I never told you at the time but he's been carrying on with that widow woman from next door to your old house. Mother found out and, every weekend, she leaves him to fend for himself and he goes to that woman.'

Alice sighed. 'I had heard the rumours. You poor thing!'

'I've been sick every morning for the last week.' Tears rolled down Hannah's cheeks. 'I haven't known what to do with myself. There was no one I could talk to in work or at home, so I decided to come and see you but you weren't here, so I thought maybe you'd gone to see Sebastian.' She winced as pain struck her again.

Alice shot to her feet, her small pretty face wore a scared expression. 'Are you OK? Should I get help? Perhaps Miss Secombe can do something?' She headed for the door.

Hannah shook her head. 'I'll be OK as long as you and Kenny stick by me. Besides…' She squirmed, trying to get comfortable, 'the pain I'm having… maybe it's a good pain.'

'You mean?'

'Granny Popo's castor oil might have worked!'

Chapter Fourteen

'I'll ask at our place about jobs.' Alice placed the frying pan on the fire. 'Three shillings'll do for her keep for now, won't it, Kenny?' She glanced in his direction. He nodded and smiled at Hannah.

Five days later and Hannah was feeling much better. She liked living with Alice and Kenny. They didn't have much room but it was peaceful, not like at home, and at the moment it was peace that she needed. Besides, she had decided she could no longer live under the same roof as Bert; Kenny had returned the handcart and dropped a note through her parents' letterbox, saying she was safe with friends.

Hannah had thanked him, wondering what her dah had told her mother when she arrived home, and found Hannah not there. Maybe he had pretended he did not know why she was staying with friends. She wished Jock could have beaten Bert black and blue but it would have turned her mother completely against him. Besides, he had never raised his hand to any of them.

Even so, Hannah sensed the conclusion would be the same, even if Jock told the truth; her mother would tell him to wash his mouth out with soap. She was just thankful that the *curse* had come. Whether that was the result of taking the castor oil she was uncertain, remembering how terrible she had felt before being dosed. Perhaps it had been the start of a miscarriage because, surely, if castor oil could get rid of an unwanted baby that easily, there wouldn't be any need for back street abortionists. That thought reminded her that Alice needed three shillings from her.

'I'll get the money now,' she said, rising to her feet. She wobbled slightly and Kenny put out a hand to steady her. He had given up his bed for her and Alice to share. He slept on the sofa. She smiled up at him, wondering whether he had realised what had been wrong with her. Whatever the case, she would never forget his unquestioning help.

She took the money her father had given her and also a screwed up ball of greaseproof paper out of her coat pocket. She thought it was an old sweet bag and was about to throw it on the fire when she felt something inside, a last sweet or some sherbet perhaps. She placed it on the table and counted out the money for Alice before sitting down and unscrewing the paper. She gazed at the white powder, a frown puckering her brow. She sniffed it, but the smell of frying liver and onions was now so strong in the room that she could not smell anything but cooking.

'What's that?' asked Alice.

Kenny glanced up from buttering bread.

'I thought it might be sherbet but it doesn't feel, look or smell like it. I don't know where it's come from,' said Hannah.

'You don't think Granny Popo gave it you?' said Alice.

Hannah shook her head. 'I wouldn't have thought so. I hope Mother doesn't go there looking for me. I wouldn't have thought she would because she and Granny have little to do with each other now Mother's back on her feet. But if she were to… Granny, doesn't have this address, does she?' she said, suddenly alarmed. 'I don't want to be dragged back home.'

Alice shook her head. 'I suppose I should have given it to her in case anything was to happen to Tilly but they've never asked and it's not something I think about when I'm there.'

Hannah sighed with relief. 'I like it here. Mother would ask too many questions and I don't want to answer them.' She smiled at Alice. 'And we can be a foursome again when Sebastian comes back.'

Kenny was pleased she said that and, sitting beside her, he took the powder. He dipped a finger in it and cautiously tasted it. He pulled a face and then reached for his pencil and pad. *I'll take it to the chemist.*

Hannah had not thought of that and was pleased that he should. 'Thanks.'

No more was said about the powder that evening. The following day Alice arrived home from work saying Hannah was in luck depending on which way she looked at sewing on buttons. 'It's tedious but if you feel you've got to leave the bakery, then give it a try. I'm working in millinery now. Because you haven't got a reference I told them you'd been looking after your mam and just been bereaved. It's almost the truth. You were looking after her not so long ago.'

Hannah hugged her. 'Thanks for that and for taking me in. I don't know what I would have done without the pair of you.' She knew she would miss dealing with the public, but sewing on buttons was better than not having any money and, besides, it hadn't been the same at the shop since Agnes had committed suicide. At least she would be working in the same place as Alice and that was something she was pleased about.

With the three of them sharing the one-roomed apartment there wasn't much space and hardly any privacy but none of them complained. Hannah mentioned that she would have to get herself some used clothes from the market and also some extra sheets. Having the time to get there was the problem. To her delight, on the following Saturday, Kenny came home with a pair of neatly darned sheets, a skirt, a blouse, and a jacket. Hannah was touched, especially to find when she tried on the clothes they fitted perfectly. 'How did you get my size right? And you picked my favourite colours, maroon and blue.' She reached for her purse. 'You must let me pay you.'

He shook his head, a faint smile in his eyes. But she insisted. His quiet, gentle thoughtfulness was exactly what she needed at the moment. The male charge-hand at work was loud and overbearing, and it was a struggle to stay in one spot and to carry on sewing when a voice in her head was urging her to get out of there. Saying that here was a man, who at heart was just like Bert, Mr Bannister and Alice's father, determined to lord it over women to make themselves feel important. If Alice had not worked nearby, perhaps she would have run out screaming. She felt her nerves were in shreds.

The following day was fine for February, so Hannah sat on the front step when she arrived home, taking the air. It was Alice's turn to prepare their evening meal. She heard footsteps on the path and glanced up. Kenny bent over her and placed a sheet of paper on her knee. She read, *Diachylum – lead plaster.*

She could scarcely believe it. 'Lead's poisonous in large doses, isn't it?' He nodded, frowning and lowered himself onto the step besides her. 'Where could I have got it from?'

Kenny shrugged. It was a puzzle he'd like to solve. Who could have put the powder in her pocket? Could somebody from the lead works where his father had once worked have given it to her? Although the factory mainly made lead shot, still someone might have been able to get hold of lead plaster. But why? It didn't make sense. The chemist had asked him where he had got it from but Kenny had shaken his head and walked out. He took out his pencil and notepad and wrote down, *Retrace your steps that day.*

She placed her chin in her hands. 'I told you. I called here and then went to see if you were over at Queen's Park with Seb, then I went home.'

Did you talk to anyone in that time? When did you start feeling ill?

'Before I arrived home – definitely after I crossed the Dee and was on this side.' She frowned in thought. 'The only person I saw was a young woman sitting in a motor outside the house where we saw Sebastian. Someone shouted my name but I had to get home, so I ignored it.'

Male or female?

'Male.' Hannah stared at Kenny and then the truth dawned on her. 'It was probably Sebastian! But if I went to find him in my search for you and Alice, why didn't I stop and ask him where you were? All I could think of was getting home.' Kenny looked as mystified as she did. Suddenly she remembered something else. 'The motor wasn't there earlier, so I must have gone somewhere in between.' She bit on a fingernail. Where had she gone? Wherever it was she couldn't remember a thing about it. It was as if her mind had been wiped clean.

Kenny wrote down the obvious. *We'll have to speak to him.*

She nodded vigorously, her eyes wide and slightly scared. It had occurred to her that someone might have given her some of the lead powder with the intention of killing her. But why should anyone want to do that? Unless Bert had slipped some in her drink and put the rest in her pocket after she arrived back at the house? But when and where would he have got the opportunity? No! She wasn't thinking straight. Hadn't she told Kenny she had started to feel ill before arriving home?

'You two ready for supper?' Alice stood in the doorway smiling down at the pair of them.

'Yes!' Hannah accepted Kenny's helping hand up. 'And Alice, we need to see Seb urgently. That white powder! It contained lead.' On their way upstairs, she told her friend what she and Kenny had discussed.

Alice said, 'I've got a date with him in a couple of days. He was busy the other Sunday so we didn't get to see him. I'll ask if he saw you talking to anyone then.'

But Alice was to see Sebastian the following evening when she and Hannah came out of work. He was leaning against a lamp-post on the other side of Northgate Street reading the *Chester Chronicle.* She spotted him immediately and called his name. He folded the newspaper as Alice, followed by Hannah, hurried past the Scotch Wool and Hosiery Store and Lipton's Grocer's, and down the steps to the street.

His eyes fixed on Hannah. 'What are you doing here?'

'She's working at our place now. I'm glad to see you.' Alice beamed at him and slipped her arm through his. 'We've something to ask you.'

He looked down at Alice's hungry-for-his attention face. 'Hannah was seen walking past Mrs Waters' house the other Sunday.'

'So it was you who called me,' said Hannah, and bit on her lip.

Sebastian nodded. 'You remember? Miss Victoria recognised you from that time we were all talking outside in the rain last year. She's got a good memory for faces. I just caught the back of you and when she said that she thought you were Alice's friend, I called your name, but you ignored me. I thought *Odd!* Miss Victoria thought the same. It was as if you were in a trance.'

'A trance!' A shiver ran down Hannah's spine.

'She wondered if you'd been to see Mrs Black,' said Sebastian.

'But why should I go and see Mrs Black?' asked Hannah, dumb-founded.

'There's all kinds of rumours going round about her. One is that she is an hypnotist.'

'Y-You think she hypnotised me? But why?' cried Hannah, incredulous.

Alice stared at her. 'Exactly! The thing is did you or didn't you see her.'

'I don't remember, so stop looking at me like that!' Hannah's voice rose several octaves. She felt hot and uncomfortable.

'Then maybe she did hypnotise you because where else could you have been,' said Alice, frowning. 'I wonder what you told her?'

The question worried Hannah, although how did they know she had gone in to that woman's house? 'Did you see me going in or coming out of Mrs Black's house?'

'No.'

'Did Miss Victoria?'

He shook his head.

'There you are then,' said Hannah, her voice quivering. 'No proof I even saw the woman.'

Alice said uneasily, 'Except you ignored Seb's calling your name. Why should you do that? I hope you didn't tell her where we lived.'

'Why should it matter?' Then Hannah thought why it might and gnawed on her lip. 'I don't remember,' she mumbled.

There was silence.

'This isn't getting us anywhere,' said Sebastian.

'No,' murmured Hannah unhappily and dug her hands deep into her coat pockets. 'I'm going home.'

'I won't come yet,' said Alice, gripping Sebastian's arm tightly. 'Tell Kenny about this – and tell him I've gone for a walk with Seb.'

Hannah nodded, wondering if they would talk about her as soon as they were alone. It would be natural, yet she felt hurt by the thought, excluded. Suddenly she wanted to be with Kenny. He would be kind and understanding and would hopefully get to the truth without having to confront Mrs Black.

Kenny was already at the apartment when Hannah arrived there, having stopped on the way for their evening meal. He was stripped to the waist, sluicing himself down.

'Sorry!' She would have gone out again to allow him some privacy but he signalled that she come in and reached for a towel. She noticed there was a puckered silvery scar on his back. For a moment all thought of Mrs Black and what she, herself, might have said to her was forgotten.

'How did you get this?' Her fingers explored the scar. She felt his skin quiver beneath her touch and slowly removed her hand. She'd had such a temptation to continue caressing his skin, to put her arms round him and rest her face against his back but it wouldn't be fair to encourage him to think that there could ever be anything serious between them. Bert had spoiled that for her. She cleared her throat. 'Seb was waiting when we came out of work. Alice has gone off with him. They're probably talking about me right now, thinking I might have betrayed your whereabouts to Mrs Black.' Her voice broke on a tiny laugh.

Kenny stilled in the act of pulling on a vest and his startled eyes flashed a question.

'I'll tell you over our meal,' she said, and removed her outdoor clothes and put on the kettle. He donned a clean shirt and waistcoat. She opened the steaming package that she had bought from the cooked meat shop and sliced the stuffed hearts in gravy and buttered a good third of the fresh loaf Kenny had brought in.

They sat at the table, across from each other and, while he ate as if half-starved, she picked at her food and told him about the conversation between herself, Sebastian and Alice. 'I hope I didn't tell Mrs Black anything that might harm the pair of you if I did go in there. Apparently there's a rumour going round that she's an hypnotist.'

Kenny picked up a pencil and wrote down. *What? That as well as a property owner! Seems odd to me. Anyway we don't know if you did. So stop worrying. Although, I'm being contrary now, if you did go to Mrs Black's, then she might have given you the powder.*

Hannah gaped at him. 'But why? Was she trying to kill me?'

Why should she want to do that? Unless she told you something that she didn't want you telling someone else. He paused and scribbled the last sentence out. *That doesn't make sense. Why should she tell you anything? It's more likely she wanted information from you.*

Hannah gnawed on her lip. 'I wish I knew what I said to her if I did go there. And it's going to drive me mad trying to figure out why she should give me the powder, if she did. Perhaps I saw something in her house that made her want to shut me up forever.'

If she hypnotised you there was no need to shut you up. You don't remember anything about being there.

'That's true. But… Oh, I wish I knew what I'd said, if I said anything at all.' Then she giggled. 'This is a bit ridiculous, isn't it? All supposition. But it's going to niggle me.'

And, looking at him, she guessed it would niggle him, too. But it wasn't going to help them find out what she had said, if she had said anything important. Hell, she was getting muddled.

Kenny mouthed *I'm glad to get a smile out of you. You mustn't worry.*

She reached across the table and covered his hand with hers. 'You're such a comfort to me. At least I know you'll never deceive me, that I can trust you. You'll never raise your voice and shout me down.' For a moment he looked as if he was about to say something but that was impossible! His fingers curled about hers and he raised her hand to his lips and kissed it. She smiled at him. 'Thanks for everything.' For a moment they just stared at each other and she felt her heart increase its beat. No! This couldn't be, she thought, and clearing her throat, said, 'Now tell me how you got that scar on your back?'

He hesitated, then wrote *I've always had it. At least as long as I can remember. It was there before we came to live in Chester.*

'D'you think your father did it?'

Kenny clenched a fist on the sheet of paper. He mouthed *I don't remember. But what do you think?*

'Yes. Who else would have been so cruel? It looks like a burn.'

A flash of memory, and for an instant he could smell burning flesh and see a woman lying on the floor, her long dark hair pulled across her face. The vision gave him such a shock that he began to shake and hurriedly got up, walked across the room, opened the door and went out.

Hannah was astonished. Had she somehow hit the mark, touched a nerve? She rose from her chair and went after him. He had moved fast and was already halfway down the stairs. She hung over the banister. 'Kenny, come back! I didn't mean to upset you. I won't ask any more questions.' He ignored her. She watched his retreating figure, wishing she had kept her mouth shut, and hoping this would not spoil things between them.

When Alice arrived home, she said, 'I told Seb that I wouldn't put it past the old witch to have dragged you into her house. The Lord only knows what goes on in there.'

Hannah could not help laughing. 'You make it sound like a house of ill-repute.'

Alice said darkly, 'You may mock! But who's to say she isn't a fraud who diddles people out of their money by hypnotism?'

'We don't know that. Anyway, why should she if she owns property and has rents coming in.'

Alice grimaced. 'You're right. But I really do hope you didn't tell her where we lived if she did hypnotise you.'

Hannah hoped that, too. The last thing she wanted was for Mal Moran not to be dead and to come storming after Alice and Kenny breathing fire and brimstone. 'Perhaps we should move?'

Alice sighed. 'We'll see what Kenny says. Where is he, by the way?'

'He got upset about something I said.' Hannah hesitated. 'You must have seen that scar on his back?'

Alice nodded. 'Dad probably did it. I remember asking Mam about it. She said he had it when he came to live in Chester but that Dad denied causing it. I didn't believe him, of course.' She made herself a sandwich with the sliced hearts and changed the subject. 'Seb says he'll carry on keeping an eye on her place and so will his ma and that Miss Victoria.' She sighed. 'Not that I really want her involving herself in our business. She has too much to do with Seb as it is, considering. But at least if my dad turns up we'll get to know about it.' She bit into her sandwich as Hannah poured her a cup of tea.

On Sunday Hannah was asked whether she was going to church. She was about to refuse when she realised she had something to be thankful for. Afterwards Alice visited Granny Popo's to see Tilly and to assure the old woman that Hannah was fine and to ask if any of the Kirks had called to see if she had been there. She was glad to find Dolly out.

'Yes, duck!' Granny lit her pipe and drew on it vigorously. She cocked a bright eye at Alice through the smoke. 'Mrs Kirk came to call, looking something dreadful. She asked if I'd seen Hannah because she knew that sometimes she came here. I said I had and that I gave her a dose of castor oil but that I haven't seen her since.'

'You didn't tell her that she went off with Kenny?' said Alice swiftly.

Granny shook her head. 'I was about to when it struck me that she might just lay the blame for Hanny's trouble on him.'

'No!' gasped Alice. 'He wouldn't. He thinks too much of her. Besides she told me that it was a drunk on New Year who raped her.'

'So that's what she says happened...' The old woman drew on her pipe, looking thoughtful but made no further comment.

Alice said, 'So you didn't mention that she's with me and Kenny then?'

Granny shook her head. 'I don't have your address, anyhow, so it wouldn't have helped.'

Alice nodded. 'Hannah doesn't want her family to know where she is.'

'I gather that and it makes me wonder why. It couldn't just be because of the upset between her parents, surely?'

Alice was silent a moment, then she said, 'Could be. She has been through a lot since her mother's fall.'

Granny gazed at her a moment, puffing jerkily on her pipe, then she removed it from her mouth and said, 'Tell her I'll keep mum and hopefully Dolly'll do the same. Fortunately Mrs Kirk seems to think that Tilly is my granddaughter's. I think that damage to her head has caused something to go wrong with her brain, if it wasn't those rays they shot through her with that new-fangled X-ray machine.'

Alice said sadly, 'Poor Mrs Kirk. She really is having a hard time of it.'

Granny agreed, and changed the subject to talk about Tilly.

When Alice arrived home, she told Kenny and Hannah all that Granny had said. Hannah was upset that her mother should be hurt but determined to stay where she was. 'I'm happy here. I just hope she doesn't start to haunt Granny's place.' She smiled tight-lipped, and expressed a need to get out for a while.

So after tea they went to the Gospel Hall in Frodsham Street, where the singing was lusty and a lantern slide show promised, presented by a visiting missionary from Africa. Being reminded that there was a big wide world beyond their small part of it helped to take their minds off things.

That night, as Hannah slipped between the darned sheets, she thought how much her life had changed in the last week and wondered, not for the first time, how things were between her parents. What had her dah told her mother exactly? She doubted it was the truth. Perhaps her mother had reported her disappearance to the police. Strangely she had not thought about that before and could only hope that she hadn't. Perhaps she should write a letter herself and post it to her parents this time.

Chapter Fifteen

'I don't understand my own daughter!' Susannah's voice shook. She slapped the letter down on the newspaper spread out in front of Jock on the table. He was reading about the outbreak of anthrax in Cheshire and feeling sorry for the farmers, so she took him by surprise. He looked down at the letter and his heart felt as if it was tying itself up in a knot when he recognised Hannah's writing. His fingers trembled as he made to pick up the letter but Susannah snatched it away before he could read it.

Jock felt furious with her and himself. 'What are yer playing at?' He missed his eldest daughter more than he could say, and couldn't bear the sight of his eldest son. They left the house together but no longer did he walk to work with him or talk to him if he could help it. He'd have had him out of the house if it hadn't been for the need to explain to his wife.

He glanced up at Susannah. Her expression was strained and she held herself stiffly. 'You can read it after you tell me what's going on. I've been to Granny Popo's house, but all she'd tell me was that Hannah felt ill and so she dosed her with castor oil. She hasn't seen her since. I went down to the bakery and had words with Mr Bannister, but he's as annoyed as I am for her going off without a word. You and that woman are to blame!' Susannah's small, dark eyes glinted like black beads. 'Hanny couldn't bear the atmosphere in this house anymore, that's why she was sick and got out.'

'You read the other letter. She needed to get away, so she's staying with friends.' A muscle tightened in Jock's jaw. 'It didn't mention anything about me and Nora.'

'Don't mention that woman in this house,' she yelled, thumping her fist on the table. 'I was ill and you betrayed me! If it hadn't been for Hanny and Bert, God only knows what would have happened to me. I've always known you never loved me—'

Jock shot to his feet. 'Don't start that all over again! If I hadn't gone out to work everrr-y morning, even though I didn't feel like it… you wouldn't have had a bed to lie in… no food in your stomach, no fire in the grate!'

'I don't care about that! Perhaps you should have let me die! What kind of husband is it who goes to another woman and leaves a sick wife and children alone in the house at night?' she asked scornfully.

Jock groaned. 'I told you I didn't mean for it to happen. It was weeks before I – we – she was lonely, I was lonely. I didn't intend ta-' He stopped. 'What's the use of going over it all again? I only wish that Hanny hadn't got to know. Bert must have told her. That so-called perfect son of yours.'

Her head, which had been bowed, reared up like a snake about to strike. 'Don't blame this on Bert. You've always been jealous of the affection between us.'

'Rubbish! And let's drop his name before I get really angry. Let me see that letter.' He reached out for it, but she scrunched it up and sat on it.

He was astonished. 'Don't be so bloody childish – she's my daughter.' He pulled his wife to her feet and picked up the screwed up letter before releasing her. He opened the sheet of paper and brought it close up to his face. After a minute he said, 'At least we know she's safe.' He handed it back to her.

'And that makes everything all right? She tells me not to get the police and that Mal Moran's probably dead, killed in an accident. As if I cared about Mal Moran when I'm worried sick about her! It's not good enough her writing there's nothing for me to worry about. I am worried! A day doesn't go by without me thinking about her being in trouble and not coming to me for help. It's a married man she's living with, I bet.'

Jock was astonished. 'It wasn't our Bert who suggested a married man, was it? Because if it was, I wouldn't believe him.'

Susannah's eyes darted venom. 'There you go again! What are you accusing him of? He'd never cause trouble for his sister.' Her voice broke and, for a moment, she could not speak. Then she cleared her throat. 'It was something someone said to him. He said he told them that it wasn't true.'

Jock stiffened. 'What wasn't true?'

'You tell me.' She took out the handkerchief Joy had made and embroidered for her for Christmas, and wiped her eyes. 'You know the truth, I can tell. So out with it or I'll go round to the next street and smash all that bitch's windows.'

Jock was furious with his son. The crafty sod! Bert was taking a big risk, thinking that he would continue to stay silent about his part in Hannah's trouble. But he didn't have time now to break it to his wife, even if he could have found the right words. 'I've got to go to work.' He got to his feet and went for his overcoat.

Susannah got to the front door before him and put her back to it, bristling like a fighting cock. 'Tell me the truth, Jock, or I'll go to our Joan's and never come back. I'll leave the children with you and you can see how your fancy piece likes that.'

He growled, 'Ye'd never leave the children. And I'll tell ye now, if yer stopped going to yer cousin's every weekend, I'd have a good reason to stay at home. I'm ashamed and sorry for what I've done. But you've got to take your share of the blame. If ye hadn't rebuffed every approach I made, then maybe Hanny would have been saved a lot of heartache. I gave her money because she said she would go to Granny about some trouble. I was wrong. I should have kept her here for you to see to, but we've both been so wrapped up in our own affairs that our child has suffered.'

The colour drained from Susannah's face and her mouth trembled. 'So it is that kind of trouble. And who do you think Hanny's staying with if it isn't a married man?'

Jock shook his grizzled head more in pain than in anger. 'How the hell should I know? I thought she'd have stayed with Granny but I was wrong. At least she has some friends, Mother, and we should be glad of that, even if we know nothing about them.'

She stamped her foot like a frustrated child. 'Stop calling me Mother! I'm not your mother!'

He raised his eyebrows. 'You've acted like one. Bossying me around since I came to this house as a lad. It's you that wore the trousers because you bloody wouldn't let me.'

Her face turned a fiery red and she put a hand to her breast. 'You never argued with my decisions.'

'I don't like arguments. I'm a peaceable man. Now out of my way, I've got work to go to.' He placed his hands on her waist and lifted her up.

'No!' Susannah was now white to the lips. 'Forget us for now. Hanny! You say you gave her money. Granny Popo said she gave her castor oil. Hannah says that she's fine? Is it true? Or is she lying?'

He said heavily, 'She was worried sick about what yer'd think about her. She wanted to protect ye. So she might be lying but all might be well with her now.'

Susannah felt as if she might faint and clung to him. 'Who is he?' she whispered. 'Did she tell you?'

'You wouldn't like the truth,' said Jock, sick to his soul, thinking about his son's wickedly devious nature. 'You brought her up to be a good girl.'

'Yes, I did,' she murmured, wondering what had gone wrong to make Hannah behave so foolishly.

He held Susannah against him a moment and then put her down. He paused on the step. 'Give it time. She'll come home when she's ready, Sue, luv.'

She stared at him, her heart thumping. It had been so long since he had called her by name and held her that she had almost forgotten what it was like. 'Are you sure you don't know where she is?'

Jock sighed. 'I'll see yer later, Sue.'

Susannah watched him walk down the street. Her heart ached, remembering how it had been when he had courted her and in those early days of marriage. She had believed then that he could love her despite the eight-year age gap between them. She heard movement behind her and turned. Bert was placing his carry-out in his coat pocket before lifting his coat down from its hook. She wondered if he had been listening to their conversation, but she was in no mood to discuss Hanny with him right now. She wanted to be alone, to think.

Bert placed an arm about her shoulders and kissed his mother's hair. 'See you this evening.' He went out, closing the door firmly behind him.

As he walked up the street, his mind was working busily, even as he smiled at several of the neighbours. So Hanny thought Mal Moran was dead and how did she know that unless she'd been in contact with the dummy and his sister? He wished he knew where they were. On the other hand, it was probably best for him if Hanny continued to stay away. She'd been a bit hysterical the last time he'd seen her and might say the same kind of thing to Mother that she'd said to their dah. In which case, it might be a good thing to press the point home with his mother about that boss of hers fancying her.

–

'I don't believe it,' whispered Susannah, her round face working in her agitation. 'Your dah says it's not true… and besides Mr Bannister isn't a married man.' Her hands twitched in her lap.

Bert had forgotten that fact and could have kicked himself. Who else could he blame? He considered and again that piece of information his parents hadn't seemed to pick up on, struck him afresh. 'Mother, haven't you wondered how Hanny knows that Mal Moran is dead? Who could have told her that?' He got down on his knees and gazed up at her as she perched on the edge of the armchair.

His mother stared at him blankly and put a hand to her head. 'I can't think.'

'His children, of course. Kenny or Alice! Our Hanny was always close to them. She felt sorry for them, especially the dummy.'

'The dummy?' Susannah's face screwed up as if trying to remember.

Bert felt a rising exasperation. 'Kenny, Mal's son. You've got to remember what a terrible upbringing he had.'

'A gentle soul,' murmured Susannah, her face relaxing. 'Our Hanny was fond of him. He'd never hurt her.'

Bert gritted his teeth. 'Mother, he could have changed. You've got to remember that he's got Mal's blood in him.'

'Florrie was good to him.'

Bert nodded in agreement. 'Yes, but she wasn't his mother. He doesn't take after her. He's Mal's son. Mal who pushed you down the stairs and could have killed you.'

Susannah moistened her lips; her head ached and, for once, she wished Bert would leave her alone. 'Mal's Kenny's father?'

'Yes.' He beamed at her. 'And Kenny's probably the one who's got our Hannah into trouble. Blood will out, Mother. As for Hanny, she should have had the courage to tell you the trouble she was in. I don't suppose she meant to be cowardly and selfish, but she probably just didn't think how you'd have much rather she'd have come to you with the truth. You wouldn't have turned her away, would you, Mother?'

Susannah's head sank onto his chest and she wept. She felt so confused. Bert reached up and touched her shoulder. Then, hearing footsteps behind him, turned and saw Joy watching the pair of them. Smiling at her, he thought how nicely she was growing up.

'Is Mother OK?' she said, her expression unfriendly as she met her brother's gaze.

'Yes, is Mother OK?' echoed Grace, who followed hard on her sister's heels.

Bert studied his sisters, two of them growing up nicely. He flashed them a dazzling smile. 'Of course, she's OK. Aren't you, Mother?'

She lifted her head, wiped her eyes, and then looked at her younger daughters. 'Where's Freddie?'

'Still playing out,' said Joy. 'Any news from Hanny?'

Susannah nodded. 'Yes, this morning. She's fine.'

'When's she coming home? We miss her.'

'We all miss her,' said Bert with a sigh.

Joy ignored him and focused her gaze on her mother. 'But when will that be, Mother?'

Susannah released a long sigh. For a moment she did not know how to answer Joy. She was hurting inside, really hurting. Bert must be right. Hanny and Kenny, Mal Moran's son! The man who was responsible for all her troubles. How could Hanny have anything to do with him? She felt a stir of anger against her daughter. She was selfish! Didn't care about how they were feeling about what she was doing... not giving tuppence about the pain her family were going through. How could she prefer to be with the Morans instead of them? Her anger grew. Let her stay away! They'd manage without her. She would explain her absence to the neighbours by putting it out that Hanny was staying in Moreton, helping Joan. Her cousin was getting frail and Hanny was to stay with her to the end. She now told her girls and Freddie that same lie.

Grace's thin face was despondent, but she responded by saying, 'I want to see Hanny, of course, but if she's all right, I can get by without seeing her for a while. I don't really feel like going to Moreton anymore. I've had enough being there weekends. It was so cold in cousin Joan's house.'

'That's fine,' said Susannah, glad to have the flaw in her tale pointed out to her. 'I've had enough of being away from home at the weekends, too.'

All through their chattering over supper, Susannah's thoughts ran on as she sought to remember more of the past. Flashes of memory came back to her of the tussles she'd had with Hanny as a child. She remembered going to Moreton one day, when Joy was only a baby, and warning Hanny to stay away from the water's edge, but would she? She kept going a little bit closer and then a bit closer still. She wouldn't be told. If Bert hadn't moved so fast she could have drowned. Then she'd had the nerve to say Bert had egged her on. Children! They were always a worry. But never would she have believed that Hanny would bring such shame to their door. But, then, never would she have believed that Jock would go with another woman.

She felt that choking sensation in her chest, just thinking of Nora Taylor. If only she had never found out, then none of these things would have happened, she felt certain. But until she knew for sure that he had stopped seeing that woman, she had no intention of welcoming him to her side of the bed.

In the meantime, she determined not to talk about her daughter unless asked. Hanny had made the decision not to ask for her help. If she were living with Kenny, and he was just like his father, then hopefully she would realise her mistake and come flying home.

Chapter Sixteen

Summer 1906

Hannah woke with a start and sat up, hugging her knees.

'What's wrong?' murmured Alice sleepily.

'I had a nightmare.'

'Not about Mrs Black again?'

'Yes. Somehow she'd got me in her power,' lied Hannah, unable to tell the truth that it was Bert coming in search of her that haunted her dreams. Fortunately he had no idea where she was, and even if he were to visit Granny she wouldn't tell him because the old woman respected her wishes. 'Perhaps she's put a spell on me,' murmured Hannah, remembering Alice calling Mrs Black a witch.

Alice looked horrified. 'Don't be daft! You don't really believe in such things, do you?'

Hannah shrugged and smiled.

Alice pulled the bedcovers over her head. 'I told you Seb said she's gone away. Part of the house has been let to three sisters who teach music.' Her voice was muffled but audible.

'I know. But I think I preferred it when she was there. At least we knew where she was.'

'It's ages since she let part of the house and vanished. We've moved since anyway, so everything's fine. We're both safe; get back to sleep.'

Hannah thought how swiftly the months had passed. There had been a General Election; in the run-up to which, the suffragettes had made their presence felt. Sebastian had told them how Miss Victoria had been among the banner wavers in Liverpool, harassing the Prime Minister, Sir Henry Campbell Bannerman, to take up their cause.

She'd had to rest in bed for a couple of days afterwards but she had said it had been worth it, maintaining she was not going to be forced into living the life of an invalid. Women still didn't have the vote and those in government had to be made to realise that the topic was not going to go away. She was determined to play her part in the struggle for women's emancipation.

Hannah would have liked to attend the meetings to which Sebastian ferried Miss Victoria. Better education, working conditions and wages for the 'poorer sisters' would only come as a result of women getting the vote and changing the laws. And Hannah was all in favour of that.

Hannah lay down and tried to relax, thinking about how Alice was no further on with her plan to separate Sebastian from the Waters than she was in trying to forget what Bert had done to her or what she might have said to Mrs Black. At least they were now safe in an apartment over a shop in Northgate Street, which sold furniture and household goods.

The move had been a good thing. Kenny had his own bedroom, she and Alice shared and they had a large living room, a small kitchen and an upstairs WC. The only drawback was that they didn't have their own front door but had to come through the shop to get upstairs. So they had the keys and acted caretaker when the shop's owner and his assistants went home.

The three of them got on well although there were times, lately, when she and Alice disagreed, but that was mainly due to Alice, who would celebrate her nineteenth birthday in a couple of months, going on about trying to get Sebastian to change his job and marry her. Sometimes Hannah felt like throwing something at her friend. The last thing she wanted her to do was to get married because then she and Kenny wouldn't be able to live under the same roof anymore and then she would have to go home.

Occasionally Hannah was swamped by guilt for not visiting her family, but she knew that if she went to see them then her mother would want answers to questions and Hannah had no wish to be interrogated about the reasons why she had left home and stayed away. While Bert still lived in the family home she would stay as far away as possible.

She worried occasionally about her sisters, but was comforted at such times with the thought that Bert would not dare touch them now Jock knew about the terrible thing he had done to her.

Hannah knew the story her mother had put about as to why her eldest daughter no longer lived at home. Alice had returned from Granny Popo's one day and told her that she was supposedly staying with her mother's elderly cousin, who'd gone 'queer in her attic'. Hannah had wondered what her sisters made of the tale, because apparently they stayed home weekends since she had left. Did that mean her dah was no longer seeing the widow Taylor? Or did he just see her once a month when her mother visited Moreton, supposedly to see her eldest daughter, and brought home fresh cockles and messages of love from Hannah. Surely they must suspect something?

She sighed. Her mother was living a lie, but perhaps that was the only way she knew how to cope with Hannah's disappearance. The girl yawned. Why couldn't something heavy fall on Bert's head at work or he be run over by a tram? But, even if something did happen to him, would she go home? Despite sweating six days of the week for a pittance, sewing on buttons, hooks and eyes, Hannah had never had so much freedom.

There were walks along the river and picnics in the countryside. Once a month she, Alice and Kenny went to the theatre or the music hall. If Sebastian was available he joined them. They would suck oranges or sweets and, if the turns did not please then, like many another, they would pelt the performers with orange peel. It was all part of the entertainment. So far they had seen an acrobatic troupe, the Colibris Midgets, and Madji the Dusky Queen who was a marvellous Hindoo dancer and contortionist. They had watched animated pictures of *The Grand National* and a morality film *The Road to Ruin* approved by the church. It was wonderful to see moving pictures but some people said they'd never catch on. Watching real people perform was much more interesting. They had also seen the play *How Dare You, You Blackguard!* starring Mr Bert Gilbert, which had been a laugh. All in all, these outings helped Hannah to forget her troubles for a while but she only had to smell bay rum hair lotion or peppermints and she would feel cold all over.

Kenny was of a different breed altogether. She felt safe and relaxed in his company. He often made her laugh with some of the cartoons he drew in his writing pad. The speech bubbles were funny and, occasionally, romantic and Hannah told him how much she enjoyed his cartoon tales. 'Although in real life, Kenny, your hero probably would have made a mess of things, unless you showed him rehearsing and rehearsing his exact words to get them right. That's the thing with writing things down. It takes longer than saying it so there's less chance of saying the wrong thing in haste.'

He had stared at her as if she had just said something he had never thought about. Hannah believed he was wasted as a coal man and told him so. 'If only we knew someone who could help you do something with your cartoons and writing, I'm sure you'd find an audience.'

Kenny was bowled over that she held him in such high regard.

Still, she was careful not to encourage him to hope that their friendship could develop into anything deeper. She was terribly fond of him but that was as far as she must allow it to go. Marriage was not for her. Instead she was content to continue to live as they were doing.

One summer evening, they decided to take the train to New Brighton and walk along the Ham and Egg Parade. Alice was in the kitchen preparing their meal. Kenny had washed and was now shaving in front of the mirror. He had allowed his sideburns to grow in the last few months, which made him appear more dashing. Hannah was glad he did not favour a moustache or beard. She noticed coal dust lodged in the hair that almost touched his chin and, licking a finger, she reached out and rubbed at it. He squinted in his attempt to see what she was doing. 'You missed a bit,' she said, twinkling up at him.

He gave her such a smile that she felt quite peculiar and had to turn away quickly. Alice was so lucky to have him as a brother, she would never be in danger from rape when he was around. Why couldn't Bert have been more like him? Their dah had never acted violently towards them or wanted them to suffer. So why was her brother the way he was? It was inexplicable. Kenny with a wife beater for a father and the frustration of never being able to express his feelings by having a good slanging match when angry, was not the least bit like Mal. His life had been full of rage and violence and yet he was so restful to be with.

Despite a strong breeze blowing up from the Irish Sea that caused the girls to hold on to their beribboned straw hats, it was warm on the Egg and Ham Parade. The stretch of shops, cafes, booths and arcades on the New Brighton promenade was somewhere different to walk and enjoy the sea air, and it didn't matter that they didn't have much in the way of money to spend.

'I wish, I wish...' murmured Alice against the background of screaming gulls.

'Don't be predictable,' said Hannah, laughing. 'We know you wish Seb was here.'

With Kenny in the middle, the three of them set out arm in arm to walk the length of the parade that, in days gone by, had been far from respectable with more than ham and egg on offer. They paused to gaze down at the beach where children were still making sandcastles and young people playing rounders. Several brave souls dared the waves to swim the murky waters of the Mersey. Hannah suddenly remembered how Kenny had prevented her throwing herself in the canal, and felt a rush of warmth and squeezed his arm. He smiled down at her and she returned his smile, not wanting him to think that she didn't appreciate him.

Suddenly Alice said, 'I'm worried Seb might be going off me. You know he's spending hardly any time with me lately. But then why would someone as good-looking as him want me?' she added forlornly.

'Don't be so modest! You know it's his job that takes him away,' said Hannah. She considered how Alice had blossomed. Her figure was shapely and she had improved in the way she dressed. The skirt she was wearing, striped cotton in black and white with a flounce about its hem, and the white muslin blouse with its high mandarin collar and short puffed sleeves suited her down to the ground. She had made them herself, having copied the design from a fashion article in the Wirral edition of the *Daily Post*. She was really pretty now, her sparkling emerald eyes her best feature. 'I'm sure there's lots of fellas who'd count themselves lucky to have you on their arm. Isn't that right, Kenny?'

Kenny nodded. He would have had to be blind not to notice the improvement in his half-sister and, although he had begun to accept the idea of Sebastian as a future brother-in-law, just like Hannah, he hoped that day was a distant one. Of course she could not marry without his permission. With their father dead, Kenny stood in the role of guardian. He wanted her to be happy, but selfishly he wanted her to stay living at the apartment. With Alice around it was OK for him and Hannah to dwell under the same roof, so he could see her every day and know she was safe from the swine who had got her into trouble.

He often wondered who the man was, angry every time he thought about how the brute's behaviour had changed Hannah. She had always had her serious side but was quick to spot a joke or see the funny side of life; and she still could, but she did not laugh so readily. Even now, over eighteen months since that terrible time when he had thought she might kill herself, the corners of her mouth would suddenly droop and her eyes wear a sad expression. One day, he thought vehemently, he'd find out who the man was and do his best to beat him into pulp. In the meantime perhaps he should be practicing a proposal. It could be that when Alice did marry Sebastian then Hannah might be prepared to marry *him*, rather than the pair of them separate? But he was apprehensive about how she would react when that moment came.

–

The three of them were pleasantly drowsy when they made the return trip on the train but, as they clattered up the metal steps onto the overhead foot bridge, Alice caught sight of a face that she had convinced herself she would never see again. 'Down, down, down!' she ordered in a shaky whisper, clutching Kenny's sleeve.

'What's up?' asked Hannah, startled, gazing round.

'Dad!'

Hannah gasped, unable to believe it.

Kenny, his heart beginning to pound, took both their hands and, keeping his head down, hurried as best he could down the steps, making sure they kept with the other passengers spilling out of the train and heading for the exit.

'I thought you were going to say it was Bert,' whispered Hannah.

Alice shook her head, wondering why Hannah should think she would hide from Bert. She would not have minded seeing any member of the Kirk family believing that, for pure wickedness, none of them could measure up to her father. She just couldn't understand Kenny and Hannah's attitude. But that should be the last thing on her mind right now. She could hear the blood beating in her ears and feel the thud-thud of her heart. She did not dare look around in case he spotted her. Why had he survived? And what lousy luck that, on the one evening they had decided to go to New Brighton, he should turn up! What was he doing here? Was he with Mrs Black? Alice had given herself no time to notice. She desperately wanted to get out of the slow-moving crowd and run but Kenny was showing amazing self-control, his wrist steely, forcing her to be patient.

Past the chocolate machine and the magazine stall, platforms one and two, and they were out of the station. Still Kenny forced them to walk normally, not to draw attention to themselves. It wasn't until they turned into Northgate Street that his grip slackened. No voice had shouted out their names and the relief at not feeling the weight of Mal's hand upon their shoulders was immense.

Both girls rubbed their wrists. 'I didn't realise you were so strong, Kenny,' said Hannah.

He smiled faintly.

Alice slipped her hand into his arm, her small face pinched and drawn. 'At least now we know he's alive. But I'm not going to worry too much. There's no need, is there, Kenny? After all he doesn't know where we live,' she babbled. She knew she was trying to convince herself. Chester wasn't such a big city and it was more than possible that, one day, their father might run into them. Still, the three of them had managed to avoid meeting any of the Kirk family, so their luck might hold.

Hannah felt a rush of guilt. Was Mal's reappearance anything to do with her possible visit to Mrs Black? Perhaps his being here had nothing to do with her. Maybe he had been a long time recovering from the accident, and when he got better, had found work to earn the money to pay for the fare to return here. But why return if he believed he had killed her mother? Of course someone might have told him that Hannah's mother had survived, and also that his son and daughter were still living in Chester. She felt sick thinking that person might be Mrs Black. Where had she been staying while away from her own house?

As soon as they reached the apartment, Kenny lit the fire. Hannah made cocoa when the fire was right and, all the time, Alice sat staring into space.

'Take that look off your face,' said Hannah, as she handed her a mug. 'He's not going to find you. You've got to convince yourself of that.' It was what she was trying to do herself. It was what she had done when worried that Bert would come looking for her.

Alice sipped the hot drink gratefully. 'I know but, to be honest, I'm still terrified,' she said, her hand trembling so much that she had to put down the cup.

'What about asking Seb if your father's been seen hanging about outside Mrs Black's? If he's arrived here under his own steam, he mightn't know she's rented part of the house out and gone away,' said Hannah, who felt rather sick herself. What if he was to find out about Tilly? He might lay claim to her. She was very fond of the little girl.

Alice calmed down a little and her face brightened. 'There's a thought! And besides what am I worrying about? Seb'll look after me. And he'll be back in Chester tonight. I could go and see him tomorrow. Although, we will have to be careful, in case Dad is at Mrs Black's.'

'I'll come with you,' said Hannah, thinking she would feel much better if she was proved wrong and Mal's presence in Chester did not have anything to do with Mrs Black.

The girls were so absorbed that Kenny felt they had both forgotten about how he might be feeling. There was also something else they had forgotten. He tapped the table with his pencil to draw their attention, then wrote *He might go to the old house looking for us? I'll have a little wander round the old streets. I'll also drop in on Dolly and Granny, see how Tilly is – warn them about Dad. They might know if anyone's seen him hanging around. We don't know how long he's been back here.*

Hannah looked at him with concern. 'You'll be careful, won't you?'

Kenny nodded, and his love for her seemed to expand his chest. If only he could convince her that what that swine had done to her hadn't made any difference to his feelings for her. No, that wasn't true, it had made him realise that she was vulnerable and needed someone to care for her. The trouble was that just as years ago fear had tied up his tongue, so love did so now.

Having made their plans, they finished their cocoa and, tired out by work, exercise and the sea air, went to bed. Even so Alice could not sleep. She was filled with dread.

Something terrible was going to happen. She just knew it.

–

Alice and Hannah stood in the shade of a tree, the sunlight filtering down through the branches. Voices and the chug-chug of a boat's engine floated up from the river, while church bells called the faithful to prayer. Alice gazed in the direction of old Mrs Waters' house. Sebastian was definitely there because the motor was outside.

'Here he is!' hissed Alice. 'Oh lord, here are the Waters' women, too.'

Hannah took her eyes off Mrs Black's house, and saw Sebastian cranking the engine, and then he opened the door of the motor for the ladies to climb in. It struck her that it was going to be difficult getting a chance to speak to him with them there. Then she saw Alice hurrying forward. In her haste not to miss anything Hannah dashed after her, only for her heel to catch in the hem of her damson cotton skirt. She fell headlong, banging her nose and scraping the palms of her hands on the ground. She gasped as the breath knocked out of her.

Alice glanced over her shoulder but, before she could retrace her steps and help her friend, a light pleasant voice said, 'Sebastian, that girl looks like she's hurt herself. We must help her.'

'Really, Victoria! Do you have to be playing the good Samaritan all the time?' said her grandmother wearily from her place in the rear of the car. 'She has her friend. You don't know what you might catch from some of these poor people, my dear. Drive on, Sebastian!' She tapped his shoulder with her sunshade.

'No! Wait! She's cut her hands and her nose is bleeding,' said Victoria, her voice filled with concern.

Hannah scrambled to her feet, knowing that if she did not get up, Alice would be torn between helping her and wanting to speak to Sebastian. She took the decision out of her friend's hands, limping towards Victoria. 'I'm fine, thank you.'

'No, you're not.' Victoria gazed at her intently. 'I thought I wasn't mistaken. You're Hanny aren't you? Sebastian's told me all about you and I've caught sight of you once or twice.' She smiled.

Hannah bobbed her head in acknowledgement of Victoria's higher station in life. 'Not all, I hope.'

Victoria laughed. 'Not one of us can know all there is to know about another person. He told me you're interested in the Cause.'

Hannah hesitated, aware Alice was whispering to Seb. 'Yes, Miss. Although, in my opinion, us working class women haven't had much of a chance to say anything about what would be the best way of going about things for us.'

Mrs Waters gasped and her eyes were shocked as she gazed at Hannah. 'I should think not, girl. Really, Victoria! I don't know what your father would say if he was here.'

'I know exactly what Papa would say.' Victoria smiled sweetly, and turned again to Hannah. 'Go round to the back of the house. Gabrielle, Sebastian's mother, should be there. Say I sent you and that she is to let you wash your hands and face, make you a cup of tea and give you some of her macaroons.'

Hannah was amazed at her thoughtfulness. 'Thank you, Miss! That's kind of you.'

Victoria smiled. 'You're welcome. Come along, Sebastian, it's time we were on our way.'

Hannah stepped back and Alice came to stand beside her as the motor moved off.

Alice linked her arm through Hannah's. 'You couldn't have timed that better. I just had time to arrange a meeting this evening.'

'You didn't get to mention your father?'

Alice shook her head. 'Are you OK?'

Hannah grimaced. 'Miss Victoria told me to go to the kitchen and get Seb's mother to allow me to wash my hands and face... to make me a cup of tea. You coming?'

Alice looked uncomfortable. 'No. I've never met her.'

Hannah could not believe it. 'You mean after all this time he's never introduced you to his mother?'

Alice fiddled with her hair. 'He wanted to but I refused.'

'You what!'

'Don't look at me like that,' said Alice crossly. 'She's not going to approve of me, is she? I'm not a Catholic and I want him to leave the Waters' service.'

Hannah was dismayed. 'I wish you'd give that idea up. He's happy where he is. Anyone in their right mind can see that.' She opened the gate to Mrs Waters' house and began to limp up the path.

Alice hurried after her. 'As I've told you before, he's too fond of the family, especially Miss Victoria.'

'She seems a decent sort. I'd say if you can't fight them, then join them.'

Alice stopped dead, her green eyes flashing with annoyance. 'Are you saying that I should try and get a job in service here?'

Hannah shrugged. 'If there was a job going, why not? The servants' garret probably has a lovely view over the Dee.' A snatch of a song suddenly flashed into her mind as they went round the side of the house. *There was a jolly Miller once lived on the river Dee.*

Alice said swiftly, 'I don't want to be a servant! I want my own home, not to be at the beck and call of others.' Her expression was stormy as they came to the back of the house, stopped and gazed up at the windows. 'I don't want to share Seb with his mother and the Waters'. I wish I could run away with him. If we lived somewhere else, Father wouldn't find me.'

'You're a dreamer.' Hannah shook her head, and a strand of blonde hair came loose. She tucked it behind her ear and looked at her friend. 'I'm going in. Are you coming? Say hello to Seb's ma?'

Alice turned her back on her.

Hannah sighed. 'I think you're making a mistake. Come on, it's not too late to change your mind.' Alice ignored her. Hannah knocked on the back door and was told to come in.

There was a smell of roasting meat and something sweet. Condensed milk? A woman stared at her, fine dark eyes taking in Hannah's appearance, looking her up and down as if she was the mistress of the house instead of a servant. Hannah could have been annoyed but instead chose to be amused. She gave her name and explained about her fall and what Miss Victoria had said. 'Ha! My son has spoken about you. You are lucky to find me here. The other servants have gone to church.'

Hannah's spirits rose; perhaps she wasn't a Catholic after all. 'You don't go to church?'

She said indignantly, 'Of course I go to church. Already I have attended Mass and my son with me.' She burst into *Ave Maria!* Bustling about the kitchen, which had onions and herbs hanging from the ceiling, she put the kettle on the gas stove, ran water in the large porcelain sink, took a tin from the shelf of a pale oak dresser, and placed a plain white cup on a saucer. Then she switched off the tap. 'Here!' Seb's mother beckoned Hannah over to the sink.

Oh Lord! She was a Catholic, thought Hannah, and a hard-working one at that. How much had Sebastian told her about Alice? If she knew of Hannah's existence, then surely he had told her about the girl he had been walking out with for at least two years. She washed her hands and face carefully, pondering on the problems religion could create.

Gabrielle took a towel from near the black leaded range and handed it to her. Hannah dabbed her face and hands dry and decided to ask Sebastian's mother about Mal Moran, explaining how Alice had seen him at the railway station.

'But your friend should have found a policeman and had him arrested.' Gabrielle stilled in the act of placing macaroons on a plate.

'He is a dangerous man. He punched my son in the face and bruised his ribs. He should be punished.'

'She was scared.'

'What use is it being scared? It gives a person power over you. My papa he taught me to look an enemy in the eye and show no fear.' Her dark eyes flashed. 'Even if inside it was as if a hawk had his talons dug into my belly, I spit in my enemy's face.' She spat in the sink.

Her words and action were so dramatic that Hannah wanted to laugh. It was difficult to imagine Alice spitting in her father's face and him backing off. Hannah sighed, thinking both she and Alice needed someone strong to fight their battles for them. Yet if Alice could steel herself to stand up to this woman, then maybe they'd not only have respect for each other, but she might prove a powerful ally against Alice's father. If only Sebastian could bring the two of them together.

'Sit and drink your tea.' Gabrielle pulled out a chair from the table, lit the gas and then placed the copper saucepans of vegetables on the stove.

Hannah drank the tea and scoffed several macaroons. 'These are good. I used to work in a bakery so I know what I'm talking about.' She smiled.

Gabrielle beamed at her. 'My papa had a woman who showed me how to make them. I never forget her. I was only a very small girl at the time but she taught me many things. Your mama, she taught you to cook?'

'Not much. She said she couldn't afford to waste food while I learnt.'

'Ahhh! I understand. But I give you my recipe for my macaroons and you make them. When my son comes to visit then you make them for him.'

'Me?'

Gabrielle's eyes twinkled. 'You and Kenny are his friends. It will give him a surprise. Although I think you will not make them as good as I.'

Hannah did not argue with that. She was pleased that Sebastian had spoken to his mother about her and Kenny. Of course it would not matter what their beliefs were to this woman. She was tempted to ask her what she thought of Alice but decided that perhaps she should not interfere, so changed the subject, asking about Miss Victoria.

Gabrielle fixed her with a stare. 'My son is very fond of her. He has known her forever. He worries about her. She has a damaged heart. You know that? Never would he leave her papa's service while either of them needs him.' There was a note of warning in the older woman's voice.

Hannah was taken aback. Had Sebastian dropped hints to his mother that he might be leaving? She was surprised but knew Alice would be delighted. Suddenly Hannah knew she had to say something. 'But what if that was what he really wanted? Miss Victoria seems a kind person; wouldn't she tell him to go?'

Gabrielle did not answer, but picked up a knife and set about peeling a baking apple. 'It is time for *you* to go.'

Hannah knew she had overstepped the mark. She stood up, thanked Sebastian's mother and let herself out.

Alice was leaning against a wall looking thoroughly fed up. 'You've been ages. What was she like? Was she annoyed with you for bothering her?'

'No!' Hannah told her all that had been said as they walked down towards the Old Dee Bridge.

As they paused in the middle, gazing down at the weir, Alice said with shining eyes, 'Now you see why I've got to get him away. His mother will bully me. I'm not tough enough to stand up to her.'

Suddenly Hannah wished she had not told her about that. 'I thought you'd be more concerned over the differences in your religion.'

Alice's green eyes widened and she cried, 'I am, of course. That's why I want to get him away from her. Once he works at something else and isn't seeing the Waters' and his mother so often, I'll be able to bring him to my way of thinking.'

'Have you discussed your faith?'

Alice looked uncomfortable and avoided Hannah's stare. 'What's the point? Besides, other things got in the way.'

Hannah gave up on the discussion, deciding it was a waste of time.

When they returned to the apartment, Kenny was already there. 'Well?' asked Hannah. He shook his head and lightly touched her cut nose. 'I fell over,' she said in answer to his unspoken question, and went to prepare Sunday lunch as it was her turn.

As they ate, Alice concentrated on looking forward to her rendezvous with Sebastian, planning how she would persuade him that he had to marry her and leave Chester. She would live in a garret with Sebastian as long as he agreed to take her away somewhere her father would never find them.

Chapter Seventeen

Alice stood near the Ship Gate in Grosvenor Park, her shoulders flung back, her head held high, chewing her lower lip, waiting for Seb to arrive. She could smell the heady perfume of roses and was reminded of that first time she had seen him. Suddenly he was coming towards her with that loose-limbed stride of his, and she experienced that familiar marshmallow feeling inside her.

Sebastian took her hand. 'You all right? You look—'

'Upset? I am upset.' She had not meant to say that and could have bitten her tongue off.

He looked concerned, his dark eyes gazing at her intently. 'What is it? You didn't say why it was so urgent we met this evening.' He held her hand tightly. 'I haven't much time. We're going back to Liverpool later.'

Alice was hurt. 'I've seen so little of you lately and now I need you, all you have to say is that you're going back to Liverpool.'

His forehead creased in a frown. 'Is this about your father? Ma told me that Hannah said something about your seeing him. Are you certain it was *him*?'

Alice burst out, 'Of course, I'm sure! Do you think I'm stupid or blind?' She clung to his arm. 'You must take me away, Seb. Get me out of Chester. I'm scared he'll find me and make me go with him and make my life a misery like he did in the past. I'm scared he'll separate us and I'll never see you again.' Her eyes were wild in her blanched face.

'OK, luv. Calm down.' He put an arm about her shoulders and hugged her against him. 'You know I wouldn't let him hurt you. Let's get walking or you'll end up getting cold. There's a bit of a breeze off the river this evening.' He had much on his mind and was finding it difficult to accept that Alice could be so scared of her father, when he didn't even know where she was living. Of course it was always possible that she'd mistaken someone else for her father and was worrying about nothing.

'But you know what he's like! He just might—'

'Beat me into pulp?' He smiled, gazing down into her anxious face. 'I'm prepared to take my chances.' His lips brushed against hers. Then he removed his arm, took hold of her hand and began to walk towards the ornamental gardens.

'I don't want you to take chances,' she said vehemently. 'I don't want ever to see him again. I've felt guilty about taking his money when he was unconscious but now I realise that was stupid of me. He didn't deserve any consideration from me. If he finds me, though, he… he…' She stopped, unable to go on, and gazed up into Seb's frowning face. 'Maybe we could live in Liverpool! There must be plenty of motor engineering yards over there.'

She felt the sudden tension in him. 'I wouldn't be able to earn the kind of wage to support a wife if I left the Waters' and did what you suggest. It's not that I don't want to marry you, there's nothing I'd like more, but it would have to be-'

She felt a deep disappointment and interrupted him. 'You wouldn't even consider leaving the Waters', that's what you're going to say, isn't it?' Her tone was bitter.

He sighed. 'At the moment I have to stay. Ma doesn't even know this yet, but Mr Waters' business interests in the cotton trade are in trouble. A bloke he took on last year has lost him a helluva lot of money. He acted like a loony! Paying for cotton before it was actually loaded on the ship and checked out in America. The harvest was a failure, so there's no cotton and the bloke with the money has disappeared. Mr Waters is planning on getting rid of the house and staff in Liverpool except for me, and he and Miss Victoria are moving in with his mother. I can't leave him when he's said he doesn't want to lose me and is prepared to carry on paying me the same wage.'

Alice's spirits plummeted. Seb move over here! Once that would have made her happy but not now. 'Why didn't you tell him that wasn't what you wanted?'

He looked at her with disappointment in his eyes. 'I thought you'd be pleased at me coming to live over here. And I accepted his offer because it's what I want,' he stressed. 'I'm to be his right hand man, general dog's body, running him here and there, standing shoulder to shoulder with him at the cotton exchange and helping at the farm when necessary. I'd hate to spend all my time tinkering with motor engines. So once and for all will you forget that idea.'

He had silenced her.

'Don't look like that, Alice. It'll all work out for the best.' His voice had softened and his eyes pleaded with her.

She looked up at him, unable to understand his attitude. 'A general dog's body! What you mean is he'll carry on treating you like a lackey, a slave.' Her voice shook with the strength of her despair. 'Do this, do that, run here, run there. Are you sure you're not only prepared to put up with that because you're in love with Miss Victoria?'

He stared down at her as if she had run mad. 'That's a ridiculous thing to say. I love you.'

Only one thing would prove it to her at that moment. 'I want you to leave the Waters',' she said, struggling to keep her voice level. 'I don't want to live in that house with them and your mother. I want us to get away from Chester. I want us to have our own dear little place just the two of us – well, three, with Tilly.'

'Tilly?' He looked incredulous. 'You expect me to find a job in a trade I've no training for, a house and to support three of us. On what exactly?'

'I… I know it's a lot to ask but you could do it if you wanted.'

His eyes met hers and they were hard. 'I don't want, Alice. I want you but not on your terms.' He reached for her hands. 'You're overwrought, and I understand. But if you met Ma then maybe we could sort something out so we could be together and you'd no longer fear your father.'

She shook her head. Seeing her father had really shaken her. And, if she was honest, so had Sebastian's continued loyalty to the Waters' and refusal to do what she asked. She felt that he didn't love her enough and that she would always be playing second fiddle to Miss Victoria.

'Mr Waters and Miss Victoria are good people, Alice. As for Ma, she's wanted to meet you for some time,' he said earnestly. 'I know she can be a bit scary if you don't know her but all you've got to do is to stand up to her, be yourself; she'll respect you for it.'

Alice let his words sink in, but she knew her weaknesses. She wasn't very good at standing up to people, and what Hannah had said about his mother had left her feeling she would never be able to match up to Gabrielle. She sounded such a strong, colourful character who, if she wanted something, went all out to get it. She would insist on Alice becoming a Catholic and that would be a betrayal of all her mam had suffered for her faith.

Alice drew away from him. 'I'm going home. I think that perhaps we shouldn't see each other again,' she said in a small voice.

He looked dismayed. 'That's not funny, Alice.' He attempted to take her hand but she snatched it back.

'It wasn't meant to be funny. It's a goodbye.' She turned and walked away.

'Alice, don't be like this!' Seb followed her, seized her by the shoulder and forced her round to face him.

She would not look at him. 'It's over.' She wrenched herself free, then, knowing she was about to give way to tears, ran. But she need not have worried that he would try and stop her again. He let her go, although he did call after her, 'Remember, Alice, I didn't want it to be like this. I love you.'

She could only think that he didn't love her as much as he loved Miss Victoria Waters.

-

'That's the tenth time you've looked out of the window,' said Hannah, taking the flat iron off the coals and spitting on it. She rubbed the surface of the iron over an old rag before placing her work blouse on the folded towel on the table. She felt so sorry for Alice, despite believing she had gone about things the wrong way. Although, if she were honest with herself, she would want to believe that, if a man loved her as much as Sebastian said he loved Alice, then he would turn the world upside down if necessary to make her happy. But real life, more often than not, didn't live up to one's dreams.

'I think Seb's got the message now that you meant what you said. The only thing that would convince him that you didn't, would be for you to write to him, care of the Waters'.'

Alice swallowed the lump in her throat and let the curtain fall back into place. He had been round to the apartment twice while she was out. 'I can't do that. He cares about them too much. Besides, I'm not looking for him. I'm… just watching people. You want to see this woman's hat. I'd swear she has a whole bird on it. If I was to be watching out for anyone it's my father.'

Hannah almost dropped the iron. 'That's a stupid thing to do. The action might be party to bringing him here. Telepathy! That kind of thing! You're best not thinking about him at all. Or if you must, imagine him in a dark hole and shutting a manhole on him.'

'You've said that before,' said Alice crossly, fidgeting with a button on her frock. 'I know you're only trying to make me feel better but it's not helping.'

Hannah glanced in Kenny's direction and he shook his head. 'OK. You believe she saw him so that's good enough for me.'

'I keep wondering why did God let him survive when he's such a horrible man!' moaned Alice, now sprawled in a chair, reaching for the hat she was making. Life had lost its savour since she had finished with Sebastian and the hours seemed to drag by. 'I wonder how long Dad's been back,' she murmured, threading a needle with navy blue thread. 'At least he won't know I stole his money. He was out for the count and, if your mam couldn't remember his pushing her down the stairs, then he might have forgotten how he came to be in Scotland and on that train.'

'Let's hope you're right,' said Hannah, suddenly overwhelmed by a longing to see her own family. The other Sunday, she had acted on impulse and gone along to the mission hall where Joy, Grace and Freddie attended Sunday school, hoping to catch sight of them but they hadn't been there.

She was startled out of her reverie by Alice bursting out with the words, 'He might have guessed I took it! You said your mother did remember some things. If he remembers me being with him in the Isle of Man, he'll work it out. That's why he's back in Chester.' She dug the needle into the fabric with a trembling hand. 'He's big on *an eye for an eye and a tooth for a tooth*. His God is the one from the Old Testament.'

Hannah placed the flat iron on the fire again and went and placed an arm round her. 'He's not going to find you, so stop worrying. We're all going to be fine.' Alice turned and hugged her back, praying that she was right. 'What are we doing later? Nothing interesting I suppose.'

Kenny looked up from the boot he was mending, a couple of tacks in his mouth.

'Sorry.' She smiled wanly. 'I know I'm like a bear with a sore head these days.'

Hannah moved away and took up the iron again. 'How about you making us all a cup of tea?' she said with a cheerful smile.

Alice returned the smile. 'Right you are!' Hannah was often right. How was her father going to find her when he had no idea where she lived these days?

–

Mal stood in the doorway of the tobacconist shop out of the rain. The bowler sat awkwardly on his cropped hair but, so far, no one had recognised him. He had grown a beard and taken to wearing a pin-striped suit and a collar and tie every day of the week. Eudora Black had said it always amazed her how clothes could so change a body. She had sent a detective up north to find out what had happened to him. Once she had discovered he had survived the accident that had cracked his skull, broken his shoulder and wrist, she had reserved a seat on the next train to Glasgow. By then Mal had left the hospital but she had set her bloodhound on the trail, asking questions, until he got the right answers and found out where he was living. Then she'd done battle to get him away and now here he was back in Newtown.

He drew back into the shadows as Susannah Kirk came out of the fried fish shop. He had been watching her for a fortnight. Hannah was the one he had wanted to talk to but, so far, he hadn't seen sight or sound of her. He was convinced, though, that sooner or later one of the Kirks would lead him to his daughter. And when he found her… His face set like granite and he flexed his fingers. Alice had to learn not to break the rules; she had to honour and obey him if she wanted to live to a ripe old age. If it hadn't been for her friend visiting Eudora and being persuaded to spill the beans, he would never have worked it out that it was his daughter who had robbed him.

Now where was the bitch going? Back home by the look of it! Standing on the corner of the street, he listened to her calling to her two younger girls to stop Freddie splashing in a puddle. She called them twice but whatever she said the third time brought them running. They all went into the house, and, as it looked like the rain was set for the rest of the evening, Mal decided to call it a day.

–

Susannah placed her shopping basket on the table and eased her back, which still caused her discomfort at times. 'If you're to have your treat, then you've all to be good.'

'Can't we go with you tomorrow?' asked Grace, gazing up at her. 'I don't understand why we can't see our Hanny. I know I didn't want to go when she first went there but it's been ages and ages!'

'Shut up, Grace. Mother has her reasons,' said Joy, holding Freddie still on the dining chair by clamping her arms about his shoulders and pressing down. Bright as a button, he was now attending elementary school, but, once set free of its confines, it was as if he had ants in his pants and had to be permanently on the move until bedtime when he went out like a light. It was hard work, keeping an eye on him. But Susannah cared for him most of the time and, even when she went to Moreton, she seldom spent the night there. The times she did were generally after Dah came in late. Then they went for each other hammer and tongs, their arguments revolving around *that woman*. Once Jock had smashed all the crockery and then stormed out of the house. It had frightened Grace when he did that but Joy calmed her down, saying it was probably only a one-off as it would cost money to keep replacing the crockery.

'Aunt Joan can't cope with youngsters anymore,' said Susannah firmly, thinking she had enough of a job herself. She felt the flush warming her from head to toe. They were worth a sovereign, her mother used to say.

'Why doesn't Hanny ever come and see us?' It wasn't the first time Grace had asked that question, but she had yet to get an answer that satisfied.

'She doesn't love us anymore.' Bert's mournful voice from the doorway caused their heads to turn.

Susannah's face broke into a smile. 'Had a hard day, son?'

'No different than any other.' Bert kissed his mother's cheek. 'I'd love to see Hanny, too. Why don't we all go and visit her in Moreton?'

Susannah reproached him with a look, glancing up as she unpacked the shopping. He knew Hannah wasn't there. It was naughty of him to tease. 'You can't be that flush, son, to be paying out on rail fares.' Having served his time as an apprentice, he now earned a man's wage and had bought a bicycle several weeks ago.

'Perhaps not.' He shrugged.

'You could bicycle there,' said Grace, her eyes shining. 'You could give me a ride on the crossbar.'

'I could,' he said solemnly.

'Don't you dare!' cried Susannah, alarmed.

'And I could sit on the carrier above your back mudguard,' said Freddie, eyes bright, jigging about on the chair. 'I'd need a cushion.'

'Enough,' thundered their mother. 'None of you is having a ride on Bert's bike.'

Freddie piped up again. 'Bert, you could make me a little cart and I could sit in it, you could pull me along behind you.'

Susannah laughed. She couldn't help it. 'That's enough! I'm going to cook tea. Joy, you can peel and slice the potatoes for scollops to have with the chops. Grace, you set the table.'

'Can I go out and play again?' asked Freddie, his head on one side. He had recently had all his curls cut and was no longer the cherub Hannah would have remembered.

'No! You can wash your mucky knees, hands and face. Then recite your three times table to me while I fry the chops.'

Jock arrived home to find his family, all sitting round the table, waiting for him. 'You're late!' Susannah's face was unsmiling.

'We were just thinking of starting without you, Dah,' chimed Freddie.

Jock sprayed him with the raindrops from his cap. His youngest son giggled and shouted at him not to do it again.

'Get your coat off and wash your hands,' ordered Susannah.

'You don't have to tell me,' he murmured, catching her eye. 'I wasn't planning on sitting in my wet things or eating with mucky hands. If you thought about what you said more, we'd argue less.'

'It's not me that wants to argue,' she said sharply, folding her arms across her pinny.

'Then don't start,' he said gruffly, before going into the scullery. Bert smiled at his mother. The girls glanced in the direction of the open scullery door. Freddie picked up his fork and stabbed a scollop. His mother told him sharply to wait. She reached for the teapot, removing the hand-knitted tea-cosy, and began to fill Jock's cup, slopping the tea in the saucer. She knew it would annoy him, also that he would know she had done it deliberately. It was a petty thing to do, but she didn't care. He had gone out after tea yesterday evening and twice last week he had done the same. He hadn't given her any excuses for why he was late. She suspected he knew where that Taylor woman had moved to and was visiting her.

Jock kept his anger under control and, as soon as the meal was over, he donned his damp coat and cap and went out. He knew it would drive Susannah up the wall, but he no longer cared. He had done as she had asked and given up Nora ages ago, determined to be home nights, having let Hanny down. He had kept a good eye on his eldest son, and Bert didn't seem to be putting a foot wrong. Although the way he sucked up to his mother sometimes turned Jock's stomach.

Bert had sworn to his father, one night after one of those arguments with Sue, that he loved Hanny, that he loved all his family. That he hated listening to his parents arguing. Jock had heard that about loving all his family before, but now he prayed that Bert had learnt his lesson, and that he had got it into his thick skull that the love he felt for his sisters, meant *Hands off! That any decent bloke never forced a woman against her will. Part of being a brother was to protect his sisters from the kind of man who did what he'd done to Hanny.* He prayed again that his words had gone in. Jock wanted Hanny back, living under his roof. It wasn't right that she had to stay away because of Bert. A neighbour had let drop that he had seen Hanny with Kenny and Alice in New Brighton. He had wondered how she had met them again and whether they now lived in the seaside resort. Anyway, he had started to go there, walking along the Egg and Ham Parade and its back streets, hoping to spot his daughter. So far he'd had no luck.

That evening was no different.

In bed that night he got the customary cold shoulder from his wife. He could have told her the truth but she never mentioned Hanny to him, keeping up this pretence that she was living with Joan. It appeared to him that she no longer cared about her daughter. It was a strain doing without his marital rights but he looked upon it as punishment for what he had allowed to happen to his daughter. When he awoke, it came as no surprise to discover that Susannah had already left the house to visit her cousin.

'Why won't she take us with her, Dah?' Grace was bold enough to ask, as he ate the salt fish Joy had boiled up for him. 'It would have been lovely having a day out today.' She glanced out the kitchen window. Yesterday's rain had cleared overnight and the sun was shining.

Bert glanced at Jock. 'You doing anything today, Dah?'

'Maybe.' He pushed his plate aside and getting up, left the kitchen.

'Are you doing anything, Bert?' asked Grace, sitting down in her father's place. She reached for a slice of bread and mopped up melted butter and tiny morsels of fish.

'I thought I'd go out on the bike.'

'To Moreton? Take me with you!' said Grace, her tone eager.

'You know what Mother would say to that,' said Joy, frowning at her.

'Bert would look after me, wouldn't you, Bert?' Grace looked at her brother.

He smiled, but made no reply.

Joy cleared the table and took the crockery into the scullery. Freddie followed her out. 'Maybe Dah would take us somewhere?'

She smiled down at him. 'There's no harm in asking.'

Freddie left her and ran upstairs. She filled the kettle to wash the dishes, then put it on the fire, and went in search of her father and younger brother.

They were in her parents' bedroom. Jock had just finished knotting his tie, and reached for his Sunday suit jacket.

'He's going to New Brighton,' Freddie informed her, sitting cross-legged on his mother's pillow.

Suddenly frightened, Joy sank onto the bed. What was he doing going to New Brighton all spruced up? Could he be meeting that woman?

'Take us with you, Dah?' she said rapidly. 'It'll be nicer for you if you have us with you.'

'I've already asked him,' said Freddie.

Jock turned towards his middle daughter. 'I said "Aye!" lass. So yer'd better get yerself ready. Go tell Grace, as well.'

Delight flooded Joy's face. She kissed her hand and blew the kiss towards him. Then she hurried downstairs. The kettle was steaming but there was no sign of Grace or Bert in the kitchen. Neither were they in the scullery or parlour. She called down the yard but got no answer. She ran to the lavatory just to make sure there was no one there. Then she noticed Bert's bicycle was missing, and her heart sank. She went back inside.

Jock had removed the kettle from the fire to the hob. 'She's gone out for a ride on Bert's bicycle,' she said, her worried chubby face turned up to her dah's. 'Will we go without her? I'd rather not but... but if she's gone there's nothing we can do about it, is there, Dah?'

Jock thought for a moment. Out in the fresh air, amongst people, his youngest daughter should be safe with her elder brother. 'We'll wait for half an hour, and if they haven't turned up by then, we'll go.'

'Promise,' said Freddie, swinging on his father's hand.

Jock promised.

The half hour passed quickly and was spent by Joy in changing into her Sunday best; a pink frock with a black flounce at the hem and black puffed sleeves. She tried not to worry about Grace, deciding that her father would have gone to look for them if he was worried. When Bert and Grace still hadn't returned, Joy said with a sigh, 'They must have gone to Moreton, Dah. They both said they wanted to go and see Hanny.' Jock decided there was nothing he could do in the circumstances and wondered what Sue would tell Grace about Hanny when she got there, but that was up to his wife. He would tell Joy a watered down version of the truth, not mentioning Bert's name. She was no longer a child and it was time Sue told both girls a few facts of life and warned them that there were men in this world who would try and take advantage of their innocence.

Chapter Eighteen

'*Daisy, Daisy, give me your answer do! I'm half-crazy all for the love of you…!*' sang Bert, peddling vigorously along the towpath of the Shropshire Union Canal.

The top of Grace's head brushed his chin as she turned her head to gaze at a flotilla of ducks swimming by. 'Aren't they sweet, Bert!'

'Lovely! Just like you.' He dropped a hasty kiss on her hair. Oh, how he adored his sisters. There was nothing sinful about what he felt for them and it was a pity that Hanny hadn't understood that. Grace, however, was a different creature altogether. She worshipped him and he felt certain would do anything to please him. Not that he would go as far as he had with Hanny or that stupid bitch, Agnes. The last thing he wanted was to get Grace into trouble. Still, a nice, friendly little cuddle wouldn't do any harm. He knew a lovely little dell further on a bit but they hadn't come to it yet. He resumed singing, '*But you'll look sweet upon the seat of a bicycle made for two!*' It was a glorious morning. After the rain everything smelt so fresh. The meadowsweet bloomed, there were poppies in the corn, and it wouldn't be long before the blackberries would be ripe for picking. He loved his mother's blackberry and apple pie with hot, thick custard. They passed a barge heading in the direction of Ellesmere Port and Grace waved to the children sitting on the roof of the cabin.

'This is a nicer way to Moreton than on the train,' she said ten minutes later. There were fields on either side of the canal. She leaned against him, gripping his jacket with one hand and the crossbar with the other.

'We're not going to Moreton.' Bert resumed humming the song. She twisted her head, looking up into his face. 'Keep still! You'll have us over,' he warned.

'What about seeing Hanny?'

'Hanny's not in Moreton.'

She shifted slightly and looked up at him again. 'B-but she has to be! Mother said she's there.'

'Keep still, Gracie. That's just a story Mother put about for the neighbours. Hanny did a naughty thing and ran away.'

'What naughty thing?' The wheels hissed through a muddy patch.

Bert did not answer immediately. Ahead, he could see a lad leading a horse towing a barge.

'Bert, what naughty thing?'

He frowned, remembering how he had rescued Hanny from that little fat boss of hers when she worked in the bakery. He had wanted to hit him for daring to touch his sister. But she hadn't been a bit grateful for his protection, so why did he still want her?

'Bert, answer me!'

'It's not for your ears.'

Her young, innocent, eager-to-appear-grown-up face gazed up into his. 'I'm not too young, Bert. Honest!' She tugged on his sleeve.

'Don't do that!' The bicycle wobbled and he struggled to keep it upright. He seemed to be succeeding, when suddenly the front wheel hit another patch of mud, skidded, and left the path. Frantically he tried to back-pedal, but his left foot slipped off the pedal. He heard Grace scream as the bicycle left the bank. She reached out for him but missed and fell into the water. He scrabbled wildly to free his legs, but went under, still with a leg caught up in the front wheel. He hit the bottom but managed to free his leg. Thank God Dah had taught him to swim at an early age, but where was Grace? She couldn't swim. He headed for the surface, lungs bursting, looked around for his youngest sister on the way but the water was too murky to see much. He only allowed time to take a lungful of air, was barely aware of someone shouting, before diving under the water again, knowing he had to carry on trying to find her.

There was weed, but not lots of it because the barge traffic ensured it never had a chance to grow out of control. He lost all sense of direction, couldn't see her, his lungs were bursting, and he resurfaced again. Only to find himself immediately berated by the bargee in the boat he had seen ahead.

'You stupid bloody fool! The towpath's not the place for them bloody bi-cycle machines.'

'My sister!' gasped Bert, aware that the lad who had been leading the horse was pulling off his boots. He dived into the water a few seconds before Bert plunged beneath the surface again. His heart was hammering with terror. He was beginning to believe that he wasn't going to find Gracie in time to save her.

It was the lad who brought Grace to the surface. The man in the barge helped lift her out the water. Bert dragged himself onto the bank and ran towards where she lay. He tried frantically to save her, pushing down on her chest in an attempt to force the water out of her lungs. Again and again he tried, but it was too late. The man and boy dragged him off her and Bert collapsed on the bank weeping. How the hell was he going to tell Mother? How the bloody hell was he going to get out of this?

The man took pity on him and helped him aboard his barge. His wife placed a blanket about Bert's shoulders, and gave one to her son. Then she handed tin mugs of hot sweet tea to both. Bert shivered and sobbed as he cradled the mug between his hands, his teeth chattering against its rim.

'Get a hold on yourself, man,' rasped the bargee. His weather-beaten face was tight with disapproval. 'Tell us where you've come from and maybe we can take you and the little girl's body as close to your home as we can.'

Bert managed to stammer out that he lived close to Egerton Street, which was near the canal in Chester. The man nodded and left him sitting on a wooden bench while he went and brought Grace's body aboard. Bert wept all the more when he looked upon her pale dead features. He was worried sick wondering whether his Mother would be able to bear seeing his poor, poor sister like this or whether it would send her completely out of her mind. The woman covered Grace's face with a lace doily and made another mug of tea for Bert.

By the time the barge reached the bottom of Egerton Street, Bert had barely managed to pull himself together. It was a struggle to stand and to take the weight of his dead sister's body in his arms. He forced himself to climb out of the barge, thank the man, wife and son for their help, and to take one step at a time in the direction of home. It was a good ten minutes walk away and he was aware of passers-by staring at him and a neighbour speaking to him, but he couldn't respond.

When he arrived at the house there was no one there. He couldn't make sense of why no one answered, that only his voice echoed back at him when he called out for his dah, Joy and Freddie. He sat down on the sofa in his damp clothes, still clutching Grace's body against him. He felt exhausted, as if the river had stolen his life, too. He closed his eyes and was still in that position when his mother came home.

As soon as Susannah saw her eldest son sitting with her youngest daughter on his lap and the pool of water on the linoleum, she sank onto her knees; her heart felt as if caught in a vice. What had happened? She lifted Grace's head, but within seconds knew her youngest daughter was dead. From somewhere, she heard a woman wailing, a deep, keening cry.

Bert's eyes opened. 'Mother!' His eyes filled with tears, and he reached out a hand to her. She took it, clinging to his fingers as if he had offered her a lifeline.

She caught her breath on a sob. 'What happened?'

He couldn't think straight enough to come up with a lie. 'We went into the canal. I-I tried to save her.'

'What d'you mean you went into the canal?'

'I-I was cycling. She started wriggling. We hit a patch of mud and skidded.'

Susannah's eyes bored into his. 'You took her out on that bicycle when I told you not to?'

He nodded miserably.

She screamed and scrambled to her feet. Then she hit him with her handbag, and went on hitting him until blood ran from his cheek where the metal clasp cut into the flesh. He made no move to defend himself, even when she threw the handbag aside, boxed his ears and kicked him in the shins. Then suddenly she stopped, knelt and, putting her arms about her dead daughter, wept.

By the time Jock arrived home, carrying a sleepy Freddie with a yawning Joy trudging beside him, the curtains were drawn. Grace's body had been stripped of its sodden clothing. She had been washed from head to toe and clad in her best frock. Hearing the sound of the key being dragged through the letterbox Susannah fled out of the room.

Jock had barely set foot inside the house when she threw herself at him. He was so taken-aback that he nearly dropped Freddie. 'What's up?'

Her arms tightened about him and her younger son, and she pressed her head against that part of Jock's chest she could reach. Bert appeared in the kitchen doorway. His father stared at him above Susannah's head. He had never seen his eldest son look so dreadful. His face was bruised and cut and he looked as if he had been crying. His heart sank.

'What is it?' Joy brushed past her parents and went to Bert. 'You tell us?' she demanded.

Bert managed to dredge up the words from deep inside him. 'Grace is dead.'

'I don't believe it!' She whirled and stared at her mother. 'It's not true!' Her voice cracked.

Susanna, lifted her head and gazed up into her husband's stricken face. 'It's true,' she said with only a breath of sound. 'It's true.'

-

That night they lay in each other's arms, knowing no one else but the other could share the depth of their grief. Their child was dead; she had been difficult, an unwilling helper, not the most favoured of their children. But that did not lessen their sadness, only deepened it. The opportunity to show their daughter that she had still been precious to them would never occur again. What had divided them no longer seemed of any importance in comparison with the loss of their youngest daughter.

'We have to let Hanny know,' said Susannah agitatedly. 'I need Hanny.'

'I've been searching for her. I'd heard she'd been seen in New Brighton, so I went looking for her,' he said wearily.

Susannah lifted her head from his shoulder and tried to see his face. 'Why didn't you tell me?'

'I didn't think you wanted her home – but I did.'

'I want her home.' And, as she repeated the words, her voice broke and she wept again.

Jock nursed her in his arms. 'Then let's have another think about who might be able to help us find her.'

She looks like an ol' crow dressed all in black, thought Mal, as he stepped out of the shop doorway and followed Susannah down Francis Street. She walked slowly as if in a dream, along Crewe Street and into Egerton Street. She crossed the canal and entered Seller Street. When she came to a house and knocked on the door, he crossed to the other side of the street, so he could have a better view of who answered her knock. He had hopes of it being Hannah or his daughter, but when the door opened it was a young woman, who was a stranger to him. She had a little girl with ginger curls in her arms. He caught the murmur of their voices and wished he could hear what they were saying because, whatever Susannah had said, it had plainly upset the younger woman. The next moment the door closed and he had to wait for a while before Susannah came out and then he followed her home. Once back in the house the door remained firmly shut. Mal decided to call it a day and return to Mrs Black's house the other side of the river; the ground floor of the house was still occupied by the sisters who taught music but he avoided them.

–

'Anything?' Jock pushed himself up out of the chair and looked at his wife as she entered the kitchen.

'Dolly says she's living with Kenny and Alice but not in New Brighton; they're here, in Chester. They visit regularly to see Florrie's little girl; I thought she was Dolly's.' Susannah's eyes filled with tears. 'Why is it my daughter feels she has to keep her whereabouts a secret from me? Why didn't she tell me that Florrie's baby was alive?'

'She kept it a secret from me, too. Did Dolly say anything else?'

'Alice and Kenny haven't been sticking to any one time of the week – so she can't say when they'll come for definite.' Susannah removed her black lace mittens and he helped her into the chair he had vacated.

Jock was worried as he knelt on the rug and rubbed his wife's hands. Despite the time of year, she never seemed to get warm since Grace had died. 'Let's hope Alice comes tomorrow or Hanny'll miss the funeral.'

'It might never have happened if I hadn't told lies about her staying with Joan.' Susannah took out one of the handkerchiefs Joy had made and dabbed her eyes.

'There, Sue, don't take on so.' He put his arms round her and held her. 'Bert's to blame. If it wasn't so obvious he's suffering I'd have him out the house.'

She was silent, pressing the handkerchief to her lips. 'It was an accident!' She had repeated those words at least ten times since Bert had broken the news to her.

'Aye.' Jock doubted he would ever be able to tell his wife what her precious son had done to Hanny. It might just kill her. His chest ached with grief. Yet he had to take his share of the blame. If he had not gone with Nora, then maybe Bert wouldn't have done what he did, and they wouldn't be living through such a sad time.

Bert came into the kitchen half an hour later and asked if Hanny was coming home. They had to tell him they didn't know but that she was staying with Kenny and Alice. For an instant, the strain vanished from his face to be replaced by a flicker of anger, but he kept it under control, and said that he was glad Hannah had been traced. They did not offer him any comfort and after his supper he went out.

–

Alice glanced over her shoulder. Why was it she felt as if she was being watched? Her green eyes scanned Abbey Square with its Georgian houses but she could see no suspicious characters or curtains moving at windows. It was not the first time she had felt that she was being followed lately, but Hannah had said it was her imagination playing tricks on her because her father was so much on her mind.

She tried to relax, but that was extra difficult since hearing the sad news about Grace, and also because Mrs Kirk had decided to accompany her back to the apartment. Alice was worried about how Hannah would react to her mother's sudden appearance and the news about Grace. She glanced at Susannah, who was pushing the pram with the three-year-old Tilly inside. Freddie had come with them as well and, despite his six years, had been ordered to sit at the foot of the pram by his mother. With a firm grip on the handle, she was now forging along Northgate Street like a ship heading for home port.

Almost at the shop now Alice wished Hannah and her mother were being reunited under different circumstances. It was going to be a very emotional meeting and she wished her mam were there to help her say and do the right thing. Still, she would just have to do her best. Make lots of hot sweet tea and have a handkerchief handy.

–

Kenny stood near the window gazing at Hannah's tear-stained face, wishing he could do something for her. Freddie sat between her and his mother. Tilly was asleep in the pram at the foot of the stairs. His heart was heavy, not only with sadness for the dead Grace but also because he guessed that Hannah would probably decide to go home with her mother. Susannah had given him such a cold look; he knew she was blaming him for keeping her daughter from her. Hannah had wept on the older woman's shoulder, and she had tried to comfort her but Hannah had been inconsolable, blaming herself for not being around to keep an eye on her sister. Now she had control of herself and was talking to Freddie as if all was right with their world instead of it having been torn apart once more. Kenny admired her courage. He felt at a loss, wishing he could take on her pain.

He gazed out of the window and across the road, thinking about how women were so much better than men at doing and saying the right thing at such times. His gaze wandered idly over the scene below. A man in a bowler stood in a doorway of the ironmonger's. A girl was skipping with a rope and a boy was bowling a hoop. A toddler sat on the kerb with a kitten on her knee. Somewhere a street organ was playing and there must be a couple of women standing outside the shop because he could hear them talking. Kenny's eyes wandered back to the man in the bowler and pinstriped suit. That was some ginger beard he had! He looked like he was talking to himself because his lips were moving and then he removed the bowler and rubbed the back of his neck, and then his eye. Kenny frowned. There was something familiar in the way he performed the act.

Suddenly the man looked up. Kenny's stomach clenched into a knot and he hurriedly drew back from the window. It couldn't be him! Yet the way he had rubbed his eye and the colour of his hair and beard caused Kenny to take another look. Cautiously he peered out of the window and, this time, there was no doubt in his mind. The man was crossing the road and the way he walked was enough for Kenny. How the hell had he found them? Kenny's mind worked swiftly despite his fear. His father must have been watching the Kirks' house and followed Mrs Kirk. Kenny knew he had to get Alice out of the building without alarming her.

'I want the lav, please!' said Freddie startling Kenny.

He glanced round and saw the boy clutching his crotch.

'I'll show you where it is,' said Hannah, rising to her feet and leading the way out of the room. Kenny slipped out after them. He found the lavatory door closed and Hannah standing outside. She attempted a smile. 'What is it, Kenny?'

He reached into his jacket pocket for his notebook and pencil but they were not there. At that moment he heard footsteps in the shop. He froze.

The lavatory door opened and Freddie stood in the opening. Kenny acted on instinct. Swiftly he pushed him back inside along with Hannah. He closed the door, keeping hold of the handle.

'Kenny, what the hell are you playing at? Let us out of here!' cried Hannah, thumping on the door.

He thought frantically, opened his mouth but at first no sound came out, despite his having practiced asking her to marry him when alone up on the cart. Then, as if a dam had been breached, the words came. 'D-D-Dad's d-downstairs!' His throat felt strange and he coughed to try and clear it before adding, 'A-A-Alice – an-and your m-m-mother must have l-l-left the shop door open.' His voice sounded croaky but deep, its resonance was something he had not been expecting.

Inside the lavatory Hannah almost fell over with shock. Fortunately she had hold of the doorknob. 'Kenny! You – was it you who spoke?'

He nodded, swallowed. 'You've got to… to get Tilly out of here.'

Hannah didn't know what to think or to say. Kenny speaking out of the blue, on top of the shock of her mother's appearance and sister's death, was all too much and, for a moment, she thought she must have imagined it. 'Could you say all that again?' she asked. 'It really was you that spoke?'

'Yes! But n-no time. Got to hurry.'

She could only think of one thing to say after that. 'It's a miracle!'

He shook his head as if to empty it. 'No! I'm not d-dumb! I was… just scared to open my mouth. But-but we've got to hurry.' He turned the handle and pushed the door open. It would have hit Hannah in the face if she had not moved back in time.

She grabbed Freddie by the arm and, for a moment, could only stare at Kenny. 'You've never been dumb?'

He eased his throat. Hell, it ached. Muscles, long unused, were already reacting to the unaccustomed movement. 'No! I'd like you to t-take Alice with you as well – bu-but I don't think there's time.' He could tell from Hannah's expression that she was not only shocked, but also struggling with some other emotion. He was aware of how strange it felt talking to her instead of considering every word before he wrote it down. If he'd thought first, not been in such a panic, then he would have said things differently.

Hannah made no move to go anywhere. She was too shocked and besides she had a bone to pick with him. 'How could you keep such a momentous thing from me?' she cried, thumping him in the chest. 'I thought we were close. I believed I really meant something to you.'

'Of-of course you do!' He staggered back. 'B-But we've no time to talk now!' He drew away from the banister rail and seized her arm. 'You've got to get Tilly out of here and go for help.'

Angry, Hannah wrenched herself free. She was tired of running, tired of being a victim. She dug in her heels. 'Like hell I will! My sister's dead and my mother needs me here.'

'Sorry!' He looked anguished. 'B-but you can't stay. Dad's coming! Just get going!' He forced her towards the stairs.

She refused to go down, clung with one hand to the knob on the banister. 'You do something, Kenny. Act like a man for once.'

Kenny's face paled and he felt icy cold. What he feared would happen was happening. Hannah despised him, thought him a coward. He heard the sound of the door that shut off the apartment from the shop open, and glanced over the banister. His heart seemed to stop as he saw his father standing next to the pram.

Kenny did not waste a second. He grabbed Hannah's wrist and seized the openmouthed Freddie and thrust them back inside the lavatory and closed the door. 'Dad's coming. Stay there until he's passed. I'll look after Alice and your mother!' He ran along the landing.

There was a shout from below but he did not stop, aware of the thudding of boots on the stairs. He burst into the sitting room. Alice and Mrs Kirk looked at him in surprise.

'What is it?' asked Alice. 'Where's Hanny and Freddie?'

Kenny did not waste time explaining but closed the door and looked wildly about him for something to put against it, picked up a chair and jammed it beneath the handle.

'Kenny, what's happening?' said Alice, suddenly frightened, having heard Hannah and a man's voice on the landing.

A fist slammed into the door and her father said, 'I know you're bloody in there, the pair of ye. I'm going to have your guts for garters!'

Alice almost died on the spot.

–

Hearing Mal's voice, Hannah wasted no time, but tiptoed out of the lavatory with a struggling Freddie in her arms, a hand over his mouth. She crept down the stairs, her heart hammering in her breast, still trying to come to terms with the shocks of that day. She told him to get into the pram, helped him as he put his foot on one of the wheels, and with a push up on his bottom he fell into the pram. Tilly woke and let out a cry. Hannah froze with fear; had Mal heard? She was almost glad to hear a crash, which she guessed was him getting to work on the living room door. For a moment she hesitated, then knew there was nothing she could do for any of them in the room upstairs. She had to get help. She hadn't been fair to Kenny calling him a coward, knowing what a brute his father was, but she was hurt and angry. He had deceived her and she was having difficulty coming to terms with that. She had believed she had known him through and through but she had been mistaken.

Trying to keep calm, she manoeuvred the pram through the door and between the furniture in the shop. Mal had left the shop door open and two women were having a nose inside. 'Out the way!' she cried. They pressed themselves against the door and Hannah was out and running, ordering Freddie to hold tight.

–

Upstairs, the door shook as Mal put his shoulder to it once more; already the wooden frame had splintered. Kenny had fetched another chair and placed that against the door but knew the chairs wouldn't keep his father out for long. He turned to Alice and Susannah. Both were white to the lips and clinging to each other.

'I knew it. I knew he'd find us,' said Alice, trembling all over.

Kenny tried to speak, to say that with the racket Mal was making someone was bound to hear and come and see what was going on. He hoped Hannah had done what he asked. Again he tried to voice the words but no words came out. Panic seized him and, for a moment, he could not move. He managed to pull himself together and, signalling to Alice, pointed at the sideboard.

She did not move and he knew why and went over to her. He seized her arm and dragged her towards the sideboard. Placing her hands at one end, he got the other and heaved the piece of furniture into the air.

Susannah watched them, trembling with fear. Somehow Mal's voice had roused emotions inside her that shook her to the depths of her being. This man was dangerous! He was responsible for Florrie's death and causing herself such injuries that her marriage had almost been destroyed. Her nerves were in shreds.

There came the sound of splintering wood again and Mal's hand appeared. She recognised the wiry red hairs on that hand and, suddenly, the sight was enough to send her flying to Alice's side; panic gave them strength. They slammed the sideboard against the door just in time. Mal yelped with pain as his fingers got caught but managed to wrench them free. He let out a stream of bad language.

'That's lovely language that is! My friend's gone to get the bobby.' The Welsh voice took them by surprise.

Mal recovered first and stared at the outraged figure in a pinny, recognising her as one of the women who'd been talking in the street. 'Shut yer bleedin' mouth!' He hit her.

Alice shrieked. 'Go away, missus! He'll kill you if you don't!' She wondered where Hannah and Freddie were? Hoped they had got away with Tilly.

Mal snarled, 'I'll kill yer, girl, when I get me hands on yer.' Another crash as his shoulder hit the door. The sideboard shifted. Kenny threw himself against it. Alice could only watch as if in a trance, convinced he was wasting his time. Hannah's mother appeared to have given up too. She had gone over to the window and was staring out, her shoulders shaking as if she was crying. Alice could hear her father's heavy breathing as he collected himself once more. More wood split. The girl stared as blunt fingers snaked round the door and gripped the edge; he pushed with his shoulder at the same time. She could see his eyes through the widening gap between the door and the doorjamb and the expression in them made her blood freeze.

'I'll beat the living daylights out of ye for putting me to all this trouble, girl! Yer effin' little thief!' he yelled.

Kenny had moved to the fireplace and picked up the poker. She wanted to laugh and cry at the same time because it was shaking in his hand. Their father would have it from him in no time but at least her halfbrother was no longer shivering in a corner. Alice considered taking a knife from the cutlery drawer but feared her father would wrench it from her hand and turn it on her. No! She could take a beating. Her mother had done so and survived dozens of times. She stood as still as a statue, her muscles aching with tension, watching the sideboard move. The gap was growing, another two inches and he would be inside the room. The sideboard creaked as he pushed it out of the way and slid round it, breathing heavily.

Kenny stepped in front of Alice. His mouth was dry, he desperately needed a drink but there was no time for that. He must not allow terror to paralyse him. He gripped the poker with both hands and, from somewhere deep inside him, came a yell as he went for his father. If the poker had found its target it would have knocked Mal out but he brought up his arm and deflected the blow. Kenny stepped back hastily to give himself the space to raise the poker again but his father seized the end of it. They struggled for possession, but Kenny was not watching Mal's other hand, and before he could get out of the way, Mal's fist landed such a blow on the side of his head that the poker slipped through his fingers as he was sent halfway across the room. He hit the wall and slumped to the floor.

Alice, who felt strangely calm now her worst terror was about to be realised, knew it was going to be as bad as she feared. She could see the madness in her father's eyes. As his fist came towards her, she turned her head, otherwise the blow would have broken her nose. Instead his fist crunched into her jaw and she fell senseless to the floor.

Mal was furious with himself. He wanted his daughter to feel every blow. It had hurt him that she could steal from him and leave him for dead. She had to be punished for making him feel that enormous ache inside his heart. He wanted her to remember how it felt when he hit her, a constant reminder never to betray him again. He kicked her limp body but it gave him no pleasure. Even so, in his frustration, he kicked at her prone figure.

'What the hell d'you think you're doing?'

Mal had been too absorbed to hear the noise at the door but when he saw the young bobby he was relieved, knowing he still had plenty of strength to see this one off. 'Keep out of it and yer won't get hurt, laddie,' he growled.

The policeman went for him with his truncheon but Mal grabbed hold of it. They wrestled and Mal won. He hit the bobby behind the ear with his own weapon and he went down like a ninepin. A bellow that sounded like an angry bull caused Mal to turn. Another copper, older and thickset, was edging his way into the room.

Kenny came to, his ears were ringing and he felt dizzy but he managed to stagger to his feet and go over to Alice. She was still out for the count. He put his arms round her, aware that Hannah's mother was screaming. He ignored her, unable to take his eyes from the struggle going on in front of him.

It seemed to go on forever, both men wielding batons as if they were swords. The thought that they wouldn't have any furniture left flittered incongruously across Kenny's mind, as chairs were sent crashing to the floor. He wanted to believe his father could be defeated, but at the moment he seemed to have the upper hand. Suddenly, he was aware of Alice stirring in his arms. Then, completely unexpectedly, Bert Kirk entered the room and thrust himself between the policeman and Mal.

'I've been waiting a long time for this,' said Bert, and thumped Mal in the chest. The older man staggered but, still game, he came roaring back. However Bert was young, strong and fresh; his fists rat-tatted on Mal's chest, arms, head and stomach. With a left to the older man's jaw he sent Mal crashing to the floor.

The older policeman stared down at him, and gave a lop-sided smile that showed a loose tooth. Then he stumbled over to Bert and thrust out his hand, thanking him for his timely assistance. Kenny swore under his breath.

'Anytime!' said Bert, blowing on his grazed knuckles and thrusting out his chest.

Five minutes later Mal was handcuffed and dragged to his feet. The older policeman said he would call the horse ambulance for the still unconscious man on the floor and went out with Mal.

To Alice, who had regained consciousness just in time to see Bert knock her father to the ground, Bert was a hero. She could not take her eyes from him, gazing at him with admiration. She tried to voice her gratitude but could only mumble indistinctly.

'You OK, Alice?' he said, coming over to her. 'No, you're not, are you, girl?' He ignored Kenny as he touched her jaw with gentle fingers. She winced, tried to smile, but that was beyond her, too. 'We'll talk later,' he said. He walked over to his mother, but Susannah was having no truck with him; she averted her eyes from his face and, brushing past him, went over to the young bobby.

Kenny left Alice to have a closer look at the policeman. He knelt down the other side of him, opposite Susannah, who was feeling for his pulse with a trembling hand. 'He's still alive, thank God,' she said. Then seemed to notice it was Kenny a couple of feet away from her. 'You! You ruined my daughter. You got her into trouble, you kept her from me. If you hadn't then Grace might still be alive. Don't you ever let me see your face round at my house near my girl in the future!'

Kenny stared at her flushed, wild-eyed face, and was about to deny the truth of her accusations. Then he heard Bert laugh. 'That's right, Mother! You tell him. Why should I be the only one in your black books.'

Kenny got up, stared at him with loathing.

Then he glanced at Alice, who was looking at him as if she had never seen him before, staring as if she believed what Susannah had just said. He was stunned, his head was throbbing. He needed fresh air and time to think. He blundered out of the room.

Kenny had only been gone ten minutes or so when Jock and Hannah turned up, having left Freddie and Tilly with Joy. She was amazed to see Bert there, sitting next to Alice. Susannah went straight into Jock's arms, babbling out what had happened. Hannah sat the other side of Alice, reaching out a hand to her and holding it tightly. She did not look at her brother, but glanced round for Kenny, only to see that he was not there.

'Where's Kenny?' she demanded.

'Gone! Thank God,' said Bert, his eyes running greedily over her. 'What a coward! I don't know what you ever got yourself involved with that dummy for.'

'He's not a dummy! Kenny's twice the man you are.' Before she could say anything more, she was interrupted.

Susannah said, 'I don't want you having anything to do with him, Hanny. You've got to put the past behind you and start again. I need you!' She held out a hand to her eldest daughter.

With a sinking feeling in the pit of her stomach, Hannah reluctantly left Alice's side and went over to her mother. She did not know why her mother should have taken against Kenny and could only hope that she would soon see him again.

Chapter Nineteen

Alice winced beneath the doctor's fingers and tried to pull back. He straightened. 'I can't really swear to it because of the swelling but it is my belief your jaw is cracked. I recommend a liquid diet and that you talk as little as possible the next few weeks, Miss Moran.' He pursed his lips. 'I suppose I could send you to have one of those new-fangled X-ray photographs taken just to be sure.' His eyes brightened.

Bert noticed the alarmed expression in Alice's eyes, such lovely bottle-green eyes, and smiled faintly but then almost immediately assumed a protective attitude. 'I think she'd rather not, doctor,' he said firmly. 'We'll take your word for it.' He wondered whether the experimental machine could have done something to his mother's brain but it was too late to worry about that now. He felt bereft every time he thought of her attitude towards him. 'Could you give her something for the pain?'

The doctor's black eyebrows bristled. 'If you had the money I could prescribe laudanum but, as you haven't, I can only say no.'

Bert would have liked to say *I have the money* but all his cash had been spent purchasing the bicycle that now lay at the bottom of the Shropshire Union Canal and he felt angry about that. If only Grace had done as he said and kept still, she wouldn't be dead.

'If Miss Moran does what I say then, hopefully, she will have no lasting ill effects.' The doctor's smile was austere as he dried his hands. 'Witch hazel on the bruising should help.' He turned to the nurse. 'Tie up her jaw. It'll encourage her to keep her mouth shut. Just take sixpence fee.' He placed the towel over the rail, adjusted his cuffs, and indicated they could leave.

Alice wanted to thank Bert for being so kind as to accompany her to the infirmary, but she could not even smile. She thought of Hannah, whose attention had naturally been more for her mother. As for Kenny, she had no idea where he was, and was worried because he'd sustained a heavy blow to the head. Having given credence to Hannah's story of the stranger who had raped her at New Year, Alice was still shocked by the idea that Kenny was to blame for her condition. If that was the case, then it made sense for Hanny to have come running to them. What she couldn't understand was why he hadn't offered to marry her? It was obvious that he loved her, and she herself knew how easy it was to get carried away if you loved someone. She was also upset that Hanny had lied to her, instead of confiding in her. There was something else at the back of her mind, but she could not remember what it was. Nothing seemed to make sense to her, anymore, and now she was in so much pain that it made her feel dizzy. She was glad to lean on Bert's arm.

As they walked back to the apartment, he explained how he had managed to get there before Jock. 'I knew Mother wanted to see Hanny, so I've been following her about. I was worried in case things got out of hand when the pair of them met. So when she wasn't at home I went to that old woman's house – Granny Popo?' Alice nodded, then winced. He squeezed her hand sympathetically. 'You'd already left a good half an hour before. Fortunately you remembered to give her your address in case Dah went round there looking for Mother. So I just headed for your place.' He smiled down at her. 'A good job, too, as it happens.' Alice could not have agreed more.

When they arrived back at the shop, to her dismay, she found the owner waiting in his shirtsleeves with her clothing and bedding in a pillowcase and her hat-making equipment in a cardboard box.

He did not mince words. 'You're out! I'm sorry for what's happened to you, Miss Moran, but I can't tolerate what went on here a few hours ago. The worst of it is that the shop door was left open for all and sundry to come in and help themselves. Several items are missing.'

'That's wicked in the circumstances,' said Bert, frowning. 'Just look at Miss Moran's face! And now you're going to kick her out. You ought to be ashamed of yourself.'

The man drew himself up to his full height of five foot six inches and said coldly, 'What's it to do with you, young man? She wants to be glad I'm not demanding money for the things that have been taken but I will keep the furniture that's still in one piece as payment.'

Bert was about to say something else but Alice tugged on his arm and shook her head. 'My brother?' she managed to croak.

'I've no idea,' said her ex-landlord, allowing himself a pitying smile. 'Perhaps you can take his things also.'

Bert was pleased. A plan had been forming in his mind and it would be so much easier to carry it through if the dummy was not around.

The man held the door wide. 'Good day, Miss Moran! I do hope you get better soon.' He inclined his head.

Alice thought he could keep his good wishes. After the way they'd looked after the shop, she expected more consideration. Still, at the moment, her concern was for Kenny, as well as herself. It was possible that he had gone to Granny Popo's or maybe Mr Bushell's house. She would have to go and see but did not want to go alone; her nerves were still in a state. But at least she was rid of her father at last. They'd put him away for a long time for what he did to that policeman. The important thing now was to find Kenny and give him a good talking to! She gazed at Bert beseechingly.

He smiled, inwardly rejoicing at the expression in her eyes. How dare she and that dummy keep Hannah hidden from him for so long? It was obvious his sister hadn't told her anything about what had happened between them, so he could use Miss Moran accordingly. 'Don't you worry, Alice. I'll look after you.' His voice was like a caress.

'Will you take Miss Kirk's property, too. She forgot it.' The shop owner pointed at the other pillowcase. 'If you please.'

Bert picked up the box and one of the pillowcases. 'Come on, Alice. I'll take you back to our house.'

She shook her head, and stayed him with a hand, having picked up the other two pillowcases. It was so frustrating not being able to talk. She remembered how Kenny had written down what he needed to say and mimed writing. Bert looked at the man.

'Can you help us out here?'

The man sighed, then nodded, and searched in a drawer for a pad of bills of sale and a pencil. He tore the top blank sheet from the block and handed it and the pencil to Alice. She placed the pillowcase on the floor and wrote *Please help me find Kenny. He could be at Granny Popo's.*

Bert nodded, and said he'd go with her to the old woman's house. He'd like to punish her, too, but at the moment couldn't see how.

Granny's mouth fell open when she saw Alice's face. 'What's happened to you, duck? You look like you've been in the wars. And where's Tilly and the pram?' she added, looking past them, and up and down the street.

In that moment Bert knew exactly how to get at her. 'She'll be round at our house.' Granny Popo looked him up and down and her eyes narrowed. 'Our Dolly told me you'd been here. What's been going on? Who did this to Alice?'

'I'll tell you what I know but don't keep us waiting on the doorstep. Alice needs to sit down,' he said in a lofty voice.

'Alright, alright, Mr High and Mighty!' The old woman chomped on the stem of her pipe and led the way inside, saw Alice into a chair, and even placed a stool beneath her feet.

Alice wrote in tiny letters on the back of the bill slip, *Kenny can't have been here.* She nudged Bert, who was standing beside her chair, and showed it to him. He nodded. 'Where else do you think he might be?'

Before she could write a suggestion, Granny said, 'Hang on, hang on, who are we talking about here?' She sounded exacerbated.

'Kenny!' snapped Bert.

'I see. Tell me what happened to Alice?'

Alice looked up at Bert and wrote, *Tell her!*

He launched into the tale, making sure that he shone in it, which of course, he did. Hadn't he arrived like a knight in shining armour to rescue Alice from her wicked father? She should be suitably grateful.

As Alice listened, she could have wept. Not only was she in pain but her father had lost them their lovely apartment and ruined most of their furniture. Even so, she found her admiration for Bert growing.

He had been so brave, so strong; just like a hero in a penny dreadful. How she needed someone just like him to take care of her – and he must be out of his time, too, and on a man's wage.

Granny patted Alice's knee. 'Prison's the best place for your father. Although it sounds like he's turned into a right loony if you ask me, having a go at the bobbies.'

At that moment the kitchen door opened and Dolly stood in the opening. Immediately, her startled gaze went to Alice's face and her expression froze. 'Bloody hell! What happened to you?'

Granny said, 'I'll tell yer it all later, duck. But the gist of it is that Alice's dad's broken her jaw, has been arrested and her landlord's thrown her out.'

'Her father must be mad! Poor Alice. She'll have to stay here, Gran.' Dolly looked at Bert. 'Obviously, you found her but where's Kenny and Tilly?'

'*Hanny* and Tilly are with Mother. God only knows where Kenny is,' said Bert, resting a hand on Alice's shoulder. 'He took offence and seems to have disappeared.' He did his best not to smile at this last remark.

Granny stared at him thoughtfully. So that's the way the land lies, does it, me buck? You want him out of the way, don't like the lad.

'So what exactly happened? Was Kenny there when his father arrived?' asked Dolly, impatiently.

Granny said, 'He was, duck! Got a clout across the head. His ears could still be ringing for all we know.'

Alice nodded.

Granny said, 'You should go round to Mr Bushell's to see if he's there. Yer'll do fine with him on your own. I'll go with Bert and fetch the pram and Tilly. I'll visit the herb shop on the way. I know a sure cure to help with the pain yer must be suffering, duck.'

Bert wasn't too pleased with this latest suggestion. What if Kenny was at the coal merchant's? He might try and put a spoke in his wheel; not that he doubted his own ability to draw Alice away from him. The trouble was that she had a soft heart. He would have much rather gone with her but, equally, he didn't want the old hag going round to their house on her own and his mother meekly handing Alice's sister over to her. He had plans for that child. He made a decision and smiled dazzlingly. 'Whatever you say, missus, is OK by me.'

It was OK by Alice, too, and she wrote it down on the available space left on the piece of paper she had and added, *Thanks for all your help. Give my love to Hanny and tell her where I am. It's possible, I suppose that Kenny might have ignored what your mother said and has gone round to your house?*

Bert doubted it. His mother had laid it on nice and thick that she believed that Kenny was responsible for Hanny's troubles. She wasn't going to allow her to see him. Gently he kissed the top of Alice's head. 'I'll come and see you tomorrow.' Her eyes shone with gratitude; Bert's star was, once more, in the ascendant.

Alice left the house a few minutes after Bert and Granny, crossed the canal and headed in the direction of Black Diamond Street. Close to the coal depot and the railway, it was home to a number of coal merchants.

Mr Bushell opened the door and let out a shocked exclamation at the sight of Alice's bruised and swollen face. 'What's happened to you, girl?'

It was obvious to her that Kenny had not been here. Deeply disappointed, Alice mimed writing on the palm of her hand. Stupidly, she had forgotten to pick up paper and pencil.

Mr Bushell placed a hand behind his ear and bent his head towards her. 'What's that?' She put a finger to her mouth and shook her head, and them mimed writing again.

He beamed. 'Ah! I get you! You'd best come in.'

Alice had never been in his house before, so was surprised when she found its interior to be as neat as a new pin. The man fussed around her making tea and offering her angel cake. She managed to drink some of the tea without spilling too much down her front but had to refuse the cake.

He handed her pencil and paper and sat across the brown chenille cloth-covered table from her, watching as she wrote. He held his head tilted to one side like a bird. When she had finished, he read what she had written. Alice watched his expressive face and, by the time he reached the end of her note knew that he was as almost upset as she was.

'That wicked, evil man,' he said, his fingers trembling on the paper. 'Florrie was always so loyal to him but I knew how much she suffered at his hands. I'm glad he's been arrested and I hope he comes by his just deserts. But where's Kenny? If he's not here and not at Mrs Popodopalous's house where could he be?'

Mrs Popo – who? wrote Alice.

'Ahhh! You didn't know that's her name. A bit of a mouthful, isn't it?' said Mr Bushell, smiling. 'Her husband had Greek blood in him and was a fierce man. Their fights used to be the talk of the neighbourhood where we came from,' he said reminiscently. 'They met in Liverpool but he worked in the boatyard down at Ellesmere. I was only a youth then and he's long dead. They were passionate about each other.'

Alice was amazed at this altogether different picture of Granny Popo. She now saw a fierce, passionate younger woman married to a swarthy, handsome foreigner, who knew more about love than she had ever imagined. Sebastian filled her thoughts and, for a moment, she wanted to cry. Then she told herself she wasn't to think about him. He hadn't been prepared to do what she wanted. What had been between them was over.

She stood up, wanting to get back to Granny's house quickly in case Kenny had arrived there after she had left. Mr Bushell offered her another cup of tea, but she refused, and he saw her out, telling her to let him know when Kenny turned up.

Only on the way back to Granny's house did it occur to Alice that, at last, she would be living under the same roof as her sister, and be able to help take care of her. But, when she got there, Granny was sitting in the rocking chair across from Dolly and both were looking angry and upset.

'Are we glad you're back, duck,' said Granny, her voice shaking. 'Mrs Kirk had the nerve to tell me that she was keeping Tilly. I think she's gone off her head! That was after keeping me waiting for ages on the doorstep. I asked to speak to Hanny but she said her daughter was too upset about Grace to be talking to anyone. I tell yer I was dumbstruck and that's saying something for me!'

Dolly put her chapped hands over the old woman's trembling ones in an attempt to calm her down but her expression was angry. 'She can't keep her, Gran. I've told you that. We've got Alice with us now. She'll get her back for us.'

Alice was stunned. What was Hannah's mother thinking? She couldn't possibly keep Tilly. Oh, she felt too exhausted and in pain for all this. She noticed the pencil on the table that she had used earlier and mimed writing. Dolly tore off part of a porridge packet and handed it to Alice, who wrote *What exactly did Mrs Kirk say?*

'Does it matter?' Dolly's voice was tight.

Alice nodded.

Granny sucked on her pipe. 'She said that she'll look after her really well… that in a way she has a right to her. She brought her into this world and saved her life, that Florrie would be happy to see her taking care of Tilly. I know your father caused her a lot of pain and trouble but that doesn't give her the right to our Tilly. So what do we do, duck?'

Alice thought, Our Tilly! She frowned and wrote *I'm not up to doing anything now. Leave it until in the morning. She'll come to no harm with Hanny there.*

Granny and Dolly did not look pleased. 'I don't think that's a good idea at all,' said the younger woman, folding her arms across her breast. 'Mrs Kirk's not right in her head at the moment if you ask me. She's lost Grace and is unlikely to have another child at her age. She could be looking for a replacement.'

Alice could scarcely believe Dolly had said that but maybe she had a point.

'Well?' demanded Dolly.

Exhaustion, pain and Dolly's hectoring began to take their toll on Alice. She could feel her annoyance increasing. Tilly was her sister! She'd make the decisions. She wrote *I'll go round the day after the funeral. Having Tilly might help Mrs Kirk get through the day. Tilly knows Hannah, so she won't feel too strange.*

'Oh, I don't like that idea,' said Dolly, tapping her foot on the linoleum. 'A day and she could get used to having her. She might even think we agree with what she's done.' Alice wrote, *I'm not up to arguing with her and demanding she return Tilly to us right now.*

'We could get the police if she refuses to return Tilly to you,' said Dolly, her eyes sparking.

'No, Doll! We can't do that,' said Granny, pressing tobacco into the bowl of her pipe with agitated fingers. 'The woman's suffered a grievous loss, we can't make it worse for her by bringing in the bobbies.'

'Then what do we do?' cried her granddaughter. 'I mean, Tilly's like my own to me!' She pressed her hands against her breast. 'I knew I'd have to give her up to Alice one day but that's only right and proper. She's her sister, but Mrs Kirk! She still has Joy and Hanny, although she's no angel, as we know.' She made a disparaging noise in her throat.

'Enough said, Doll! You leave Hanny's one fall from grace out of this.' Granny drew on her pipe and leaned back in the chair. 'We do what Alice says and wait until the funeral's over. We need to show a bit of heart.'

Alice tried to smile but the attempt was a miserable failure, but she was grateful for the old woman's words. She thought of Bert and how he had been such a support to her, thought of Kenny and hoped and prayed she would see him again soon and get some answers to why he and Hanny hadn't been honest with her. Where could he be?

Alice spent the night in Dolly's bed but, despite Granny's potion, she didn't sleep very well because her jaw made it uncomfortable. Eventually she did fall into a heavy sleep and so was unaware when Dolly rose and went out with Granny. When at last Alice did wake, her first thoughts were that she was too late for work and must have missed Grace's funeral.

What would Hannah be doing about work? Had she gone in early that morning and explained what had happened? Would she have mentioned Alice's injuries? Would she still go to work or might her mother want her to stay at home and support her through this dreadful time? One thing was for sure: despite her jaw feeling twice the size it had yesterday, Alice had to go to work tomorrow. She could not afford to take time off. All her dreams had turned to ashes and she was back living in a two-up, two-down in someone else's house, with no man to support her. But maybe Bert would be the answer to her prayers. Perhaps once her jaw healed, he would find her attractive. Alice allowed her imagination to run away with her.

Downstairs there was no sign of anyone and she presumed Granny might be helping at a birth somewhere and Dolly was out shopping. The fire was still in, and the kettle on the hob, so she made herself a cup of tea. Hunger gnawed at her insides and she decided to go and buy the makings for barley broth, hoping that she would be able to get that down her without too much difficulty.

Alice wrote down what she needed and afterwards walked to Eastgate Street. She was aware of the curious glances from passers-by. In the shop, when the shop assistant made a sympathetic remark, Alice wrote that she had walked into a lamp-post. As it was almost lunchtime by the time Alice returned to Granny Popo's house, she decided to visit Mr Bushell, before making the soup, and see if Kenny had turned up for work, knowing from her half-brother that his employer came home for lunch. She spared a thought for her father wondering whether he had been in court yet, and if he had, whether he was enjoying prison. It occurred to her, with a grim sense of satisfaction, that with all his talk about punishment and forgiveness jail should teach him a thing or two about just deserts, and serve him right.

Mr Bushell let her in and then excused his appearance, saying that he hoped she didn't mind him getting on with his meal. He sat down at the table, clad in grimy jacket and trousers to which a layer of coal dust clung, his elbows resting on a sheet of newspaper; another sheet covering the seat of the chair. She passed him a slip of paper that had written on it, *Kenny is still missing.*

He shook his head, obviously disturbed by that news. 'I don't know what to make of his disappearance. I mean, now your father's in jail there's nothing for him to be scared of. If he doesn't turn up in a day or two, I'm going to have to find someone else to help me.' He frowned, exposing white skin in the creases of his face. 'Two somebody elses probably,' he said gloomily. 'My eyes aren't so good for close work these days. As you know, Kenny took over doing my books. I taught him myself. As well as that, he was always quick off the mark to get them sacks of coal to our regular customers. Peaceful to work with and I could trust him with money. I need someone I can trust.' He sighed.

Don't we all, thought Alice, not liking the way Mr Bushell spoke of Kenny in the past tense. It was as if he was dead! He was still quick, and clever, could still write with a neat hand, even if he wasn't completely trustworthy. But where was he?

She thanked the coal merchant and got up to go. He accompanied her to the door and looked down at her and she saw the compassion in his red-rimmed eyes. 'How are you off for money, Alice? I was very fond of your mother. I miss Florrie as I'm sure you do. If there's anything I can do to help don't hesitate to ask.'

Alice was touched, remembering how he would appear suddenly at her mother's side at meetings. He might not be much to look at but if her mam had been able to marry him, she would have been much better off.

Alice hurried back to the house, letting herself in with the key on the string. There was no sign of Dolly or Granny. She made soup and managed to swallow some, it was tricky and painful, but she felt so much better for it. When she had finished and washed her cup, bowl and spoon, she decided to visit the police station to see if they could help her find Kenny. She wrote what was necessary on the torn off porridge packet and was soon on her way.

The sergeant was sympathetic at first, then exasperated, seeming to get the wrong end of the stick thinking it was Kenny had hit her in the face. He told her to get off home, adding that she was better off without him.

Alice managed to find a teeny space on the piece of porridge packet that had not been written on. She wrote *Can I have a sheet of paper, please?*

The sergeant sighed and produced paper. She wrote in detail about what had happened yesterday. He read her writing upside down as she wrote, then said abruptly, 'Why didn't you mention your dad's name earlier? We're not too happy with him, assaulting two of our men. One's still seriously injured in the infirmary. This brother of yours, most likely it was him who came in last night wanting to see your father.'

If Alice's jaw had not been tied up it would have dropped. Why should Kenny want to see their father? She thought he would never want to see him again and hoped that clout on the head hadn't sent him peculiar. She wrote, *Did he get to see him?*

He shook his head. 'He wouldn't have got anything out of him, girl. Raving, that's what your father was, raving! We had the men from the lunatic asylum here. They put a straitjacket on him and took him away.' Suddenly Alice needed to sit down, and the sergeant must have realised this because he came from behind the counter and lowered her into a chair. He left her a moment, returning with a glass of water. She looked at him and burst into tears. He placed the tumbler on the counter and took from his pocket a large white handkerchief and handed it to her. She buried her face in it, remembering the madness in her father's eyes. Strangely enough, she had not considered him a lunatic in the past but thinking about it, yes, he must have been crazy to have behaved the way he did just because her mam spoke God's name, and refused to give up her church going. Yet her mam would not have dreamed of getting a doctor in to him, could not afford it, but the police had seen that he was a really sick man. She wondered how Kenny had reacted to the news? Where had he gone after leaving here?

She wiped her damp face with the handkerchief, and would have handed it back to the sergeant, but he said with a faint smile. 'You hang onto it, Miss. Just in case you have need of it again. Want me to tell our men on the beat to keep their eyes open for your brother?' She nodded. The policeman placed a finger at the bottom of the paper. 'Write down where you're staying and, if I find anything out I'll let you know.'

Alice was relieved to leave matters in his hands and return to the house. She half hoped she would find Kenny there but she was to be disappointed. Hungry, Alice heated the soup and managed to eat some more. Exhausted after her efforts, she swallowed another dose of Granny's potion, and within half an hour, she fell fast asleep.

When Granny and Dolly came in, Alice wrote down the events of her day. The old woman didn't look a bit surprised when she read that Mal had been declared a lunatic. 'But it makes you wonder how he got into that state. He mustn't have been a loony when your mam married him, although they do say some madmen are dead crafty.'

'Perhaps it's the moon,' said Dolly, nodding her head sagely. 'That's another thing I've heard said.' She lifted the lid from the soup pan. 'You made this?'

Alice nodded. Dolly smiled with her mouth but not her eyes. 'Good! I can see you're going to fit in nicely with us. So when are you going round to pick up Tilly and the pram?'

Tomorrow, I'll go tomorrow, she wrote, still feeling exhausted. *Today will have been a bad day for Mrs Kirk.*

Shortly after, Bert called at the house. Dolly answered his knock, and gazed up at him, a severe expression on her face. 'What do you want?'

He smiled and rested his shoulder against the wall. 'That's a nice welcome. I've come to see if Alice is feeling any better.'

'She's exhausted. I don't know if I should let you in. We're not feeling too pleased with your family right now, what with your mother trying to take Tilly from Alice. She belongs here.'

He nodded gravely. 'Don't blame you feeling like that but to be truthful, it's our Hanny who seems to want to hang on to the child.'

'Hanny!'

'Yes. Anyway, I've come round to see if I can help Alice in any way. Any news of Kenny?'

Dolly scowled. 'The only news is that he called at the police station wanting to see his dad, he's vanished since then. But getting back to Tilly; I've looked after her since she was a baby.'

'Then be glad to have a rest from her,' said Bert, an edge to his voice, straightening up from the wall.

'If you're going to speak to me like that – you're definitely not coming in.' She slammed the door and then turned to see Alice standing behind her. She looked as annoyed as one could in her condition, and pushing past Dolly, opened the door.

Bert was still standing on the pavement looking angry but the moment he saw Alice, his expression changed. He smiled at her, hating the way she looked with that daft bandage round her head, but she wasn't going to be wearing that for long and her eyes told him she was glad to see him. From his pocket he took a small pad and pencil and handed them to her.

If only she could have smiled without it hurting, but she was touched by his thoughtfulness. Immediately she wrote *Thanks! How's your mother? I'm sorry I didn't make it to the funeral.*

He read the words and sighed heavily. 'Bearing up. Joy had a good cry but she seems to have bucked up. She took Freddie and your sister to the park. Hanny's not speaking to me.'

Give her time to get over Grace's death. Is Tilly all right?

He nodded. 'Seems very happy. I haven't heard any crying out of her.'

'That doesn't say she isn't missing being away from us,' interrupted Dolly from behind Alice, much to her irritation. 'She's such an easy-going little soul.'

Bert ignored her and addressed Alice again. 'I hear Kenny went the police station. What did they have to say about your father?'

She wrote in the pad *They've put Dad in the lunatic asylum.*

Bert's fair eyebrows almost shot through his hairline. 'Bloody hell!' He apologised for his language immediately, then continued, 'I always thought he was a bit mad at times but I didn't think him a loony.'

She nodded, glad that he had said that. Wasn't it just how she felt? *The police are going to keep a look out for Kenny.*

'That's good. Let's hope they find him.' Bert mentally crossed his fingers, praying they wouldn't but the news of her father had given him a shock. Alice might be tainted with the same madness. Although, he suddenly remembered that Mal had worked at the leadworks. Hadn't he read in the newspaper recently that a man had brought a case against the company because he'd got real sick from working with lead and had been having bad heads?

Alice wrote *Is Hanny going into work tomorrow?*

He shrugged. 'I don't know. She and the rest of them are treating me like a leper. I mean, no one's said anything about her behaviour and how it upset Mother and Dah.' He paused, and smiled. 'Still, maybe they'll come round to forgiving me.' Bert's voice drifted off forlornly.

They should! Grace's death was an accident. Could you tell Hanny I'll be round early to see her in the morning?

'If she'll listen to me,' he said mournfully, before gently squeezing her shoulder. 'I'll go now. I don't want to tire you out.'

She wrote *Thanks for coming.*

He brought his fair head down and kissed her lightly on the lips. 'You take care now.'

Alice thought he was a bit bold, kissing her like that, still, it showed he thought something of her. She turned to go indoors and found herself face to face with Dolly. 'You're stupid, you are,' said the older girl, her expression exasperated. 'I wouldn't trust him as far as I could throw him. Smarmy bugger!'

Alice wished she could tell her to go to hell but decided instead to make excuses for her. After all she had saved Tilly's life when she was born and taken good care of her all this time. What Dolly needed was that husband of hers to come home and give her another baby! She would pray for that.

'I'll say no more for now,' said Dolly abruptly. 'I shouldn't blame you in your condition. But tomorrow you'll get Tilly back, won't you?'

Alice nodded, and they went into the kitchen.

A short while later the sergeant turned up. Granny invited him in and made him a cup of tea. 'You've news of Kenny?' she asked on Alice's behalf.

'Not news that'll make you happy, Miss,' he said, gazing at Alice, who was sitting by the window, through which he caught a glimpse of the canal. 'One of our men remembered your brother, had him arrested for disturbing the peace three years ago. He'd been in a bad way, face all bruised, worse than it was today from what he said. He was seen at the railway station very early this morning.'

'Where was he going?' asked Dolly, glancing at Alice.

'He bought a ticket for Glasgow. Do you know anyone in Glasgow, Miss Moran?'

His words fell into a silence that grew and grew only to be broken when the astonished and hurt Alice scribbled on a sheet of paper. *My father came from Scotland, but I don't know why Kenny should go there. He was only an infant when he left.*

The sergeant sighed. 'Well, he's a free man. There's no reason for us to chase after him. Maybe he'll be in touch with you soon.'

Alice could only hope so, although she was feeling really annoyed with him for going off to Scotland without telling her. Dolly saw the sergeant out.

'That's a real blow,' said Granny, sucking on her pipe. 'What the hell is going on in his head? Why should he go up north?'

Maybe he's gone crazy like Father! thought Alice, then immediately chided herself for thinking such a thing. Kenny wasn't crazy. But why go to Scotland? She couldn't make sense of it. She wondered what Hannah would make of the news? After all, she and Kenny had clearly been very much closer than she'd ever imagined.

Chapter Twenty

Kenny was saying something to her, but she couldn't make out the words! Hannah reached out to him but all she grasped was thin air. She looked about her but there was nothing but darkness. Then she sensed a presence, and she was frightened. Someone was whispering in her ear. 'Hannee!'

She woke with a start to find Tilly snuggling up against her back, her chin resting on her shoulder and her chubby arms clasped round her. Hannah let out a heartfelt sigh of relief. 'You gave me a fright,' she said.

'Why? I only blew in your ear and then whispered "Hannee!"' Tilly butted her with her forehead.

Hannah could not help smiling. She removed Tilly's hands and rolled over carefully and gazed down at Alice's sister; her reddish gold curls were in a tangle, and her eyelashes fanned out like tiny wires. A rosy cheek rested on a dimpled hand and she grinned at Hannah, showing tiny white teeth. She really was a little love, lapping up any affection you gave her and letting it flow back to you. Her talent for mimicry had actually brought a smile to Susannah's face yesterday. Hannah sighed, remembering the funeral. She wouldn't like to go through that again.

'What's a matter? Don't look sad.' Tilly's chubby fingers, spread out like a starfish, reached out and stroked Hannah's cheek.

Hannah smiled. 'You're a tonic.'

'She's also a wriggler,' groaned Joy, opening her eyes and gazing across the top of the child's head at her sister. 'You OK?'

Hannah nodded, and then glanced in the direction of the window where the sunlight was shining through a gap in the curtains and painting a lozenge of brightness on the linoleum. 'I'm going to get up. You keep Tilly here for a quarter of an hour or so.' Joy nodded, knowing that Alice was coming early and that Hannah wanted to speak to her alone, but she was so glad to have her elder sister back home.

Hannah was thinking that it was natural for Alice to want Tilly to live with her under Granny Popo's roof, but she had come round to thinking it would be good for her mother to have Tilly staying with them a bit longer. It didn't seem to worry Susannah that she was Mal Moran's child. Who knows, maybe she could see something of her old friend Florrie in her; Florrie had, by all accounts, been a very pretty girl. If Hannah could persuade Alice to let Tilly at least spend her days with the Kirks, then she felt sure that only good could come from it. After all, Dolly had a husband who would be coming home one day and, as for Alice, she had to go out to work.

Hannah found her dah already up. The fire was glowing in the grate and the kettle was boiling. His smile held a touch of anxiety. 'How are yer, lass?'

'I'm fine, Dah! How are you?' Hannah had forgiven him. Had done so as soon as she saw her mother go into the comfort of his arms back at the apartment. But even when she had been angry with him, she had never stopped loving him. With her older brother it was different. She hated him even more since hearing of the death of her sister. At least for the moment he was out of favour with their mother, although how long that would last Hannah had no idea.

She kissed Jock's cheek, but did not linger, wanting to go to the lavatory. When she returned and had washed her hands and face, a cup of tea was already poured out for her and he held the toasting fork speared through a thick slice of bread to the fire.

'I thought you might like a piece,' said Jock, withdrawing the bread from the heat to check it wasn't too well done. He knew his eldest daughter liked her toast golden brown.

'Thanks, Dah.' She spread butter on the toast, watching it melt. Suddenly she was reminded of Kenny and how he used to toast and butter her bread. Her eyes felt damp and a lump welled in her throat. How she had loved getting up in the morning to that warm fragrant smell of toasting bread, occasionally spread with beef dripping. He had always been so caring and considerate of her comfort. She was going to miss him cherishing her, his company, his scribblings and cartoons, just seeing him every day. Not that she was in love with him. Oh no! What she felt couldn't possibly be love. Her knees had never turned to mush when she saw him. Alice had told her that hers went all wobbly each time she set eyes on Sebastian. But she was desperate to see him and could not understand why he hadn't been at the funeral. He surely didn't believe that she would still be angry with him, although she was a little, but it was wonderful that he could speak and she couldn't wait to tell him so.

Hannah bit into the toast again, melted butter dripped down her chin. Her tongue flicked out and licked it away. There was a rat-a-tat-tat of the front door knocker. Hannah hurried to answer it, knowing it could only be Alice. It was, and she looked dreadful! There were smudges beneath her eyes, and the part of her jaw that could be seen was black and blue. She felt so sorry for her.

'Hello, Alice! Are you coming in? I'm sorry I haven't been round to see you but I'm sure you know how it's been for me. Anyway, Bert's been playing the role of good Samaritan to you and I'm sure that made you happy.' Even to her own ears, that last sentence sounded bitchy but she was unable to conceal her feelings towards her brother.

Alice's lips tightened. From her pocket she took the notebook and pencil Bert gave her. *He's been very kind and I don't want you going on about him. I've come to ask if you are going into work, and let you know that Kenny was seen buying a ticket to Scotland. God only knows why. Also I want to see Tilly and take her back to Granny Popo's, that's where I'll be living for now.* She tore out the sheet of paper and handed it to Hannah.

Hannah read it and was stunned. Kenny in Scotland! How could he go to Scotland without saying a word to her… and why go there? As for what she said about Tilly – of course Alice wanted her living with her and she could understand that but before she could say so, Bert appeared behind her.

'Morning, Alice. I hope you're feeling a lot better today? Perhaps you'd like to go for a walk with me this evening; that's if you feel up to it?'

Alice tried to smile but failed. So she wrote down *Thanks! It'll help take me out of myself. Although I look such a mess, are you sure you want to be seen with me?*

Bert was wearing his working overalls but he wasn't worried about what they made him look like. His face was his fortune, he thought, and stepped down onto the pavement and placed an arm about her shoulders and hugged her. 'Don't be daft! It's not your fault you look like Frankenstein's monster,' he teased. 'I'll be proud to have you on my arm.'

Hannah glared at him, and his blue eyes challenged her. She turned to Alice. 'What nice compliments he gives a girl. Frankenstein's monster! I wouldn't take that sitting down.'

Bert said softly, 'I care about Alice. I care about you, Hanny. I know I haven't always behaved the way I should towards you, but can't we bury the hatchet?'

'In your head,' she retorted.

He laughed. 'You spoke to me! Things are looking up.'

Not if I've got anything to do with it, thought Hannah, watching him turn his gaze on Alice.

'I've got to go and have my breakfast, luv. Then it's work. I'll see you this evening about half seven.'

Alice nodded, feeling cherished.

After he had gone back inside the house, Hannah looked at Alice with a hard expression in her blue-grey eyes. 'Don't let him fool you. He's a polished git.'

Alice's mouth set in a straight line. *I like a bloke with a bit of polish. Now what about Tilly, is she still in bed? And work? Are you going?*

'He's not what you think him.'

Shut up about him. I'm not a child, I can make my own judgements about people. You're just jealous of him. You always have been.

'Like hell I have,' said Hannah, trying to keep a rein on her temper. 'But please yourself.' She tapped her fingers on the doorjamb. 'I just hope you don't learn what he's like the hard way. As for work, I managed to slip there early yesterday and when they said you hadn't turned in I explained what had happened. I won't be going in at all.

Dah wants me to stay at home for a while to keep Mother company and be a help to her. I'm going to make a suggestion now that you can take or leave. Why don't you leave Tilly here during the day? She's in bed right now with Joy. Tilly knows me and it means that Dolly and Granny will stop being so possessive. You could pick her up when you finish work.' Alice was unsure what to do. She was cross with Hannah and didn't feel inclined to fall in with her wishes. Her remarks about Bert filled her with uncertainty, too. Still, she knew what her friend said about Dolly and Granny was true, although she would, of course, have to live with them – at least until Kenny turned up again.

She wrote, *Granny said Mrs Kirk seemed to think she had a right to Tilly because she brought her into the world. I don't want your mother getting too possessive, either!*

Hannah's smile was twisted as she read the words. She looked up from the page at Alice's bruised face. 'You've got to remember that she's not thinking straight; she's been through a lot lately; even Bert's no longer her blue-eyed boy, and I'm not being nasty about him.'

Alice nodded but was still unsure what to do.

Sensing her uncertainty, Hannah threw in what she thought of as her trump card, not realising she was actually playing into her brother's hands. 'You've got to think what'll happen when Dolly's husband comes home from India. I mean, he's not going to be there forever, is he? Where will you and Tilly sleep? He'll be sleeping with Dolly. I suppose you could get in with Granny but he mightn't want you and Tilly in the house.' Hannah paused to allow the words to sink in.

Alice nodded. It would be sensible right now to do what Hannah suggested. She wrote *OK. How much will you want me to pay you?*

Hannah was delighted. 'Who said anything about payment! It'll be a pleasure to have Tilly, though Mother probably will want something for her food. I'll have a word with her and let you know.' She squeezed Alice's hand. 'I'm sure this is the right thing for Tilly.'

Alice hoped she was right and tried to smile her gratitude and left.

She decided to cut a tragic figure when she went into work. It wasn't difficult given the way she looked. When she also wrote down that her brother was missing and her father consigned to the lunatic asylum, that clinched the matter. She received sympathy not only from her workmates but also her boss – and surprisingly, he said that he wouldn't dock her wages for being absent yesterday. So Alice was in a reasonable frame of mind when that evening she called at the Kirks' home to pick up Tilly.

Bert came to the door, accompanied by her sister. Immediately Tilly placed her arms about Alice's legs. 'Hello,' she said, beaming up at her. 'You look funny.'

Bert grinned. 'Don't take that to heart! I think you look better than you did this morning.'

She placed her fingers at the corners of her mouth and eased them up.

Tilly chuckled. Bert thought Alice looked ridiculous but took her hand and said, 'Save your smiles for when you can do it properly. Want me to walk down to Granny's with the pair of you?'

The offer pleased her but, remembering the pram, she wrote the word down in her pad, and showed it to him. 'It's gone,' he said with a shrug of powerful shoulders in a blue shirt. 'Dolly came round for it, apparently.' Alice wondered what Hannah had said to her but did not ask.

They set out. Tilly between them, holding a hand of each. She lifted her feet from the ground and they swung her. It was obvious to Alice that her sister had taken to Bert, and that delighted her. When they arrived at Granny Popo's, the old woman looked a bit grumpy but she told Bert to come in. She sat in the rocking chair with Tilly on her knee, the little girl babbling happily about Freddie and Joy, as well as Mrs Kirk and Hanny taking her for a walk along the river to feed the ducks.

'Well, she seems happy enough,' said Granny with a sigh, 'But our Dolly's not going to be pleased by your decision. Still I suppose it had to come one day.'

Alice felt sorry for the old woman but, while she was grateful for all Dolly had done for her sister, she was not going to be swayed by her into changing her mind; she was certain that the decision she had made was the right one. When she put her sister to bed before going to meet Bert, she could not help but think that while her father's actions had been frightening and terrible, and Kenny's disappearance worrying, every dark cloud had its silver lining.

Over the next few weeks Alice's condition improved. She practiced moving her jaw a little day by day. It was a relief when she could dispense with the bandage and talk properly again. 'That's better,' said Bert, running a finger down her cheek before kissing her on the lips. It wasn't the first time he had kissed her but this time it was what she called a real kiss, and she could respond properly. Her response seemed to please Bert and there was a different light in his eyes the next time they met. She was convinced that he was falling in love with her.

-

Hannah watched their relationship develop with alarm. Alice had been her friend as long as she could remember. Bert knew that and appeared to be deliberately ousting her from Alice's affections. And now it seemed that the only time she saw her was when she dropped by to pick up Tilly. Sundays, which Hannah used to look forward to when living at the apartment, were different from the rest of the week only in that she didn't have to keep her mother company and look after Tilly. She so much missed her other life; spending time with Kenny, her chats with Alice and the girls at work; she definitely regretted the lack of even a little money in her pocket. She yearned for the outings to the music hall, theatre or picnics along the river when Kenny and Sebastian had been on the scene.

So far she had kept Kenny's long held secret, having gathered from their exchange on the doorstep that Alice had no idea that Kenny could speak. Should she mention it? Would it make any difference to the way Alice was behaving? She seemed so wrapped up in Bert now that Kenny did not figure at all in their brief exchanges. Kenny might have deceived them both when it came to his being mute, but Bert's deception was much worse. She thought deeply about what she should do to prevent the relationship developing into anything more serious. The problem was that Alice was inclined to cut her off in mid-sentence if she started to say anything about Bert. If only Kenny would return from Scotland or write to her as he used to then she felt certain something could be done. Her heart ached to hear from him, she was unable to understand why he should have vanished from her life so completely. She could only hope that he would get in touch eventually.

Summer passed and, in October, the suffragettes organised a mass demonstration against the Government in London. The event ended badly with eleven suffragettes in jail. By chance, Hannah read an article in the *Chester Chronicle* protesting about this but it was the by-line which offered Hannah a little ray of hope: *Miss Victoria Waters.* Hannah was immediately reminded of Sebastian and, after much soul-searching, decided to go and see him. If he still felt something for Alice then perhaps all was not lost. But when she arrived at the house it was to find the shutters up on the windows. Her heart sank and in low spirits she made her way home.

Elsewhere in the world momentous change was in the air. In Russia, the revolutionary Trotsky was exiled to Siberia, President Roosevelt visited Panama where plans were afoot for a canal to be built so ships could more easily reach the Pacific Ocean from the Atlantic. In the Transvaal, self-government had been granted to the settlers there. Closer to home, Dolly delivered the news that her husband would be coming home in the spring.

Soon it would be Christmas and Hannah could only hope that Kenny would get in touch then. She wondered how her mother would cope with this first festive season without Grace. She seemed to be managing to get through each day as long as Hannah was there to talk to and shoulder most of the responsibility for organising her days. Having Tilly with them gave Hannah the perfect excuse to make sure her mother didn't mope at home – and it seemed to work. Susannah told her eldest daughter that it was a treat after years of managing her household herself to have the time to feel free to walk, almost aimlessly, about the city, along the walls and the river. They visited the Grosvenor Museum, a place that Susannah had never set foot inside. 'I always thought it was just for the tourists,' she explained to her daughter.

'But this is where our history is, Mother!' exclaimed Hannah, thinking of the Roman remains that had been discovered during repairs to the north wall and were exhibited in the museum and drew thousands of visitors from all parts of the globe. 'Doesn't it give you a thrill to think that before Jesus was born, people lived in Chester?'

Susannah smiled faintly. 'The present is enough for me to cope with at the moment. One step at a time, Hanny! Knowing the walls were built to keep out the Welsh was what affected me most when I was a child.'

'Who are the Welsh?' Tilly tugged on Hannah's sleeve.

'I am,' said Susannah, prodding herself in the chest. 'But wasn't one of those I'm thinking of.'

Hannah began to tell Tilly how, hundreds of years ago, the Welsh used to come raiding over the borders to steal cattle from the fertile Cheshire plains. The little girl was round-eyed with wonder. She was full of questions about everything she saw, about people, places, dogs, and cats. There was no end to the things she wanted to know, and, in seeking answers, both Hannah and Susannah learnt much in the process.

The week before Christmas, Susannah dismayed Hannah by saying that she thought the time was right for Bert to be forgiven. They were standing on the old Dee Bridge, gazing down at the weir which was in full flow because it was high tide. 'Accidents do happen and he thought he was giving Grace a treat. And what with him and Alice seeing so much of each other, I do think we've got to let go of the past. I never thought I'd say this, but you know, Florrie and I used to talk about him and Alice getting married one day, and now it looks like it might happen.' She smiled happily at her eldest daughter, who had her arm round Tilly sitting on the sandstone parapet. 'She's a good girl, whatever her half-brother was, and of course, she's Tilly's sister. Which means we won't lose her, as we might if Alice were to marry someone else.'

It felt to Hannah as if the sun had gone behind a cloud. 'Mother, you can't want Bert to marry Alice just so Tilly can be part of the family? He's not right for her.'

Susannah frowned. 'How can you say that? They look well together. He loves her and she so looks up to him.'

'Which isn't good for him,' muttered Hannah, her arm tightening about Tilly, who suddenly looked up into her face and placed her fingers at the corners of Hannah's mouth. 'Smile!'

Hannah refused to do anything of the sort. How she wished she could tell her mother the truth. How would he treat Alice and Tilly if they married? Her friend could be about to make the same mistake as Florrie when she married Mal Moran! If Bert hadn't seen anything wrong in raping his own sister and getting Agnes pregnant and throwing her over, who was to say he wouldn't do things to Alice that were just as depraved?

Susannah smiled down at Tilly. 'You'd like your sister to marry Bert, wouldn't you?'

'What's marry?'

Hannah swung the child down from the parapet. 'See, she doesn't know what marriage is! She's happy as she is being with us during the week and Alice on Sundays.' Her tone was vehement.

Susannah frowned. 'Bert loves her. She'd have a father figure. They'd be a happy little family. Don't let your jealousy get in the way of seeing how fitting it would be.'

'I am not jealous,' said Hannah angrily. 'The only person Bert loves is himself!' She marched off, taking Tilly with her.

Susannah did not speak to Hannah that evening and was short with her in the days leading up to the festive season. Hannah tried not to allow her mother's coldness to hurt her. On Christmas Day, Alice and Tilly were due to have dinner with the Kirks and she was not looking forward to it.

Hannah was woken up early by Freddie climbing over her and worming his way between her and Joy. Almost her first thought was of Grace and the second of the last Christmas that she had spent with Kenny and Alice. A lump rose in her throat and, for a moment, she was unable to smile or respond to Freddie's, 'Merry Christmas, Hanny!' His bright eyes gleamed down into hers. 'I'm glad you're here with us now. You'll enjoy seeing what I've got. Grace was never interested… and Joy pretended.'

He began by dragging out a small wooden engine from one of Jock's large woollen socks. Hannah and Joy, who no longer had any illusions about who really provided the goodies at Christmas, joined him in expressing rapture over each and every item. He shared the chocolate bar he'd received and then sang *Away in a Manger* in his sweet childish treble, rubbing his toes along Hannah's shins as he did so. She kissed his dark curls, thankful for the heartwarming start to the day, if anxious about the rest of it.

She went downstairs to light the fire and peeled the vegetables before taking up cups of tea, boiled eggs and buttered toast for her parents.

'This is good of you, Hanny,' said Jock, placing his pillow behind his back as he sat up. He shook his wife gently, 'Wake up, Sue! Hanny's brought you breakfast.'

Susannah's eyes fluttered open and she smiled sleepily at her eldest daughter. 'Thanks, lovey.'

It appeared that she was forgiven, thought Hannah and kissed her mother's cheek but the words *Happy Christmas* stuck in her throat, knowing that this special holy day would be tinged with sadness for them now and in the future. They would have to make the best of it, though, for Freddie's sake.

So there were no long faces when the whole family eventually got up around ten o'clock. Jock took some of the blazing coals from the kitchen fire on a shovel and carried them into the parlour where the Christmas tree stood. He soon had another fire blazing in the tiled grate there. He set up the wooden tracks for Freddie's engine to run on and soon he and his youngest son were absorbed and talking trains.

Bert put on his new suit and told his mother that he was going round to Granny Popo's to fetch Alice and Tilly. 'Don't get caught talking too long with Granny,' said Susannah, flicking a speck of almost invisible dust from his lapel and smiling up at him.

'I won't,' he said, returning her smile and kissing her.

Hannah wanted to wipe that smile off his face. She turned her back on them and got out the cutlery. Joy was spreading the spotless white damask cloth her mother kept for special occasions over the table.

'So what d'you think?' whispered Joy, meeting Hannah's eyes across the table. 'Is there going to be a special announcement today?'

'Dear God, I hope not,' said Hannah in a low voice, and gnawed on her lower lip. 'He doesn't deserve to be happy.'

'No,' murmured Joy. 'But have you noticed in this world that people don't always get what they deserve? And truthfully, I'll be glad to have him out of the house, won't you?'

For a moment the sisters' gazes held. 'Did he ever…' Hannah paused.

Joy hesitated and then shook her head and whispered, 'He'd look at me in a way that made me feel uncomfortable. I didn't really understand what was going on at the time when you… when he…' she stumbled over the words. 'But I knew you were terribly upset about something, and I felt it wasn't just because of Mother. When you disappeared I was angry with you at first because the atmosphere in this house was terrible and Mother expected so much more of me. After a while I stopped being angry and began to think. You loved us and I knew you wouldn't just leave without having a good reason. So when I was asked to go to Moreton for the day by a friend with her parents during the school holidays I accepted, but I lied to Mother about where we were going. You weren't amongst the cocklers but cousin Joan was, so I went to the house and no one was there. I guessed then that Mother was lying but I never let her know that I knew. I often caught *him* murmuring things to Mother and it made me wonder.' Her eyes darkened. 'I wish he'd have drowned instead of Grace.'

'Me, too,' said Hannah, just as vehemently.

Before anything else could be said, Susannah called to them to stop standing like statues, whispering, and get a move on; so the rest of what the sisters might have said went unspoken, but Joy's words comforted Hannah.

It was towards the end of the meal when the sherry glasses had been refilled that Bert stood up and announced that he had asked Alice to marry him and she had agreed. Susannah beamed at them both. 'But that's lovely!' She got to her feet and going round the table, first kissed her eldest son and then Alice. 'Florrie would be so pleased if she were here.'

Alice's eyes shone with tears. 'I'm glad you're glad! I wasn't sure you would be after what my dad did to you.'

'Forget about that,' said Jock, rising out of his chair and patting Alice's shoulder. 'You weren't to blame for his actions.' He turned to his son, thinking that maybe marriage to Alice would sort him out. She was attractive enough to keep him from straying, as well as being a good, religious girl like her mother. He held out his hand to Bert, 'Well, son, I hope yer realise how fortunate ye are, and do yer best to make Alice happy?'

'I do, Dah, I do,' said Bert, grinning. He pumped his father's hand.

Hannah felt unable to offer her congratulations. 'And when's the wedding to be?' Her voice was cool.

'When we find a house,' said Alice, both her arms wrapped round one of Bert's.

He gazed down at Hannah, the triumphant expression in his eyes made her want to spit in his face.

'I think Alice is making a mistake.'

'Hanny!' Her mother stared at her in astonishment. 'How can you say that?'

'I don't find it easy, believe me.' Hannah's voice shook.

'Don't be like this, Hanny,' pleaded Alice, looking uncomfortable. 'Be happy for us. Bert's told me he's done things in the past that he's truly ashamed of but he's really sorry.'

'I bet he hasn't told you it all,' muttered Hannah, her heart beginning to thud.

'Alice knows about Grace,' said Susannah, her face pale and tense, both hands gripped tightly so that the knuckles showed white. 'Stop this at once!'

Hannah stared at her father. 'Well, Dah?' There was a long silence and she could feel the tension in the room like tightly strung wire waiting to snap. Even Tilly and Freddie had stopped fooling about and were looking at Jock. He cleared his throat and said weakly, 'I think we should let the past go, lass.'

Hannah was so disappointed in him, she spat out the words, 'Well, I don't!'

Bert said, 'Say what you're wanting to say, Hanny. You tell Alice what you think I wouldn't dare tell.' He rubbed his chin against his fiancee's hair. 'She's got her mam's capacity for forgiveness.'

Hannah stared at him. Could it be true? It wasn't possible, surely? It didn't put him in a good light, and her brother was someone who needed to be well thought of... and Alice, could she accept what he'd done to her, without being revolted? Hannah did not know what to say. Couldn't bring herself to speak aloud the words. *He raped me. Is that what he told you? He got me pregnant, made me feel so bad I wanted to kill myself.*

'Forgiveness, Hanny. It's the only way you'll ever get rid of that burden of resentment you carry,' said Bert with a gentle smile. 'Look at Mother and Dah; she's forgiven him.'

'Since when have you suddenly got so wise?' said Hannah scathingly, and walked out of the room. Joy made to follow her but Susannah spoke to her sharply, 'Let her go! I need you here.' Joy had no choice but to do as her mother said.

'Poor love,' said Bert, drawing Alice over to the window. 'Hanny's her own worst enemy.'

'I feel guilty about her.' Alice's green eyes were sad. 'I wish she'd find someone to love.'

'Me too,' lied Bert. 'I wonder if she'll come to the wedding.'

'Of course she'll come to the wedding,' said Susannah, overhearing him. She seized hold of Tilly and Freddie. 'Come on, you two, into the parlour and play. Joy, you wash the dishes.' Again Joy had no choice but to do as she was told. Even so, as she did the dishes, she was watching Bert and Alice.

Alice was looking flushed and ill at ease. She wasn't so sure that Hannah would come to the wedding. She had always had a thing about Bert, always envied that love his mother had for him. Yet she cared for people, must have cared for Agnes. Bert had told her about the shop girl, and how she had thrown herself at him. How he had been weak and given in and lain with her, of her pregnancy and how Hannah had blamed him when Agnes had committed suicide. How it had hurt him to the quick, especially when he'd suspected Agnes had been seeing another bloke for some time. Bert had been so repentant, so obviously upset about the girl's death that, despite being shocked by his revelation, Alice decided to forgive him. She did not want anything to get in the way of them getting married. With Dolly's husband coming home in the spring, she knew that she had to get out of Granny's house. She wanted her own little place. Bert had agreed to Tilly living with them, saying that he loved her like one of his own family. It was what Alice wanted to hear.

But how she wished Hannah could forgive Bert. Suddenly it struck her afresh that it was Kenny's absence that was causing Hannah to behave the way she did. Now that he was no longer around, it probably made her jealous of anyone else in love. Where was Kenny? Why hadn't he got in touch? Why go to Scotland? It was a mystery that she felt would only be solved by his return. Yet here they were on Christmas Day and not a single person had heard from him. Surely he couldn't be dead. She dismissed the thought quickly, not wanting to believe it was possible. Sooner or later, he would be in touch, she was sure of it.

Chapter Twenty-One

Hannah left the house in a blazing temper and walked swiftly in the direction of Cow Lane Bridge, near to tears. She had to stop the wedding taking place but how? She felt so hurt and angry that her dah hadn't supported her, but instead seemed pleased that Bert and Alice were engaged. How could he when he knew what sort of monster his son was? If only Kenny was here. Why hadn't he come home to Chester for Christmas, or at least written?

She walked along the towpath, thinking about how he had saved her from throwing herself in the canal, and could almost feel the strength in his wrists and the warmth of his coat as he had pushed her arms into the sleeves. He had always been so thoughtful yet what had she given him in return, very little. She felt ashamed, looking back on the times they had spent together and how she had always kept him that little bit at a distance. With a head full of memories she made for the Phoenix tower.

As she walked along the walls she gazed across the fields that were hoary with frost, and recalled their shared interests and how he could make her feel safe, as well as make her laugh.

She turned and gazed down into the city. It being Christmas Day there were very few people about. When she came down from the walls she went and stood opposite the shop, looking up at the windows of the apartment where they had been happy.

Why had Kenny gone off the way he had? Surely it couldn't have been her telling him to act like a man and accusing him of having deceived her? And why go to Scotland? Who did he know there? He'd only been little when he left. Surely he wouldn't remember where he had lived, unless someone told him, and the only person she could think of who might know where Mal Moran had stayed in Scotland was Mrs Black. Hannah was feeling desperate enough to snatch at any straw thrown at her. Could Kenny possibly have gone to the house in Queen's Park? Maybe he had felt a need to go and tell Mrs Black that his father had been committed to an asylum. It could be whatever she had said caused him to go haring off to Scotland. Hannah made a decision and headed in the direction of Queen's Bridge.

An icy wind whipped her skirts about her legs as she crossed the river; shivering, she prayed that her journey wouldn't be a waste of time. She toiled up the road and it was only when she reached the top did she turn her head and gaze back the way she had come. Ribbons of mist were wreathing above the surface of the water and lights were twinkling on in the houses the other side of the river. How she loved this view, but this was not the time for romantic reverie; she would have to get a move on or it would soon be dark.

As Hannah passed the Waters' house, she thought of Sebastian but the shutters were still up and she could only suppose that the family had moved or were away for Christmas. She hunched her shoulders against the cold, gazing into the garden where frost blighted plants looked a sorry sight, remembering the first time she had seen Sebastian and how Alice could not take her eyes from him. Why couldn't she have been a bit more patient, a bit more trusting and a little less jealous? Things just might have worked out between the two of them.

Hannah carried on walking until she came to Mrs Black's place. She hesitated outside the gate, looking up the drive to the house, then taking a deep breath, she pressed down on the latch and went inside. Before she reached the front door it opened. A woman stood there, her arms folded across her bosom. Her hair was jet black and looped in braids about her ears. She was wearing a cream collared, purple satin gown with long sleeves ending in cream lace cuffs, and a cameo brooch was pinned to her frock. On her hands she wore several rings.

'I knew you'd come, Hanny Kirk,' she said gravely.

'You know me?' As soon as the words were out, Hannah knew that was a daft question. Of course, this woman knew her, because if she was not mistaken she was Mrs Black.

'Kenny put me in two minds whether I should stay here until you turned up, but I felt a certain responsibility for what happened to his father, so I've waited for you.'

Hannah wondered why she should feel responsible. It would have needed several men to hold Mal Moran down once he made up his mind to do something. 'You know where Kenny is?'

A faint smile played round the woman's lips. 'Perhaps. He said I wasn't to let you know where he was unless you came looking for him.'

So she had been right to come here! Hannah's heart seemed to leap inside her just thinking that she was so close to finding out where Kenny was. Then she shivered as a gust of wind blew up her skirts.

'You're cold. Come!' Mrs Black crooked her finger and beckoned her inside.

For a moment Hannah thought about what she knew of this woman, and felt slightly spooked, but then she thought of Kenny and followed her indoors. From a downstairs room came the tinkling of a piano and the murmur of voices and sudden laughter. So Mrs Black wasn't alone in this house. Maybe the three sisters who taught music still lived here? The prospect comforted her. She looked about her, trying to remember if she had been here before but the red and gold wallpaper of the lobby and the staircase was unfamiliar.

Mrs Black went upstairs and Hannah followed her. The well-polished wood of the banister rail felt like satin beneath her cold fingers, and she could not take her eyes from the gold twisting shapes of the dragons on the wallpaper. She was led to a room on the first floor and Mrs Black ushered her inside.

Hannah blinked. The room seemed bright after the darkness of the staircase and landing. She noticed by the light of several lamps that there seemed to be a lot of heavy mahogany furniture in the room, and a Christmas tree, decorated with tinsel and red and gold baubles stood in a corner. The long velvet curtains at the window were drawn, and in the fireplace a fire burned.

Hannah faced the woman, but avoided looking her straight in the eyes. 'Why did Kenny come to you? Why'd he go to Scotland? I thought he—'

Mrs Black raised her ringed hand. 'Patience, Hanny Kirk. Come and sit over by the fire and warm yourself. Perhaps you'd join me in a glass of sherry and a slice of Christmas cake.'

Hannah controlled her impatience, thanked her, and sat down in what turned out to be a wonderfully comfortable chair covered in green leather. She held her cold hands out to the fire, wishing she had thought to put on her new Christmas gloves, and hoped she would not get chilblains.

A glass of sherry was handed to her and a china plate with slices of Christmas cake was placed on an occasional table close to hand. 'Your good health, Hanny Kirk.' Mrs Black lifted her glass.

To her surprise Hannah found herself toasting the woman's good health as well. She sipped the sherry and reached for a slice of cake, realising it was a few hours since she had sat down with her family to Christmas dinner.

'Naturally it came as something of a shock to you when Kenny spoke,' said Mrs Black.

Hannah stilled in the act of breaking off a piece of marzipan, which she loved, and looked at her. 'He told you that of his own free will?'

Mrs Black smiled. 'Yes. I don't always have to use my powers to get information out of people. You were easy to hypnotise because you were weak with worry and needed help.'

'So you admit getting information about Mr Moran out of me and giving me that powder?' Hannah's voice remained calm but inside she was seething.

Mrs Black nodded gravely. 'Because of your loyalty to your friends, I knew you wouldn't have given it to me willingly. I had been so worried about Malcolm.'

'Were you in love with him?'

'Love! No! You could say that trying to save Malcolm from himself was my salvation after my husband died. I didn't succeed, sadly. Although, I did rescue him from the cause of all his troubles.'

Hannah longed to know more but guessed this woman was not going to be rushed into telling her story.

Mrs Black said softly, 'Kenny told me that you lost your sister and that your mother was in a state. If she would like to visit me we could try and get in touch with – Grace, is it?'

'What?' She stared at her, puzzled. 'What do you mean?'

'You still have no idea what I do then?' The woman laughed. 'Never mind. I'm not touting for business. I don't need to but I'm still willing to help those who find the silence of the grave too terrible to cope with.' She drained her sherry glass and then refilled it, remembering the first time Malcolm spoke to her after attending one of her meetings fifteen years ago. He was in such a state that she had agreed to see him privately. At first she had thought the problem was his wife Janet whom, he had told her, he loved dearly. She had died in Scotland, but in truth the real trouble was his mother. She had been evil. Her husband had deserted her and she had taken it out on her only son.

Mrs Black leaned towards Hannah. 'Malcolm's mother's religion was the kind that gave her no pleasure. To laugh on the Sabbath was a sin to her. Imagine a young boy trying to live up to her standards. She was forever trying to beat obedience into him. He managed to escape when he was twenty-one, having met the lovely Janet McDonald. Unfortunately his mother tracked them down and that was the end of what might have been a long happy marriage, which could have been the saving of him.'

Hannah, who had been hanging onto every word, said, 'Why are you telling me this?'

'I'm telling you because Kenny has gone to see his grandmother.' She held up a hand as if to ward off the words Hannah was about to speak. 'Not his father's mother but his mother's mother.'

Hannah was flabbergasted. She had never thought about Kenny having grandmothers. She tossed off her sherry in one go and almost choked, breaking into a flurry of coughing. Mrs Black patted her sharply on the back and offered a glass of water. Hannah shook her head and managed to stop coughing. 'How did he find out about her?'

Mrs Black smiled. 'His father left certain information in my possession. More sherry?'

Hannah shook her head. 'I don't understand. His father was always horrible to him.'

Mrs Black rose to her feet and went over to a polished mahogany bureau over by the window. She unlocked the flap and took an envelope from the blotter there, and handed it to Hannah. 'I thought Christmas might be the time when you would come. His grandmother's address is in there.'

Hannah recognised Kenny's handwriting and her heart seemed to turn over in her breast. She thanked her profusely.

Mrs Black raised a hand. 'It's the least I can do. I should have known better than to believe the different methods I tried could heal all the damage that woman did to him – the guilt he could never be rid of for long. Then he worked with lead, too, you see. It all took its toll.' She sighed. 'You'd better go now, dear, it's dark and your family might worry about you. Come again if you can. I get lonely sometimes. Perhaps I need to rethink the future.' There was a wistful expression on her face.

Not likely, thought Hannah, as the older woman saw her out. Although Mrs Black had helped her and so maybe… Hannah decided to think about it another time.

It was not until Hannah reached Northgate Street, where there was enough light by which she could read, that she tore open the envelope, too impatient to wait any longer.

Dear Hanny,

It seems that most of my life I've lived in fear, silenced by something I buried deep in my mind. Sometimes in dreams images would come to me. A woman lying on the floor, her face covered by her dark hair. I couldn't remember who she was, but now I know she was my mammy, and that she was dead. Did I see what happened? I'm not sure but one thing I've always been sure about, there was someone else in the room. Now I know what happened that day. Dad wrote down my grandmother McDonald's address for if I ever wanted to trace my mother's side of my family; it must have been during one of his saner moments. I have to see her, so I'm off to Scotland. Maybe I'll stay there. It all depends if you get to read this letter. If you can accept me as the person I am then, perhaps, there could be a future for us together. I love you. I've always loved you. If you write to me at the address at the bottom of the page I'll be home on the next train.

Kenny.

Hannah read the letter twice, tears trickling down her cheeks. A future for them together meant marriage, and she had convinced herself that it was not for her. Perhaps she was wrong. Kenny knew she was no virgin and yet he still loved and wanted her. Perhaps they could make some kind of life together. At least they could give it a try. One thing was for sure and that was that he was the only man she could marry and be happy with. He would have to know the whole truth, of course. Suddenly it occurred to her that he made no mention of Alice in his letter. Perhaps Mrs Black had another letter in that bureau of hers addressed to his half-sister.

Hannah stared at the address at the bottom of the page. Then she folded the letter and walked the rest of the way home, scarcely aware of the damp slippery cobbles beneath the thin soles of her shoes. She was going to have to wait until the day after Boxing Day before she could buy notepaper and a stamp and write to Kenny, but tomorrow she would go and see Alice and tell her about the letter.

–

'Hello, Hanny!' Alice did her best to put on a smile as she held the front door open, but since Christmas Day, she felt nervous just looking at her old friend. Having made up her mind that nothing was going to stop her marrying Bert, she did not want Hannah persuading her otherwise.

Hannah smiled. 'You got a few minutes? Only I've something to tell you.'

Alice's eyes clouded. 'Oh no! If it's about Bert I don't want to listen. He might have done things wrong, but so did you and Kenny.'

What was she talking about? Hannah rested her shoulder against the doorjamb. 'It's about Kenny. I got to thinking and so I went to visit Mrs Black. She invited me in, gave me tea and Christmas cake. She wasn't a bit like I thought she'd be… and I found out what she does. She's a medium.'

'She's what!' Alice's jaw dropped and her eyes were like saucers.

'A medium – and she told me where Kenny was.' Hannah smiled.

'You must be mad! It says in the Bible you shouldn't consort with mediums,' gasped Alice, horrified.

'Let me finish!'

'No!' said Alice angrily. 'I'm-I'm not interested in anything that woman has to say. I can't understand you, Hanny, going to her. She's trying to trick you. I'll not believe a word she says.' Alice slammed the door in her face.

Hannah was speechless. She could scarcely believe that her friend had intended that. She hammered on the door. 'Alice, you've got to listen to me. She gave me a letter from Kenny.'

'I'm not listening. Go away! All you want to do is spoil my life. You're just jealous.'

Jealous! There was that word again. Hannah almost choked on her anger. She could have a man, one who was worth at least ten of Bert! But if Alice wanted to believe she was jealous then let her. She would keep what she knew about Kenny to herself and Alice would have to live with her mistake.

The next day, though, Hannah changed her mind. She had to get Kenny to stop the wedding. She had been given money for Christmas by her dah, so bought what she needed to write to Kenny and set about penning a long letter. She unburdened herself, telling him of what Bert had done, and that although she loved Kenny more than she had realised, she was damaged goods, and would understand if he didn't want to marry her. She told him about Alice and Bert being engaged and of the plan for Tilly to live with them and why that worried her. She signed it, *All my love Hannah*. She did not read the letter over in case she changed her mind about being so honest with him, then she posted it.

A week passed, and Hogmanay arrived, but there was no party and 1907 came in like a damp squib. There was still no Kenny, and no letter from him. Another week passed, and there was news of an earthquake devastating Kingston, Jamaica, which helped Hannah to put her worries into perspective for a short time. But she could not settle, anxious and nervous that perhaps Kenny had changed his mind since going to Scotland. Maybe he had met another girl, who was unsullied, and prettier.

Another week passed in which Hannah and Alice did not exchange a word. Jock read out with satisfaction that Lloyd George wanted to reduce the powers of the House of Lords. 'The working man's day is coming, lass. You just wait and see,' he said.

Hannah was glad of it but it didn't make her day. She wrote again to Kenny just in case the postal service had let them down.

In February, King Edward and Queen Alexandra visited Paris. Hannah wished she was going to Paris with Kenny on their honeymoon. She was completely down in the dumps. Still no letter or Kenny. Perhaps the grandmother no longer lived at that address. Perhaps she had waited too long before trying to find him; maybe he had believed that she didn't want to get in touch with him and had moved on. That she might never see him again struck her like a physical blow. It hurt so much; she felt like a wounded animal, wanting to nurse the ache inside her. She could not bear to be near people, nor did she feel she could cope with the plans that were being made for the wedding, which had now been brought forward because Bert had found a house for his would-be bride and three-and-a-half-year-old sister-in-law. As well as that, Dolly's husband was sailing home from India, so it made sense to be out of his way. Besides, according to Granny, Dolly wasn't making life easy for Alice these days.

The final straw came when Alice surprised Hannah by asking if she would like to be her bridesMald. Hannah did not hesitate in refusing. For a moment she thought Alice was going to cry, but then she buttoned her lips tightly in a way that was becoming familiar to Hannah, and walked away.

Her mother was angry with Hannah. 'You're spoiling it for everyone with your moods. Perhaps you should go and stay with Joan until the wedding. Maybe by then you'll have got over whatever's wrong with you.'

The suggestion did not please Hannah because how would a letter from Kenny get to her, if her letters had been sent on to wherever he was now. She knew that she was clutching at straws but waited another week. When still no letter came, she packed some clothes and left for Moreton. Joan was glad to see her and set her to work.

–

Alice was upset. She stood on the pavement gazing up at the windows of the house where green damask curtains hung, thinking she should be happy, but instead she was miserable. For weeks she had tried to forget what Hannah had said about Mrs Black telling Hannah where Kenny was living. Now, with her wedding only two days away and the house probably ready for her and Bert to come home to, she could not stop thinking; not only about her half-brother, but Sebastian as well.

As she stood in front of her future home, she felt as if butterflies wearing football boots were zooming inside her stomach. Bert had painted the outside woodwork green, her favourite colour. While the house was not the one of her dreams, she knew that she was lucky having a home at all. Yet, here she was considering calling the whole thing off.

Taking a deep breath, she climbed onto the step and banged the knocker, knowing that Bert's plan that evening had been to come here straight from work. The noise seemed to vibrate up the street causing several of the women gossiping outside their front doors to look her way. She heard her name mentioned and heat rose in her cheeks. *Please hurry, Bert, I don't like standing here with them all looking at me. Probably saying her father's in the asylum, you know. That Bert Kirk really is a good bloke taking her on.*

The next moment she heard the soft padding of feet inside, then the door opened and Bert stood there in his stocking feet. The sleeves of his shirt were rolled up revealing bulging muscles. The handsome face looked pleased to see her. She was filled with dread. He was going to be hurt and who could blame him, but it would be wrong of her to go through with the wedding when she didn't love him.

'Hello, Alice! You all right?' He did not wait for her answer but seized her arm and drew her inside. 'Come and see the latest thing I've bought.' He closed the door but instead of leading her into the kitchen he brought her against him and crushed her mouth with his open one.

She struggled, taken by surprise. It was not like him to be so rough. He released her abruptly and gazed down at her, a faint smile in his eyes. 'Sorry! It's just you're so lovely. I can't wait to make you mine.' He fixed her with a stare. 'You do understand? You do forgive me?'

'Of course, I forgive you,' she said instantly, rubbing her arms where he had grabbed hold of her. Oh God, this was going to be difficult. She didn't know if she could go through with it.

'What is it?' He took hold of her chin and dropped a light kiss on her bruised mouth. 'You're looking worried. Something wrong?'

She took a deep breath. 'Let's go inside. I've been working hard all day. I'm tired.'

Reassured, he took her hand and led her into the kitchen. He had forbidden her entry into the house for the last fortnight, saying that he didn't want her to see it until he had it all ready for her.

She sniffed cautiously. The house smelt differently from the last time she was here. Her eyes widened as she gazed at walls papered in a floral pattern and the new linoleum on the floor. There was even a carpet square in front of the fireplace. Oh, hell, he had gone to town doing the place up. This was going to be terrible! At the same time, she remembered how she had wanted to share in choosing how it was to be decorated, but he had insisted on his doing that, saying as it was his money, so his choice.

It had been the same with the furniture. Embroidered cushions were scattered on a country style sofa and a dark oak drop-leaf table was placed near the window. A clock ticked on the mantle-shelf that also held a matching pair of pottery dogs, two candlesticks and a jar of spills.

He took out a cigarette and taking a spill put it to the fire. 'Mother chose the cushions and the dogs,' he said, lighting his cigarette.

'It's nice.'

He frowned as he smoothed his fair hair back with a hand that trembled slightly. 'Is that all you've got to say? It's more than bloody nice and a whole lot better than you were used to.'

'Yes, yes, it is,' she said quickly. 'It's-it's lovely, Bert. You've really worked hard.'

He beamed at her and rubbed his hands. 'Shall we have a cup of tea?'

'Let me make it,' suggested Alice, taking the kettle from the hob and placing it on the fire. 'I wasn't sure whether you'd be alone.'

'Mother's not long gone. Hanny's still away, you know.' He looked morose. 'I thought you might have got her to change her mind about being bridesmaid. I'd like her to see us get wed.' He sat down on the sofa and patted the seat beside him.

Alice ignored the gesture. She did not want to talk about Hannah either. 'Did she have Tilly with her?'

'Sure she did.' He smiled, placing his arms along the back of the sofa. 'I love that kid. I want lots of daughters. It'll be fun making them. You like children, don't you, love?'

'Of course, although I think a son would be nice,' said Alice, flushing slightly, fetching the teapot shaped like a cottage from the table.

Bert fixed Alice with a stare. 'You are pure, aren't you, Alice?' The cigarette stuck in the corner of his mouth jiggled up and down as he spoke.

She felt a tremor go through her. 'Of course!'

He relaxed. 'I thought so, only Dolly said something about you having a boyfriend once. I wouldn't like to think you'd done anything with him.' He drew on his cigarette while at the same time flexing his fingers.

That bitch Dolly, she thought, staring at him, a trickle of apprehension running down her spine, remembering her father's habit of flexing his hands before he hit her mother. She couldn't really believe Bert would hit her or do… anything at all but, suddenly she knew she had to get what she had to say over with quickly or she wouldn't be able to go through with it. 'Bert, I can't marry you! It wouldn't be fair on you.'

He froze. His expression was one of disbelief. Then he took the cigarette out of his mouth and said, 'That's not bloody funny.' He got to his feet.

'I-I… it's not meant to be a joke!' She clasped her hands tightly together to try and stop them from trembling. 'I'm sorry.'

'Sorry! Is that all you can say – sorry?' His mouth trembled and he blinked his eyelids rapidly. 'It's our Hanny, isn't it? She's told you.'

'Told me what?' She backed away from him.

'Don't play games with me!' His hand shot out and grabbed hold of her. Before she could prevent him, he pressed the lighted end of the cigarette on the side of her neck. She screamed with pain and tried to pull away from him but he slapped her across the head. 'She told you! The bitch told you and you're not prepared to forgive!' He hit her again on the other side of her head and she would have fallen to the floor if he had not held her by the neck of her blouse. Slowly she lifted her eyes to him and saw his hand coming down again and knew that she should have listened to Hannah.

Chapter Twenty-Two

'I'll not go to the wedding, I will not go to the wedding, I will not!' muttered Hannah as she worked. It was three hours after high tide and scurrying clouds raced each other before the wind, over the Irish Sea, above the glistening sandbanks, across the Wirral peninsula and towards the far distant Welsh hills. A horse-drawn cart stood several yards away waiting for the cocklers' harvest.

Hannah had pulled her back skirts between her legs and pinned them to the waist at the front, so she looked like she was wearing baggy trousers.

Splay-legged, bent almost double, she used the short-handled rake to scrape through the inch deep water to where the cockles lived just beneath the surface of the sand. She thought of Joy having to help her mother with the preparations alongside Alice, but determined not to let that thought sway her. She felt sorry for her sister but was completely out of tune with her mother and Alice.

She sieved the cockles, taking out the smaller ones and returning them to their home in the sand to grow, while emptying the larger ones into a bucket. She felt mad at her dah, prepared to fork out half the money for the whole shebang. He knew what his son was but seemed able to put it out of his mind and let Alice walk down the aisle to her fate. Hannah's expression was grim as she bent once more to her task. It seemed to her that the Berts of this world could get away with murder and rape, and come out smiling. While she... Sod Kenny! A tear rolled down her cheek and she brushed it away.

'Hanny!'

She thought, What now? There was always one of the men ready to tell her she was doing something wrong.

'Hanny!' The voice was closer.

'What?' she said crossly, straightening up and turning round to confront whoever it was. She froze. Bert was coming towards her.

'Why did you have to do it?' he said, flexing his fingers. His mouth was fixed in a smile but his blue eyes were cold.

'Do what? What are you doing here? Shouldn't you be at work?' Hannah's hand tightened on the rake and she glanced swiftly in the direction of Joan and the other cocklers. The nearest was twenty feet away.

'Don't play the innocent with me. I know too much about you,' he sneered. 'Why did you have to go and ruin everything?' He took another step towards her.

'I don't know what you're talking about?'

'Don't play the innocent with me!' He shouted the words so loud this time that heads turned and Hannah jumped out of her skin. 'You told Alice,' yelled Bert.

Hannah's spirits soared. 'You mean she's thrown you over. Thank God!'

Bert covered the ground between them in a rush, heedless of the seawater ruining his boots. Hannah tried to back away but the wellies she wore were too big for her and her left foot went over and she almost fell. He grabbed hold of her and shook her. 'You bitch.'

'So you didn't tell her everything after all!'

'Some things are private. I don't know how you could have told her,' he said, his jaw rigid. 'I loved you, Hanny.'

'Love! You don't know the meaning of the word,' she said in a scathing voice. 'Now let me go!' She tried to pull herself free.

'Not until I make you suffer.' His voice was almost unrecognisable. He began to force her down into the water, heedless to the shouts of Joan and the other men. Hannah struggled to keep on her feet but he kept forcing her down, down. She attempted to hit him with the rake.

Then a voice said, 'You heard her, Bert! Get your hands off her!'

Earth and sky seemed to shift, and the rake slipped from fingers that were suddenly nerveless. She grabbed hold of her brother's trousers to prevent herself from falling flat on her back and gazed sidelong at the man a few feet behind him.

'I got here as soon as I could,' said Kenny.

She had never seen him looking so good, and her heart seemed to swell inside her. His face was tanned and he was wearing a seaman's navy blue gansy and canvas trousers. His brown hair ruffled in the breeze, and his jaw was set firm. His arms hung straight at his side but his fists were clenched. His hazel eyes rested only a moment on her face before shifting to Bert, who was staring at Kenny as if he had seen a ghost. Bert grabbed hold of his sister as she attempted to move out of his reach.

Kenny said in a harsh voice, 'Let her go, Bert.'

The colour returned to Bert's face and he seemed to pull himself together. 'And if I don't? You're going to make me? I beat you up once before, I can do it again.'

Kenny's expression was steely. 'You can try. But I intend giving you a taste of your own medicine… not only for what you did to Hanny but what you've done to my sister, you swine.'

'You and whose army?' Bert smirked and pushed Hannah into the water and brought up his fists.

Hannah picked herself up and scrambled out of the way; her eyes not leaving Kenny's face. She wondered what Bert had done to Alice and prayed it was not what he had done to her. It struck her that Kenny had something to prove, but it worried her that Bert was at least a couple of stone heavier and several inches taller than her love. Oh God, help him, she prayed, thinking that if he didn't, then she would hit Bert with the rake.

The men had stopped their cockling and were watching, some had moved closer to where Kenny and Bert were squaring up to each other. Joan, too, was eyeing the pair of them up. She squeaked, 'Queensberry Rules! Queensberry Rules!' She might as well have saved her breath.

Kenny let out a roar and shouted something in a foreign tongue, then lowering his head, charged Bert. He caught him in the chest, and sent him sprawling backwards into the water. Before Bert could recover, Kenny was on top of him and had pinned down Bert's arms with his knees. He then proceeded to punch the hell out of him, managing to resist all Bert's attempts to throw him off.

Hannah rejoiced in what she was seeing. Where had Kenny learnt to fight like this? She expected Bert to fight back but, amazingly, the battle was soon over and Kenny the victor; swifter than she would have dreamed possible. Her brother lay spread-eagled in the sandy water, his face bloodied and bruised. 'I'll get you for this, Kenny Moran,' he gasped.

Kenny shook his head slowly. 'I wouldn't try it, Bert Kirk. I'm a peaceable bloke but I could get to enjoy knocking you down. I'm hoping once will be enough.' He turned and held out a hand to Hannah. 'Let's go.'

She stared at him, mesmerised, and her fingers caressed his bloodied knuckles. Her heart swelled with pride. He had fought for her! There was so much she wanted to say but the words seemed to have stuck in her throat. She knew there was only one way to express her feelings at that moment and, reaching up with her free hand, she brought his face down to hers. She kissed him long and deep. He returned her kiss with passion, lifting her off her feet. Her heart performed the polka. Then he lifted his head and rested his cheek a moment against her sea-breeze-tangled hair, and said, 'I love you. I want you to marry me.' It was the sweetest of moments and she wanted to cry, but then he kissed her again, ignoring the catcalls from the cocklers nearby.

'This is a fine carry-on,' burst in Joan in her squeaky voice. 'Stop it at once, Hanny! I don't know what Sue would say.'

Hannah and Kenny drew apart and smiled at the old woman. 'We're going to get married,' said Hannah.

Joan's face, weathered by wind and sun, broke into an almost toothless grin. 'Thank God for that. I knew you were moping for someone.' She reached out and shook Kenny's hand vigorously. 'Off with you both then. And I'd like an invite to your wedding. Bert, I never could abide. Smarmy bugger! Don't you worry about him. I'll get him sorted out.'

Hannah laughed out loud. Kenny kissed the old woman's cheek.

It was a long time since a man had kissed her and Joan stared at him with as much wonder in her eyes as Hannah. 'Well, you saucy thing!' she cried.

Hannah winked at Kenny. 'You have come out of your shell. What have they been feeding you up there in Scotland?'

He grinned and then, with his arm about her waist, he ran with her, splashing through the water until they reached the dunes. Beyond them lay a flat coastal expanse, Leasowe lighthouse, and trees that were bent double with the strength of the saltladen winds from the sea. Yet Hannah felt there was nowhere else she would rather be at that moment. She could not take her gaze from Kenny's face. There was a new strength there that caused her to feel such respect for him.

'What took you so long coming?' she said.

'My granny got ill six weeks after I got to Glasgow and so her daughter came down from the north and whisked the pair of us to her place on the coast in Argyllshire so she could recuperate. My cousin's husband is a fisherman, so I used to go out with the fishing boats. Then when Granny got better, we returned to Glasgow.' His voice sounded excited. 'Hanny, I've got cousins and three aunts, as well as a couple of uncles. One cousin works on a newspaper and he thinks I've got talent. That I could be a cartoonist for a newspaper!' He wore a bemused expression. 'Think of me doing such a thing.'

'Will it make us money?' she said seriously.

He smiled down at her. 'Don't you worry, I wouldn't let us starve. I'll carry on doing Mr Bushell's books until that day.'

She freed a deeply satisfied sigh. 'Tell me everything, right from when you visited Mrs Black.' She kissed him again. In fact she did it again and again, feeling that she could never get enough of the feel of his lips against hers.

Hand in hand they walked along the path that led to Joan's house, where Hannah planned to change out of her wellies and wet clothes and pick up the rest of her things. Kenny would have to wait until they reached Chester before he could change but he seemed oblivious to his damp clothing.

She asked him what Bert had done to Alice and his expression darkened. 'He beat her up. She was only saved from worse, I reckon, by your mother popping back with something else for the house and finding him at it.'

'Poor Alice.' Hannah's face was distressed. 'He thought I had told her about what he did to me.'

'But it wasn't that at all,' he said with a loud laugh. 'Suddenly she couldn't go through with it! Realised she was still in love with Seb and decided it wouldn't be fair on Bert to marry him the way she felt. She tried to tell him but...'

'That took some courage,' interrupted Hannah.

He nodded, and said softly, 'She's almost as courageous as you are.'

Tears filled her eyes and she went into his arms. They hugged and kissed again. It was some time before he managed to tell her all that had happened to him since last she saw him.

She listened intently as he explained how Mrs Black had hired a private detective to trace his father. It wasn't easy but, eventually, he had been discovered living in a village just outside Greenock with his mother. Her eyes widened as he spoke of how she had conveniently died of some kind of stomach upset after Mrs Black arrived, freeing the hold she had over his father and enabling him to return to Chester. 'When you say conveniently...' butted in Hannah.

'Rough justice,' said Kenny in clipped tones.

'You think Mrs Black helped your grandmother on her way to the Other Side?' Hannah gasped.

'God only knows,' said Kenny with a shrug. 'I'm glad she's dead.' He smiled grimly.

'She said that your father's mother was evil.'

Kenny nodded, and he was suddenly pale beneath his tan. 'She killed my mammy.'

They had come to Joan's house. Hannah stared at him, feeling his anguish, yet wanting to know the rest of the story. She decided it could wait until they were indoors.

Half an hour later they were sitting at the table under the window, which faced out onto the heath. 'So what happened?' asked Hannah.

Kenny warmed his hands on the steaming mug of tea, his expression was sombre. 'Granny Moran hated Mammy, not only because she took her son away, but because Mammy liked pretty clothes and dancing, had a family who loved her and showed affection. They treated me the same way as a child, and were even getting round Dad to relax and believe that he could be one of them. But Granny Moran couldn't bear that.' He paused and Hannah reached across the table and covered his hand with hers.

He lifted her hand to his lips and kissed it, then held it against his chest. He continued with a faraway look in his eyes now. 'She turned up at our house unexpectedly one Sabbath and found Mother dancing with me in the kitchen. Dad was down the yard in the privy. I can picture Granny Moran now because I've seen a photograph. She's tall and bony, and with a face that would have been nice if she'd only smiled.' His voice grew husky. 'She took the poker, which had been left in the fire and hit Mammy with it across the head twice. She didn't get up again and I went to her. Granny Moran turned on me and whacked me across the back with the hot poker. I had undergarments on and a shirt but, even so the poker burnt right through them. I must have let out such a scream that it brought Dad running.'

'That's how you got the scar on your back?'

He nodded. 'I hid under the table, sobbing, and she was screeching at him. He was yelling at her that Janet was dead, dead, dead and how had it happened? Eventually all went quiet.'

'How could he let her get away with it?'

Kenny made a sound in his throat, somewhere between a sob and a laugh, and he toyed with Hannah's fingers. 'I know how strong the fear of someone can be. It paralyses part of you, makes you behave differently. She told Dad it was an accident and that Mammy fell and hit her head on the hearth. But there was me with the burn on my back and hysterical because I'd seen her murder my mother. Apparently I babbled on about it in my sleep. I drove him crazy and that's when he told me to shut my mouth and threatened me with the kind of beating his mother had given him, but he never did it. The truth of the matter was that he was wracked with guilt and self-hatred, believing that if it hadn't been for him, Mammy would have still been alive. The McDonalds tried to find out what happened but he couldn't bring himself to tell them what he believed to be the truth. In the end we left Scotland, but the damage had already been done. He became bitter and twisted.' Kenny took a deep breath. 'I never thought of Mammy after that, and the memory of the McDonalds faded.'

'You've remembered all this since you started talking again?' said Hannah.

He shook his head, and then told her how Mrs Black had given him pages of scrawled handwriting, written by his father when he had first visited her. 'He went to one of her meetings. Did she tell you that she's a healer and a medium and used to travel round the country? People like my father went to see her because they were grieving or had unfinished business with their dead. I think he might have written the pages under hypnosis. Whatever, it didn't get rid of his guilt and his need to punish anyone who reminded him of his mother! But if only he hadn't been so twisted, he would have realised my stepmother wasn't at all like his mother.' A muscle in his throat tightened.

Hannah rose from her seat, went round the table to him and drew his head against her breast. For a long moment they did not move or speak and then he lifted his head and smiled. 'At least some good came out of it. If he hadn't left Scotland and come south, then I'd never have met you. I think we're meant for each other.'

She said unsteadily, 'You do say the nicest things, Kenny Moran. Don't ever stop talking again.'

He hugged her and then they kissed. Eventually they drew apart and she asked him how he had found out about Alice.

He told her how he had got back yesterday and called at Hannah's parents' house. Joy had answered the door, and had appeared delighted to see him and amazed that he could talk. 'But, once she got over the shock, she told me about the wedding being brought forward, said that she felt sorry for Alice. I told her that I was going to stop the wedding. It was at that point that your mother entered the house with Alice; her face was all bruised and bleeding.'

'So how did Mother react to you?' breathed Hannah, as tense as a coiled spring.

He smiled faintly and toyed with Hannah's fingers. 'I don't think she took in who I was. She was in a real state! Alice was holding her up as much as she was Alice. She'd discovered to her horror that Bert was not the person she believed him to be.'

'Did you… did you tell Mother about… what he did to – to me?' Hannah's face was pale.

Kenny said quietly, 'I would have, if I'd thought it necessary, but I think we'll leave it to your dah to explain about that. I think she's probably in a mood to believe it now. It needs to be said, though, because when I left the apartment she seemed to be suffering from the illusion that I was responsible for your trouble. She told me that I wasn't to see you again.'

'So that was why you disappeared?'

He nodded. 'It was probably Bert who put it into her head.'

Hannah agreed, feeling disgust with her brother, but sad that her mother had believed what he had said about Kenny. She felt no joy knowing that Susannah knew her terrible secret at last. She was more worried that her mother might never get over the shock. Yet, thinking about it, maybe her mother had to carry part of the blame for spoiling Bert. She had made him believe that he could do anything he wanted and get away with it. That whatever he did was admirable. Maybe Bert would have been different if their dah had not been so weak-willed, or was it that Bert was just bad? What would happen to him now, she wondered. Hopefully he would go away, so he would no longer be a constant reminder of what he had done.

She turned in Kenny's arms and held him tightly, praying that she would be able to give him all the love and affection he deserved. They'd both need to be there for Alice, now that she had found out the truth about Bert the hard way. So she was still in love with Sebastian, but was he still in love with her? Poor Alice!

Epilogue

Alice gazed at the stained glass window of the Cathedral but saw it through a blur. She lifted her arm from the pew and scrubbed her eyes for the umpteenth time, still hardly able to believe that she could have been so deceived in Bert over so many things. A fortnight had passed since Kenny's return. His being able to talk had come as a great surprise but a good one, nonetheless. She was glad he and Hannah were to marry. She could squirm with embarrassment when she thought how she had believed Kenny responsible for getting Hannah into trouble; she must have been mad! She wished them the best.

She had seen nothing of Bert and for that she was thankful. None of the Kirks had seen him either but his mother was managing to hold her head high, although she had lost weight, so it was obvious she was grieving over yet another loss.

Alice sighed, and went back to thinking about Kenny, recalling how he had yelled something as he had gone for their father with the poker at the apartment. She had recognised the Gaelic and thought the noise had come from her father.

She shivered, and thanked God for the lucky escape she'd had. She also asked Jesus for forgiveness for being so pig-headed in not believing Hannah or Kenny, when they had tried to impress on her time and again that Bert had another side to him.

She closed her eyes and put her hands together, knowing she should pray for him and her father but, at that moment, it was beyond her. Instead she asked, 'Lord, what am I going to do about Tilly? Where are we going to live?' She needed a quick answer to her prayer but, in her experience, it was true what it said in the Bible; one had to wait upon the Lord.

If only she had shown such patience where Sebastian was concerned they might have been married by now. Was there a chance that he still loved her? She thought back to the days when life had been so full of fun and happiness. She remembered how he had made her feel, then felt guilty for thinking such thoughts in God's house. She stayed a moment longer to think about what she should do, then got up off her knees.

Her footsteps rang on the decorative tiles as she swiftly walked up the aisle. She left the cathedral and came out into the evening sunlight. She was going to risk having mud thrown in her face, and try to see Sebastian.

There was a motor outside the Waters' house. Did that mean Sebastian was here? Alice took several deep breaths trying to calm her nerves. She must not let her courage fail her now. Yet how could he possibly forgive her for refusing to see his side of things, and walking away? She had tried to force him to do what she wanted, and, because he wouldn't, she had flounced off like a spoilt child.

Someone jostled her arm, then murmured an apology. She turned and saw a woman dressed in black from head to toe. At a glance Alice guessed her to be a woman of some substance. Her skirt was of silk and the black braided jacket was real velvet.

'Perhaps you can help me,' said the woman, lifting her veil.

It was a question often asked by trippers; generally they wanted to know where Brown's Emporium was or God's Providence House, but this woman was well away from the track beaten by most visitors. 'Where are you looking for?' asked Alice.

'I'm looking for a Mrs Black. I was given the name of this road but the woman couldn't remember the number.'

Alice shook her head in disapproval. 'You're newly bereaved, are you? Wouldn't you be better going to church?'

The woman drew herself up to her full height. 'I beg your pardon? I am a regular communicant of the Church of England.' Her tone was haughty. 'Mrs Black has been highly recommended, she has the gift.'

Oh dear, thought Alice. The woman was already hooked. Let her find out for herself what a phony the medium was. Still, the woman looked like she could afford to pay for what she wanted. Alice pointed out Mrs Black's house and watched her go in, before turning to survey the Waters' house again.

A tall young woman, wearing a long driving coat, gauntlets, and an outrageous hat with a scarf tied round it, came out of the gate. She glanced at Alice and then her eyes widened and she fixed her with a stare. 'You!' she exclaimed.

Alice recognised her. 'You're Miss Waters!'

'And you are Alice Moran, if I am not mistaken.' Her voice was cool. 'What are you doing here?' She opened the door of the motor and climbed into the driving seat.

Alice walked slowly towards the car, her hands clasped behind her back. 'I had hoped to see Seb.' Her voice quivered. 'I suppose he hates me now. No doubt he told you what happened.'

Victoria raised her eyebrows. 'You flatter yourself. But, as it happens, it was apparent to me and his mother that your relationship had come to an end, due to no fault of his own.'

'It wasn't what I wanted,' said Alice frankly. 'I behaved stupidly.'

Victoria surprised her by smiling. 'Now there's an admission.' She tried to start the engine but it refused to do so. 'Drat! You wouldn't be a dear would you, and crank the engine for me? Sebastian says you don't really need strength – just persistence. Even so, he's forbidden me to do it myself. I have a weak heart, you know!'

Alice thought, I do know. But she took the cranking handle from Victoria and fitted it into its hole. Within minutes the car began to shudder and then the engine roared.

Victoria smiled at her. 'Thanks! Get in, why don't you? I can give you a lift into town, and on the way you can tell me what went wrong between you and Sebastian. He's not here by the way, he's in America with my father.'

Alice was so disappointed she could have cried. Instead, after the barest of hesitations, she got into the motor. As they sped down the road in the direction of the old mill, Alice began to unburden herself, telling the sympathetic Victoria what a mess she had made of everything. They crossed the bridge with the weir roaring below them and chugged up Lower Bridge Street.

By the time they reached the Music Hall, Victoria had convinced Alice that it would be worth her trying to win back Sebastian's love. 'He hasn't met anyone else and, if he loved you once, then perhaps he will love you again if you can prove to him that you've seen the error of your ways and really do love him still.' She paused and seemed to be thinking deeply. 'He might take some convincing but your presence in the house could wear him down.'

'What do you mean – in the house?' asked Alice.

Victoria smiled. 'Why don't you work for me and join the fight for women's rights? I need an assistant, someone to help put letters in envelopes, stick on stamps and take messages. There's plenty of room in the house. Although do you think that Kenny and Hannah might take in your sister? You're going to be too busy to look after a child.'

'But-but I'm a trainee milliner,' stammered Alice, but then remembered that was no longer true. She had given in her notice because she had been going to marry Bert.

Victoria's dark eyes twinkled down at her. 'Then you can make my hats for me as well. I'll pay you a fair wage.'

The prospect of living under the same roof as Seb – and his mother – made Alice hesitate. But if she were to win him, then she had to win his mother over to her side, too. She made up her mind. 'I'd like that! In fact, why don't I start right now? I'd like to come to the meeting with you, if I may? I wasn't doing anything important this evening.' She could explain everything to Granny, Kenny and Hannah later.

'That suits me. You can move into the house tomorrow.'

Alice beamed at Victoria, and followed her up the path, taking a deep breath before walking into the Music Hall. Life had suddenly taken on a whole new colour. It was no longer grey but golden. A new job, a place where she could stay, and Sebastian's homecoming to look forward to. But she mustn't go rushing ahead of herself. She must take one step at a time. Even so she couldn't resist imagining a rosy future.